英文達人必讀系列

英文寫作有訣竅！

Making Sense of English Writing

三句話翻轉英文寫作困境

交大外文系、外文所

劉美君 教授——著

ABCDE
FGHIJK
LMNOP
QRSTU
VWXYZ

在英文寫作越來越重要的今天，英文達人的你，可以回答下面幾個問題嗎？

- 面對英文作文、考試、履歷、自傳，到底要寫什麼？
- 想要寫的，又該如何下筆、組織、鋪陳？
- 如何建構英文式的思路，避免寫出中式英文？
- 雖然看得懂英文文章，卻寫不出有條理、有邏輯的英文作文，怎麼辦？

看完本書，你也可以

- 培養英文思考習慣，決定英文寫作習慣！
- 善用「G-S-G 三句話原則」構思鋪陳，輕鬆達陣！
- 不再用「中翻英」的方式，寫硬拗的中式英文！
- 熟悉英文文法句型，不再錯誤百出！

翻轉你所有的英文寫作觀念，建立三進式的構思模式，

寫出重點清楚、文意明確的好文章！

前言

在新竹縣英語輔導團所辦的研習會上，我問在座近 40 位國中英語老師：「你還記得大學的英文作文課嗎，老師教了你什麼？你學到什麼？」老師們一一發言：

> 「要有主題！」
> 「要有邏輯性！」
> 「前後思路要連貫！」
> 「要用英文思考，不要寫中式英文！」
> 「一開始要有 topic sentence，要破題！」
> 「文章分三段，每段都要有重點！」
> 「要注意文法，標點符號也要注意。」

對！這些都是重要的原則，但我進一步問：

> 「什麼是主題？如何凸顯主題？」
> 「什麼是邏輯性？如何建立邏輯性？」
> 「什麼是英文式的思考？如何養成英文式的思考？」
> 「什麼是 topic sentence？如何破題？」
> 「段落怎麼分？重點又如何釐清？」
> 「文法要注意什麼？如何避免中式英文？」

這些進一步的問題，卻沒有答案。

翻開坊間有關英文寫作的書，也沒有提供明確的答案。

但這些進一步的問題才是作文最難的地方。我們都知道要分三段：Introduction-Body-Conclusion，但是接下來呢？第一句話到第二句話該如何鋪陳？每一段當中的重點如何交代？如何延伸？段落和段落間又要如何連接？

這些細節才是我們需要學清楚的！

這本書的出版，就是要明確回答這些不容易回答的問題！

《英文寫作有訣竅》是我的第一本書《英文文法有道理》的續集，因為作文是句子的延伸，文法的道理在於搞懂英文的標記原則，標記正確的句子又是怎樣串連成一篇有意義的文章？從語法的結構到文章的結構，其實有異曲同工之妙，二者所依循的原則都是一樣的，都表現出英語獨特的「語性」！本書主要的目的就是要教你建立英文式的思考模式，唯有 Think English，才能 Write English。而英文式的表達就是養成主從分明，重點先講的「三句話」習慣：

第一句：最重要的話　　　　-> 重點
第二句：最有說服力的話　　-> 細節
第三句：最令人感動的話　　-> 結論

這種講三句話的習慣，構成「三進式」的思維模式，在英文寫作的每一個層次都表露無遺。本書的第一部分將以實證說明這種思考模式的精髓，藉由不同程度的文本，帶您透析構思英文的訣竅，繼而靈活運用在各種寫作需要上。第二部份針對最被詬病的「中式英文」，整理出各種問題類型，找出問題的癥結，對症下藥。

寫這本書的目的很簡單，因為大家都想把英文作文學好，卻不知如何下手，這本書要清清楚楚地告訴您：英文寫作不但有訣竅、有方法，更有無窮樂趣！

交大外文系

劉美君

推薦文

英文寫作能力越來越重要，我能用英文開會，看英文資料也沒問題，可是到了要英文寫作時，卻永遠要面對著三個困擾：

1. 我的文法對嗎？
2. 表達得夠清楚嗎？
3. 我寫得好不好？

去年聽到劉老師的演講，覺得 G-S-G 公式非常奇妙，這個公式讓我在英文寫作的時候有一個很簡單而又可行的概念，而且這個概念寫短文的時候可以用，在寫段落時候也可以用，真的簡單又實用，就非常希望劉老師能出一本書，把文法標記與寫作兩個主題結合在一起，更全面的提升我的寫作功力。

現在終於等到這本書出版，劉老師在 Part I 中討論英文寫作的構思原則，在 Part II 中探討我們老中英文寫作的常見問題，而且她花了很多時間在每一個章節的後面加了「寫作練功坊」跟「寫作修理廠」，讓讀者把每個章節所學到的重點能夠寫一下，再確實的修一下，這種練習對寫作能力的提升，非常有幫助。不過我全力推薦大家努力閱讀的是 Part III「生存遊戲」，在這個部分中劉老師分別用大學入學考試、多益測驗、托福測驗、SAT、履歷表撰寫，分別讓讀者模擬實戰一番，充滿了臨場感。我自己特別把多益測驗的實戰題部分，好好的挑戰了一番，再看老師的修理與修正，非常過癮，大有收穫。

如果你想提振你的寫作能力這本書當然是本好書，不過請你務必要下定決心，做一個負責任的讀者，認真的參與「寫作練功坊」與「寫作修理廠」的活動，這樣你很快就能成為一位擁有優質英文寫作能力的國際人了。

ETS 台灣區代表 王星威總經理

英文寫作是思考的歷程

我閱讀過作者劉美君教授的第一本書《英文文法有道理》，也在一場演講中聽過她逐條說明的此書的道理後，對於續集《英文寫作有訣竅》能先睹為快自然欣喜不已。大約半年前我知道劉美君教授正在寫一本有關寫作有道理的新書時，充滿期待與好奇。因為我們都知道，文法是英文寫作的根基，而英文寫作是文法的延伸，但如何在「文法有道理」後接續說出英文寫作的一番道理來說服人呢？

閱讀後充滿發現後的驚喜，劉教授以「獨特的道理」將這兩個在英文學習上的大議題緊緊相扣、缺一不可。劉美君教授最令我印象深刻的一句名言是「文法的道理在於英文語言系統的標記原則」，標記原則如同標示一個人的鮮明個性，讓英文文法的獨特語性形成一種道理，進而易認、易懂、易記及易學。我完全同意劉美君教授所說的「唯有 Think English，才能 Write English」，這與我自己在英文寫作課程中強調的理念 "A writer as a thinker" 極為相似，因為沒有思考即沒有寫作這件事存在。我相信英文寫作者必須先學習的是寫作思考的歷程，讓每一環節緊緊相扣。英文寫作之困難也在於要在寫作歷程中建立思考的邏輯與組織。至於如何思考，正是本書最重要的學習點：學習到英文寫作的道理，進而建立英文式的思考模式三大關鍵「重點、細節、結論」。

本書由英文寫作上的基本概念切入，說出嚴實的一番道理，接續以最常見的五大問題類型來說明如何避免中式英文常見錯誤，例如：何謂嚴句子、動詞出場的時態、主動被動責任的釐清、動詞類型搭配用法等，劉教授用心思考命名，讓此書的每一個章節名稱都變得十分生動、有趣，自動吸引人繼續讀下去。亦能在瞭解英文寫作的大道理後，逐漸走出中式英文的寫作困境。

我也欣賞每一章節最後的設計：「寫作練功坊」及「寫作修理廠」，不以長篇大論的理論來講解英文寫作技巧，而是以中式英文的寫作者的範例直接說出寫作道理。這是本書特色，讓英文寫作更淺顯易懂，也更充滿了挑戰成功後的小確幸與學習樂趣。

國立中正大學 語言中心

林麗菊 主任

目錄

Contents

Part III   Actions Speak Louder Than Words
生存遊戲：實戰演練

本書架構導覽

英文寫作基本功

Part I
Think English, Write English
思考習慣決定寫作習慣——
英文構思的五大基本原則

Chapter 1　講什麼？三句話法則
Chapter 2　如何連貫？主詞相關，話
　　　　　　題相連
Chapter 3　如何破題？找出主控點，
　　　　　　為文章定調！
Chapter 4　如何交代主旨？提綱挈
　　　　　　領，言明主旨！
Chapter 5　如何拓展全文？善用
　　　　　　G-S-G 推進法，層層開展

Part II
To Be or Not to Be Chinese
如何避免中式英文——
最常見的五大問題類型

Chapter　6　英文嚴句子
Chapter　7　名詞出場必有標記
Chapter　8　動詞出場時態相隨
Chapter　9　主動被動釐清責任
Chapter 10　説文解字，善於用詞

英文寫作應用

Part III
Actions Speak Louder than Words 生存遊戲：實戰演練

Chapter 11　大學入學考試 作文訣竅應用
Chapter 12　TOEIC 寫作測驗訣竅應用
Chapter 13　TOEFL / SAT 作文訣竅應用
Chapter 14　如何撰寫履歷：申請工作與學校

Think English, Write English
思考習慣決定寫作習慣

寫英文作文時，一般人都有兩怕：一怕不知道寫什麼，二怕不知道怎麼寫。這兩個問題沒有解答前，往往寫出來的就是「中式英文」，為什麼會寫出「中式英文」呢？又該如何轉換成英語的腦子？

我們必須由思考模式出發，理解英文與中文在構思條理、鋪陳方式上的差異：前者開門見山，務求重點清楚，

條理分明；後者迂迴漸進，強調起承轉合。兩者在思考架構的本質上截然不同，正因為如此，如果想要寫出一篇道地的英文作文，絕不能單純地按照中文寫作的習慣，套入英文的詞彙，直截了當地翻成英文就好；而是需要建立英文式的思考模式，依照「三句話原則」來發想、組織內容，按照 G-S-G 三進式的推展原則來進行鋪陳、安排敘事架構。

Part I：英文構思作文的五大基本原則，要強調的就是在篇章的內容與結構上，要知道如何「Think English, Write English!」，避免直接將中式思維翻譯成英文，寫出重點不清、文意不明的「中式英文」作文。

Chapter

講什麼？——三句話法則

01

如何切入主題？

如何令人印象深刻？

如何訓練英文式思考？

What to write about?

1.1 　困境1：不知道要講什麼？

　　英文作文到底該寫些什麼？這是最令人頭痛的問題！寫作能力是評量一個人英文好壞非常重要的一環，因此，越來越多的考試或測驗將寫作納入考量。這令很多人十分驚慌，因為常常看著作文題目，卻不知道到底要寫些什麼，即使想破頭擠出一篇作文，往往只落得言不及義，東拼西湊，囫圇帶過的下場。今天要傳授的第一招，就能夠讓你從惡夢當中醒來。寫作文不需要多、不需要長、不需要詞藻華麗，只需要：「三句話」！

1.2 　訣竅1：請講「三句話」

◎ 寫作是一種溝通，有效的溝通來自三句話：

→ 最重要的話

→ 最具說服力的話

→ 最令人感動的話

　　真的只要三句話嗎？是的，在交大的 EMBA 課程中，柳中岡教授一語道破在這個步調快速的社會，和老闆溝通的要領就是只能講三句話。老闆的時間有限，只想聽重點，這三句話就是重點！

　　作文也一樣！閱讀者的時間一樣有限，言簡意賅、條理清楚的寫作就是以「三句話」為基底！這三句話代表講求效率的英文式思考的三個要素、三個步驟：交代關鍵重點 →列舉具體事實→提出生動結論。重點要簡潔有力，事實要具體細緻，總結要生動感人。依照這「三句話」來構思，才能掌握有效、有重點的溝通技巧。因此，不知道該寫什麼時，請問自己三個問題：

→ 最重要的關鍵點是什麼？　 - key point

→ 最具說服力的細節是什麼？ - supporting details

→ 最令人感動的結語是什麼？ - memorable conclusion

　　總之，要如何讓讀者清楚快速地了解自己想說什麼呢？就是說三句話。哪三句？「最重要的話」、「最具說服力的話」及「最令人感動的話」。

知易行難。到底英文作文要如何只說三句話便可以清楚表達重點？舉個例子，假設今天的作文題目是 My Mom，該怎麼下筆？

第一句：最重要的話 → My mom is beautiful.

第二句：最具說服力的話 → She has big eyes, soft skin and long hair.

第三句：最令人感動的話 → She looks like the super star Lin Zhi-ling（林志玲）.

這三句話說完了是不是讓人印象深刻？看到 My Mom 這個題目後，先決定最重要的關鍵點（key point）：My mom is beautiful.。既然重點是 beautiful，那是怎麼樣的漂亮法呢？為什麼很漂亮？憑什麼說她漂亮？為了言之有據，所以接下來提供最具說服力的細節，就是 She has big eyes, soft skin and long hair.。描述完了客觀的美女條件以後，那主觀的感受是什麼呢？如何寫出一個生動感人的結語？那就是 She looks like the super star Lin Zhi-ling（林志玲）。

說清楚了嗎？再清楚不過了。只說三句話，就把重點說清楚了，簡潔有力、乾淨俐落。好的開始是成功的一半。只要開頭的三句話寫好了，就不用擔心接下來的文章會不知所云。說完簡單清楚的三句話後，一切將會水到渠成。

1.3 條條大路通佳作

俗話說得好，一樣米養百樣人，這樣的概念也可以延伸到英文寫作上，一樣的三句話結構，可以發展出各式各樣不同的文章，就端看所選取的「**關鍵點**」為何，這個關鍵點主控以下的內容，所以又可稱為「主控點」（controlling idea）[1]。一樣是 My Mom 這個題目，也可選擇不同的主控點來發揮：

My mom is _____.

(intelligent, open-minded, quick-tempered....)

---

1 "Controlling idea" 一詞出自 *North Star: Reading and Writing Level 4*, Unit 2, p.42, Longman.

究竟該如何發想？首先，這個題目會激發出許多靈感。「我的媽媽」可以是很和藹的，很會煮飯的、很漂亮的、或是很忙碌的等等，這些想法在腦海中浮現：

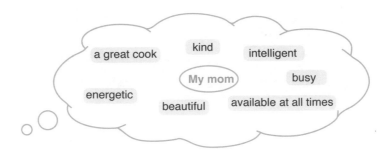

這些不同的**面向**都和 My Mom 有關，那下一步該怎麼做呢？請選擇一個最重要的**主控點**（controlling idea）。在各式各樣的想法之中，選一個主控點來發展，就像遇到岔路的時候，必須選一條路走下去。若選擇的這條路是 a great cook，那這篇文章就可以如此發展：

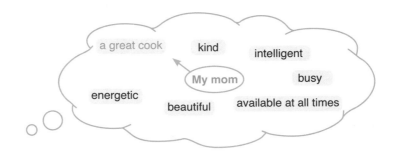

My mom is a great cook.→**最重要的話**

She can cook all kinds of delicious food, Chinese or Western.→ **最具說服力的話**

Everyone likes the food she makes and calls her A-ji-sao（阿基嫂）.→ **最令人感動的話**

最重要的第一句話說明主題與主控點，也就是媽媽是個很棒的廚師。那為什麼是很棒的廚師呢？接下來提供有說服力的細節，因為她可以煮各式各樣好吃的菜。最後，最令人感動以及印象深刻的結論，就是每個人都愛吃她做的菜，並且稱她為「阿基嫂」。

那麼，如果選擇的主控點變成 kind，又能如何發展成一段呢？

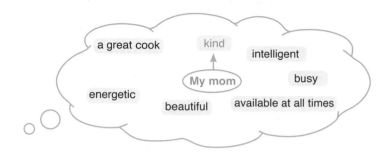

同樣，最重要的主題與主控點先提出來，之後提供有說服力的細節，最後給個印象深刻的結論：

My mom is very kind. → **最重要的話**

She cares about everyone around her and is always willing to spend time helping people in need. → **最具說服力的話**

She is like the sunshine of my community that gives out light and warmth.
→ **最令人感動的話**

最重要的主控點是媽媽非常「和藹」，她非常關心身邊的人，也樂意幫助有需要的人，用這兩個事實來說服讀者，並且下一個令人感動的結論──她有如我們社區的陽光。

此外，在一開頭最重要的話當中，也可以用一些具象化的物體來比喻 my mom。比方說，如果主控點落在 My mom is available at all times.

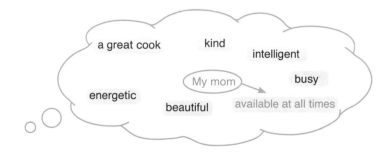

那麼用 7-11 便利商店的特性──隨時可以提供服務，來做比喻，會讓這個段落極富新意：

My mom is like a 7-11. → **最重要的話**

She is available 24 hours for her work and her kids. → **最具說服力的話**

She is the most energetic and hard-working person I know. → **最令人感動的話**

用一個同樣的思考流程，形成三段式的結構：

這三句話代表英文式思考的三個步驟：**交代重點 → 列舉事實 → 概括總結。主題與主控點說明重點 → 列舉事實、細節來做為最有力的證據 → 概括總結整個段落**，使人印象深刻。從溝通技巧來說，重點要簡潔有力，事實要具體細緻，總結要生動感人。這種思考方式其實是英語母語人士從小的訓練。證據為何？讓我們繼續看下去。

1.4 原來如此！透視英文式的思考模式

「三句話」不是「只能寫三句話」，而是代表「英文式思考」的**三個要素、三個步驟**。從訊息的**粗細度**來說，這三句話之間存在一種「粗 → 細 → 粗」的關係，意即 General → Specific → General 三進式的推展關係。

這個原則符合英文學術論文寫作的基本流程，在 *Academic Writing for Graduate Students* [2] 一書中提到：

...A type of text (is) sometimes called general-specific (GS) because its structure involves general-to-specific movement. ...As their name implies, GS texts move from broad statement to narrower ones. However, they often widen out again in the final sentence.

通常寫開頭段落（introduction）最簡單的方式就是遵守這三個步驟、三個進程。所謂 **G-S-G** 文本是一種文章前進的方式，從較廣泛的主控點陳述進入明確細節的交代，再推展至較開闊的結語。

重點
General

細節
Specific

結論
General

這種 General → Specific → General 三進式的思維方式，成為英文寫作的特色，在各式各樣的英文出版品中皆清楚可見。三進式思維的第一步，是由 General → Specific 二進式的思維發展而來的，首先要了解二進式思維的推展關係。以下以各個年齡層的英文讀本為例，說明二進式思維是英文寫作的基本訓練：

General → Specific 二進法
訊息由「粗→細」的進程。廣泛的重點提出之後，都要列舉細節來支持。

比如說，在兒童讀物 *It's Mine* [3] 這本書中，一開始的第一頁只有兩句話，這兩句話就呈現重點與細節的分別：

---

2. John M. Swales and Christine B. Feak, *Academic Writing for Graduate Students: Essential Tasks and Skills*, Unit 2, Writing General-Specific Texts. pp. 44-47. The University of Michigan Press.

3 *It's Mine* by Leo Lionni.

G-交代重點

In the middle of Rainbow Pond there was a small island.

⋮
▼

S-列舉細節

Smooth pebbles lined its beaches, and it was covered with ferns and leafy weeds.

這兩句話的「粗細程度」可以由以下的圖來表示，場景的重點在於小島，那小島上有什麼東西呢？細節說明小島有小石子、蕨類植物以及海草。

In the middle of Rainbow Pond there was a small island.

What's special about it?

Smooth pebbles lined its beaches,
and it was covered with ferns and leafy weeds.

交代完場景之後，第二頁隨即又出現兩句話，介紹主角出場，這兩句話也呈現重點與細節的分布：

G-交代重點

On the island lived three quarrelsome frogs.

⋮
▼

S-列舉細節

They quarreled and quibbled from dawn to dusk.

這時候重點轉換成了愛爭吵的青蛙，也就是主控點落在愛爭吵的特色上面。那麼是如何愛爭吵呢？細節就是證據：他們從早吵到晚！

On the island lived three quarrelsome frogs.

How did they quarrel?

They quarreled and quibbled from dawn to dusk.

這樣的二進法在給青少年的讀本中，慢可見，像是在 *Flipped*[4] 這本小說中，一開頭就是使用二進法的兩句話：

G-交代重點

All I've wanted is for Juli Baker to leave me alone.

S-列舉細節

For her to back off – you know, just give me some space.

二進法使文章順利推展，前後句之間存有「粗到細」的延伸關係。這樣的二進法不一定是存在於兩個分開的句子。同一個句子當中，也會有二進式的關係，例如在 *Sequoya's Gift*[5] 這個文章當中所出現的句子：

G-交代重點 ▸ **S-列舉細節**

Sequoya was a remarkable man – a silversmith, painter, and soldier,

G-交代重點 ▸ **S-列舉細節**

who is famous because he is the only person in history known to have invented a written language.

在這同一個句子當中，出現了兩次 G-S 的語意關係。第一個重點是 Sequoya 很優秀，細節則點出優秀的原因——因為他身兼三職。而第二個重點是 Sequoya 很有名，為什麼有名呢？細節說明了原因——因為他發明文字。這樣的進程可轉換成如下圖示：

---

4 *Flipped* by Wendelin Van Draanen

5 *Sequoya's Gift* 此篇文章來自 Kenneth Hodkinson and Sandra Adams 所著之 *Wordly Wise 3000, Book 1*, Lesson 1.

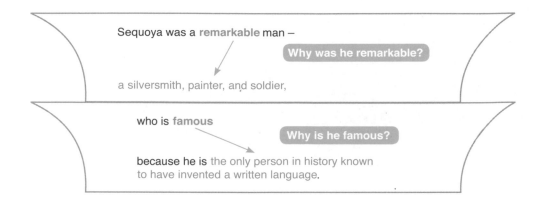

Sequoya was a **remarkable** man –

Why was he remarkable?

a silversmith, painter, and soldier,

who is **famous**

Why is he famous?

because he is the only person in history known to have invented a written language.

上述例子來自於英文童書以及小說，都顯示了「**粗 → 細**」的語意連結，也就是 General → Specific 的推展關係。在書寫英文的過程中，一個重點必定要有事實或細節來說明。而在陳述事實與細節之後，可進一步加上一個概括的總結，而形成「**粗 → 細 → 粗**」的關係，意即 General → Specific → General 三進式的推展關係：

General → Specific → General 三進法

訊息由「粗 → 細 → 粗」的進程。提出每一個廣泛的重點之後，都要列舉細節來支持，最後加入概括總結，以承上啟下。

在先前提過的 *It's Mine* 這本書當中，主角出場後：

G-交代重點：They quarreled and quibbled from dawn to dusk.

S-列舉細節："Stay out of the pond," yelled Milton.

"The water is mine."

"Get off the island!" shouted Rupert.

"The earth is mine."

"The air is mine!" screamed Lydia as she leaped to catch a butterfly.

G-概括總結：And so it went.

一開始的重點在於他們吵個不停，細節的部分以對話來顯示吵鬧的過程，最後來個概括的總結，他們就這樣一直吵個不停，用來承上啟下。

General
They quarreled and quibbled from dawn to dusk.

Specific
"Stay out of the pond," yelled Milton.
"The water is mine."
"Get off the island!" shouted Rupert.
"The earth is mine."
"The air is mine!" screamed Lydia
as she leaped to catch a butterfly.

General
And so it went.

另外，我們在 *I Remember...When I Was Afraid*[6] 這本書中也看到三進法的運用：

G-交代重點：Sometimes I have trouble remembering things.

S-列舉細節： It's not because I'm too old and it's not because I'm too young. It's not that I try to forget.

G-概括總結：It's just that I don't remember to remember.

一開始的重點說明廣泛的概念：我記不得事情。接下來列舉細節說明這是怎麼一回事：不是因為年紀太老或太小，也不是因為我試著去遺忘。而最後總結是：我只是會忘記要去記得。

General
Sometimes I have trouble remembering things.

Specific
It's not because I'm too old and it's not because I'm too young.
It's not that I try to forget.

General
It's just that I don't remember to remember.

再舉一例，我們也在 *Our favorite Creatures*[7] 讀本中看見三進法的出現：

G- 交代重點：Going off on wildlife adventure is exciting!

S- 列舉細節：You meet all kinds of funny, bizarre, fascinating, weird, and wonderful creatures. Sometimes you have to hike high up the mountains or dive deep in the ocean; but that's not the hardest part of going on a wildlife adventure.

G- 概括總結：The toughest part is trying to decide of all the creatures you've met, which is your favorite.

首先文章交代了重點——去野外探險很有趣，然後細節說到你會遇到各式各樣的生物，有時候必須辛苦地爬上爬下。但是這些辛苦不算難，難的是什麼呢？最後點出結論：最難的是決定你最喜歡哪個生物。

General
Going off on wildlife adventure is exciting!

Specific
You meet all kinds of funny, bizarre, fascinating,
weird, and wonderful creatures.
Sometimes you have to hike high up
the mountains or dive deep in the ocean;
but that's not the hardest part of
going on a wildlife adventure.

General
The toughest part is trying to decide of all the creatures
you've met, which is your favorite.

從英語母語人士的讀本出發，觀察其寫作的流程，不難看出，其實英文寫作有「理」可循。要寫好英文作文，就必須了解英文式的思考模式，也就是「**粗 → 細 → 粗**」的三進原則，意即 General → Specific → General 三進式的推展關係。把這層關係帶到寫作中，將會使作文更流暢、更有邏輯。

---

7 *Our Favorite Creatures (Kratt's Creatures)* by Martin Kratt and Chris Kratt

1.5 中英比一比：由遠而近 vs. 由近而遠

General → Specific → General 三進法反映了英語的**「語性」**。《英文文法有道理》這本書中清楚提到英文有十個語性特點，如**「重點在前」**、**「主從分明」**，以及**「由近而遠」**。文法如此，作文也是如此。句子的結構和文章的結構有異曲同工之妙，因為作文其實是文法的延伸。

英文是「重點在前」、「主從分明」的語言，習慣先呈現最重要的關鍵點，跟隨在後的則是補充的細節。這個特色在中文與英文的比對之下，會更為明顯：

> 昨天晚上八點我去看電影。
> I went to see a movie at 8 pm last night.

這句話最重要的關鍵點在「我去看電影」這件事情上，但是中文與英文的處理方式大不相同。中文習慣先交代時空背景，再說重點。然而，英文通常會先提出最重要的重點，隨後才是時空細節的描述，符合「先講重點」的語性：

> I went to see a movie at 8 pm last night.
> 　重點　　　　　　　 細節
> 　主　　　　　　　　 從

重點和細節的區分就是主從之分，由下面的例子更可以清楚地對照出英文「主從分明」的語性：

> 中文傾向「先因後果」：為了避免傷亡，請繫緊安全帶
> 英文傾向「先果後因」：Please fasten the seat belt to avoid death or injury.
> 　　　　　　 主　　　　　　　　　　　　從
> 　　　　　　 重點　　　　　　　　　　　原因

中文習慣先交代背景原因，在提出重點結果。然而，英文的思路恰恰相反。英語使用者習慣先講目的，再闡述相關的理由與細節。這樣的對比，在 G-S 的用語上更加明顯：

| 英文：**Turn right** in 2 miles. | → 重點在前 |
| 中文：兩公里後**向右轉** | → 重點在後 |

因此，在英文寫作流程當中，習慣將重點，就是最「重」要的主控「點」，放在開頭的第一句直接點明。說清楚「最重要的事」以後，再提供相關的細節，列舉「最具說服力的事實」，最後再加上生動的結語，令人在感動中印象深刻，這就是 G-S-G 二進法的精髓。

承襲「重點在前」的語性，英文也是一個**「由小而大」、「由近而遠」**的語言。就如同拍電影時，先聚焦在最重要的景物上，再逐漸擴展納入其他相關細節。英文的視野也是「由近而遠」。這個原則不僅表現在個別的語句中，也反映在段落與整篇文章的結構上。因此，英文的思考模式是直接了當、開門見山。相對於英文的直接，中文則推崇「不直接」，重點留到最後，這是截然不同的溝通模式。中文作文強調「起承轉合」，就是先「迂迴曲折」漫談背景前提，然後才峰迴路轉，點出重點。

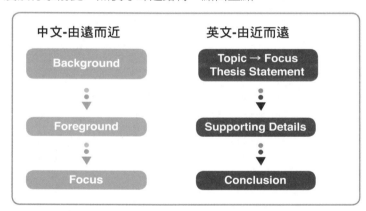

1.6 教材總體檢

先前提到的例子，大多來自於英語母語人士所寫的讀本，從這些讀本當中，可以歸納出「講三句話 G-S-G」的英文思考寫作模式。但這種建構模式是否有納入現今台灣教材的編撰呢？學生在學習英文的過程中，是否有足夠的閱讀範本，來培養這種英文式的建構模式，並將 G-S-G 內化為思考寫作的自然流程？接下來將實際檢測台灣的教材是否反映 G-S-G 三進法的架構。

我們來看看下面這個例子是不是有符合英文寫作原則呢？

A Hard Lesson for Jason

G

G: Jason was sick because he ate too much on Saturday night. → 全篇最重要的話

S: He had hamburgers, French fries, pizza, fried chicken, and a lot of ice cream.
→ 何謂 too much？

S

G: He couldn't sleep that night, so he went to the doctor the next day. → 小段重點

S: The doctor said, "You're sick because you ate too much. Take some medicine and stay away from fast food." →doctor 說什麼？

G: Jason took the medicine right away, but he still had to lie in bed all day. → 結果

G

G: It was a hard lesson. → 整個事件的總結

S: He is now very careful about food. → lesson 的內涵

（南一教科書 第三冊）

　　這篇的標題是 A Lesson for Jason，首先講出「最重要的話」：Jason 因為吃得太多而生病了，點出全篇的主題與主控點（G）。接下來第二句話就交代吃太多的細節（S）→ 到底是吃了些什麼？頭兩句話已形成一個 G-S 小段。然後進入第二小段看醫生的過程，由於第二小段的內容是針對第一段主題（G）提供「具有說服力的事實」（S），因此第一段與第二段間又形成一個 G-S 的關係。接著，進到第二小段內部的三句話，其中也存在 G-S-G 的關係：第一句是重點，第二句是實際引述醫生說的細節，第三句再作個小結。最後，在這些經歷過後，Jason 有什麼改變呢？他學到一個教訓，變得很小心，不再亂吃食物。最後這兩句話作總結，提出一個「令人印象深刻的結語」。這篇文章反映了三進式的鋪陳架構，是很好的範例。

　　然而，如果把下面這篇文章用「三句話」的原則來分析一下，是不是好像缺少了一個總結全文的結語呢？

They Are Going Home

G: The students and their teacher are going home now.

S: On the bus, Miss Wang is talking on the cellphone. Stacy is listening to music. Jason is eating cookies. Denny is playing a video game. And Michael and Emma are sleeping.

G: ?

（南一教科書 第一冊）

上述主題是老師跟學生要回家，那回家途中每個人在做些什麼呢？接下來細節提到每個人從事的活動，但細節說完以後並沒有稍作總結，好像還沒有說完，也無法令人「印象深刻」。

若是加上一個簡單的結論，是不是比較有結束的完整感呢？

They Are Going Home

G: The students and their teacher are going home now.

S: On the bus, Miss Wang is talking on the cellphone. Stacy is listening to music. Jason is eating cookies. Denny is playing a video game. And Michael and Emma are sleeping.

G: They are all very happy to go home.

這樣修改以後，整段文字有了一句簡單的總結：他們都很高興要回家了！這樣是不是更完整了呢？

以上示範如何用 G-S-G 三進建構法來討論文章的好壞，這個原則可運用在教學討論上，不管教科書的內容有沒有符合三進法原則，都可以作為閱讀分析的課題。如果有符合，那老師帶著學生欣賞英文寫作的結構，可以強化學生的構思能力。如果沒有符合，那老師可以帶著學生一起動動腦、想想看，這個段落怎麼樣可以更完整。相信學生經過這樣的分析訓練，一定能夠培養出道地的「英文式思考」！

1.7 英文式思考的養成訓練

「寫三句話」如何落實到整篇文章的鋪陳？本書強調 G-S-G 三進法是文章每一個層次的基本架構，句子到句子，段落到段落，都依循這個原則。英文寫作的習慣是在文章的首段點出全篇的重點，也在每段的首句交代全段的重點。所以，G-S-G 三進法的英文寫作流程不只是說三句話而已，而是能夠應用到不同層次的段落當中，作為最基本的結構流程。

根據 G-S 或 G-S-G 原則，相連的 2、3 個句子間彼此關係密切，圍繞同一個小話題，構成一個「話題組」，成為文章最小的建構單位（a building block）。就像堆積木一樣，

每個含有 G-S 或 G-S-G 關係的 block 就成為可用來堆疊的積木，由下而上，層層建構。所以，2 到 3 個句子（2-3 sentences）相互聯結，就可以形成一個「話題組」（a block）：

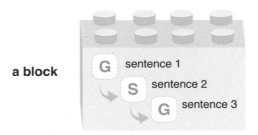

2到3個「話題組」（2-3 blocks）相互聯結，就可以組成一個段落（a paragraph）：

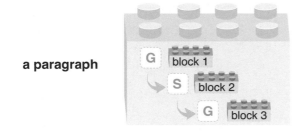

更上一層，2 到 3 個段落（2-3 paragraphs）相互聯結，就可以變成完整的篇章（a composition）：

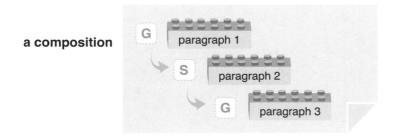

因此，一篇英文作文當中，有好幾個階層的 G-S 或 G-S-G 組合！ 層層鋪展的結果就如下圖所示，由上到下，由裡而外，一層層的 G-S 或 G-S-G 結構，逐步推疊，建構出一篇架構完整，段落有序，內容豐富的好文章：

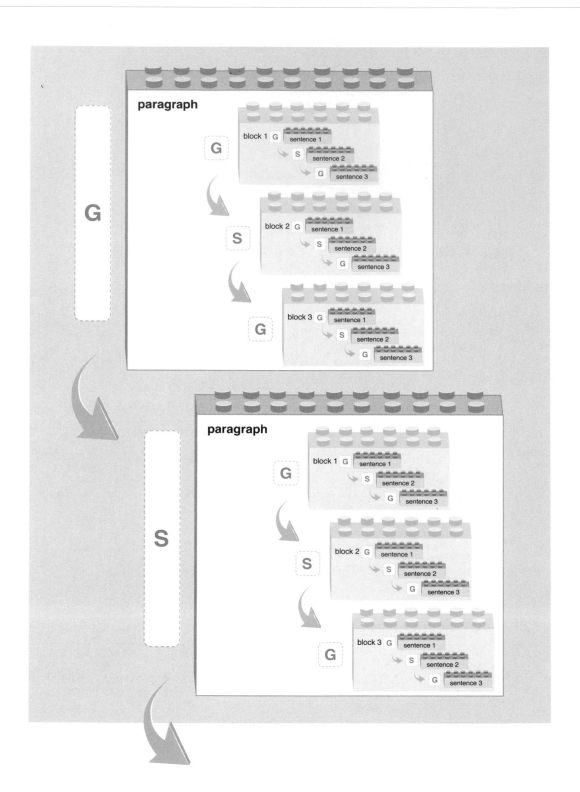

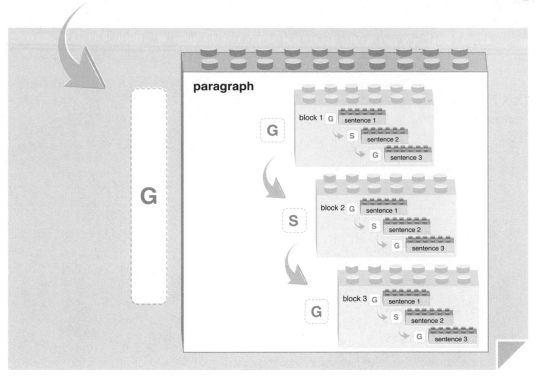

這一章開宗明義，指出寫作的內容以「三句話」為原則。建立了「三句話」的思考模式之後，接著該採取什麼步驟將原則落實到實際的寫作中？從文章的開始到結束，還有什麼值得注意的呢？我們將在以下四章中，針對最困擾台灣學生的四個問題，分別傳授四個訣竅，提出四項具體的作法：

> 主詞必相關（詳見第二章）

Q：什麼是連貫性（coherence）？如何建立連貫性？

A：主詞要相關，話題要相連！主詞連貫代表話題連貫！

Boy[1]

<u>My mother</u>話題 heard me out in silence. She asked no questions. <u>She</u> just let me talk, and when I had finished, <u>she</u> said to our nurse, 'You get them into bed, Nanny. I'm going out.' ← 話題組的主詞必相關

---

1 *Boy* by Roald Dahl

➤ 主題必聚焦（詳見第三章）

    Q：如何破題？如何寫 topic sentence？

    A：主題句不是只有「主題」，還要有「主控點」（controlling idea）！

Sequoya's Gift

Sequoya 話題 is a remarkable 主控點 man.   ←　明確的形容詞帶出主控點

He was a silversmith, painter and soldier 細節.   ←　細節說明主控點

➤ 主旨必承上啟下（詳見第四章）

    Q：如何交待主旨？如何寫 Introduction？

    A：第一段中要有「主旨句」（thesis statement），摘要論點，提出焦點
        （narrow focus）！

Our favorite Creatures

Going off on wildlife adventure 主題 is exciting 主控題!

You meet all kinds of funny, bizarre, fascinating, weird, and wonderful creatures 細節.

The toughest part is trying to decide of all the creatures you've met, which is your

favorite. 主旨／焦點 ←　第一段最後一句話為主旨句，承上啟下

➤ 段落必循序推展（詳見第五章）

    Q：如何分段推展？條理分明、言之有物？

    A：依照 G-S-G 法則，層層堆疊！

My trip to Japan 全篇主題 in May 2010 is the most unforgettable 主控點.

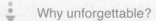
Why unforgettable?

It was my first trip to Japan and I learned a lot about this interesting country 原因細節.

It opened my eyes to the unique culture 焦點 1 and the natural beauty 焦點 2 of Japan 全篇主題.

第二段主題	第三段主題

小結

思考習慣決定寫作習慣。經由閱讀大量的英文作品，分析文章架構，就可歸納出典型的英文式思考與寫作模式。這本「教戰手則」不但讓你了解英文母語人士的溝通方式，也深入剖析 G-S-G 三句話法則。若您能融會貫通這些實戰步驟，確實把握這些寫作訣竅，就能夠寫出道道地地，原汁原味的「英文作文」。

寫作練功坊

1. 以下這篇作文題目，請你寫出一句話，代表本篇的主控點。

運動：說明你最常從事的運動是什麼。（101 年大學指考）

_____

_____

2. 承上的題目，文章分為兩段，請接續上面的第一句話（主控點），再發揮寫出兩段落，每一段請各寫三句話。

(1) 第一段描述這項運動如何進行（如地點、活動方式、及可能需要的相關用品等）

G: _____

_____

S: _____

_____

G: _____

_____

(2) 第二段說明你從事這項運動的原因及這項運動對你生活的影響。

G: _____

_____

S: _____

_____

G: _____

_____

範 例

1. Swimming is my favorite kind of sports.

2. (1)**G:** I usually go swimming at the sports center in my community.

   S: To swim there, I need to wear my swimming suit, swimming cap, and goggles. I also need things for a shower afterwards.

   G: Although it is kind of troublesome to bring a huge bag to the pool, I still enjoy my weekly swimming very much.

   (2)**G:** Swimming helps me relax and forget about pressure at school.

   S: In the water, I gently exercise my whole body with my favorite free-style.

   G: When swimming, I feel like a fish in the water and feels no worries at all.

Chapter

02

如何連貫？
主詞相關，話題相連

中文、英文思路有什麼不同？

主詞為何不能跳來跳去？

每句話如何轉接才自然？

What is coherence?

上英文作文課時都聽過老師說：作文要有 coherence！但究竟什麼是 coherence？每個句子的文法都對了，兜在一起，就組成了一篇好作文嗎？如何將一個個句子組成有條理又有連貫性的文章？

在討論連貫性之前，先來看看什麼叫作「不連貫」！第一章提到英文寫作由最重要的三句話開始：「最重要的話」、「最具說服力的話」、及「最令人感動的話」。下面三句話分開看，似乎符合三句話的內涵，但是整個讀起來是否有點「跳 tone」的感覺？

My mom is beautiful. → 最重要的話？？

Her dresses are expensive and tailor-made. → 最具說服力的話？？

My father loves to take her to travel. → 最令人感動的話？？

這個怪怪的感覺，其實源於這三句話的「不連貫」。何謂「不連貫」？就是**主詞不相關，話題不相連**。細細觀察，主詞從 my mom → her dresses → my father，跳來跳去，一下說媽媽，一下說衣服，一下又要說爸爸。另外，每一句所帶出的話題也不相連，從「媽媽很漂亮」說到「衣服很貴」，再說到「爸爸很愛帶她去旅行」，這三個話題的相關性實在無從得知，彷彿話題彼此之間隔著一條鴻溝，無法跨越。

學生寫作時，常常會有這種「不連貫」的問題。下面這一篇是台灣學生[1]寫的作文，題目是如果人能夠活一千年，那會是什麼樣的生活呢？跟現在又有什麼差別？請讀讀看，有沒有 coherence？

Living a Thousand Years

Through the past of my 200 years, I have many delightful moments. Since the life-span of humans has extended, the lives are longer than before. The summer vacation is lengthened to 4 months a year.

這一段說到了過去兩百年的生活情況，仔細讀過，是否感到有些不連貫？原因為何？若把主詞抽出來比照：I → the life-span → the lives → the summer vacation，因為主詞不停變換，而且彼此之間沒有相關性，造成了彷彿話題不停跳換的現象。所以，「不連貫」

---

1 本書所引用的學生作文片段僅用為範例且皆經學生許可。

的問題之 是「主詞變來變去」

再看看另一位學生寫的作文，在文章開頭的第一段，也示範了另一種「不連貫」：

Is Homeschooling a Good Choice?

More and more people are promoting homeschooling in Taiwan. They consider that homeschooling can help children to develop their interests and get more information than school education. However, society in Taiwan does not seem to be the same as western countries. For example, the poverty gap in Taiwan is a big problem, and it may lead to a disorder of education between children.

上述例子的主詞分別為 more and more people → they → society in Taiwan → the poverty gap in Taiwan，若單看主詞，似乎是有相關性，但是這些主詞和主題 homeschooling in Taiwan 的關聯是什麼？顯然這個段落是要探討「台灣在家自學」的現象，所以第一句指出越來越多台灣人提倡在家自學，第二句則說明原因。但是在第三個句子中，卻突然將 society in Taiwan 和 western countries 做比較，這種比較與 homeschooling 的關聯性在哪裡？這句話之前的文字中並沒有提到 western countries 與 homeschooling 有何相關。因此，文章內部的思路出現不連貫的「跳接」（jump in thought），也會導致讀者混淆。所以「不連貫」的第二個問題是「話題跳來跳去」。

看完了上述兩個例子，對於什麼是「不連貫」，是否有了基本的認識呢？基本上，造成「不連貫」的原因有兩大點：

1. 「主詞」變來變去
    → 同一個話題組的主詞沒有相關，東扯一個，西扯一個！

2. 「話題」跳來跳去
    → 新的話題與前一個話題連接不上，造成文章思路「卡卡」！

現在知道了問題所在，那麼解決的辦法是什麼呢？讓我們繼續看下去。

維持英文寫作「連貫」的兩個訣竅分別是：

1. 保持**主詞**間的連貫 → 建立「主詞」相關的「話題組」
   Write a topic-sharing, subject-related block:

   Subject 1 → Subject 2 → Subject 3

2. 保持話題間的連貫 → 以「舊話題」引進「新話題」
   Introduce a new topic by mentioning it in the previous block:

   Block 1 Topic X...Y... → **Block 2** Topic Y...Z... → **Block 3** Topic Z...

　　首先，如何保持句子間的連貫？訣竅在於了解英文的「主詞」（subject）即是「句子的話題」（topic of the sentence）。因此，主詞必須保持相關的一致性，才能保有話題的一致性。主詞相關、話題一致的 2、3 句話結合在一起，就形成了一個「話題組」（a topic-sharing block），這是作文最基本的 G-S-G 建構單位。「話題組」顧名思義，必然是話題一致，但如何顯出話題一致？最重要的就是主詞要相關！

　　接著，組成一個主詞相關、話題一致的「話題組」後，該如何變換成另一個「話題組」呢？話題組的轉換，就是話題的轉換，保持 coherence 的祕訣是前後相連、新舊交替！話題轉換的過程中，想辦法將新的「話題」融入到「前一個」話題組中，藉由前一個話題組中提到的某個元素（a mentioned element）帶出新的話題。這樣的步驟強調話題間的銜接，要在語意關係上環環相扣，由第一個「話題組」轉為第二個「話題組」，語意上既要有交集，也要有延伸。藉由主詞後提到的成份轉入新的話題，這樣的轉換才不顯突兀，而且文章才會順暢，到達「船過水無痕」的境界。

　　說了這麼多，到底該如何實際操作呢？那來試改一下先前看過的文章吧！

　　如果主詞相關，文章看起來是不是就會好多了呢？

> 主詞要相關

Living a Thousand Years （修改版）

Through the past 200 years, I have many delightful moments. Since my life span has been extended, I enjoy more vacation time in each season. My summer vacation is lengthened to 4 months a year and it's the best time for me to travel around the world.

如此改寫以後，把原本八竿子打不著關係的主詞，變成 I → my life span → I → my summer vacation → it，文章看起來是不是通順多了呢？主詞的相關性提高，才能維繫一致的話題！從 I 到 my life span 到 I 是一個話題組，再發展到另一個話題組 my summer vacation。從 I 到 my summer vacation 是藉由主詞後的成分 more vacation time in each season 作為連結，將新話題與前一個話題連接起來。

因此，主詞後所提到的「後敘成分」，是連接話題的關鍵！在另一個例子改寫中，也可以看到話題與話題間的思路連結：

> 話題要連貫

Is Homeschooling a Good Choice? （修改版）

More and more people are promoting homeschooling in Taiwan. They consider that homeschooling can help children develop their interests and get more information than school education. However, homeschooling is not as popular in Taiwan as in western countries due to societal differences. For example, the poverty gap in Taiwan is bigger, so fewer people can afford homeschooling which costs a lot.

在這段文章中，把第三句改寫一下，使這句話承上啟後，先清楚提到台灣在家自學並不像西方國家如此普遍，再提到原因是兩方的社會差異。如此一來，新話題「台灣與西方國家的差別」就可以跟上一個話題有所連接。那麼差別在哪呢？後面舉出例子說明，因為台灣的貧富差距大，能夠負擔在家自學費用的家庭並不多。整段看下來，這樣的開頭是不是通順多了呢？

由上面的兩個例子改寫，印證了維持英文寫作「連貫」的兩個訣竅就是：建立「主詞」相關的「話題組」，以及利用「舊話題成分」引進「新話題」。有了這兩個訣竅在握，就不怕寫出「跳 tone」的文章！英文寫作不再「痛」！

2.3　以不變應萬變

　　把握上述的原則之後，接下來要探討更細部的訣竅，也就是「何謂相關」？首先，在許多英文讀本當中，可以觀察到同一個話題組的主詞常常保有相關的一致性，像是 *Boy* 一書中所提到媽媽跟他的互動：

> My mother 話題 heard me out in silence. She asked no questions. She just let me talk, and when I had finished, she said to our nurse, 'You get them into bed, Nanny. I'm going out.'

　　首先，最一開始的「主詞」是 my mother，說明了主要的「話題」是「我媽媽」。她在互動當中做了哪些事情，說了哪些話，這些句子的主詞都是 my mother 或是代替 my mother 的代名詞 she。由此可知，一個話題組中不會隨意地變換主詞，因為一個主詞代表一個句子的話題。主詞相關的幾句話就會形成一個「話題組」（topic-sharing block），所有的句子都用高度相關的主詞來延續這個話題。

　　但是所謂相關就是「重複」同一個主詞嗎？其實不是。如果不重複主詞，那主詞要如何相關呢？在 *Stealing the Show* 的讀本中，就可以找到主詞高度相關卻不重複的「話題組」：

> Josh and Katie were still in the living room. Their father had gone back to the kitchen, and upstairs they could hear the sound of running water and muffled screams.

　　這個「話題組」當中高度相關的主詞 Josh and Katie、their father，以及 they 告訴讀者這一段落的話題是 Josh and Katie。可能有人會問，Josh and Katie 不等於 their father 啊？為什麼它們是高度相關的主詞？那是因為關聯性就顯現在 their 這個字上。因為 their father 代替的是 Josh 跟 Katie 的父親，當然跟 Josh and Katie 有關囉！

　　主詞相關之外，還要講求話題相連，從一個話題到另一個話題要有順暢合理的轉接。以下，在讀本當中，能夠看到話題之間的轉換過程。在 *The Promise*[2] 這本書中，發現了這樣的例子：

2　*The Promise* by Jackie French Koller

We pushed the barn door open a crack and slipped inside. The air within was warm and moist and scented with the sweet-sour mix of animal smells and fresh hay. The cows stirred and mooed, and Bessie and Ned, our work-horses, stomped and blew us a welcome. Old Snoops, the barn cat, and her assorted sons and daughters came running from all corners.

從這個段落中，我們可以清楚的看到這段有三個「話題」：第一是 we，也就是主角的出場；第二是 the air within，也就是在穀倉裡的空氣；第三是 the cows 以及穀倉內其他的動物。若把代表話題的主詞抽出來看，似乎天差地遠，那這一段是如何把它們連結在一起的呢？就是藉由主詞後提到的「後敘成分」。下面的圖示很清楚地說明了連結的流程：

話題一：
We pushed the barn door open a crack and slipped inside.

話題二：
The air within was warm and moist and scented with the sweet-sour mix of animal smells and fresh hay.

話題三：
The cows stirred and mooed, and Bessie and Ned, our work-horses, stomped and blew us a welcome. Old Snoops, the barn cat, and her assorted sons and daughters came running from all corners.

這個流程中，可以很清楚的看到，藉由第一個話題 we 進入穀倉 barn 帶出第二個話題 the air within，然後再藉由 barn 裡的 animal smells 引出第三個話題。由此可得知，在英文寫作中，所謂話題的連貫，意思是「新話題」必定是由前一個話題之中所提到的「後敘成分」（elements after the subject）來發展。這些後敘成分，就成為語意連接的關鍵詞！

從許多的英文讀本中，可以發現，文章連貫的方式，就是主詞相關，話題相連。如前所述，英文當中，主詞就代表話題。因此，主詞相關的幾句話合起來，就變成一個「話題組」。在「話題組」當中，主詞必須高度相關，如下圖所示：

知道了英文的主詞代表話題，那麼主詞相關就是連貫嗎？一個段落中，每個句子之間的主詞關聯好了，接下來要關心的是，怎麼換話題？換話題就像介紹新朋友的過程，一個人要介紹新朋友，總是會先說「這是我的朋友，他叫 ×××」，而不是直接說「他叫 ×××」就結束。為什麼？因為新朋友對其他人來說，是完全陌生的人，但是因為有「我」這個中間人，所以新朋友才會藉由「我」來連結到其他人。因此，在寫作的時候，新話題出現之前，必須依附在前一個話題的內容上，與其產生關聯。由於每一個主詞所代表的話題與其後敘成分（predicate）是息息相關的，因此，新的話題就是要藉由前一句主詞後的敘述成分來帶出。也就是說，前一個句子的「後敘」成分可成為下一個句子的話題，這就是所謂的「舊訊息」（old information）帶出「新訊息」（new information）。

這樣的關係如同下圖所示：

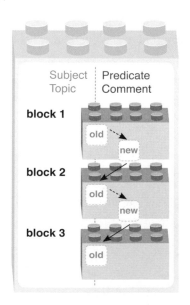

「舊訊息」帶出「新訊息」的連貫性也可以很清楚地在下面的段落[3]中看出：

> **The introduction** is the first paragraph of your essay. **It** includes a thesis statement which introduces the topic and states the main idea. **The introduction** should capture the reader's attention and make them want to read on. **Many introductions** begin with general background information and end with the thesis statement as **the last sentence** of the paragraph. In an opinion essay, **the thesis statement** should state your opinion about the topic.

上述例子搭配下列的圖解，可以看出，第一與第二個話題組皆圍繞在 "the introduction" 上，而第三話題組為 "the thesis statement"。那他們是如何轉換的呢？第一組與第二組因為話題類似，因此主詞沒有太大的轉變。而在第二組與第三組的轉換過程，利用舊訊息 many introductions 引出新話題 the thesis statement，之後話題就此轉移為 the thesis statement。

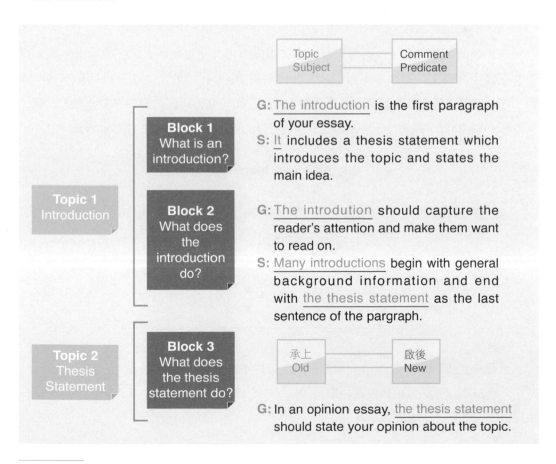

3 此段落出自 *NorthStar: Reading and Writing Level 4*, Third Edition, Unit 3, p.62.

再強調一次，英文寫作要思路通順、連貫，到底訣竅何在？在於了解英文主詞即是話題，主詞必須保持相關的一致性，才能保有話題的一致性。而換話題的時候，要藉由前一句話的「後敘成分」（predicate）來銜接，在敘述中清楚「提到」下一個話題。如此前後呼應，語意上下承接，才能達成通篇作文的思路連貫。

2.5 中英比一比：主詞為大 vs. 主題為大

建立主詞相關的話題組，難就難在「相關」二字。寫出主詞相關的「話題組」，對台灣學生來說很困難的原因在於，中文與英文呈現主題的方式大不相同。哪裡不同呢？首先，請仔細觀察下列句子的主詞：

- 他的家很漂亮，客廳很大，廚房很新，浴室還有自然採光，我們都很喜歡_____！
- His house is pretty. Its living room is big. Its kitchen is newly equipped, and its bathroom has natural lighting. We all like his house!

在主詞的表達方式上，有沒有看出什麼端倪？中文可直接談客廳、廚房、浴室，但英文要加上使各主詞關聯在一起的所有格代詞 Its。在《英文文法有道理》一書中提到，中文與英文最大的不同在於中文是情境導向，而英文則是語句導向。中文以「主題」（discourse topic）為大，一旦主題確立後，相關的句子可以有不同主詞（subject）：

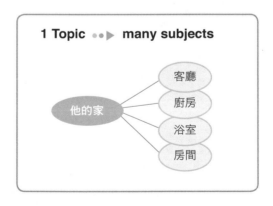

一旦中文提到以「他的家」為主題，之後的主詞可能是「客廳」、「廚房」、「浴室」、「房間」，都與這個主題相關。因此，中文的基本句式是以主題為一個單位，同一主題底下又細分許多小主詞。

但是，英文以「主詞」（subject）為大，每個句子的主詞都是獨立的代表一個話題（topic of the sentence）。客廳、浴室、廚房有了相關的所有者（its）才能和 His house 關連起來。因此要藉由相關的主詞連結為一個單位，對應到一個較大的話題（topic of the block）。也就是說，彼此相關的主詞（群）才能指向同一個話題（a topic-sharing block）：

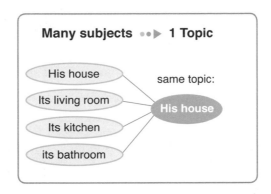

　　因此，中英文的不同在於表達主題方式不同。中文先決定主題（discourse topic），再發展出與主題相關的主詞。反之，英文則是藉由幾個相關的主詞一起導向同一個話題（topic of the block）：

Chinese vs. English

Chinese →「主題」（topic）為大

- [他的家] 很漂亮，客廳很大，廚房很新，浴室還有自然採光，我們都很喜歡！

English →「主詞」（subject）為大

- **His house** is pretty. **Its living room** is big. **Its kitchen** is newly equipped, and **its bathroom** has natural lighting. We all like **the house**!

　　中英文的寫作方式承繼兩個語言不同的特性：中文以「主題」（discourse topic）為大，一旦主題「他的家」確立後，相關的句子可以有不同主詞。但是，英文以「主詞」（subject）為大，每個句子的主詞都代表句子的話題（topic of the sentence），因此唯有藉由相關的所有格才能將不同的主詞連結為一個話題單位（"His house"），對應到一個話題組（a topic-sharing block）。同一個話題組的主詞之間彼此高度相關。

在此特別一提，英文的 topic 可以翻譯為中文的「主題」或「話題」。本書使用「主題」來表示大範圍的 topic，如全篇文章或段落的主題（theme of the essay/paragraph）；「話題」則用來表示小範圍的 topic，如句子的話題（topic of the sentence/block）。

由於中英文有不同的語言表達方式，台灣學生很容易寫出「中式英文」，把中文的習慣帶到英文，也就是沒有保持主詞的相關性，主詞變來變去，也使得話題變來變去，缺乏一致性。舉例來說，下列兩個句子的好壞之分，差別在於主詞是否一致：

Bad → 主詞變來變去：<u>My house</u> is big. <u>I</u> have a large living room and <u>there</u> are three spacious bedrooms. <u>Most people</u> like to have a big house.

Good → 主詞一致：<u>My house</u> is big. It has a large living room and three spacious bedrooms. It is the dream house most people would like to have.

因此，在寫英文的段落時，特別要掌握的一個原則，就是不要輕易變換主詞。這就是一般所說的文意通順連貫（coherence）的「訣竅」之一。因為主詞等於話題。如果一段文字當中，所要描述的是同一個話題，最好的方式就是主詞維持一致，並藉由舊主詞引進「後敘成分」，作為另外一個話題，然後再換主詞，進入另外一個話題組。

2.6 教材總體檢

了解英文中主詞即是話題之後，可以依此來檢視台灣的英文教材，是否有依循英文不隨便變換主詞的原則呢？這樣的觀念是否能夠透過教材來讓學生熟悉英文「主詞」為大的特性？

以下台北樹蛙的例子可以作為一個好的範本，因為這篇文章的主詞相當一致，主詞彼此高度相關，全篇維持一貫的主題：

A Taipei Tree Frog

Hello, everybody! <u>My name</u> is Fred. Look at my green skin and big eyes. <u>I</u> am a Taipei tree frog.

<u>I</u> was not a frog a month ago. What was <u>I</u>? <u>I</u> was a cute tadpole at that time. <u>My skin</u> was dark, and <u>my legs</u> were short. <u>My brothers and sisters</u> were with me in the pond.

Now <u>I</u> am a frog, and <u>I</u> don't live in a pond. <u>I</u> live in trees. Look! <u>I</u> can climb trees.

（翰林教科書 第二冊）

這個範本當中的主詞從 my name → I×3 → my skin → my legs → my brothers and sisters → I×4，這些主詞彼此都高度相關，都是以台北樹蛙為第一人稱來描述故事。

然而，以下的閱讀範本讀起來，是不是有比較「跳 tone」的感覺？

Birthday Gifts for Cody

<u>Today</u> is Cody's birthday. <u>The Browns</u> are busy. <u>Mrs. Brown</u> is preparing hot dogs, Cody's favorite food. <u>Peter and his father</u>, Mr. Brown, are building a new house for Cody. <u>Amanda</u> is painting it. <u>Cody</u> is very happy. <u>He</u> is running and jumping around.

（康軒教科書 第一冊）

這篇的標題為 Birthday Gifts for Cody，話題應該圍繞在 birthday gifts 以及 Cody 身上，也就是說，主詞應該與這兩個話題相關。但是看完整篇，發現主詞由 today → the Browns → Mrs. Brown → Peter and his father → Amanda → Cody → he，主詞之間的關係不清，話題不停地轉換，而且主角 Cody 到最後才出現，所以整篇似乎給人重點不明、思緒混亂的感覺。

假如要符合英文的寫作原則，保持主詞的一致性，使主詞圍繞在同一個話題上，該如何改寫呢？也許可以這麼做：

Birthday Gifts for Cody （修改版）

<u>Today</u> is Cody's birthday. <u>Cody</u> is very excited, because everyone in his family is preparing a gift for him. <u>His mother</u>, Mrs. Brown, is grilling the hot dogs for him. <u>His brother and father</u>, Peter and Mr. Brown, are building a new house for him. <u>His sister</u>, Amanda, is painting the house for him. <u>Cody</u> is so happy that he is running and jumping around!

除了主詞相關以外，建立coherence 的第二個重點在於新舊訊息的轉換。新的話題就是要藉由前一句主詞後的敘述成分（predicate）來帶出。前一個句子的「後敘」成分可成為下一個句子的話題，也就是所謂的「舊訊息」帶出「新訊息」的方法。

在高中的教材中，有一篇文章在介紹便利貼與跳跳彈簧的兩個發明，其中在談論便利貼的部分，可以清楚的看到「舊訊息」帶出「新訊息」的過程：

<u>A man named Spencer Silver</u> was working in the 3M research laboratories in 1970 trying to find a strong adhesive. <u>Silver</u> developed a new adhesive, but <u>it</u> was even weaker than those 3M manufactured. <u>It</u> stuck to objects, but could easily be lifted off. It should have been super-strong, but <u>it</u> turned out to be super-weak instead.

（遠東教科書 第四冊）

從上段可以發現，原本的話題是在介紹 Silver 這個人，後來說到他發明了新的黏著劑，但黏著劑不怎麼黏。到這邊為止，其實新話題已經悄悄地被引介進來，與舊話題結合。這個引介的過程在第二句話的鋪陳就非常明顯，這句話同時包含了舊訊息 Silver 與新訊息 a new adhesive。原本環繞 Silver 的主詞也從第三句開始變成環繞 a new adhesive 的主詞（It）了。這樣的轉換，在英文當中，是非常自然的，也是學生可以學習的範本。

然而，就在同一篇課文中，介紹跳跳彈簧 Slinky[4] 的段落，似乎出現了轉換「卡卡」的現象：

---

4 標題為了讀者方便暫訂為 Slinky，此非原文標題。

> ### Slinky
>
> The no-battery-required toy has fascinated three generations of children and adults alike. According to one estimate, more than two million Slinkys have been sold and the only change in the original design has been to crimp the ends as a safety measure. Betty James died in November 2008, aged 90, after having served as president of James Industries from 1960 to 1998. But the Slinky is still hopping, skipping, jumping, and bouncing across floors and down stairs all over America.

（遠東教科書 第四冊）

這個介紹 Slinky 的段落，前兩句的主詞圍繞在 Slinky 這個話題上，但是在第三句話中，突然出現一個不相干的主詞 Betty James，顯得有點突兀，此段當中的前後文也沒有提及 Betty James 為何會突然出現在這裡。隨後又馬上回到原本 Slinky 的話題上。第三句話的突兀使得這個段落似乎有個斷層，語意不連貫。即使文章的第一段有提到 Betty James 是跳跳彈簧的創始人之一，但是若光從這一段文字敘述來看，並沒有辦法了解 Betty James 出現的原因。因此，怎麼樣的寫法比較有連貫性，而且不會改變太多原意呢？

> ### Slinky（修改版）
>
> The no-battery-required toy has fascinated three generations of children and adults alike. According to one estimate, more than two million Slinkys have been sold and the only change in the original design has been to crimp the ends as a safety measure. Although one of Slinky's investors, Betty James, died in November 2008, aged 90, after having served as president of James Industries from 1960 to 1998, the Slinky is still hopping, skipping, jumping, and bouncing across floors and down stairs all over America.

在第三句話當中，把 Betty James 的身分跟 Slinky 關連起來，使 Betty James 的出現不再突兀，那麼這個段落的主詞群也能夠導向同一個話題：Slinky，並且讓文章讀起來通順許多。

小結

英文寫作時，如何保持「句子」間的連貫？訣竅在於英文的「主詞」必須保持相關的一致性，才能保有話題的一致性。那麼，話題與話題之間該如何轉換呢？必須藉由前一句中的「後敘成分」新舊話題轉換的過程中，要在前一個「話題組」中，想辦法融入接下來要談論的「新話題」，藉由「舊訊息」（old information）來引進「新訊息」（new information）。這樣的轉換才會通順，而且文章的語意才會流暢。顧好了句子間的連貫，以及話題間的連貫，就可以大聲的保證：I can write a COHERENT composition!

寫作練功坊

題目

這一章我們學到了英文作文很重要的觀念：話題要連貫。

請檢視以下作文，試問各句話題的銜接是否都有相關性？如果沒有連貫的地方，請試著改寫看看，如何改寫才能比較通順？

請以運動為主題，說明你最常從事的運動是什麼。文分二段，第一段描述這項運動如何進行（如地點、活動方式、及可能需要的相關用品等），第二段說明你從事這項運動的原因及這項運動對你生活的影響。

One of my favorite sports is badminton. Near our office, there is a gym of the community. Recently, I joined a group. There are about 20 members in it for now. The leader of this group booked three fields in two hours every Sunday. Each person just needs to pay 1000 NT dollars per season. We can play men's doubles, women's doubles or mixed-doubles. Because the leader will provide enough badminton, all we need is to prepare our own racquet.

Badminton lovers are often played indoors, because the shuttlecock would be affected by wind. We can play badminton in any weather. I think it is necessary to join an indoor sports group in Taipei. Everybody knows the rainy season in Taipei is very notorious and annoying. People usually couldn't play basketball outsides in summer. Beside of that, this kind of sport demands agility, speed, precision and technique. Power or Strength does not absolutely decide the affect. Even a child with excellent technique can defeat an adult person easily. Badminton is really a very interesting sport.

 寫作修理廠

 修 改

I love sports. One of my favorite sports is badminton. Near ~~our~~my office, there is a ~~gym of the~~ community gym. I often played badminton with my colleagues there. Recently, I joined a badminton group. There are about 20 members in it for now. The leader of this group books~~ed~~ three fields ~~in~~ for two hours every Sunday. Each ~~person~~ player just needs to pay 1000 NT dollars per season. We can play men's doubles, women's doubles or mixed-doubles. Because the leader will provide enough ~~badminton~~ shuttlecocks, all we need is to prepare our own racquets.

Badminton ~~lover are~~ is often played indoors, because the shuttlecock is light-weighted and would be easily affected by wind. ~~We can play badminton in any weather.~~ In order to play it in any weather, I think it is necessary to join an indoor sports group, especially in Taipei. ~~Everybody knows~~ The rainy season in Taipei is ~~very~~ notoriously ~~and~~ annoying, but since I joined the indoor group, I have been playing it in all seasons. It helps to keep my body fit. ~~People usually couldn't play basketball outsides in summer.~~ Besides ~~of that~~, this ~~kind of~~ sport demands agility, speed, precision and good techniques. Physical power or strength alone does not ~~absolutely decide the affect~~ determine the result of the game. Even a child with excellent techniques can defeat an adult ~~person~~ player easily. To me, badminton is really a very interesting and challenging sport.

（參考範例）

 修改建議

1. 中式英文的一個大問題就是人稱變來變去，原文中第一句用第一人稱的觀點：One of my favorite sports，第二句就變成 near our office（our 從哪跑出來的？）。因此要儘量保持一致的人稱：one of my favorite sports、near my office。

2. 前後句子間的事件也要相關，語意的連結要清楚！原文第一句提到 badminton，第二句跳到 gym，第三句又突然提到 a group。三句話間有什麼關聯？修改時加了一句話使前後語意連結：I often played badminton with my colleagues there.

3. 第二段中也有人稱變來變去的問題，連續四句話的主詞都是不一樣的人稱：

We can play badminton.... I think it is necessary ....

Everybody knows.... People usually couldn't play....

這樣跳來跳去，真是叫人摸不著頭緒！請依主題群（topic block）的概念，每兩三句話的主詞要相關，以連結成一個語意相關的主題鏈！

4. 第二段另一個問題也仍是句子間的相關性，文中先提到在室內打球，因為球會受風影響，又提到必須要在台北加入室內團體，然後又描述台北的天氣，接著又突然移轉開始說羽毛球需要快速和技巧，這些和第二段的主題（你從事運動的原因及對個人生活的影響）有什麼關係？因此修改時加上一些連結語意的句子，強調從事該運動對個人的幫助和挑戰！

修改後版本

    I love sports. One of my favorite sports is badminton. Near my office, there is a community gym. I often played badminton with my colleagues there. Recently, I joined a badminton group. There are about 20 members in it for now. The leader of this group books three fields for two hours every Sunday. Each player just needs to pay 1000 NT dollars per season. We can play men's doubles, women's doubles or mixed-doubles. Because the leader will provide enough shuttlecocks, all we need is to prepare our own racquets.

    Badminton is often played indoors, because the shuttlecock is light-weighted and would be easily affected by wind. In order to play it in any weather, I think it is necessary to join an indoor sports group, especially in Taipei. The rainy season in Taipei is notoriously annoying, but since I joined the indoor group, I have been playing it in all seasons. It helps to keep my body fit. Besides, this sport demands agility, speed, precision and good techniques. Physical power or strength alone does not determine the result of the game. Even a child with excellent techniques can defeat an adult player easily. To me, badminton is really a very interesting and challenging sport.

Chapter

03

如何破題？
找出主控點，為文章定調！

開頭怎麼寫？

如何定主題？

如何延續寫下去？

How to begin?

　　萬事起頭難，常常有學生問：「作文到底要怎麼開頭？」可能得到這樣的回答：「英文一定要先破題，要有 topic sentence！」但究竟要怎麼破題？怎麼寫 topic sentence？是否只要寫出一成不變的 I am going to talk about...，就算是有了 topic sentence 嗎？什麼樣的開頭才算是好的 topic sentence？而開了頭之後又要如何繼續？學生常常困在作文的泥淖裡，就是因為不知道如何開頭。所以本章要教給你的訣竅，就是如何破題，如何兼顧「開頭」與「延續」。

　　在說明如何寫「好的開頭」以前，先來看看什麼樣叫作「不好的開頭」。近來風行的 Mind Map 成為許多學生的作文教材。寫作文以前，先胡思亂想，天馬行空，這對於發想的練習是非常好的。比方說，My Mom 這個主題，可以有很多的發想。我媽媽有哪些特質呢？她很漂亮、很聰明，平常很忙碌而且待人和善：

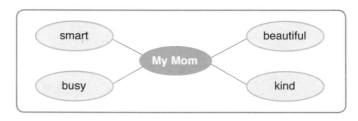

　　想好了這些特質以後，是把想到的東西全部都丟到作文裡嗎？

My mom is beautiful. She is also smart. She is busy every day. She is kind to others.

　　仔細觀察一下這樣的作文，感覺怎麼樣呢？這些的確都是媽媽的特質，但是不知道哪一個才是重點。而且這些特質間有什麼關聯？細節又在哪？媽媽哪裡漂亮？怎麼知道她很聰明？她每天在忙什麼？她很和善的具體作為是什麼？太多的重點放在一起，就變成了沒有重點。因此一篇好的文章，是不是需要經過篩選重點、去蕪存菁呢？理想的開頭會有一個清楚的**「主控點」**，為全文定調！

　　再者，為了鼓勵學生開始寫簡單的作文，常會以「My Daily Routine」為題，要學生記下日常生活中做的事情。這種條列式的練習，有助於熟悉時態與句型，但作為寫作練習，就變成流水帳的紀錄，今天七點做什麼、八點做什麼、九點做什麼，就這樣一路寫到晚上十點。每個細節都寫得清清楚楚：

```
7 am: I eat breakfast.
8 am: I go to school.
9 am: I study English.
10 am: I study math.
…
7 pm: I eat dinner.
8 pm: I watch TV.
9 pm: I do homework.
10 pm: I play the computer.
…
```

　　整篇讀下來，給人什麼樣的感覺呢？是不是有點太過瑣碎？不知道重點在哪裡？這樣的練習，對於訓練英文寫作的效果有限。 畢竟英文寫作不等於流水帳啊。流水帳的特性就是條列細節，但英文寫作講求重點清楚！只有在細節前加上一個「主控點」（controlling idea），才能為文章定調：

I have a **busy and stressful** schedule.
At 7, …
At 8, …

　　總結上述，可以知道，「太多的重點」及「毫無重點」都不是好的英文寫作開頭。那麼，到底該怎麼開頭，才能夠說出「恰恰好」的重點呢？祕訣就是要在 topic sentence 中帶出一個「主控點」（controlling idea）！

3.2　訣竅3：找出主控點，為主題定調

　　「恰恰好」的英文作文必須有它的條理，那麼何謂條理？條理從何而來？條理其實來自於「一開始」就定調於一個新鮮的**「主控點」（controlling idea）**[1]，也就是控制主題接下來的走向。根據國外編撰的英文寫作教材 *NorthStar*[2] 對 topic sentence 所下的定義，其中就提到主控點的重要性：

1　*NorthStar: Reading and Writing Level 4*, Third Edition, p.19.

2　*NorthStar: Reading and Writing Level 4*, Third Edition, Unit 2, p.42.

The topic sentence introduces **the main idea** and **the controlling idea** which is your idea or opinion about the main idea. The topic sentence controls what you write in the rest of the paragraph. All the sentences in the paragraph must relate to, describe, or illustrate **the controlling idea** in the topic sentence.

所以 topic sentence的功能在於介紹與主題相關的控制點（the controlling idea），我稱為「主控點」，段落中其餘的部分都得依循這個主控點來發揮。主控點不能缺少，也不能太多，通常一個主題只需要搭配一個主控點（a controlling idea），一條路走完了才接續走下一條。比方說，在第一章談到的 My Mom 的例子中，示範了如何選擇主控點：

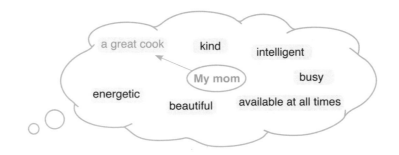

在許多 My Mom 的特質當中，只選一條路來發展，例如 a great cook。主控點確立了，接下來就要提供佐證，也就是具有說服力的細節。媽媽為什麼是一個好廚師呢？因為她會煮各式各樣的菜！主控點與具體細節的結合，就是所謂的「開頭」與「延續」的結合。

My mom is a great cook. → 以主控點開頭
She can cook all kinds of delicious food, Chinese or Western.→ 以具體細節延續

首先要了解「破題」之後必須「控制」文章走向，所謂主題句就是最直接點出主題並為主題定調的那句話，要有一個明確的主控點（controlling idea），才能確定主題的走向，也才能決定「延續」的內容，知道要加入什麼樣的「具體細節」。定調之後，再具體鋪陳！台灣學生在思考及寫作上，常犯了「重點不清」或「言而無據」的大忌。問題就在於缺乏控制文章走向的「主控點」，或是缺乏支撐這個主控點的相關細節。洋洋灑灑的作文中，不但要說出最重要的話，也需要補充最具說服力的「證據」，才不至於空泛無力。最給力的論述需要最給力的論點與證據，而證據如何提供？在於先確立「主控點」，然後才知道要描述哪些「具體的細節」！

依照這樣的邏輯，如果作文練習只是請學生以時間來記錄事件，可能會誤導他們，使他們誤把事情的細節（如時間地點），當成重點來講。其實真正的重點應該是事情本身某個凸出的面向，也就是能夠為全篇定調的一個主控點。因此，假設以 The School Anniversary 為題，一篇好的作文不能只是流水帳，不能只是一一記錄校慶這一天所發生的事情，而是要先找出一個能聚焦的面向，為校慶這整件事情定調，然後再描述細節。校慶可以有很多個面向，它可以是好玩的、忙碌的、無聊的，或是累人的等等。那麼，你的選擇是什麼？開放的 Mind Map 提供了零散的各種面向，但文章要能深刻感人，就得選擇一個最能凸顯特色的主控點！

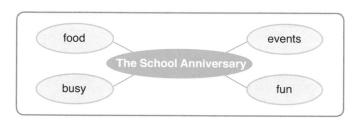

　　對你而言，校慶最深刻的一點是什麼？請先選擇，而所選擇的主控點將會決定作文的走向。例如：

The school anniversary is _____.

fun—How fun? Why is it fun? What are the fun things?

busy—How busy? Why is it busy? What makes you busy?

tiring—How tiring? Why is it tiring? What makes you so tired?

boring—How boring? Why is it boring? What makes you bored?

　　The school anniversary is _____. 就是全文的主題句（topic sentence），文章的主題是校慶（The school anniversary），這很清楚。但框框裡要填的是什麼？就是你要強調的主控點。主控點清楚之後，必須要進一步凸顯主控點的可信度，選擇可用來說明、具有說服力的細節，繼續寫下去。你想說校慶很好玩，那就要接下去說怎樣好玩？為什麼好玩？好玩的事情有哪些？如果說校慶很忙，那就要接下去說怎樣忙？為什麼忙？忙些什麼？依此類推。

　　這就是英文先破題，再延展一個構思的方式。許多的故事書，甚至童書，都是如此鋪陳的。英文母語人士從小就開始訓練這樣的思維方式，所以只要學會了這樣的結構，寫作就不會是難事，而且可以寫得很「道地」。

表現主題的方式有很多種，提出主控點的方式也很多樣。topic sentence 可以因為主控點所控制的方向不同，而有不同的發展，並且會有許多不一樣的寫法。因此，除了寫了無新意的 I'm going to talk about... ，還可以這麼寫：

在 *Sequoya's Gift* 這個故事的開頭，用一個形容詞來破題：

Sequoya `topic` is a remarkable `controlling idea` man.
He was a silversmith, painter and soldier `detail`.

⋮
▼

He is famous because he is the only person in history who has invented a written language.

這個 topic sentence 中，Sequoya 是主題，其後用了一個「形容詞」remarkable來帶出主控點，說明他是一個了不起的人。那接下來要說什麼呢？按照 G-S 原則，他如何了不起？為什麼了不起？因為 He was a silversmith, painter and soldier.。一個人身兼三職，的確不簡單。那這個主控點如何控制全文走向呢？接下去是與主控點相關的另外一個形容詞 famous。他為什麼有名呢？因為他是發明文字的人。整個段落圍繞 Sequoya 這個主題，並定調於他卓爾不凡這個面向。作者在 topic sentence 中用 remarkable 這個形容詞來凸顯全篇的主控點，再用相關的形容詞繼續鋪陳，並各自舉了具體的細節來支持這兩個抽象的形容詞：

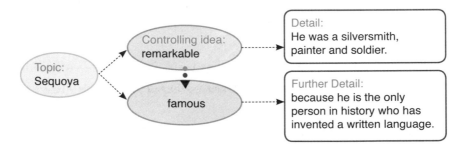

另外，在第一章提過的 *It's Mine* 的例子中，我們也可以看到這樣的「開頭」與「延續」：

On the island lived three quarrelsome frogs controlling idea, named Milton, Rupert and Lydia detail.

⬇ elaboration of the controlling idea

They quarreled and quibbled from dawn to dusk.

⬇ illustration of the controlling idea

"Stay out of the pond," yelled Milton. "The water is mine."

"Get off the island!" shouted Rupert. "The earth is mine."

"The air is mine!" screamed Lydia as she leaped to catch a butterfly.

　　第一句 topic sentence 使用了「倒裝句」，先把地點提出，再將主角引介進來，同時點出主控點，用包含形容詞的名詞片語呈現：three quarrelsome frogs。How do they quarrel? 接下來是進一步的說明：他們從早到晚吵個不停，並提供具體的細節，也就是他們之間的對話，來顯示他們「愛吵架」的特色。

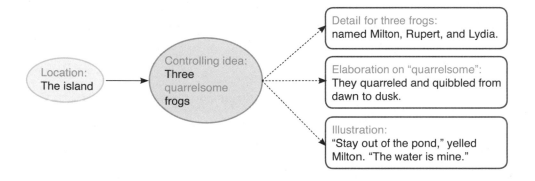

　　除了使用形容詞與倒裝句，在 *Flipped* 這本書中也可以看到「強調句」的用法：

　　All I've wanted is for Juli Baker topic to leave me alone controlling idea. For her to back off – you know, just give me some space explication of "leave me alone".

　　這個 topic sentence 中，使用強調句來說明「我最想要的就是……」，這也是介紹主控點出場的一種方法，也就是說，主控點不一定要是形容詞或名詞，也可以是動詞片語，表達一件事，或一個動作。書中主角希望這個女生 Juli Baker 放過他，而怎麼樣叫放過他呢？就是接下來的細節說明：離我遠一點，給我一點空間！

　　另外，在典型的 SVO 句式中，主控點常出現在受詞的位置。在 *I Remember...When I*

Was Afraid 這本書中，害怕的對象 our old Westinghouse washing machine 放在受詞的位置引介出來以後，作者特別強調 this was a strange washing machine：

> When I was little, I was scared to death `topic` of our old Westinghouse washing machine `controlling idea`. I know it was a strange thing to be afraid of, but, well, this was a strange washing machine `key feature`. It had a round window in front. To me, the window looked like a mouth with rubber jaws `detail 1`. It had two dials on top. To me, the dials looked like eyes `detail 2`.

這是一個講述小男孩害怕很多東西的故事，而其中一個東西就是「老舊」的洗衣機。因此，這個 topic sentence 把使小男孩害怕的主體「洗衣機」放在受詞的位子，並且再加以定位 old → strange，之後的細節進而介紹這個洗衣機為什麼 strange。

除此之外，topic sentence 還有什麼樣的方式呢？其實也可以用「問句」來引起讀者的興趣，再逐步帶出主控點，漸進式的聚焦，如 *Boy* 這個讀本的封底介紹：

> Where did Ronald Dahl get all of his wonderful ideas for stories `topic`? From his own life `controlling idea`, of course! As full of excitement and unexpected as his world-famous, best-selling books, Ronald Dahl's tales of his own childhood are completely fascinating and fiendishly funny `feature of his life`. Did you know that Ronald Dahl nearly got lost his nose in a car accident? `detail 1` Or that he was once a chocolate candy tester for Cadbury's `detail 2`? Have you heard about his involvement in the Great Mouse Plot of 1924 `detail 3`? If not, you don't yet know all there is to know about Ronald Dahl. Sure to captivate and delight you, the boyhood antics of this master storyteller are not to be missed `conclusion`.

首先第一句先使用了問句來引起讀者注意，到底作者的故事題材都來自哪裡呢？然後再自問自答：是從他的生活而來。在這裡可以看到主控點是「他的生活」，但是這個主控點還太籠統，因此筆者又縮小了主控點的範圍，聚焦在「他的童年」，並進一步定調為「completely fascinating and fiendishly funny」。由此可以知道，這本書是在講述這位作者童年所發生的趣事，而這些趣事包括了那些事呢？之後的細節便提到了三件在書中會詳述的趣事，讓讀者有大概的了解，最後再給一個總結。這樣的逐步問答若換成平鋪直敘的

說法就變成：

Ronald Dahl got his wonderful ideas for stories `topic` **from** his own life `controlling idea` ,
which is completely fascinating and fiendishly funny `further characterization` .

綜觀上述，是否有感受到寫 topic sentence 其實可以很多變呢？如果文章的開頭不再只是 I'm going to talk about... 或是 Today my topic is...，是不是會更加生動呢？掌握了 topic sentence 的訣竅，就不用再為開頭而煩惱，而且更能感受到寫作的樂趣！

3.4 原來如此！透視英文式的思考模式

很多人對 topic sentence 的理解僅止於 topic，以為把「主題」交代一下就好了。本書在第二章提到，英文中所謂 topic，可以是大範圍的主題（topic/theme of the essay/paragraph），也可以是小範圍的話題（topic of the sentence/block）。所謂的 topic sentence 通常是指篇章或段落大範圍的主題，但因為往往是第一句，當然也成為第一個 block 內小範圍的話題。不過本章的重點是要強調「主題句」的功能，除了說明 What is the topic? 更要強調 What is the topic about? 除了指出主題是什麼，更要有一個「清晰明確」的主控點！

何謂清晰明確？這是沒有絕對標準的。最基本的要求就是能夠提出一個支撐全文的焦點，為全篇定調。它可以是直接了當的形容，如：

Going off on wildlife adventure is exciting!

也可能由事件的角度切入，點出主控事件：

The story is about a boy who went forth to learn fear.

所以，主控點的清晰度，端視所要談論的內容而定。在 *Boy* 這本書中，主題當然是七歲那年的 boy，但主控點是男孩的那所「適當的男校」a proper boy's school，這是整個章節的軸心：

> When I ⬚Topic was seven, my mother decided I should leave kindergarten and go to a proper boy's school ⬚general controlling idea. By good fortune, there existed a well-known Preparatory School for boys about a mile from our house ⬚specific 1. It was called Llandaff Cathedral School, and it stood right under the shadow of Llandaff cathedral ⬚specific 2. Like the cathedral, the school is still there and still flourishing ⬚conclusion.

這一段的「主題」圍繞在主角七歲時發生的事情，而「主控點」將整段導向他就讀男校的經驗上，詳細的介紹這所著名的學校。即使中間小話題有轉換，目的是要漸漸聚焦，從 a proper boy's school，到 a well-known Preparatory School，再到明確的 Llandaff Cathedral School，主控點本身的明確度越來越清晰，焦點也越來越清楚。

更重要的是，這個主控點，也同時也與第二、三、四段的 topic 息息相關。怎麼說呢？因為二、三、四段也在說明他就讀男校的經驗，只是說得越來越詳細：

> When I was seven, my mother decided I should leave kindergarten and go to a proper boy's school. By good fortune, there existed a well-known Preparatory School for boys about a mile from our house. It was called Llandaff Cathedral School, and it stood right under the shadow of Llandaff cathedral. Like the cathedral, the school is still there and still flourishing.
>
> But here again, I can remember very little about the two years I attended Llandaff Cathedral School, between the age of seven and nine. Only two moments remain clearly in my mind. The first lasted not more than five seconds but I will never forget it.
>
> It was my first term and I was walking home alone across the village green after school when suddenly one of the senior twelve-year-old boys came riding full speed down the road on his bicycle about twenty yards away from me...
>
> My second and only other memory of Llandaff Cathedral School is extremely bizarre. It happened a little over a year later, when I was just nine...

事實上，一到四段的主題分別是：

一：The boy entered a proper boy's school.
二：In the two years of school, he only <u>remembered</u> two things.
三：The first thing is...
四：The second thing is...

第一段的 topic sentence 牽連到二、三、四段的主題，因為有一個明確的支點——男孩就讀的男校，才能繼續談男校的生活經驗。

所以，由此可知，英文文章中第一段的 topic sentence，通常帶出一個核心焦點，牽連之後各段落的主題，只是內容上會有訊息粗細之分。也就是說，在寫作時，要注意第一段的 topic sentence，是否指出一個關鍵點，並呼應到之後各段的主題上，這樣才能讓每一段的 topic sentence 息息相關。有了主控點，內容才會通順有條理。

3.4　中英比一比：清晰主控 vs. 情境暗示

中英文基於不同的語性，破題的方式也不一樣。中式寫作承襲中文「重點在後」的語性，習慣將重點放在最後，所以破題的方式越朦朧含糊，越有意境。

應變

一睜眼，望著病房裡慘白的唯一光源——一支日光燈。我即刻從簡陋的沙發床上彈起，接近母親的床沿。她安詳的笑容如每次確認我在她身邊時一般，安心且無惦念。

這段開頭取自99學年度指定科目考科的國文考科作文佳作[2]，題目是「應變」。但讀完第一句話，甚至整個第一段，都不太確定要講的重點是什麼，這是中文的好文章。

但英文卻恰恰相反，破題的方式講求直接了當、開門見山。英文傾向「主從分明」、「重點先講」，這樣的特性也落實到主控點的陳述上。像是以下在 *Boy* 這本書當中任選的三個例子，可以看到 topic sentence 都用簡單直述句，都是主詞配一個術語，即後敘成分（predicate）的基本句型，直接帶出主題和主控點：

2　因篇幅過長，未全部引用，刪減部分文字

This topic is not an autobiography controlling idea . I would never write a history of myself. On the other hand, throughout my young days at school and just afterwards a number of things happened to me that I have never forgotten thesis .

Everyone topic has some sort of a boat controlling idea in Norway. Nobody sits around in front of the hotel. Nor does anyone sit on the beach because there aren't any beaches to sit on...

This man topic was slim and wiry controlling idea 1 and he played football controlling idea 2 . On the football field he wore white running shorts and white gymshoes and short white socks...

為了直接了當也破題，通常段落的第一句不會用太複雜的句子。但是如果使用複合句，那麼重點會落在主要子句的動詞述語上：

Mr. Lexington topic , his apron still on, appeared in the hall controlling event . "Is this a friend of yours?" he whispered to the kids...

又如讀本 *Boy* 裡這段文字的第一句，藍色部分是主要子句的後敘成分，帶出主控事件，其餘的片語或是關係子句都是補充説明：

In slow motion and with immense reluctance, little Perkins topic , aged eight and a half, would get into his dressing-gown and slippers and disappear down the long corridor controlling event [that led to the back stairs and the Headmaster's private quarters]. And the Marton, as we all knew, would follow after him...

因此，英文「主從分明」、「重點先講」的特性，也在 topic sentence 中顯現。因為主要子句之於附屬子句，如同重點之於背景，所以關鍵性的主控點往往會落在主要子句上。

3.6 教材總體檢

英文文章的開頭可以千變萬化，但基本原則是要有明確的主題與主控點，作為後續細節鋪陳的依據。而在台灣的英語教材當中，是否也如此講究呢？

觀察一下這篇文章的開頭，有沒有明確的 topic sentence？

The Talent Show

Look! *Super Singer* is on $\boxed{\text{topic}}$. The three singers $\boxed{\text{controlling figures}}$ are from the UK. The little girl is Connie. She is six years old $\boxed{\text{singer 1}}$. The tall and heavy woman is Susan. She is from a small town $\boxed{\text{singer 2}}$. The man is Paul. He is a cellphone salesman. He is shy $\boxed{\text{singer 3}}$. Listen! Their voices are so beautiful $\boxed{\text{conclusion}}$.

一開始先點出主題，也就是選秀節目 *Super Singer* is on. 那麼主控點是什麼呢？什麼是這段真正要介紹的？應該是節目中的三位選手。三位選手都來自 UK，那他們各自的特色為何呢？特色就出現在接下來的細節陳述。

大致上，這篇文章有主題，也有主控人物，但是介紹的方式卻將這三位選手 the three singers 直接當作主詞，加上 **"the"**，認定為「已知」人物，主控人物的出場少了一個適當的出場介紹。若要使訊息的傳遞更為順暢，可考慮改為：

The Talent Show（修改版）

Look, *Super Singer* is on! There are three singers on the show today. They are all from the UK....

如此，三個主控人物先經由 "There are..." 的句式，有了出場介紹，才不會顯得太突兀。再仔細觀察以下這段介紹合歡山的文字，是否有明確的 topic sentence？作者想要談論的主控點是什麼呢？

Hehuanshan

Hehuanshan `topic` is a tall mountain in Taiwan. It is famous for its beautiful flowers and snow `controlling idea` . From May to September, it is sunny and cool at Hehuanshan. People go there for the mountain flowers. In winter and early spring, it sometimes snows there. People watch snow, play with it, and make snowmen there. Winter is a busy season at Hehuanshan `conclusion` .

　　一開始看到開頭的兩句話用來破題,主題是合歡山,接下來的主控點是山上漂亮的「花與雪」。但在第三句當中,卻換了一個話題,只提到了氣候,主詞 it 也換成指天氣。之後第四、五、六句才又回到山上的花與雪。雖然用意是想藉由不同的天氣來介紹主控的兩項特色「花與雪」,但對於主控點的訊息承接卻似乎出現中斷,最後面的結論也只針對冬天是個忙碌的季節,似乎沒有完整呼應這段的兩個重點:花和雪。如果依照話題連接的原則,稍作修改,讀起來是不是比較通順呢?

Hehuanshan(修改版)

Hehuanshan `topic` is a tall mountain in Taiwan. It is famous for its beautiful flowers and snow `controlling idea` . People go there for the mountain flowers from May to September when it is sunny and cool. In winter and early spring, it sometimes snows there. People watch snow, play with it, and make snowmen there. Hehuanshan is a popular place in all seasons `conclusion` .

　　依照話題相連的原則,第三句延續主控焦點,重點先說,之後再補充說明季節氣候等原因,如此一來,訊息是否較為流暢?最後的結論也須關照到兩個不同時節的主控點,強調合歡山每個季節都受人歡迎。

小結

　　因此，何謂「破題」？如何「開頭」與「延續」？「破題」就是要指出主題為何，以及主控點何在！有了清楚聚焦的主控點之後，才能為文章定調，進而依循主控點繼續發揮，描述具有說服力的細節來支持主控點，這樣就兼顧了「開頭」與「延續」。但是，接下來還有一個問題沒有解決：文章的第一段有了好的開頭，然後又該如何結束呢？如何寫出全篇的主旨摘要，作為第一段的結尾，同時承上啟下開啟後面各段的主題？這就是第四章要教給你的訣竅！

寫作練功坊

題 目

我們在這一章探討了一篇文章如何下筆破題，首先就是要找出主控點，為文章定調。再繼續依主控點來發揮，以細節支持主控點。

下面這個作文題目，請分為兩段，各寫出每一段的主控點

你認為畢業典禮應該是個溫馨感人、活潑熱鬧、或是嚴肅傷感的場景？請寫一篇英文作文說明你對畢業典禮的看法，第一段寫出畢業典禮對你而言意義是什麼，第二段說明要如何安排或進行活動才能呈現出這個意義。　　　　　　　　（100 年大學指考）

第一段
第一段寫出畢業典禮對你而言意義是什麼
主控點：

_____

_____

細節：

_____

_____

_____

_____

_____

_____

第二段

第二段說明要如何安排或進行活動才能呈現出這個意義

主控點：

_____

_____

細節：

_____

_____

_____

_____

_____

_____

解答 （學生作文示範）

第一段

主控點：

To me, the graduation ceremony means both a start of another unknown phase of life and a milestone of the previous stage of life.

細節：

It sums up not only the knowledge I have gained but also the friendship and enjoyments I have shared with my schoolmates and teachers. The graduation ceremony is a time to remind me how much I love these people, and how important it is to cherish every stage of my life.

第二段

主控點：

How should a graduation ceremony be held? In my opinion, we don't need overelaborated decorations or the presence of some celebrities, neither of which has any connections to our memories of school life. Frankly, a simple, warm and meaningful graduation ceremony can be more satisfying.

細節：

I would suggest the following things to do. First, play some recorded videos to recall the fun experiences of daily school life, showing what we've done together in the past few years. Secondly, spend a period of time giving thanks to our teachers, as they have devoted themselves to helping us in our studies as well as in our behaviors. Finally, the rest of the time is for all of us to talk to someone about something we kept in mind for a long time. It is a chance to apologize, to forgive, to show appreciation, or to make peace. Needless to say, it is hard to say goodbye in the graduation ceremony. But without an end of the past, how can we open the door to a promising future?

Chapter 04

如何交代主旨？
提綱挈領，言明主旨！

主旨如何呈現？

為何需要小結？

句與句、段與段，如何串連？

Please summarize your points in ONE sentence!

What is the thesis statement?

一篇作文的開頭，有主題，有主控點，也略述細節，那麼接下來呢？該怎麼結束最重要的第一段？答案是：必須用一句話來統整全篇的主旨，總結作者的立場，並且介紹之後的段落出場。這一句話就叫做第一段的「小結」，又稱為「主旨句」（thesis statement）。「主旨句」通常出現在第一段的最後，是整篇文章當中最重要的摘要提示，因為它扼要說明全篇的論點主旨，是所有段落圍繞的軸心，具有「提綱挈領」、「承上啟下」的功用。

因此，了解「小結」的作用與寫法，就知道如何畫龍點睛，交代文章的核心論點。「小結」的好壞往往能夠決定一篇作文的優劣！

既然「小結」是在第一段的最後簡要說明主旨，就是最關鍵的一句「摘要」，必須「承上啟下」：承接上面的主控點，同時開啟以下各段的重點。但什麼是「承上啟下」？了解這個問題之前，先來看看什麼樣的句子「沒有承上啟下」。這是一篇學生撰寫關於校園志工活動的作文，來觀察一下它第一段的「小結」：

The Volunteering Program

I always take the volunteering program seriously, because I think it does us good. Hence, I support that every student has to devote to the volunteering program. In my opinion, it is important to experience these things. However, I don't agree that the hours we spent can affect our score. The volunteering program could be required. But once it could influence the scores, it would definitely lose its meaning.

The reason why I support volunteering program is that we can learn a lot from every activity. Take my experience as an example; I did obtain a large number of knowledge which we will never learn from the textbook from the project. When I was in senior high, I joined a recycling group in my neighborhood. At first I didn't know even recycling can shock me. The trash piled up to the sky, giving off horrible smelling. After attending this program, I know how important recycling is. I knew the garbage we made was blocky and they all do harm to earth, even if they could be recycled. Besides, I learned some details about recycling, and the way we handle the dump is too crude. These surprising facts only can be learned through joining the process in person.

第一段開宗明義指出作者「支持」志工活動，但在第一段的最後只説志工活動可列入要求，但若變成一種影響成績的標準，就會失去活動的意義。以這句話作為「小結」，也就是全篇的論述主旨，接下來要説明的應該是「為什麼」志工活動若會影響學業成績，就失去了意義？但是接下來的發展好像不是這樣。

看到第二段的第一句話，突然話鋒一轉，説到了作者支持志工活動是因為可以獲益良多，但是這件事跟主旨有何關係呢？第一段的最後跟第二段之間，是不是有很大的鴻溝，導致文意連接不上呢？

從這篇文章來看，第一段的最後少了一句「主旨句」（thesis statement），來承上啟後。如果把第一段的最後改寫一下，凸顯論點主旨，並關照下一段，就會銜接得更順：

> ### The Volunteering Program （修正版 1）
> .... The volunteering program could be required. But once it could influence the scores, it would definitely lose its meaning. The program is meant to enhance students' knowledge and learning experiences without burdening them with grades.
> The reason why I support volunteering program is that we can learn a lot from every activity. Take my experience as an example; I did obtain a large number of knowledge which we will never learn from the textbook from the project. When I was in senior high, I joined a recycling group in my neighborhood.

在主旨句中提到 to enhance knowledge and learning experiences，接下來的第二段就可以繼續談 we can learn a lot from it。

本章的目的就是要教你如何寫 thesis statement，發揮「主旨句」的功能，使文章有一個簡短鏗鏘的「小結」，能夠點明主旨、提綱挈領、承上啟下！接下來，這個訣竅將隆重登場。

4.2 訣竅 4：言明主旨，總結立場，承上啟下

怎麼樣寫第一段的「小結」才不會使頭腦「打結」呢？其實很簡單：結構上「小結」就是第一段的結尾，按照 G-S-G 推進原則，文章第一段 introduction 也需具有三進式結構：

G – Topic sentence   主題句 → 點出主控點
S – Supporting detail   延伸句 → 支持主控點的細節
G – Thesis statement   主旨句 → 摘要説明主旨

以內容而言，主旨句一定要講出一個貫穿全文的「論述立場」！在國外的寫作教材[1]當中，是這樣定義 thesis statement 的：

> **The thesis statement** communicates **the main idea of the essay**. It reflects the writer's <u>**narrow focus**</u> and **point of view**, **attitude**, or **opinion**, and it also **forecasts** which aspects of the subject the writer will discuss to support the thesis in the body of the essay. A good thesis statement should have all of the criteria mentioned above.

寫主旨句最重要的一點是，發揮「摘要」的作用，簡潔扼要地交代全篇的主旨，「預告」接下來的二、三、四段要寫些什麼！它必須有「論點」，也就是作者自己的立場、看法、意見，及態度。説明了自己的「立場」以後，後面幾段就開始以這個立場為軸心，繼續發展下去。

依照這個邏輯，若要改寫第一節的文章，一定要先找出一個論述的主軸。依照這個主軸來發揮，才能使文意通順連貫。為要凸顯這個小結，確實説明全篇主旨，也可以這麼改：

> **The Volunteering Program** （修改版 **2**）
>
> I always take the volunteering program seriously, because I think it does us good. Hence, I support that every student has to devote to the volunteering program. In my opinion, it is important to experience these things. However, I don't agree that the hours we spent can affect our score. The volunteering program could be required. But once it could influence the scores, it would definitely lose its meaning. In my opinion, it is more important to "learn" than to score!
>
>
>
> <u>The reason why I support volunteering program is that we can learn a lot from every activity.</u> Take my experience as an example, I did obtain a large number of knowledge ...

由於文章有了明確的「立場」，「支持」志工活動的原因就更鮮明，因此，把第一段最後加上一句承上啟下的「主旨句」，就可以銜接第二段説明「支持」志工活動的「原因」，是不是通順許多呢？

---

1 *NorthStar: Reading and Writing Level 5*, Third Edition, Unit 2, p.39.

4.3　十面埋伏，暗藏玄機

　　概要的説，何謂主旨句（thesis statement）？就是文章第一段與第二段之間的小結，故事第一部分與第二部分的連結。這是非常重要的一步，因為第一段的小結（thesis statement）關係到整篇文章的走向。比如說，如果我要寫一篇文章敘述一段難忘的旅行，該怎麼開始第一段？怎麼樣的小結可以承上啟後的呢？

An Unforgettable Trip

- 　Topic ：I went to Japan with my mom on July 20, 2010.
- 　Controlling idea ：It was an eye-opening trip I will never forget.
- 　Detail ：The trip was 5 days long and I had a chance to closely observe the Japanese people.
- 　Thesis ：I learned a lot about their unique social norms, especially the way they talk, the way they eat, and the way they dress themselves.

　　這個例子中，主題是去日本這件事情，主控點則是這是一場大開眼界的旅行。既然定調於「eye-opening」，細節部分繼續提到 5 天的旅程可以近距離觀察日本人，但究竟觀察到什麼？最後一句簡短說明學到很多日本的社交模式，特別是說話、飲食、和穿衣這三方面。這句「主旨句」，承上也啟後：既呼應上面的主控點，也開啟下面各段的主軸。接下來談什麼呢？當然是日本文化在這三方面的特殊之處！

　　同樣的題目，也可有不一樣的破題，不一樣的鋪陳主軸：

An Unforgettable Trip

- 　Topic sentence ：On June 20, 2010, I took a trip with my mom topic to visit my dream country – Japan controlling idea .
- 　Detail ：We visited three different places: Tokyo, Kobe and Kyoto.
- 　Thesis statment ：During the trip, I was most impressed by the natural beauty of Mount Fuji and the flavory beef steak of Kobe.

　　一開始就破題點出旅行的目的地是日本這個最嚮往的國家，接著補充地點細節，至此主題句與細節皆已描述完成。最後以一句小結，點出這趟夢想旅程中印象最深刻的是富士

山的美景以及神戶的美味牛排。此話一出，讀者便會期待接下來的鋪陳主軸，一定是與富士山及神戶牛排相關的旅遊經歷相關。文章至此，筆者已經非常自然流暢地交代了全篇的「主旨」。正所謂「焦點」在前，「細節」相隨，既然第一段的最後點出兩個重點作為「鋪陳主軸」：富士山與神戶牛排，那麼理所當然，隨後出現的二、三段必然繼續提供有關這兩者的「細節」。

同樣地，在 *Our favorite Creatures* 中，也可以看到「小結」具有「承上啟下」的功用：

Going off on wildlife adventure `topic` is exciting `controlling idea` !
You meet all kinds of funny, bizarre, fascinating, weird, and wonderful creatures.
Sometimes you have to hike high up the mountains or dive deep in the ocean `detail` ;
But that's <u>not the hardest part</u> of going on a wildlife adventure.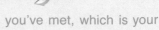
The <u>toughest</u> part is trying to decide of all the creatures you've met, which is your favorite `thesis statement` .

在這個例子中，第一句已破題指出 Going off on wildlife adventure is exciting，在「exciting」的前提下，全篇真正要講的是 which is your favorite creature? 這段最後的主旨句清楚交代論述主軸，接下來各段就是要介紹各種不同的 creatures。最後這句話總結了前面所說的，也同時開啟了後面的話題，選一選你最喜歡的動物。

主旨句可長可短，也可能只有短短幾個字。在 *Just Joking*[2] 讀本中發現這樣簡短呼應前文的 thesis statement：

Thursday night `topic` . Mom and Dad have gone out and left me at home all by myself `controlling idea` . Normally, I would be making prank phone calls, setting up buckets of water over half-opened doors, and putting rubber snakes underneath pillows `detail` —but not tonight `thesis statement` .
Tonight I'm standing on a ladder polishing the lightbulbs in the living room with Dad's CD cleaning cloth...

這段的第一句點明時間主題 Thursday night 及主控情境 I'm home by myself。接著詳

---

2 *Just Jokings* by Andy Griffiths

細說明獨自在家我通常都會做些什麼事，然後筆鋒一轉，but not tonight! 點出全篇主旨：今晚不一樣！那麼讀者一定會很好奇：今晚你做些什麼事呢？於是，接下來第二段就說明了今晚做了些什麼事。從這個範例可知，第一段與第二段的內容，藉由簡短的「小結」承上啟下而彼此呼應，密切相關。

看了這麼多，來小試身手吧！讀過《英文文法有道理》這本書嗎？你會怎麼介紹這本書？以下範例運用「主旨句」的訣竅，以一句話來總結這本書的特色：

- This book `topic` probes into the unique characters of English `controlling idea` .
- It proposes that languages, like human beings, may have different "personalities" `detailed elaboration` .
- The book describes how the personality of English is different from that of Chinese with TEN important features `thesis` .
- In the following, the 10 features will be presented in full detail.

上述這段 introduction 旨在介紹《英文文法有道理》這本書，其主控焦點落在英文獨特的語性上。先說明了語言像人一樣，有不同的「個性」，然後以小結「主旨句」來承上啟下，提綱挈領的交代了全文的主旨：該書描述英文不同於中文的十項語性特點。這十項特點就成為以下各段的陳述主題。

綜觀以上，可以知道「小結」的功用是簡述全文主旨，總結文章第一部分的 introduction，開啟第二部分的 body。「小結」位於第一段的結尾，必須「預告」整篇作文的論點及走向，以求「承上啟後」，銜接後面段落的內容。因此，要快速的了解一篇文章的主旨是什麼，看它的「主旨句」便可以一目瞭然！越清楚明確的「主旨句」越能完整表達全文的大意！

4.4 原來如此！透視英文式的思考模式

英文寫作中，第一段是最重要的，因為最重要的訊息都在第一段。除了破題、定調之外，第一段的最後一句話要講出全篇的主旨（thesis），做一個「小結」。這個「主旨句」（thesis statement）像一句簡短而完整的「摘要」，提綱挈領地交代全篇內容的重點，概述作者的論點、立場、意見，做「大綱式」的提示。因此讀完了第一段的 introduction，就

會對全篇要講的內容主軸有所了解——「主旨句」擔負「提綱挈領」、「承上啟下」的功能，角色重要。

但大多數的人只知道英文作文要寫 topic sentence，對於要寫「主旨句」就比較陌生，其實主旨句就是第一段的結論，既然第一段是 introduction，做「小結」時就要介紹全篇的主旨，同時呼應其餘段落的內容。這樣的講究很符合 G-S-G 三進法原則，將這「寫作三部曲」運用在 introduction 的寫作上：第一步就是 G – topic sentence，點出主題與主控點，接著是 S – elaboration 延伸說明，最後的 G 就是 thesis statement，做一個小結，提示重點內容。由下圖可知，「主旨句」關係全篇段落的發展：

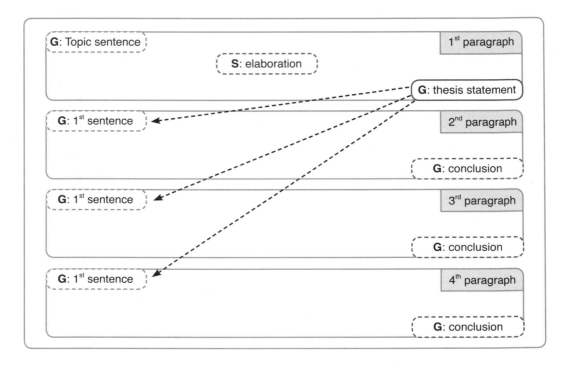

上圖顯示，主旨句既是第一段的總結，也是其餘各段的「提示」。就如前面提到的例子，介紹《英文文法有道理》這本書時，第一段最後加上一個 thesis statement，把整本書的特色做個扼要說明：English is different from Chinese with 10 features.，這個主旨句也預告下面要繼續發展的內容重點。

有些人以為作文的各個段落自成一格，彼此獨立，不一定要有關連，這是一個不甚美麗的誤會。事實上，文章各個段落都與第一段有關，特別是 thesis statement，這是全篇論點的總結，同時提示各段的內容大綱。有人也許要問：像這樣的結論不是該放在最後嗎？

為什麼在第一段的 thesis statement 就先說了呢？別忘了，英文的語性是「重點先講」，「細節留後」；英文式的溝通原則是開門見山、直接了當。還記得第一章談的「三句話」原則吧！這也是「三句話」原則的體現，「最重要的話」一定要先說。所以，開頭第一段裡就把最重要的訊息都概括陳述，先把重點說清楚了，才來描述相關細節。以下我們要看看中英文在主旨的處理上有何不同？透過中、英文的對照，進一步闡明「主旨句」的功能角色。

4.5 中英比一比：結論先講 vs. 結論留後

學生之所以覺得 thesis statement 困難，是因為中文寫作中沒有這樣的習慣。英文喜好「重點先講」、「主從分明」，但中文恰恰相反，重點通常要到最後才出現，例如以下 99 學年度指定科目考科的國文考科作文佳作，可以細細觀察一下它的鋪陳手法：

應變

一睜眼，望著病房裡慘白的唯一光源——一支日光燈。我即刻從簡陋的沙發床上彈起，接近母親的床沿。她安詳的笑容如每次確認我在她身邊時一般，安心且無惦念。

在我十七歲那年，母親罹患癌症。

在接下學校辯論社社長，被選為優良學生，並沉浸在明星學校的光環中，突來的噩耗……

剎時得知媽媽隱瞞的病情竟是癌症……

在理性與感性之間，我打理好情緒，準備迎向不同的人生。

無論是怎樣的變故，任何人的行程皆不為我而耽擱……

在變故之中，我鮮少恣意地釋放情感。應該做的，總是比想去做的來的重要，在經歷這場意外後更是如此。回望媽媽的病房，在紛紛細雨中，只希望雨別壞了媽媽的心情。十七歲那年，我的肩膀更寬了，足以擔起人生的責任。我的應變，即是勇敢地負責。

99 學年度指定科目考試　國文考科作文佳作

在這篇佳作當中，第一段從病房裡的一盞燈開始娓娓道來，從場景、發生的事實、醫院的情況、到自己的情緒，細細鋪陳，建構出整篇文章的「背景」，到最後才破題並總結，提出最重要的焦點：「我的應變，即是勇敢地負責。」

反觀英文，在 *Flipped* 這本小說中的第一章 Diving Under，第一句話就點明了整章的焦點，先講出結論：Juli Baker 真的很煩！我只想要她離我遠一點！然後才娓娓道來時空背景，細述 Juli 到底做了哪些事情讓我煩。

Diving Under

All I've wanted is for Juli Baker to leave me alone. For her to back off—you know, just give me some space.

It all started the summer before second grade when our moving van pulled into her neighborhood. And since we're now about done with the eighth grade, that, my friend, makes more than half a decade of strategic avoidance and social discomfort.

She didn't just barge into my life. She barged and shoved and wedged her way into my life. Did we invite her to get into our moving van and start climbing all over boxes? No! But that's exactly what she did, taking over and showing off like only Juli Baker can...

這樣的反差，實在很明顯！中文借景喻情，越不直接，越有美感；但英文強調直接了當，廢話少說，重點先講。中英寫作上的根本差異，清楚反映了兩個語言獨特的語性差異。語言反映文化，文化影響語言。一般而言，「有話直說、先講主旨」的溝通習慣也成了英語人士思考、認知、待人處事的習慣。因此，要學會寫 thesis statement 的訣竅，就要先改變中式的思考模式，養成先做「小結」的習慣。

4.6 教材總體檢

關於「主旨句」（thesis statement）的角色功能，相信讀者已經能夠心領神會。但是，在英語的養成訓練中，是否也提供了適當的教材範例來深化「主旨句」的寫作習慣。現今的英文教材裡是否體現 thesis statement 的重要性呢？來一探究竟吧！

首先，以下這篇介紹泰姬瑪哈陵的教材當中，第一段的最後用兩句話點出全篇主旨：The Taj Mahal – one of the most impressive and glorious wonders of the world to date. 這個「小結」說出了這篇文章的主旨：介紹全世界最榮美華麗的殿堂之一：The Taj Mahal。「小結」的作用是一方面總結第一段所說的這是一個代表愛的建築物，同時又開啟第二段

陳述建築物背後的愛情故事，這樣的 thesis statement 的確達成提綱挈領，承上啟下，點出全篇焦點的功能。

The Taj Mahal

There are a million ways to express deep affection for our loved ones. To Shah Jahan, a Mogul of India, building an incomparable mausoleum was how he memorized his love. Finished more than three hundred years ago, this tomb remains one of the most impressive and glorious wonders of the world to date. It is known as the Taj Mahal.

In fact, behind this grand structure is a touching story. Legend has it that Shah Jahan had numerous wives. Among them, Mumtaz Mahal was his favorite. He felt extremely depressed after she passed away while giving birth. Therefore, he recruited twenty-thousand workers to construct a mausoleum in memory of her...

（三民教科書 第四冊 Unit 7）

然而，嚴格檢視下面的例子，第一段的最後一句話，似乎少了能夠總結全文、承上起下的力道。這句話只提到了宮崎駿會把很妙的場景放進電影裡，但第二段就直接講述他的童年，兩段之間的連結不是很清楚。「小結」即代表全篇的焦點，若焦點就落在電影裡這些特殊的元素，讀者便會期待，也許在第二段可以讀到相關的特點介紹。然而，第二段卻開始介紹宮崎駿的家庭背景，與第一段的小結似乎有點連接不上。

Mizayaki's World of Fantasy

Some call him Sensei of Anime and others the Japanese Walt Disney. He is Hayao Miyazaki, a great animator and director from Japan. For many years, he has taken his fans to his world of fantasy. He is fond of putting in his films such scenes as flying machines, strong females, and funny pigs.

Miyazaki was born into a wealthy family in Tokyo in 1941. His family grew prosperous by making parts for fighter aircraft during World War II. That was why he lived a life of ease as a little boy. It was during that time that Miyazaki began to draw airplanes and developed a fascination with flying, which consequently became a recurring theme in his films...

（遠東教科書 第四冊 Unit 7）

如果要讓第一段與第二段連接得更順暢，或許可以加上一句更給力的主旨句：

Mizayaki's World of Fantasy（修改版）

Some call him Sensei of Anime and others the Japanese Walt Disney. He is Hayao Miyazaki, a great animator and director from Japan. For many years, he has taken his fans to his world of fantasy. He is fond of putting in his films such scenes as flying machines, strong females, and funny pigs. These "features" characterize the unique style of Hayao Miyazaki films, which may have started to develop in his childhood years.

Miyazaki was born into a wealthy family in Tokyo in 1941. His family grew prosperous by making parts for fighter aircraft during World War II. That was why he lived a life of ease as a little boy. It was during that time that Miyazaki began to draw airplanes and developed a fascination with flying, which consequently became a recurring theme in his films...

加上這個 thesis statement，就把「電影」與「童年」串連起來了，是不是讀起來比較通順呢？這樣一句「小結」是不是為第一段添上一個較完整的總結，同時也承接下一段的主題，發揮「題綱挈領」、「承上啟下」的特質呢？

小結

「主旨句」（thesis statement）其實是一篇文章的心臟，寫得好，文章內容就主旨清楚、文理分明；寫不好，文章就有可能不知所云，條理不清。這個「小結」（concluding statement）的功用很大，放在第一段中言明主旨、總結立場，才能如蓋房屋一樣，先立下大樑支柱，建立文章的發展主軸，落實英文「重點先講」的特性。至此，文章第一段的開場、延續與小結都已詳細說明，下一章中，將繼續探討整篇文章的架構，段落與段落之間是如何連結發展的呢？這就是第五章所要探討的訣竅！

寫作練功坊

題 目

我們在這一章學到了英文文章鋪陳的方式，需要將結論先提出來，寫出精簡的主旨句，這種寫法和中文式的作文有所不同。

1. 請檢視以下這個題目和一位同學的練習寫作，看看這篇文章有沒有運用英文式的寫作方式，發揮主旨句的功能？

在你的記憶中，哪一種氣味（smell）最讓你難忘？請寫一篇英文作文，文長至少 120 字，文分兩段，第一段描述你在何種情境中聞到這種氣味，以及你初聞這種氣味時的感受，第二段描述這個氣味至今仍令你難忘的理由。 （99 年大學學測）

When I was an eight-year-old girl, my family moved to Chiayi city. As soon as I stepped into our home, a strange smell assaulted my nostrils. I couldn't use any words to describe it but only strange. As I was wondering what was it, my dad told me that the person living next door is making stinky tofu. And I finally realized it was the smell of stinky tofu.

A few days later, when I went to night market with my friends, the air was filled with a familiar smell. "It was the smell of stinky tofu!" I told to myself. Because of curious about what does it taste like, I ordered one for a try. To my surprise, it was delicious and not stinky at all. It was really amazing and just couldn't forget the smell and taste. When mention an unforgettable smell, I would say it is the stinky tofu, because of its strange smell.

2. 承上題目，請以中文寫作方式，寫一篇文章。

3. 承上題目，請以英文寫作方式，寫一篇文章。

4. 請檢視一下你自己前兩題的作文，比較自己寫的中文式文章和英文式文章，是否達到了這一章所教你的要領？

寫作修理廠

1.

(1) 本篇學生的作文雖有小地方需修正，但第一段描述與氣味的「初相見」，人事時地物的交代都有切中主題，並且盡量明確地形容這個氣味。本文將氣味定調於 "strange" 保持一貫又加入新意，最後由 "strange" 連結到 "familiar"，多了語意層次的變化。

(2) 第一段最後一句要發揮主旨句的功能，提供精簡的小結。

(3) 第二段要寫出懷念氣味的理由，不能只是說很難忘，還要說清楚為什麼不能忘。因此加上了兩句話來解釋氣味由「奇怪」變為「熟悉」，因為由氣味聯想到小時候友善的鄰里與無憂無慮的童年。

這篇文章可修訂如下：

When I was an eight-year-old girl, my family moved to Chiayi City. As soon as I stepped into our new home, a strange smell ~~assaulted my~~ came into my nose. ~~nostrils.~~ I couldn't use any other word~~s~~ to describe it but ~~only~~ "strange". As I was wondering what it was ~~it~~, my dad told me that the ~~person~~ neighbor living next door ~~is~~ was making stinky tofu. And I finally realized it was the stimulating smell of stinky tofu.

A few days later, when I went to the night market with my friends, the air was filled with a familiar smell. "It was the smell of stinky tofu!" I told ~~to~~ myself. Because ~~of~~ I was curious about what ~~does~~ it ~~tastes~~ tasted like, I ordered one for a try. To my surprise, it was delicious and not stinky at all. ~~It was really amazing and~~ Over the years, the strange smell became a familiar and memorable smell that I just couldn't forget. ~~the smell and taste. When mention an unforgettable smell, I would say it is the stinky tofu, because of its strange smell.~~ It reminds me of the friendly neighborhood and the carefree childhood I had enjoyed in Chiayi.

2. (略)

3. (略)

4. (略)

Chapter

如何拓展全文？
善用 G-S-G 推進法，層層開展

05

寫完第一段之後呢？

如何循序鋪陳文章？

如何寫得有條理？

中文、英文作文有什麼不一樣？

How to write a
whole article?

　　前面幾章，不斷地說明如何把作文的第一段寫好。為什麼呢？因為第一段寫得好，之後的段落就會自然順應第一段的脈絡寫下去。尤其第四章中提到，「小結」的優劣往往決定一篇作文的好壞，因為它就是全篇的主旨及脈絡。也就是說，小結必定與其後的段落息息相關！那麼，以下的段落是如何鋪陳的呢？如何能開展全文，使段落有序、內容豐富、結構嚴謹？在討論鋪陳的脈絡以前，先來觀察以下這篇學生的文章，總共有兩段，兩段各自的內容是如何推展的，兩段間又是如何連結的呢？

My High School and College Life

　　I love my high school life. I consider it one of the most important stages of life because I learned a lot when I was a senior. I studied in JMGSH that only allows girls to enroll. **The homework** in high school was really heavy, but I'm kind of missing the days that I sat at the desk and did homework intently. **The friends** I made in my high school were very nice and easygoing. That was a little bit out of my expectation because I used to think that a big group of girls was so hard to deal with. **Teachers** always taught us the specific answers to questions instead of telling us how to find an answer. I joined **a club called "English Conversation Club"**, and it was filled with fun when I got along with people in that club.

　　Now, I'm a college student, studying in NCTU. This is a college where males are more than females, so. **The homework** part is also a little bit different. It's not heavy but I need to make more effort to complete a report or something else. **Making friends** in college is a challenge because you have to do it actively on your own. It's not like high school that you can meet the same group of people at the same time every day. **Professors** are teaching us how to figure out an answer, not telling us what the answer is. I attend **the guitar club** in NCTU, and I'm really into this club and have a lot of fun. For me, the college life is also colorful and interesting.

　　第一眼所觀察到的是：這兩段分別講述兩個階段——高中生活與大學生活，且各段內談的小話題也很一致：homework, friends, teachers, and club 不過細細體會一下，這樣的描述方式是不是少了什麼？是否有點東扯一點，西扯一些的感覺？這篇文章到底有什麼問題？我們來檢視一下：

- ➢ 一開始的主題句才提到 I love my high school life，讓人以為全篇的重點是 high school，但下一段又跳到 college，為全文定調的主控點何在？
- ➢ 接下來好幾個小話題各自為政，話題本身的鋪陳少了 general to specific 的推展，話題與話題之間也缺乏「關鍵詞」的連結。
- ➢ 然後是段落間的連結，第一段與第二段完全是脫鉤的，彼此的關係何在？雖然題目是：My High School and College Life，並不等於可以各寫一段，互不相干，還是要找出兩者的關連，並交代全篇的主旨！

　　整篇文章像是在說分開的兩件事情，先說高中生活，再說大學生活，然後就結束。這樣的文章是否給人一種沒頭沒尾、各自為政的感覺呢？這篇文章的基本問題在於每個句子似乎都寫對了，但是湊在一起，了無章法，脈絡不清，主題不明，與前幾章所談的寫作原則大相逕庭。

　　本書一直強調英文寫作要有條理，英文式的溝通方式要先點出重點與主軸，有了大方向之後才詳述細節。在讀者還沒搞清楚全篇的主旨概念時，就直接開始介紹細節，難免有些唐突。另外，各段之間的連結必須息息相關，各段的內部也要話題相連。

　　到底段落內部應該遵循怎樣的邏輯結構？外部的分段鋪陳該如何進行？如何在第一段埋下之後段落的伏筆？其後段落又如何與第一段相呼應？接下來就要傳授給你推展全文的訣竅！

5.2 訣竅5：善用 G-S 與 G-S-G 推進法，拓展全文

　　首先，段落當中應該遵循怎樣的邏輯來步步推展？祕訣就是依照 G-S 二進法與 G-S-G 三進法，層層推展。「G-S 二進法」與「G-S-G 三進法」在第一、二章中已初步介紹，接下來的問題是：如何善用於文章當中？「G-S 二進法」包含 General-to-Specific「二個進程」，就是一再提到重點先講、細節隨後；先提出一概括的重點（G），再提供具體的細節來說明（S）。以下的文章[1]示範了這樣的進程是一種基本的思考模式：

1　取自 *The Bronze Bow* by Elizabeth George Speare

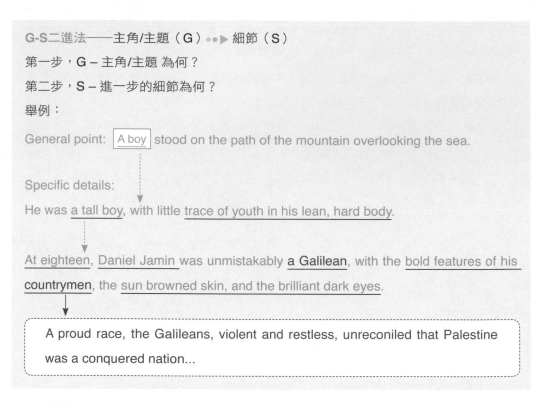

G-S二進法──主角/主題（G）••▶ 細節（S）

第一步，G – 主角/主題 為何？

第二步，S – 進一步的細節為何？

舉例：

General point: A boy stood on the path of the mountain overlooking the sea.

Specific details:

He was a tall boy, with little trace of youth in his lean, hard body.

At eighteen, Daniel Jamin was unmistakably a Galilean, with the bold features of his countrymen, the sun browned skin, and the brilliant dark eyes.

A proud race, the Galileans, violent and restless, unreconiled that Palestine was a conquered nation...

　　上例中很明顯地看到，第一句點出主角人物，然後就一層層展開細節，從身形到年紀、姓名、種族、相貌特徵：

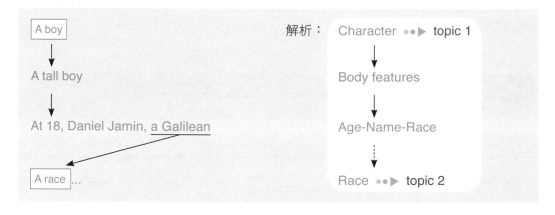

　　有趣的問題是：主角人物出場後，到底要選擇什麼樣的細節來鋪陳？答案很簡單：要鋪陳的細節必須和「上文」有關，又能帶出「下文」，可用來連結下一個話題。上例中特別提到主角的身形外貌，是要帶出他的種族特徵，然後銜接下一個話題 a proud race！

一般說來，General-to-Specific「二個進程」可以繼續延伸進化成 General-Specific-General「三個進程」，使文意更完整，這就等同於先前提出的「三句話法則」。所謂「三句話法則」其實不是「只能寫三句話」，而是英文作文的每一個段落都可以由簡單的 General-Specific-General「三個進程」組成：

G-S二進法 先說主控點（G）再進入細節（S）最後總結（G）

第一句，**G** – 主控點為何？ ●●▶ 最重要的話

第二句，**S** – 進一步的細節為何？ ●●▶ 具說服力的證據

第三句，**G** – 概括結論為何？ ●●▶ 印象深刻的總結

三段式文章結構：

第一段：**G**eneral Introduction

第二段：**S**pecific details

第三段：**G**eneral conclusion

這樣三進式的結構，我們稱作「G-S-G 三進法」。三進法是由「G-S 二進法」衍生而來，其基本要件是 G-S 二進式的思維，最後在需要總結時加上一個 G。這種推進原理不只是撰寫文章時可以運用的最佳模板（template），也是文章「前進」的最高指導原則，可運用在文章的每一個層次上。「G-S-G 三進法」可用在三句話間的關連，形成一個小話題組；也可運用在三個小話題組，形成一個段落的結構，更可以運用在段落和段落間，形成整篇文章的架構。

比方說，還記得前一節提到的問題範例嗎？學生的作文當中提到了高中與大學生活的比較，但是只提到了細節（S）的部分，找不到文章的主旨（G）與結論（G）。那麼，要如何運用「G-S-G 三進法」來改善這篇文章呢？

如果開頭加上一個介紹主旨概念（G）的第一段，整篇文章的脈絡就會更清楚。第一段先清楚說明文章的主旨為何，在小結的部分就提到高中生活、大學生活、以及自己對於這兩段生活的感想。最後，再加上一個與小結相呼應的結論（G），整篇文章是不是就更完整了呢？

My High School and College Life

G   I am a twenty-year-old college student. Looking back, I found that my high school life and college days so far were quite colorful and memorable. In high school, I learned to open up and make friends while studying hard; in college, I learned to solve problems and find answers by myself. I enjoyed the different experiences and faced different challenges in the two stages.

S₁   I love my high school life. I consider it one of the most important stages of life because I learned a lot during the three years. I studied in JMGSH that only allows girls to enroll. The homework in high school was really heavy, but I sat at the desk and did my homework attentively. Now I kind of miss those hardworking days. The friends I made in my high school were very nice and easygoing. That was a little bit out of my expectation because there was a stereotype in my heart to regard that a big group of girls was so hard to deal with. But the fact was that I was wrong about this. I joined a club which called "English Conversation Club", and it was filled with fun when I got along with people in that club.

S₂   Now, I'm a college student, studying in NCTU. This is a college that males are more than females, so I took some time to adjust to the new environment that was different from my high school life. The homework part is also a little bit different. It's not heavy but I need to make more effort to complete a report or something else. Making friends in college is a challenge because you have to do it actively on your own. It's not like high school that you can meet the same group of people at the same time every day. Professors are teaching us how to figure out an answer, not telling us what the answer is. I attend the guitar club in NCTU, and I'm really into this club and have a lot of fun. For me, the college life is also colorful and interesting.

G   I had a wonderful time in both high school and college. I would never forget the valuable experiences I had in the two stages and I expect myself to keep growing in the years to come.

　　多了前後兩段，有了開場與總結，先前各自為政的高中與大學生活才能串連起來，文章的結構才趨於完整。因此，先說重點（G），再進入細節（S），最後下結論（G），這是每一個層次都蘊含的基本文章結構，也是內容鋪陳的最佳途徑！

5.3 結構與內容相互搭配，層層堆疊，息息相關

英文寫作特別強調結構與內容的搭配。在先前 My Mom 的例子中，如果根據 G-S-G 三進法，試寫 My Mom 這個主題，將主控點放在媽媽很會煮菜這件事情上來發展，可以寫出很簡單的段落：

G: [My mom] `topic` is a good cook `controlling idea` .
S: She can make all kinds of delicious food with an extraordinary taste `supporting details` .
G: Everyone is crazy about the food she makes `conclusion` .

在這段簡單的文字中，已確實包含了第一章強調的「三句話法則」：最重要話（破題的主控點 G）、最具說服力的話（搭配的細節 S），最令人難忘的話（動人的結語 G），內容與結構相互搭配，三句話間清楚呈現 G-S-G 的三進式關連。其實英文作文的每一個層次，都包含這三個結構性的成分：主控的重點、選定的細節，以及概括的結論，搭配 G-S-G 三進法，形成文章層層推展時最重要的結構條理。

要是主控點不只一個呢？也一樣可以照 G-S-G 三進式的推展來鋪陳嗎？當然可以！

My Mom

G: [My mom] `topic` is beautiful `controlling idea 1` and kind `controlling idea 2` .
S: She has big eyes and soft skin `detail 1` . She cares about everyone around her `detail 2` .
G: To me, she is the angel of our family `conclusion` .

這段文字中，主題是 My Mom，其後接上兩個主控點 beautiful 跟 kind。這兩個焦點分別有兩個細節：細節一（She has big eyes and soft skin.）補充說明 beautiful；細節二（She cares about everyone around her.）則補充說明 kind。最後，加上一個生動的小結來呼應這兩點。

依此類推，若今天有三段文字，每一段當中也可有三進式的安排，例如第一章所提到的範例：

Block 1 - G

G: [My mom] `topic` is a good cook `controlling idea` .

S: She can cook all kinds of Chinese and western food `supporting detail` .

G: Everyone likes the yummy food she makes `conclusion of block 1` . ••▶ `thesis statement`

Block 2 - S

G: [The spaghetti] `topic` she makes is most delicious `controlling idea` .

S: [It] has a special flavor with my favorite meatballs and mushrooms `detail` .

G: [It] tastes better than the ones sold in the restaurants `conclusion of block 2` .

Block 3 - G

G: [My mom] `topic` enjoys cooking very much `controlling idea` .

S: [She] spends most of her time in the kitchen and loves to create her own recipes ▶
`details` .

G: [She] is like a magician who can play magic on food `conclusion` .

　　這樣的三個話題組（block）之間顯示 G-S-G 的連結關係，各個話題組內部也同樣存在著 G-S-G 三進關係。事實上，英文文章中各個層次之間的連結幾乎都有 G-S 二進或 G-S-G 三進推展的運用。通常文章第一段先説明整篇的主旨（G），而接下來的二、三段就依循著這個主旨來補充説明細節（S），最後總結（G）再呼應第一段。G-S-G 三進式的結構，可配合各式各樣的內容，形成文章基本的脈絡。例如，在《多益口説與寫作測驗官方試題指南》當中，有提供寫作的範文，而這些範文之所以能夠達到 4～5 分的高分，標準即在於「結構完整」。在下列的範文中，就顯現了 G-S-G 推進法的脈絡：

The Most Important Characteristics of a Marketing Manager

My career goal is to become a marketing manager of a consumer product company. A marketing manager is responsible for the company's marketing strategies. To be successful on this role, I believe a marketing manager should possess several important qualities.

One important quality of a successful marketing manager is to stay up to date with the market. Marketing managers are expected to stay informed with the demands of target consumers. This is usually done through reading industry and trade reports or working closely with financial research firms. Understanding the pulse of the market helps marketing managers decide what product features to highlight in advertising.

Creativity is another desirable characteristic. Sometimes a product idea is difficult to convey to the customers. A successful slogan can help capture the spirit of the product and allow consumers to remember your firm and products favorably. An example of product slogan is Nike's "Just do it," which inspires young people to be active.

Finally, an effective marketing manager should be able to think in strategic terms so that the product line yields a desired profit. An example of such strategic decision is pricing. The manager must be familiar with the cost structure of the product, so he can price products properly. The manager should also be able to develop a realistic budget for the product line and evaluate the financial performance of products to make sure the profit target is achieved.

The head of marketing management plays a critical role in the success of a company, and therefore should take careful steps to hire a well-qualified manager. An ideal candidate for the position is a person who reads a lot to understand the market, is creative enough to come up with good marketing ideas, and thinks in strategic terms.

　　這篇文章的標題很清楚，要說明 market manager（行銷經理）的要件。第一段是全篇的重點，第一句直接破題指出：個人生涯規劃的目標是 become a market manager（行銷經理）（G）；然後對行銷經理的任務稍做說明（S），最後一句主旨句再點出行銷經理

必須要具備幾項重要特質（G），作為第一段的總結，同時預告下面各段的主題。接下來二、三、四段就是分別一一說明這幾項特質的細節。相對於第一段的 G 而言，第二、三、四段的細節說明都是 S：第二段指出要有熟悉市場趨勢的能力，第三段提到創意的重要性，第四段則強調必須能夠選擇適合的行銷策略，三段分別談論三個特質，呼應第一段的介紹，特別是主旨句的小結。在分述完細節之後，最後一段再將這些特點綜合形成結論，作為總結全篇的 G。

因此，這五段的結構仍然形成 G-S-G 的推展關係：

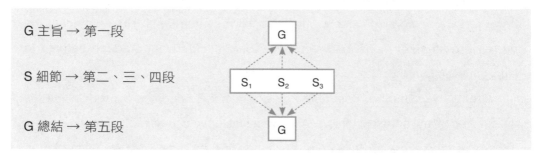

除了文章整體來看呈現 G-S-G 的推展關係，若細究這篇文章每一段的內部，也包含了 G-S-G 的推展關係，比方以第二段為例：

G: [One important quality] of a successful marketing manager is to stay up to date with the market .

S: Marketing managers are expected to stay informed with the demands of target consumers. This is usually done through reading industry and trade reports or working closely with financial research firms.

G: Understanding the pulse of the market helps marketing managers decide what product features to highlight in advertising.

第二段第一句就指明此段落的主旨（G），也就是要有熟悉市場趨勢的能力，而這個能力如何能夠累積呢？細節的部分（S）說明了兩點，分別是隨時了解顧客需求以及熟知貿易與市場資訊，最後總結的部分（G）則闡明了解市場脈動的必要性，以達到成功的推銷商品的目的。第二段呈現的 G-S-G 結構，在其他段落也一樣可見，這就是貫穿全文的基本脈絡。

以上這篇文章的中間二段列舉行銷經理的各項特質，示範了「列舉式」的細節描述。同樣在 G-S 的推展原則下，我們可以發現另一種「對比式」的細節鋪陳方式：細節的陳述彼此相對，剖析正反兩面不同的意見。以下範例[2]改寫自 *NorthStar* 閱讀與寫作教材，主題是比較兩位華裔美國人的成長歷程：

A Comparison of Eva and Elizabeth

Whoever once said [that the children of immigrants have an easy time adapting to life in their new country] was surely mistaken. As the oldest children in their families, both Eva Hoffman and Elizabeth Wong play an active role in helping their family members communicate with the outside world. As a result, they often suffer from the pain and frustration experienced by people who live in two cultures. From their self-portraying stories, we can see that although Eva and Elizabeth may have certain hopes and feelings in common, they are at the same time very different from one another thesis statement .

They both want to be "accepted" by the mainstream. Like Eva, Elizabeth tries hard to look like her peers and she is embarrassed when she is made to feel different. In the same way that Eva becomes self-conscious about expressing her feelings, Elizabeth is ashamed when she hears her grandmother speak loudly in Chinese. This brings them to another common area. Eva and Elizabeth are both unhappy about the ways in which their moms are treated. Just as Eva is angry with her sister, who challenges her mother's authority, Elizabeth views her brother's constant criticisms of her mother's English as fanatical and cruel. Both Eva and Elizabeth are more outwardly protective of their mothers' feelings than their siblings are.

Although Eva and Elizabeth share similar attitudes, they also differ from each other in many respects. Unlike Eva, Elizabeth does not feel that her identity is bound to her family's cultural heritage. While Eva embraces her Polish heritage, Elizabeth flees her Chinese background. Eva holds on to the memory of the family's sad past, but Elizabeth is happy to strive for a "cultural divorce" by not attending the Chinese school. Whereas Eva sees herself becoming bicultural, Elizabeth adores everything American and longs to be an "all-American girl." In contrast to Elizabeth, Eva is flexible: she is willing to compromise and accept the best of both cultures.

---

2 *NorthStar: Reading and Writing Level 5,* Third Edition, pp. 114-115.

Eva and Elizabeth have made different adjustments to their cross-cultural experiences. When children like Eva immigrate, they understand the sacrifices their parents have made in order to provide them with a better life. However, children like Elizabeth who are born and raised in the US often don't understand what their parents have gone through until they become adults. And when they finally do, can it sometimes be too late?

這篇文章有其獨到之處：首先，第一句以反面陳述來破題，然後提到兩位主角 Eva 及 Elizabeth，她們都是移民家庭的老大，成長的過程有其相同的痛苦之處。第一段最後的主旨句（G）交代她們雖有很多相同的感受，但也有非常不同的地方。然後第二段開始說明其相同之處，而第三段則是說明其不同之處，兩段都是細節的探討（S），彼此相對卻又相關。最後總結（G）再闡述二人的移民身分所帶來的衝擊，並以問句作為結尾，針貶之意自在其中。

「師父領進門，巧妙在各人」。以 G-S 和 G-S-G 為脈絡來層層推展，使文章每一段的連結都很緊密，不論是列舉或對比，每一段都承接上一段的話題，彼此相關。由此可知，遣辭用句可以多樣多變，但文章仍有基本的模式可循，只要依照 G-S 和 G-S-G 的推展邏輯，文意通順，架構嚴謹，就是一篇可讀的好作文。

5.4 原來如此！透視英文式的思考模式

透視英文作文內部的模組結構，其實就像下面的圖一樣，層層推展，每一段的主題互相呼應，每一段的最後小結都可承上啟後：

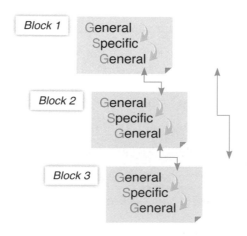

若細究各段間的連結關係，有幾種可能相關的模式。上一節中提到，有兩種基本方式：第一，第一段的主旨句直接點明之後各段落的主題後，二、三段的細節並列，如同綁粽子一樣，最後再以總結歸納各段重點，這是總結式的並列結構：

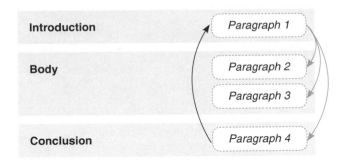

　　另外則是像鐵鍊一樣把每一段串連起來，形成「鏈結式」的對比，每一段的第一句承接前一段的最後一句，彼此呼應對照：

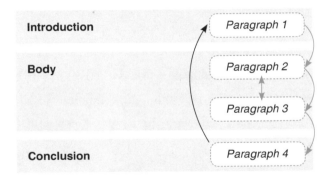

　　綜合上述的模組分析，我們來做一個簡單的分析練習，以 An Unforgettable Trip 為題：

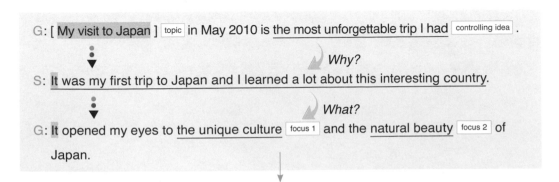

G: Japanese culture is unique in the way people interact with each other.
S: They spoke softly, smiled gently and bowed deeply.
G: They worked very hard and behaved "properly".

Extending focus 2

G: The most beautiful place I visited is [Mount Fuji].
S: [It] was covered by snow and looked magnificent from all angles.
G: [The mountain] is called "Holy Mountain" by the local people and a "must-see" for many tourists.

Echoing the thesis - Conclusion

G: Japan is very different from Taiwan.
S: It is crowded but quiet, busy but orderly, and eventful but clean.
G: My trip to Japan is truly memorable and I would like to visit it again when the cherry trees blossom.

　　如圖所示，第一段的 Introduction，其實是接下來各段發展的基礎。首先，針對題目來破題 My trip to Japan is most unforgettable，而難忘的原因在於初體驗又學到很多。主旨句再點出兩個焦點 the unique culture 以及 the natural beauty，分別作為以下兩段發展的主軸。二、三段分別描述文化特殊之處與富士山的美景，最後針對小結發展出結論，回應難忘的感受，期盼櫻花盛開時再去拜訪。

5.5　中英比一比：結構嚴謹 vs. 情境至上

　　在 G-S-G 的架構下，英文強調「開門見山」，第一段通常點出整篇文章的主旨。相對於英文嚴謹的結構，中文更重視情境的醞釀，描述手法不盡相同。中文的文章常以寫景、寫情開頭，迂迴地先說故事，或細細描繪景物來襯托心情，最後才慢慢帶出要說的重點。以下這篇大學學測的作文佳作就可以看出中文起承轉合特色，是迂迴漸進式的描述手法：

自勝者強

獨棲於舞台一角，我蜷伏著身子卻依然難以阻遏顫抖的雙腿。望著台下萬萬目企盼的目光和同學們信任的眼波，我無法克服心中的壓力，戰勝不了自己……

那是國中畢業前的一場英文話劇比賽，頂著第一男配角頭銜的我，在登台前被一頭名為「恐懼」的獸猛然吞下。那時，我竟蹲踞在後台，無法走向屬於我的舞台。我深怕自己的演出會搞砸其他演員的完美表演，我怯懼於眾人對我的期待與關愛，還有，怕輸給了強勁的對手，然而，我卻無庸置疑的敗給了自己。脆弱的精神堡壘倏地被緊張之獸的利爪給摧毀……恣縱青春韶光蒙上灰黑暗影，神傷黯然。

然而當華麗浮誇的裝扮被卸下，我重拾起久置牆角的課外書，裝扮起自我的靈魂。我彷彿騰飛至華盛頓的球場，看見身為「台灣之光」的王建民，是如此耐得住孤寂的七百五十五天復健，沉著而冷靜地克服傷痛，超越自我內心的恐懼而重返榮耀。我又好似穿越時空，聽見蘋果前總裁賈伯斯堅定而自信的說：「失敗是一種良藥」時，那般超越自我後的坦適和昇華。有時，我乘著輕舟逆流而上，又於林旁輕見蘇軾輕吟著：「誰怕？一蓑煙雨任平生」，而震懾於其豁達和無懼及其對挫折的心靈突圍，進而自我提升。逐漸，我不知不覺超越了自我的緊張和恐懼，拾起一塊塊信心的磚瓦重建心靈堡壘……

詩人何梅斯說：「人生重要的並非你站在何處，而是你向何處前行。」唯有勇敢面臨自我，超越勝敗得失，以堅持和樸實的態度戰勝自己，才能達到「自勝者強」的境界，踏出邁向強者之路的關鍵步伐。

101 學年度學科能力測驗 國文考科作文佳作

這篇作文一開頭就描述一個話劇比賽的後台場景，慢慢帶到自己的內心世界，心情起伏的轉折，最後才提出全篇作文的重點——自勝者強。其實一開始讀者並不知道話劇的場景及比賽，與標題有何關聯，但是經由意境的醞釀，聯想的引導，最後讀者就能夠領會出作者如何慢慢從這個比賽中得到「自勝者強」的啟發。

敘事文如此，甚至廣告商品的推銷文案，也是如此。一開始選擇先經營情境，細說個人故事，卻把最重要的商品連結放到最後，像是博客來站立電腦桌的廣告文宣：

自從我站立工作以來已經有 2 年時間。不論一天要寫程式多少個小時，我都是站立在電腦前。有時我會一天站立超過 10 個小時，雖然不是連續的——中間會有小憩、吃飯、冥想等。我在決定站著寫程式前並沒有測過血壓或其他身體指標，如今也沒有測過，但下面是我自己對身體上變化的感覺。

站立工作後一些我擔心會有但實際上並未出現的事情

- 我的膝蓋、腳、背、臀部並沒有發生任何病痛。
- 在一天結束時我並沒有感到精疲力盡。
- 我的工作效率和注意力並沒有降低。

站立式工作後真正發生的變化

- 我的姿勢比以前更好了。我的脖子和肩頭不再向前曲。
- 我不再有腰痛背痛；腿上有了更多的肌肉。
- 我工作期間身體有活躍的運動。

站著寫程式的副作用

- 負面效果：連續坐兩個小時我就會覺得有點不舒服。
- 積極作用：坐捷運排隊時我很少再有打不起精神的感覺。

這兩年來我的自我調整

- 以前我穿軟底的鞋，並用厚地墊。現在，不用軟鞋也不需要地墊了。
- 我把筆電提高了 5 英吋，鍵盤高度在胸部左右，視角是前下方 105 度。
- 之前我會坐下來休息，現在我做跳躍動作。跳一跳讓我的腿更有活力。

總之，這些變化讓我感到驚奇和高興。站了兩年之後，我仍然衷心的向大家推薦使用站立式電腦桌。尤其是站立式筆記本工作桌。你從這裡可以找到一個。

Homelike 時尚升降便利桌（胡桃色）

這個廣告實在將中文「情境主導，重點在後」的特點發揮的淋漓盡致，從頭到尾鉅細靡遺說了一大堆作者自身的經驗，但是到底要賣什麼卻讓人一頭霧水，直到最後才恍然大悟。這是中文「愛賣關子」獨到的藏鋒式寫法[4]。然而，英文的思路與描述手法大不一樣。即使同樣是敘事的文章，仍然強調結構嚴謹、重點清楚。像以下這篇散文[5]，一開始就直接了當，開門見山，點明他相信真理並追求真理，隨後故事的細節才慢慢出現：

There Is Such a Thing as Truth

<u>I believe in truth and in the pursuit of truth</u>. When I was 10 years old, I asked a neighborhood kid who was older than me, "Which city is further west: Reno, Nevada, or Los Angeles?" The correct answer is Reno, Nevada. But he was convinced it was the other way around.

He was so convinced that Los Angeles was west of Reno that he was willing to bet me two bucks. So I went into the house to get my Rand McNally atlas. The kid looked at the atlas and said, "The map is drawn funny." It wasn't. I showed him if you trace down the 120-degree west line of longitude—which runs almost directly through Reno, Nevada—you end up in the Pacific Ocean.

He replied that lines of longitude don't cross the ocean. What? I told him that the lines of longitude were there to indicate how far west and east some location was, regardless of whether it was on land or on sea. <u>There was one insurmountable problem, however. He was bigger than I was</u>.

<u>I drew a number of conclusions from this story</u>. There is such a thing as truth, but we often have a vested interest in ignoring it or outright denying it. Also, it's not just thinking something that makes it true. Truth is not relative. It's not subjective. It may be elusive or hidden. People may wish to disregard it. But there is such a thing as truth and the pursuit of truth: trying to figure out what has really happened, trying to figure out how things really are.

...

---

[4]　請注意廣告中對自身感受的描述，是採取小標題式的整理方式。

[5]　改寫自 *NorthStar: Reading and Writing Level 5*, Third Edition, pp. 30.

這篇散文的重點是要說「理」，並且在一開始就把「理」簡潔明確地說清楚了。接下來細細描述小孩起爭論的故事原委。故事本身是一個引子，作為鮮活的事證，生動地襯托出主旨及結論的可信度！

英文當中開門見山的例子，在廣告及商業書信之中更加明顯常見，以下多益模擬試題的選文，就示範了重點先講、再談細節的基本原則：

There's a Big Market out There!

Douglas Marketing Company is offering a new series of seminars that can help you find the markets you need to reach. Unlike many workshops that provide one-size-fits-all solutions to every business owner who attends, Douglas Marketing offers customized assistance to help you develop the plan that works for your company.

How does it work? Our initial two-day class will give you an overview of marketing basics. After that, we'll arrange a series of meetings between you and one of our expert advisors. Your advisor will visit your workplace to learn firsthand about your business and to discuss your vision for future growth. Together you'll select key strategies that will help you reach new customers. We'll help you focus on finding those customers whose needs match the products and services you provide.

Many consultants can show you how to reach a larger market, but it might not be your market. Let Douglas Marketing teach you all the basics that you need to know. Then let us help you apply your new knowledge to your own business plan.

這篇文章開宗明義就告訴讀者全文主旨，也就是這個公司能幫你找到你要的市場。第二段開頭也是開門見山，直接以問句帶出主題，詳細說明提供訓練課程的作法。結論也一樣，直接比較其他公司不及之處，再次強調本公司獨特的服務。

中、英文寫作方式的不同，反映出語性的差異，但溝通習慣其實也受到社會變遷的影響。由於現代社會已逐漸轉型，邁向工商業的時代，溝通注重效率，講求重點明確，快速掌握訊息。中文的寫作方式也受到影響，慢慢在改變，新聞報章雜誌的寫法就很直接了當，藉由標題提示主題，在第一段就「開門見山」言明主旨，再分別闡述細節：

王金平應當如何自處

王金平將回國，司法關説案亦進入升高放大的情勢。接下來，王金平如何解釋此案，以及他如何自處，將決定此案如何發展下去。

有兩種可能，一、王金平承認了本案迄今呈現的事實，並對自己的行為表達認錯及歉意；然後，或者自行引咎而有所表示，或者藉此營造出一個朝野可能形成的寬容情勢，再與各方在其中尋找轉圜的空間。

二、以目前之端倪，王金平卻好像做了第二種選擇，他似想否認此案迄今呈現的事實，辯稱電話中所説「只是安慰柯建銘的話語」。（以下略）

因此，中、英文雖有不同的講究，但在現代化社會講求效率的前提下，文章的脈絡也會受到影響。在步調快速的工商時代，中文的商業書信、新聞報導、學術論文中，往往也會注入「開門見山」、「重點明確」的元素。

5.6 教材總體檢

在英文重視結構的原則下，文章的條理很清晰，大都遵循 G-S-G 三進法前進，那麼學生在英文教材當中，是否也能夠學習到這樣的架構呢？下列這篇閱讀範本整體的條理清楚，依循 G-S-G 三進式的概念，將內容與結構緊密結合：

Inventing A Better World

As the saying goes, "Necessity is the mother of invention controlling idea ". Many times, people invent things to meet their own needs. Later, the solutions to their problems turn out to be great inventions and change our way of life thesis .
Two examples will illustrate this point.

When Teng Hung-chi was a vocational school student, he worked as a mechanic in a factory. One day, he was using the bathroom and his hands were dirty because of work, so he did not want to touch the faucet. He thought, "If I could wash my hands without touching the faucet, it would be great." Teng worked hard to put this idea into practice. Soon, he invented a faucet controlled by a built-in sensing device.

...

Since then, Teng has invented many other things. He represented Taiwan at the IENA exhibition, an international exhibition for invention in Germany. Because of his many great inventions, Teng has become known as "Taiwan's Edison."

The other great modern invention that came from a simple need is the Post-it note. Do you know where its inventors Art Fry and Spencer Silver got the idea from? At first, Silver had been trying to invent a strong glue. As he experimented with different chemicals, he found that he had made a very weak one. He wasn't disappointed. Instead, he began to think about how useful a weak glue could be...

Silver's weak glue became a great success in 1980—it glued itself to a piece of paper. When Silver's fellow worker Art Fry sang hymns during the church service, he was frustrated that his bookmarks kept falling out. Suddenly, he remembered Silver's invention. Weak glue on a piece of paper would help him mark the right page. Then, the Post-it note was born and successfully spread around the world.

As you can see, great inventors get ideas from their own experience `conclusion`. Next time you have a problem, try to think of a way to solve it. Perhaps you may become a great inventor, too.

（改寫自三民教科書 第一冊 L7）

再來觀察下面這篇文章，是否也有清晰的條理？主旨句與各段的主題有沒有密切相關？第一段的主旨點明 Silverstein 的詩作最令人喜愛之後，第二、三段就直接談論詩的特色，解釋他的詩作令人喜愛的原因。但是其中的連結比較不明顯：

A Poem for the Young Heart

Some poems are written for either adults or children, but the poems of Shel Silverstein attract readers of all ages `controlling idea`. Perhaps this is why he is one of the best-loved poets in the U.S.A. and in other parts of the world.

Silverstein's poems always bring laughter and joy to readers. A sense of humor that is neither clichéd nor offensive is the main characteristic of his poems. For example, Silverstein likes to tease adults in ways that children find funny. However, his humor is meant only to make people laugh and is never used as a way to criticize others.

Another characteristic of Silverstein's poetry is its short, snappy lines. With just a few words, Silverstein can create a strange character or a situation in an imaginary world, such as a bear living in a refrigerator, or a girl eating a whale. In his poems, he mixes the serious with the funny and the common with the strange. His poetry reminds us of the days when we were children and lived between the real and the imaginary.

Sadly, Silverstein passed away in 1999. His poetry, however, still lives on today. Around the world, readers continue to enjoy the strange and amazing world that Shel Silverstein created in his poems.

（三民教科書 第一冊 L12）

這篇文章的主題很清楚：the poems of Shel Silverstein，主控點也很清楚：attract readers of all ages。但第一段的最後一句主旨句似乎只用來小結前文，與下面二、三段之間相關連比較不明顯。雖然讀者可以在閱讀中自行補充上下文間的關係，但缺少了「啟後」的主旨句，就顯得每一段有點各自為政的味道。如果把主旨句稍作修改，點明下文將分別介紹詩作的兩個特色，在結構與內容上的連結是否比較清楚呢？

A Poem for the Young Heart（修改版）

Some poems are written for either adults or children, but the poems of Shel Silverstein attract readers of all ages. Why? Perhaps there are two reasons why he is one of the best-loved poets in the U.S.A. and in other parts of the world.

Silverstein's poems always bring laughter and joy to readers. A sense of humor that is neither clichéd nor offensive is the main characteristic of his poems....

Another characteristic of Silverstein's poetry is its short, snappy lines. With just a few words, Silverstein can create a strange character or a situation in an imaginary world,...

Sadly, Silverstein passed away in 1999. His poetry, however, still lives on today.

....

值得一提的是：這篇各段內部的鋪陳很有條理，以第二段為例：

G: Silverstein's poems always <u>bring laughter and joy to readers</u>.

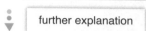

S: <u>A sense of humor</u> [that is neither clichéd nor offensive] is the main characteristic of his poems.

S: <u>For example</u>, Silverstein likes to tease adults in ways that children find funny.

G: However, his humor is meant only to make people laugh and is never used as a way to criticize others.

如果學生能夠多多接觸 G-S-G 三進法建構的好文章，就能漸漸內化這種鋪陳模式，在寫作的時候，也就比較能夠得心應手，發揮順暢的思路，使作文的條理清楚，架構明確。

小結

寫作的基本功，就是藉由 G-S 及 G-S-G 推進原則來鋪展內容，組成彼此相連的話題群，上下裡外都建構出以「說三句話」為本的結構與內涵。英文作文叫 composition ，顧名思義，就是要懂得「組合建構」。不僅文章各段內部要以 G-S-G 三進原則來組合，文章整體的脈絡也要遵守 G-S-G 的組合架構，如此一來，符合英文思考條理的道地作文便可以水到渠成！

在這一章中，我們學會了如何善用 **G-S** 以及 **G-S-G** 推進原則來堆砌建構一篇文章。

1. 請檢視以下題目及作文，標出哪些句子是 G，哪些句子是 S。看看這篇學生的作文是否條理分明、層層堆疊出一篇有邏輯的英文作文。

你最好的朋友最近迷上電玩，因此常常熬夜，疏忽課業，並受到父母的責罵。你（英文名字必須假設為 Jack 或 Jill）打算寫一封信給他／她（英文名字必須假設為 Ken 或 Barbie），適當地給予勸告。 （101 年大學學測）

Dear Barbie,

 I heard that your parents have been worrying about you for a long while. Did you spend too much time playing video games recently? It might be a problem that you need to face! The happy atmosphere of the house would go wrong if you do not solve it actively.

 As I know, your parents love you dearly and will take any action to stop you from indulging in the games. For example, they may take away your computer, or suspend you from getting monthly allowance from them. To avoid these undesirable consequences, my suggestion is that you should talk to them in this regard.

 Your parents are very open-minded and liberal. Please carefully explain why you were addicted to video games for the past weeks, and try to propose a new plan to balance your interest and school work in the future. I think they don't really want to deny your leisure time after school, but they want you to take good care of your schoolwork and not to forget all the important things to do as a student.

With my best wishes,
Jack

2. 請閱讀以下題目，運用 G-S 及 G-S-G 的積木，一塊塊建構出一篇英文思考式的作文。

請仔細觀察以下三幅連環圖片的內容，並想像第四幅圖片可能的發展，寫一篇涵蓋所有連環圖片內容且有完整結局的故事。

（103 年大學學測）

1.

Dear Barbie,

[G]

    I heard that your parents have been worrying about you for a long while (G). Did you spend too much time playing video games recently? It might be a problem that you need to face (S)! The happy atmosphere of the house would go wrong if you do not solve it actively (G).

[S]

    As I know, your parents love you dearly and will take any action to stop you from indulging in the games (G). For example, they may take away your computer, or suspend you from getting monthly allowance from them (S). To avoid these undesirable consequences, my suggestion is that you should talk to them in this regard (G).

[G]

    Your parents are very open-minded and liberal (G). Please carefully explain why you were addicted to video games for the past weeks, and try to propose a new plan to balance your interest and school work in the future (S). I think they don't really want to deny your leisure time after school, but they want you to take good care of your school work and not to forget all the important things to do as a student (G).

With my best wishes,

Jack

2.

參考範例，以下為一篇真實的學生作文，及修改建議。

Mary was watching her cellphone and I was listening to metal music when we went to school yesterday. Suddenly, Mary bumped into a tree and fell down because she focused on her cellphone and didn't notice the tree in front of her. I didn't know what happened to Mary because of listening music loudly. Meanwhile, a car driver honked the horn to me but I didn't hear. Unfortunately, car crashed into me so that I was badly injured in the accident.

After this accident, Mary and I learn a lesson that we should watch roads carefully. In addition, we talk to our friends this story, hoping everyone don't be smartphone addicts on a road and listen to music indoors. It is necessary to follow traffic rules and keep us safe.

> **修改後**

Picture 1:

G: Mary and I were on our way to school one day.

S: **Mary was watching** news on **her cellphone** with her head bowing down **and I was listening to** heavy **metal music** with my earphones on ~~when we went to school yesterday.~~

G: We both enjoyed what we were doing and did know what's going to happen next.

Picture 2:

G: Suddenly, Mary bumped into a tree and fell down, (S) because she only focused on her cellphone and didn't notice the tree in front of her.

S: I didn't know what happened to Mary (S) because of ~~listening the music loudly~~ the loud music I was listening to.

G: I kept walking with my earphones on.

Picture 3:

G: Meanwhile, a car ~~driver honked~~ was driving fast behind me.

S: The driver honked his horn ~~to me~~ as loud as possible to alert me.

G: But I didn't hear it at all.

Picture 4:

G: Unfortunately, the car crashed into me ~~so that~~ and I was badly injured in the accident.

S: I was sent to a nearby hospital and it took me a week to recover from the injury.

G: After this accident, Mary and I learned a lesson that we should watch ~~reads~~ the road carefully.

(G): In addition, we talked to our friends about this story, (S) hoping everyone of them ~~don't~~ would not be a smartphone addict or listen to music while walking ~~on a road and listen to music indoors~~.

(G): It is necessary to follow the traffic rules and keep ~~us~~ ourselves safe on the road.

修改建議 ▶

1) 看圖說故事的最佳策略就是運用 G-S-G 三進法來寫每一段，兼顧重點、細節與小結。以上的修改建議即是針對這個策略來進行。

2) 第一段描述第一幅圖時要先有一個開場（G statement），介紹人物或場景，作為 topic sentence。接著要有細節的描述，對圖中所顯示兩個人物的特徵姿態加以細述！

3) 中文說「看手機」、但在英文裡不能說（✗）"watch cellphone"，因為 watch 的是手機顯示的資訊或節目，而非手機本身。

4) 原文的第四段很長，敘事之後還有說理。這兩件事放在一起，仍可按照三進法來循序鋪陳。先談事故的發生，在敘述事故的重點之後，加上後續細節的說明就更生動，然後總結在 learned a lesson。之後若要針對這個 lesson 繼續發揮，仍可藉由三進法寫出條理分明的三進式結論！

To Be or Not to Be Chinese
如何避免中式英文

在 Part I 說明了英文式寫作的構思模式後，下一步要講究的是什麼呢？就是要寫出一個接一個文法正確、語意通順的英文句子，這就是本書的另一個重點：寫正確的句子，避免中式英文！Not to be Chinese!

英文重視結構，在篇章的組成上是如此，在句子的層次上更是如此。在了解英文的篇章結構後，我們該如何在句子的層次上寫出道地的英文呢？我的前一本書《英文文法有道理》目的就是要釐清英語的語性，指出英文「嚴句子」的十大標記特點，藉由理解形式和語意的搭配關係，建立完整有效的文法概念。這些概念也可落實在寫作上，依循英文文法的道理來寫出「形」「意」正確搭配的句子。

台灣學生在作文時常常出現的錯誤句型，其實都源於對英文標記原則的疏忽，為了讓大家有更清楚的體認，針對台灣學生的英文作文進行分析，一共歸結出**最常見的五大問題類型**。用微觀的角度，從句子的層面來剖析「中式英文」中最常見的問題。正所謂「知己知彼，百戰百勝」，期許透過明確指出中式英文的典型問題，能達到「醍醐灌頂」的效果，幫助讀者日後在寫作上更容易察覺自身的盲點，建立「準確標記」的好習慣，從而寫出「形、意」完美搭配的英文語句。

人家來找碴

首先，在進入五大問題類型之前，讓我們一起看看下面這些問題句子，有沒有看出那些地方不對勁呢？

問題示範，請改錯：

1) He attended NCTU is because he studied hard in high school. ●●▶ 動詞不可多？
2) I am so happy to meet new friend from different country. ●●▶ 名詞單複數？
3) He went for a walk after dinner and see a poor stray dog. ●●▶ 時態標記？
4) I know the pattern of questions and what should pay attention to. ●●▶ 誰注意什麼？
5) Everything became so chaos. ●●▶ 詞類用對了嗎？
6) Thank you for organizing the event and gave us the opportunity to visit Hsinchu. ●●▶ 對等連接？

這些問題句式都是作文中典型的「中式英文」，語意似乎是可理解的，但語法形式不正確。產生「中式英文」的原因都是在於中、英文有不同的標記原則。若我們從「形、意」搭配的角度來看，這些句子其實都是忘記英文在形式與結構上的要求，語意和語法必須有相對應的搭配關係，導致在「標記」上出了問題。

在《英文文法有道理》一書中，我們一再強調，語法是形意搭配的標記系統。語言藉由「形式」與「意義」的搭配，來傳達明確的語意；而語言就像人一樣，每個人都有著不同的個性，因此每個語言也有專屬的語性，從而發展出不同的標記形式。而中文跟英文在語法標記上最大的不同，在於中文「重情境」，英文「嚴句子」！中文的標記是「情境導向」，而英文則是「語句導向」。

所謂的「情境導向」，就是語境語意至上，把說話時的「情境場景」也自動納入考量，成為表達系統的一部分，因此情境中已知的成分，若已在場景中出現，就可以不必在句子中重複。例如：「我」拿著一本「書」問「你」：

問：看了沒？
答：還沒看。

單看句子，「誰」看了「什麼」？「誰」又沒看「什麼」？句子中並沒有提供足夠的資訊，但若將這兩個句子放到情境裡，「誰」和「什麼」都相當清楚了。這就是中文「情境導向」特性的展現。

那麼，「語句導向」又是什麼意思呢？「語句導向」是以「句子」為單位，每一個語意成分都得在句子的層次上嚴謹標示。句子內誰是主詞、誰是動詞、誰是賓語（受詞）都要有清楚的標記。因此，即便是我拿著書看著你，也要清楚標示是「誰」看了「什麼」：

問：Have you read the book?

答：I have not read it yet.

即使簡答：I haven't. 主詞也不可少。英文「嚴句子」，表現在語法形式的嚴謹要求上，就像是個嚴謹的英國紳士，在句子的層次上，必須遵循嚴謹的標記原則。上面的六種問題句型，就是違反了英文「嚴句子」的形式要求。我們在接下來的五章中，將從微觀的角度，提示英文寫作的要素，針對句子層面的標記特點，詳細説明：

Chapter 6　主動賓不可少，也不可多

Q: 在句子的組成上，中、英文有何不同？

A:

中文

以「主題」為核心，小句連連，自由串接：

他能夠上交大，是因為他高中很用功。　●●▶ 小句間自由連接

英文

1) 主動賓不可少、也不可多：一個句子只能有一個主詞、一個動詞

2) 主從要分明：一個句子只能有一個主要子句

[He 主詞 <u>attended</u> 動詞 <u>NCTU</u> 受詞] because he studied hard in high school.
　　　　└▶ 主要子句　　　　　　　　└▶ 附屬標記

「主從分明」的要求下，兩個子句間一定要有主從或連接標記（詳見第六章）。

Chapter 7　名詞出場必有標記

Q: 中、英文在名詞的標記上有何特性？

A:

中文

名詞不須帶有任何標記：

我很高興認識從不同國家來的新朋友！ ●●▶ 單複數只能意會！

英文

每個名詞出場都要清楚表達人稱、個體性（單複數），並考量聽者「知之否」！

I am so happy to meet new friends from different countries. ●●▶ 多數！

My friend is a vegetarian who loves animals. ●●▶ 名詞 / 動詞都有單複數標記

I cherish our friendship. ●●▶ 抽象 / 概念性的名詞才不用標記

Chapter 8　動詞出場時態相隨

Q: 在動詞的表現上，中文和英文有何不同？

A:

中文

靠情境或時間詞來表達**時間**，「了」表示已出現或已完成，動詞本身沒有變化：

我昨天吃了蘋果。　●●▶ 動詞不改變

晚飯後我出去散步，看見一群流浪狗。　●●▶ 動詞

英文

主要動詞必須標記時間，動詞隨時態改變

I ate an apple. ●●▶ 動詞標記過去

I went for a walk after dinner and saw a pack of stray dogs. ●●▶ 時態要貫徹！

Chapter 9　主動被動釐清責任

Q: 中、英文什麼時候用「主動」？什麼時候用「被動」？

A:

中文

主動、被動看詞彙、靠情境

書出版了　••▶　沒有「被」的被動關係

他被選為班長　••▶　有「被」的被動關係

他獲選為班長　••▶　由詞彙表達的被動關係

英文

必須釐清主詞與動詞間是「主控」還是「受控」關係

God created man.　••▶　上帝（主控）造人

Man was created.　••▶　人（受控）被造

Chapter 10　形式與語意的準確搭配

Q: 中、英文詞類的形式和語意如何搭配？

A:

中文

同一個詞有不同用法，詞類改變，但形式不變

這裡很混亂！　••▶　形容詞

這裡是一團混亂！　••▶　名詞

英文

1) 不同用法，詞類不同，形式也不同：

　　Everything became so chaotic.　••▶　形容詞

　　It's a total chaos!　••▶　名詞

2) 對等連接必須保持詞性一致： N and N; V and V; ADJ and ADJ

　　We often manage to show our kindness **and** friendship to them.

　　　　　　　　　　　　　　名詞 1　　　　　名詞 2

　　Thank you for organizing the event **and** giving us the opportunity to visit Hsinchu.

　　　　　　　　　動名詞 1　　　　　　　動名詞 2

Chapter

06

英文嚴句子

中文為什麼不能直翻成英文？

英文句子的必要成分是什麼？

什麼是動詞的標記？

This is very good.
I like the salad. It is fresh and crisp. I like the steak. It is juicy and flavory!

Be strict with English

《英文文法有道理》這本書一再強調：中文重情境，英文嚴句子。什麼叫做「嚴句子」？就是對句子的語法結構和語意搭配有嚴謹的要求：

1) 一個子句表達一個單一事件（發生了什麼事？），主詞、動詞、受詞都要清楚標示，語意才完整 ●●▶ 主動賓不可缺、也不可多

2) 一個句子只能表達一個重點事件（重點是什麼？），所以只能有一個獨立的主要子句，其餘為附屬，要有附屬標記 ●●▶ 主從分明

3) 一個主要子句必須有一個主要動詞，帶有時態標記，表達時間的主軸；其餘為輔，不帶時間（不定詞 to-V 或 動名詞 V-ing） ●●▶ 一主一從

這三個原則應用在寫作上，首先就是要寫出完整獨立的句子：

➢ 單一事件：單一動詞

　　　I baked a cake.

　　　I baked a cake for my mom.

　　　I baked a cake with brown sugar.

基本句式：　

➢ 兩個事件合一：兩個動詞，一主一從

　　　I baked a cake <u>to please my mom</u>.

　　　I baked a cake <u>for her to enjoy</u>.

　　　I baked a cake <u>using</u> brown sugar.

雙動詞句式：　

➢ 兩個事件分開：兩個子句，一主一從

I baked a cake for my mom [because she loves desserts].

S V O.　　　　　　　[because S V O]

My mom loves desserts　　[although she is high on cholesterol].

S V O　　　　　　　　[although S V O.]

| 主要子句 | ◀•• | 附屬連接詞**附屬子句帶時態** |

兩個子句間的語意關係，是藉由附屬連接詞（because, although, if, when）來表達，同時在結構上，附屬連接詞用來標記附屬子句，與主要子句作區隔，使主從關係清楚。由標記方式來看，英文是「標從、不標主」，兩個子句在一起時，主要子句無須特別標記，但附屬子句一定要有特別標記：

[S V O]　　[附屬標記 S V O]
主要子句　　　　附屬子句

帶有附屬標記的子句：

條件：He will go to the party [if[附屬標記] he can finish his lab work].

先後：He went to the party [after[附屬標記] he finished his lab work].

時間：He agreed to come to the party [when[附屬標記] I invited him].

原因：He worked hard [because[附屬標記] he would like to get promoted].

結果：He worked hard [so[附屬標記] he got promoted to managerial staff].

名詞子句：He told me [that[附屬標記] he had finished his lab work].

關係子句：He bought a new book [which[附屬標記] talks about English writing].

6.2 中式英文的問題

中文是語意情境導向，在結構上沒有主從之分，動詞和小句間可隨意連結，學生往往受到中文的影響，就忘記英文句子的嚴謹要求。請看看下面這兩個問題句子，從 SVO 的標記原則來看，有什麼不妥的地方呢？

（？）There are some other points should be clarified or examined.

（？）He can attend NCTU is because he studied hard.

這兩個問題句子就是典型的「中式英文」，直接將中文的說法轉成英文，完全沒有考慮英文句子的結構要求：

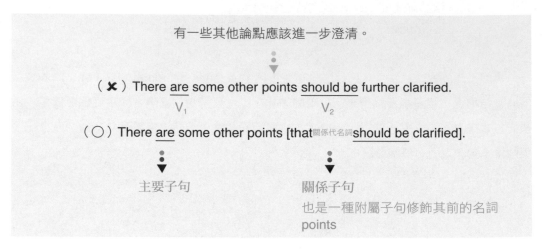

既然前面已經用了一個帶有時態的主要動詞，就不能再直接用另一個動詞，必須用附屬標記來區隔：

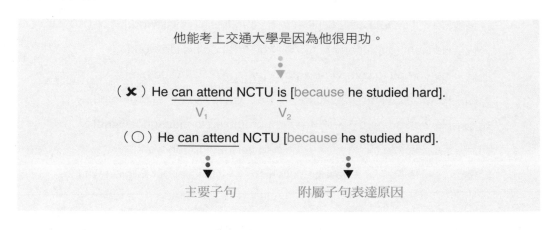

一個子句只能有一個主要動詞，只能有一個帶時態的動詞，若是同時出現兩個動詞都帶有時態，之間又沒有主從之分，就成了所謂的「run-on sentence」，違反英文「一主一從」的標記原則。這些問題的出現都是沒有掌握中英文的標記差異，直接將中文翻譯成英文的結果！

如何避免這種「中文直譯」的問題句子？我們可以有「三步」做法：

1. 養成寫完整主要子句的習慣：無論要講什麼，都先寫出主詞、動詞、補語明確的獨立主句，確立每句話要描述的重點，遵循 SVO 的原則，動詞不可多也不可少：

主句： He is able to attend NCTU.

2. 建立「主從有別」的連結習慣：再適當運用「主」、「從」分明的區隔來連接主要事件之外的成分。基本上，英文是「標從不標主」：「主要」事件獨立完整，無須特別標記，但「從屬」事件在標記上要有附屬標記（if, when, although, because...）：

[S V O] [because **S V O**]

[主 動 賓] [附屬標記主 動 賓]

[He is able to enter NCTU] [because he studied hard].

3. 把長句拆成兩個短句：太長的句子容易出錯，焦點不清，語意也較模糊，因此要養成寫短句的習慣。短句不但可以讓讀者一目了然，在標記上也容易掌握：

He studied really hard in high school. Therefore, he was admitted to NCTU.

千萬不要以為短句沒有程度。精簡的短句才是深沉的功力！在暢銷書 *The Last Lecture* 中，整本書的第一句如此言簡意賅：

I have an engineering problem.
While for the most part I'm in terrific physical shape, I have ten tumors in my liver and I have only a few months left to live.

作者是工程背景，就把自己得癌症這件事比喻為一個 engineering problem。短短的一句話點出引人好奇的重點，然後再解釋為什麼這樣說。完全符合重點先講，細節隨後的 G-S 精神！

　　下面這個句子好長，語意就顯得凌亂，請依照上述原則，改寫這個長句，分成幾個短句，記住：每個子句裡只能有一個主要動詞！

冗長凌亂：I love basketball, playing basketball with classmates every Wednesdays, watching basketball games, and am a big fan of Jeremy Lin.

簡潔有序：I love basketball. I play it with my classmates every Wednesday and watch basketball games on TV. I am a big fan of Jeremy Lin.

　　這樣改寫，每個句子在文法上都符合 SVO 不可少的標記原則，句句分明，在內容銜接上也符合 G-S-G 的鋪陳原則。

6.3　動詞不可少，也不可多

　　英文裡的每一個句子只能表達一個焦點事件，因此在標記形式上，只能有一個主要子句，包含一個主要主詞和一個主要動詞。主要動詞用來表達主要動作，並標記主要時間，不可多也不可少！

句子的必要成份 = 一個**主詞**＋一個主要動詞（帶有時態）

　　下面這兩個問題句式（run-on sentence）在動詞上出了什麼問題呢？

　　改正錯誤的第一步，就是要先找出主要子句的 SVO，每用一個動詞，都要檢視動詞的主詞是誰？動詞間有沒有區隔或連接標記：

錯誤句式：

1) There <u>are</u> many students <u>choose</u> to give up math. ●●▶ 兩個帶時態的動詞在一起？

2) <u>Try to</u> eat food produced in the country you live in <u>can reduce</u> the emissions of carbon dioxie. ●●▶ 整句的主詞在哪？

正確句式：

1) There <u>are</u> many students who <u>choose</u> to give up math. ●●▶ 加上關係代名詞

2) <u>Trying</u> to eat food produced in the country you live in <u>can reduce</u> the emissions of carbon dioxide. ●●▶ 動名詞作主詞

基本上，動詞的使用有兩個原則可遵循：

原則1：兩個動詞在一起，若沒有對等連接詞（and），一定是「一主一從」，一定要有附屬標記來區隔：

(✘) [There <u>are</u> many students] <u>choose</u> to give up math.
　　　　V₁　　　　　　　　　　V₂ → choose 的主詞是誰？和前一個動詞有無區隔

(○) [There <u>are</u> many students] who ^{關係代名詞} <u>choose</u> to give up math.
　　　　　　　　　　　　　　　　→ 加上關係代名詞，分隔主從

原則2：典型的主詞是名詞，當動詞作主詞時，形式上也須有附屬標記，才能與主要動詞有所區隔，可用動名詞 V-ing，或不定詞 to V，或 that 子句。

(✘) <u>Try</u> to eat food (produced...) <u>can reduce</u> the emissions of carbon dioxide.
　　V₁ to V₂　　（分詞修飾語）　　V₃　　　　　O → reduce 的主詞是誰？
　　　　　　　　　　　　　　　　　　　　　　　　　　和前一動詞有無區隔？

(○) [<u>Trying</u> to eat food produced in the country you live in]^{主詞} <u>can reduce</u> the emission of carbon dioxide. → 動詞原形不能作主詞，加上ing 改為動名詞，作全句的主詞！

掌握英文嚴句子的特性，就是要遵守每個子句「主動賓，不可少也不可多」的嚴謹要求，先確定主要子句，就是主要主詞加一個主要動詞。若有多個動詞，請善用「主從有別」的原則，在附屬子句上加入合適的附屬標記就可以了。

6.4 常見錯誤類型

中式英文常見的錯誤類型有幾種，在此列舉出來的目的是希望學生能知己知彼，自我警惕，避免類似錯誤。

類型一 子句間缺少必要的主從標記

錯誤句式：

1. (✗) I would be happy if you are willing to share your favorite songs or band with me, it could help me to choose songs to perform at the annual concert.
   → 兩個子句間沒有連接關係

2. (✗) Since I joined the music club, not one group I joined ever won first prize when we participated in competitions, it made me depressed and felt really miserable.
   → 連接關係不清

3. (✗) Since I am a fashion enthusiast, don't panic when you see my desk littered with nail polish and my bookcase cluttered with fashion magazines, I will do my best to make my living space as neat as a pin; I am used to getting up an hour early before class to get myself ready, I will make sure to avoid waking you up in the morning. → 連接關係不清，語意不明

正確句式：

1. I would be happy if you are willing to share your favorite songs or band with me. It could help me to choose songs to perform at the annual concert.
   → 分為兩句話，各自獨立

2. Since I joined the music club, not one group I joined ever won first prize when we participated in competitions. This made me depressed and felt really miserable.
   → 分為兩句話，各自獨立

5. Since I am a fashion enthusiast, please do not panic when you see my desk littered with nail polish and my bookcase cluttered with fashion magazines. I will do my best to make my living space as neat as a pin. Since I am used to getting up an hour early before class to get myself ready, I will make sure to avoid waking you up in the morning. → 主從有別，標示清楚

寫作原則 ：兩個完整的子句在一個句號內，一定要有連接標記，可用對等連接詞（and）連成對等的兩個子句，或用分號（；）分開，或寫成兩個獨立的句子。

上述的例子其實都是「句子太長」造成的結果。別忘了，句子太長容易模糊焦點，不但難以有效率的傳遞訊息，標記也容易出問題。因此若要解決這樣的問題，最好的方式就是將一個長句拆成短句，這個時候，連接詞及標點符號便派上用場了。一個句子的結束，可用句號（．）、驚嘆號（！）或問號（？），在這些符號出現以前，所有子句都還隸屬於同一個句子的範疇中，所以必須要有連接標記：

1) 對等連接：   [SVO] and [SVO]. → 用 and 連接兩個對等子句

2) 分號：   SVO; SVO.   → 用分號連接兩個語意相關的子句

3) 分成兩句：   SVO. SVO.   → 各自加上句號（．）

類型二 缺少動詞，難以成句

前一類問題是在句子中塞入過多動詞。第二類問題是缺少動詞，結構殘缺，語意不全：

（✘）If you want to a fluent English speaker, you need to speak as often as possible.

        動詞在哪？

（○）If you want to be a fluent English speaker, you need to speak as often as possible.

這樣的問題在台灣學生的作文中還蠻常出現的，請幫忙改正以下的問題句式：

問題句式：少了動詞

（✘）People between eighteen to thirty years old, who came from more than fifty countries including Asia, Europe, and America. → 主要子句的動詞在哪？

（✘）Peter Burk, an FBI agent who is in charge of Neal's case and tries hard to catch Neal. → 主要動詞在哪？

正確句式：

(◯) [People between eighteen to thirty years old]主詞 came 動詞 from more than fifty countries including Asia, Europe, and America.

(◯) Peter Burk 主詞, [an FBI agent who is in charge of Neal's case]關係子句, tries 動詞 hard to catch Neal.

主要子句中的重要成分是主要動詞，所以一定要把動詞找回來！

寫作原則 ： 主詞後一定要有動詞。沒有主要動詞的句子，就好像一部電影，主角出現了，卻連一個動作也沒演出，整部電影就結束了。因此，若想要寫出一個好句子，主詞、動詞缺一不可！

類型三 附屬子句的問題

前面提過主要子句用來描述焦點事件，如果想為這個焦點事件加上一些「背景」，這時候就需要附屬子句出馬了！當一個句子裡同時有主要子句及附屬子句時，要如何標記「主」與「從」呢？別忘了，常用的附屬標記有三種：(1) 附屬連接詞（although, if, because, when...），(2) 分詞或不定詞，(3) 名詞子句或關係子句。以下列舉常見的幾個問題：

1. 附屬連接詞太多：只有附屬子句，沒有主要子句

下面這個句子是將中文說「因為……所以……」的習慣帶到英文，出現兩個附屬連接詞，兩個子句都變成附屬，卻少了主要子句：

(✘) Because I knew each of the boroughs had a community center, so I hoped that he could lend us a place for three days.

(◯) I knew each of the boroughs had a community center,　　→ 主要子句

so I hoped that he could lend us a place for three days.　　→ 附屬子句

更正原則：保持句子必定要有一個主要子句，避免多餘的附屬標記。

2. 不定詞和進行貌的使用

請看看下面這個句子在動詞補語上出了什麼問題？It's time 後面接什麼？to stop 後又要接什麼？

> (✖)　It is time we human beings to stop destroy the environment and make a difference.

> (◯)　It is time <u>for us</u> human beings to stop destroying the environment and make a difference. → 在說話的同時，破壞環境的事情仍不斷發生
>
> (◯)　It is time <u>that</u> we human beings stop destroying the environment and make a difference. → 說話者呼籲大家停下手邊的工作，不再破壞環境

依照主從分明的原則，It's time 是主要子句，後面須接帶有附屬標記的補語，才能區隔主從關係，大致有兩種方式：

1) 接 that 子句：It's time **that** [someone] do [something] → 作為 time 的說明
2) 接不定詞：It's time **for** [someone] **to do** [something] → for...to 不定修飾

至於 to stop 後面該接什麼，根據《英文文法有道理》，動詞的語意類型不同，後面接的補語形式就不同。不同的補語形式有其意義：進行貌 **V-ing** 表「**動作已出現、在進行中**」，不定詞表「**目標事件，想要作的事**」。這裡的 stop 是指「停止繼續做……」，要停止中斷的事，必然已經出現、且在進行中，因此要用 stop + V-ing：

比較：

It's time to <u>stop destroying</u> the environment.　　　 → 該停止破壞了！

It's time to <u>stop to think about</u> the environment.　　 → 該停下來想一想了！

3. 名詞子句或關係子句的標記

關係子句也是一種附屬子句，作為修飾名詞之用，關係代名詞就是附屬標記。然而要注意的是：關係代名詞是代替前面的名詞，語意類別和數量人稱必須和前面的名詞相呼應，以達到「形」、「意」相符的效果。下面例子使用的關係代名詞都出了問題：

(✘) When I was seven years old, we moved to Banchiao, [where is my father's hometown].

(✘) If you want to go shopping in this city, [which the price for goods is surprisingly high], I also know some great stores where you can buy inexpensive clothes.

(○) When I was seven years old, we moved to Banchiao, [**which** is my father's hometown].

(○) If you want to go shopping in this city, [**where/in which** the price for goods is surprisingly high], I also know some great stores where you can buy inexpensive clothes.

　　在這組範例中，都用到關係子句來修飾前面的名詞，但關係代名詞的選擇卻要看它在關係子句中的角色而定。兩句看似都用來修飾地方，然而，第一句中的關係代名詞是作為主詞，單純用來代替 Banchiao（板橋）這個地方名詞，做為關係子句的主詞，是名詞性的用法，所以要用 which：Banchiao (= which) is my hometown。 第二句中的關係代詞是作為副詞，所代替的是 in the city (= in which = where)，說明事件發生之處，是副詞性的修飾語：「在」這座城市「裡」，因此要用 where 或 in which。

　　此外關係代名詞既是代替前面的名詞，其後的動詞必須和所代替的名詞相呼應，單複數要相符：

(✘) People like me, [who is lazy and still questioning my career], are not well suited for homeschooling. → 關係子句是修飾 people！，不是 me ！

(○) People like me, [who are lazy and still questioning their careers], are not well suited for homeschooling.

還有，當介係詞片語出現時，一定要搞清楚它是跟著哪一個子句走：

> (✘) When I was little, I visited my grandmother, [who lives in Hualien underline every summer].
> → every summer 是用來修飾主要主詞 I，還是 grandmother？

> (○) When I was little, I visited my grandmother every summer, [who lives in Hualien].

> (○) When I was little, I visited my grandmother, [who lives in Hualien], every summer.
> → 請注意標點符號

寫作原則：每次用關係子句，一定要釐清所代替的名詞在關係子句中的角色：

關代詞為主詞：I saw a friend <u>who</u> visited me last week.

關代詞為受詞：I saw a friend <u>who(m)</u> I visited [_] last week.

關代為地方副詞：I saw a friend in a park <u>where</u> (= in which) I took a walk every day.

關代為時間副詞：I saw a friend at the same time <u>when</u> I walked into the park.

關代加介係詞：I bought a new oven, <u>with which</u> I can bake all kinds of dessert.
I have a lot of clothes, <u>none of which</u> fits the special occasion.

類型四 分詞構句的問題

分詞是子句的簡化版，動詞以分詞形式出現時，省略了主詞，因為分詞的主詞就是主要子句的主詞。「主要主詞」是整句話的核心人物，分詞子句必須繞著它打轉。根據《英文文法有道理》，現在分詞代表主動關係，過去分詞代表被動關係，不管是主動或被動，分詞的主詞必須和主要主詞一致，這就是最容易出錯的地方。請看看下面這些分詞的主詞和主要子句的主詞？

問題句式:

(✘) Attending quite a few concerts, <u>they</u> enabled me to understand more about myself. → attending 的主詞是誰？

(✘) Wanted to become more like my brother, <u>I</u> told my mom I wanted to learn the piano. → wanted 的主詞是誰？是被動的角色嗎？

(✘) Surprising by the interesting software, I spent about two hours trying all the programs that were already in the system. → surprising 的主詞是誰？是主動 的關係嗎？

(✘) When I grew up, returning to Fu Long, it had changed thoroughly. → returning 的主詞是誰？

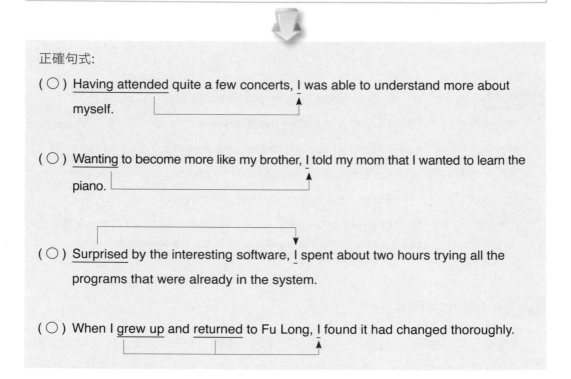

正確句式:

(○) Having attended quite a few concerts, I was able to understand more about myself.

(○) Wanting to become more like my brother, I told my mom that I wanted to learn the piano.

(○) Surprised by the interesting software, I spent about two hours trying all the programs that were already in the system.

(○) When I grew up and returned to Fu Long, I found it had changed thoroughly.

　　上列四個句子的問題，很明顯出在分詞的主詞與主要主詞的角色不一致，別忘了主要主詞是句子的主角，分詞子句必須配合主角，千萬不可喧賓奪主：

主要主詞＝分詞主詞

寫作原則：將分詞主詞和主要主詞「對齊」，並釐清分詞和主要主詞間的主動、被動關係。

類型五 直接引述 **vs.** 間接引述

　　當我們要引用別人的話時，總是有兩種選擇：直接引述和間接引述。兩者表現方式不一樣：「間接引述」是融入句子的一部分，遵照主從分明的原則，須加上附屬標記；「直接引述」則以雙引號" "來區隔兩個場景，時空人物都各自獨立：

> 問題句式：
>
> (✘) When the speaker asked "Who has questions?" several hands raised up high in the air. → 直接引述 or 間接引述？
>
> (✘) English changed my life a lot, just like the quotation says that "*Living in another country means growing another self, and it takes time for that other self to become familiar.*" → 直接引述 or 間接引述？

正確句式：直接引述

(○) "Who has questions?" the speaker asked, and several hands raised up high in the air.

或　　When the speaker asked: "Who has questions?", several hands raised up high in the air.

(○) English changed my life a lot. As the quotation says, "Living in another country means growing another self, and it takes time for that other self to become familiar."

　　直接引述的原則就是「原音重現」，通常放在句首作為重點，並用「引號」來標記所引內容。同樣的話，也可用間接引述的方式來呈現，與主要子句緊密結合，因為已經過改寫，不再是「原汁原味」，不需要「引號」來標記，但要有明確的附屬標記：

間接引述

(○) When the speaker asked who had questions, several hands raised up high in the air.

(○) The quotation says that living in another country means growing another self, and it takes time for that other self to become familiar.

間接問句與間接引述句類似，也是作為動詞補語的附屬子句，雖是疑問的語意，但在主要子句為直述句的前提下，間接問句作為子句補語，也是直述句的一部分，不須倒裝：

> I don't know who has the time to finish the book.
>
> I want to know how I can finish the book.
>
> I asked him when he will finish the book.
>
> I asked him if he would like to finish the book.

類型六　the more... the more...（愈……愈……）

　　The more...the more... 基本上是對等連接，前後子句都是由 SVO 的基本句式倒裝而來，形成對等的修飾關係。使用此句型時，要認清 the more 修飾的對象是什麼，是修飾名詞（the more N），還是修飾動詞（the＋副詞比較級）？同時，在前後子句中，仍要保持 SVO 句構的基本元素。the more...the more... 雖是強調用法，但是主詞、動詞、受詞等基本要素仍要到位，缺一不可！中式英文常出現的問題在於：少了主詞或動詞，或是修飾關係不對稱。請檢查下列兩句有沒有這兩個問題：

> 問題句式：
>
> (✘)　The more studying, the better scores you will get.　→ the more studying 是主詞還是動詞？
>
> (✘)　From the biological view, the upper species in the food chain, the more quantity of poisonous chemicals they receive.　→ 前句中的動詞在哪？

> 正確句式：
>
> (○) The more studying you do, the better scores you will get.
> 　　　　　　　O　　　　S　V　　　　　O　　　　S　V
>
> 或　The more you study, the higher you will score.
> 　　ADV　　S　V　　　ADV　　S　V

(○) From the biological view, <u>the higher</u> a species is in the food chain,

                             ADJ   S   V

<u>the more poisonous chemicals</u> it receives.

                 O   S   V

基本上，the more...the more... 的句型是由 SVO 句式倒裝而來：

A species is high in the food chain. → <u>The higher</u> a species is in the food chain.

以及

It receives poisonous chemicals. → <u>The more</u> poisonous chemicals it receives.

由此可知，無論英文的句型如何變化，都必須遵守 SVO 標記的大原則。

類型七 形意彼此搭配

「嚴句子」的最終目的是要完成「形意搭配」的講究。英文主從分明的形式，是為了搭配主從分明的內容。形式上的主要子句也是語意上的重點事件，形式和語意要相互搭配，彼此呼應。以下例句中雖有正確的主從標記，但搭配的語意卻不是很對稱：

形意不對稱：

(?)   Since [attitude toward learning and relationship] is the most important difference, I categorized it among other differences between Asian and Western people.

(?)   It was the biggest earthquake that ever occurred in Taiwan, the 921 earthquake, which deprived Taiwan of its natural beauty due to people's overdevelopment to the mountains.

這兩個例子要強調的重點都被放到附屬子句裡了！語意的重點淪為次要子句，就會顯得頭重腳輕，訊息錯置。要記住：主要子句是句子的核心，攜帶語意重點；附屬子句則描述次要的語境，扮演著補充說明的角色，兩者各司其職。「形」、「意」要互相搭配，清楚呈現所要強調的訊息究竟是什麼！

形意較對稱：

(○) Among the many differences between Asian and Western people, [the attitude towards learning and relationship] was the main difference I categorized.

(○) [The 921 Earthquake] was the biggest earthquake that ever occurred in Taiwan. It deprived Taiwan of its natural beauty as a result of overdevelopment of the mountains.

　　將重點放在主要子句中說明清楚，再加上其他附屬訊息，讓人一目了然。切記，語言中的形與意是要互相配合，相輔相成的。英文主從分明的要求便是形式（句法）與語意（內容）彼此搭配的原則，藉由「形式」呈現「語意」！把英文語句寫好的第一步就是要掌握「嚴句子」的各項妙處！

 題　目

一、英文「嚴句子」，必須謹記主動賓都不可少的最高指導原則，請改正以下的句子。

1. The temperature is lower than the day time, the breeze is comfort, the smell of grass is refreshing.

_____

2. When ask an unforgettable smell, I would say it is the stinky tofu because of its strange smell.

_____

3. Walking is a very simple way to exercise, what I need is my feet and shoes.

_____

4. It was really amazing and just couldn't forget the smell and taste.

_____

5. We spending a period of time giving thanks to our teachers, devoting themselves in helping us in our studies as well as in our behaviors.

_____

二、以下這篇填空題，請選出正確答案。

In 1985, a riot at a Brussels soccer match occurred, in which many fans lost their lives. The tragedy began 45 minutes before the start of the European Cup final. The British team was scheduled ___1___ against the Italian team in the game. Noisy British fans, after setting off some rockets and fireworks to cheer for their team, broke through a thin wire fence and started to attack the Italian fans. The Italians, in panic, headed for the main exit in their section when a six-foot concrete wall collapsed. By the end of the night, 38 soccer fans had died and 437 were injured. The majority of the deaths resulted from people ___2___ trampled underfoot or crushed against barriers in the stadium. As a result of this 1985 soccer incident, security measures have since been tightened at major sports competitions to prevent similar events from happening.

1. (A) competing

   (B) to compete

   (C) compete

   (D) competed

2. (A) be

   (B) been

   (C) being

   (D) to be

 寫作修理廠

解 答

一、

1. The temperature is lower than the day time, the breeze is comfort, and the smell of grass is refreshing.

2. When people ask me about an unforgettable smell, I would answer "stinky tofu" because of its strange smell.

3. Walking is a very simple way to exercise, and all I need is my feet and shoes.

4. It was really amazing and I just couldn't forget the smell and taste.

5. We should spend a period of time giving thanks to our teachers, as they have devoted themselves to helping us in our studies as well as in our behaviors.

二、

1. (B)
主要動詞是 "was scheduled"，所以接下來的補語必然是附屬性質的不定詞，故選 (B) to compete。

2. (C)
主要動詞已經出現 "resulted from"，所以這裡要有一個修飾 people 的現在分詞，故選 (C) being。

Chapter

07

名詞出場必有標記

你知道我所說的是哪一個嗎？

這個名詞可否個體化？

要表達的是多數？還是類別？

a book, the book, or books?

我要買書

Be strict with nouns

英文的嚴謹，表現在名詞的標記上，也是一絕。名詞表達事件相關的人、事、物，在《英文文法有道理》一書中提到，英文名詞出場必有標記。標記什麼呢？舉凡人稱、單複數、及「已知否？」，都要明確標記！例如「學生」這個名詞可用來指涉一個學生（a student），一群學生（students），或者是「聽者已經知道的」那個學生（the student）。這就是名詞標記的意義，要明確告訴聽者所指的是哪一個，是一個還是多個！

既然要標記單複數，名詞就有是否能細分為多數的問題。 當一個名詞所代表的概念是抽象的（如：health, patience），或者形體無法切割（如：air, water），又或者在日常生活中不常拿來數（如：sand, rice），就成為不可數名詞，意指這些名詞很難「個體化」，也就沒有單複數之分。

名詞第二個要標記的，就是「聽者是否已知？」，也就是 a/the 的區別。我們從小就耳熟能詳「特定的用 the，非特定的用 a」。但是什麼是「特定」？什麼是「非特定」？可能許多人還是一頭霧水。《英文文法有道理》中指出：所謂「特定」就是對方已經知道是那一個，「不定」就是對方並不知道是哪一個。例如，你問我：

Q: Where did you go?
A: I went to the park. ◀●● 你我都知道的那個公園

Q: Where did you go?
A: I went to a park. ◀●● 我認為你不知道是哪個公園

簡單的說，定冠詞 **the** 是給聽者一種清楚的「提示」（a prompt），所指的就是「你知我知」的那一個啦！若是僅用不定冠詞 a，就只是簡單地告訴對方是「某一個」，並非對方已知的。因此，除了單複數之外，每次使用名詞時也要考量所指的事物是不是聽者知道的那一個。

但是由於中文在名詞的處理上和英文不同，多仰賴情境及修飾語的幫助，而不在名詞本身的形式上變化，所以「名詞出場必有標記」這個原則就成為學生的一大罩門。常常忘了要在英文名詞的形式上注意這兩方面的標記：(1) 個體化的標記：是具體的、還是抽象的概念？具體的又有單複數之分；(2) 已知性的標記：若是對方已經知道的，是「你知我知」的那一個，就用 the。

依照這兩個考量，請檢視下面的句子在名詞標記上出了什麼問題呢？

（✘）　I am so happy to meet <u>friend</u> from <u>different country</u>.

（✘）　<u>Weather forecast</u> had already reported that this week would be freezingly cold; <u>temperature</u> would drop day by day.

第一句中，friend 和 country 都是指涉具體的個體，卻少了單複數的標記，所以要說 I met **a** friend from **a** different country。第二句中，weather forecast（氣象報告）和 temperature（溫度）雖非具體名詞，卻都是說者和聽者共同知道的，是與天氣有關的已知成分，所以要加上 the：**The** weather forecast predicts that **the** temperature would drop.。

7.2 常見問題分析

既然名詞涉及的對象，要藉由冠詞來表達，冠詞的使用就成為一大課題。

類型一 冠詞的問題

前例已說明，台灣學生在寫英文時，最常發生的問題就是名詞少了相對應的冠詞。會有這樣的問題，關鍵當然在於中英文的標記方式不同，中文名詞前不一定要有冠詞，因此中文一句「我買了書」，換成了英文就要考量單複數與已知與否，就須利用冠詞來清楚標記是哪一種可能：

I bought a book.　　●●▶ 一本書
I bought books.　　●●▶ 一些書
I bought the book.　　●●▶ 那本書
I bought the books.　　●●▶ 那些書

其實這樣的標記習慣，在溝通上會使語意比較明確。名詞和冠詞是一體的，密不可分，若能把名詞和冠詞當成一個整體來用，就能漸漸養成使用冠詞的習慣。個體化的名詞出場時，會很自然的考量該用 a 或 the？所指的名詞對聽者來說是否可以辨認，能夠認定是哪一個，是不是「你知我知」？

1. 名詞前缺少冠詞 a/an/the

原則：使用名詞指涉具體、個體化的人或物時，一定要加上**冠詞 a/an/the**

> 問題句式：名詞出場是否有適當的標記？
>
> (✘)　The storm caused <u>serious disaster</u>.
>
> (✘)　So, we made <u>conclusion</u> that people from southern and northern Taiwan say eraser in <u>different way</u>.
>
> (✘)　<u>Wright brothers</u>, who invented the world's first airplane, had faced many challenges.
>
> (✘)　This chocolate beverage was spread by <u>Spanish and Italian</u>.

正確句式：加上 a/an/the 的標記

(○) The storm caused <u>a serious disaster</u>. ••▶ 尚未提過，聽者不知

(○) So, we made <u>the conclusion</u> that people from southern and northern Taiwan say eraser in <u>a different</u> way.

　　••▶ 藉由 that 子句的說明，conclusion 是明確可知的，故用 the

(○) <u>The Wright brothers</u>, who invented the world's first airplane, had faced many challenges.

　　••▶ the ＋姓氏，代表姓氏專有的一族，用來指稱「我知你知」的那家人

(○) This chocolate beverage was spread by <u>the Spanish and Italian</u>.

　　••▶ 以形容詞來表達類型屬性，the 仍然是用來指「你知我知」的類型群體。

　　視冠詞為名詞的一部分，將指涉對象納入標記的考量，是解決以上問題最好的策略。中英文名詞標記方式不同，導致學生往往將中文的習慣套用至英文書寫上，而忘了給予聽者適當的「提示」（a prompt）。因此使用英文名詞的第一步，就是要在個體化的名詞前加上適當的 a/the 標記，以清楚提示是哪一個（which one?）。

2. 名詞前一定要有冠詞嗎？

　　在上一節中我們強調要加冠詞，並說明 **a** 和 **the** 兩者的功用在於指出聽者「知或不知」的分別。但是一再強調要加冠詞，有時又會讓人誤以為所有英文名詞前一定都要有冠詞！這又是另一個錯誤的開始！名詞前都一定要有標記嗎？除了專有名詞之外，其他名詞有沒有什麼都不加的狀況呢？

　　當然有！要充分回答這個問題，我們要再次檢視英文在名詞前加冠詞的用意。名詞前加上 **a** 或 **the**，是為了「提示」聽者所指的是哪一個（**which one?**）。但是當名詞的出現並非為了指涉個體，或是所表達的是抽象無形的概念，就根本不牽涉「哪一個」的問題，也就沒有「提示」的必要了。因此當一個名詞的功用不具個體性，或與「個別指認」無關時，即所謂「無定指」，前面就未必要加上冠詞，而成為無冠詞的「純名詞」型態（**bare noun**）。英文的名詞，有三種常見無冠詞標記的情形：

1. 用抽象名詞表達抽象的概念時：

　　　<u>Love</u> is the most important cure of depression.

　　但是，同樣的抽象名詞加上了具個別性的修飾語，就添加了個別性的定指：

　　　<u>The love</u> [from my Mom] is my most important cure!

　　　<u>The depression</u> [I have experienced] is curable.

2. 用來泛指類型、群體或種類時：

　　　可數名詞複數：I love <u>dogs</u>, not <u>cats</u>. ●●▶ 「貓狗」這一類，屬無須細究的多數

　　　不可數名詞：I eat <u>rice</u>. I like <u>brown rice</u>. ●●▶ 集合名詞，泛指類型

3. 用來表達名詞的功能性或單純的語意概念時：

　　　I went to <u>school</u> on <u>foot</u>.　　●●▶ 強調功能性，無實體指涉

　　　<u>Spring</u> comes before <u>summer</u>.　●●▶ 季節的概念，不具特定時間指涉

　　　<u>Man</u> and <u>woman</u> can get along.　●●▶ 性別概念的對立，並非指涉個體

　　簡言之，當名詞的出現不涉及數量和 **which one** 的考量，也就無須特別提示標記了。運用上述的概念，下頁名詞前的冠詞是不是顯得累贅了？

問題句式：多了冠詞

(✘) She admitted that she was always afraid of **the** heights. ••▶ which height?

(✘) In order to lower carbon emissions, it is better not to go to work or school by **the** car. ••▶ which car?

(✘) I learned that in American culture, it is not common for people to live at **the** home with their parents after they turn eighteen. ••▶ which home?

正確句式：既然沒有 which one 的問題，就無需加上 the：

(○) She admitted that she was always afraid of ~~the~~ heights.

   ••▶ 用複數 heights 泛指任何「high places」，無定指

(○) In order to lower carbon emissions, it is better not to go to work or school by ~~the~~ car.

   ••▶ 用來泛指「車子」的概念，無定指

(○) I learned that in American culture, it is not common for people to live at ~~the~~ home with their parents after they turn eighteen.

   ••▶ 用來泛指「家」的概念，無定指

    請注意，中文說「怕高」，是指高的地方，英文傾向用複數 heights，泛指這種類型的地方。有時中式英文會口誤為：I am afraid of height，這不是英文常見的用法，因為 height 做為抽象名詞時是指中性的度量概念，如：the height of the stove，不見得一定指很高的地方。一般來說，害怕的對象可能是複數的實體或非實體的概念：

   複數的實體：I am afraid of heights/snakes/small spaces.

   非實體的概念：I am afraid of death/commitment/responsibility.

「中國人」或「中國的」？國別詞性有講究

另外一個台灣學生常見的問題在於國家詞性的錯用。部分國家的形容詞與名詞相異，造成學生們在使用上的混淆。看看下列句子，冠詞標記後面的名詞用對了嗎？

問題句式：冠詞後面接的是名詞嗎？

(✘) He is <u>a Spanish</u>. ●●▶ Spanish 是名詞嗎？

(✘) She is <u>a French</u>. ●●▶ French 是名詞嗎？

正確句式

(○) He is <u>a Spaniard</u>. ●●▶ 西班牙人為 Spaniard，才能與 a 合用

(○) She is <u>a Frenchwoman</u>. ●●▶ 法國人是 Frenchman 或 Frenchwoman

許多國家形容詞和國人名詞的形式是一致的，如 Chinese 既是形容詞也可指中國人。當形式趨於一致時，英文使用者往往偏好較不易造成混淆的形容詞用法。例如：**He is a Chinese.**（他是一個中國人）在理論上似乎沒有錯，但因形式上易造成語意混淆，所以較少這樣用，英文使用者會選擇以下的說法：

He is Chinese. ●●▶ 單數時傾向當形容詞用！

He is a Chinese man. ●●▶ 或是加上顯而易見的名詞！

They are Chinese. ●●▶ 複數時兩種形式就合一了！

以下為常見的國家地名、國家形容詞及當地居民的使用形式，熟悉這些用法，有助於避免發生混淆。

Place	Adjective	Demonym
Africa	African	Africans
America	American	Americans
Asia	Asian	Asians
Europe	European	Europeans

Australia	Australian	Australians
Mexico	Mexican	Mexicans
Brazil	Brazilian	Brazilians
India	Indian	Indians

Great Britain	British	Britons/Brits
France	French	Frenchmen/Frenchwomen
Spain	Spanish	Spaniards
Sweden	Swedish	Swedes
Scotland	Scottish	Scots/Scotsmen
The Philippines	Philippine	Filipinos(m)/Filipinas(f)
The Netherlands	Dutch	Dutch
New Zealand	New Zealand	New Zealanders
Iceland	Icelandic	Icelanders

China	Chinese	Chinese
Taiwan	Taiwanese	Taiwanese
Canton	Cantonese	Cantonese

類型二 單複數標記與「個體化」的問題

　　冠詞的標記也牽涉到單複數的問題，英文名詞分為兩大類：可數與不可數。可數名詞有單複數之分，不可數名詞沒有單複數之分，但究竟如何區分這兩者？本章一開始就引《英文文法有道理》一書，來解釋區別可數不可數的關鍵就在於能否「個體化」！凡是個體獨立，可單獨談論個體的就是可數名詞。既然是有「數」可數，就必須加上單複數的標記。請記得單數名詞是談論單一的個體，而複數名詞才有可能代表整體或類型。看看下面這些從英文讀本中節錄的句子[1]，其中的複數名詞，是不是都代表那一「類」的人或物：

1　改寫自 *Wordly Wise* Book 9, Unit 4.

Ballplayers would set a good example if they would be devoted to their families.

Governments have the right to mandate speed limits on highways.

As part of my diet, I avoid fried foods. ●●▶ 用 foods 強調各式各樣的食物

再看看下列這些學生寫的句子，都在個數的標記上出了問題！

問題句式：少了複數標記

(✘)　They develop different flavor of chocolate on their own, and hope their products would be able to bring happiness to their customers. ●●▶ 口味有幾種？

(✘)　Volunteers joined some volunteering project in order to broaden their worldviews, take on new challenges and make foreign friends. ●●▶ 有幾個計畫？

(✘)　Before, group tour was quite common because travel agencies would book the plane ticket and the hotel for you. ●●▶ 有多少旅遊團？

(✘)　In his leisure time, he takes guitar lessons, studies Korean, and learns how to fly an airplane. He tries to do thing he has never done before, such as breaking into a closed theater or traveling spontaneously. ●●▶ 嘗試做幾件事？

(✘)　Cult film, also known as underground movies, is a film that gains success only within a small, specific group of people. ●●▶ 個數標記前後一致嗎？

(✘)　This kind of films has an unclear definition. ●●▶ 到底是一種還是多種？

　　要強調「多種不同」或是「一整類」的東西，就要特別注意這是「多數」的概念，要用「複數」形式來表達：

正確句式：複數名詞表多數或整類

(○) They develop different flavors of chocolate on their own, and hope their products would be able to bring happiness to their customers.

　　　●●▶ flavors 要加上複數標記

(○) Volunteers joined <u>some volunteering projects</u> in order to broadening their worldviews, taking on new challenges and making foreign friends.

●●▶ 複數的 volunteers 搭配複數的 projects

(○) Before, <u>group tours</u> were quite common because travel agencies would book the plane tickets and the hotels for you.

●●▶ group tours 也要加上複數標記

(○) In his leisure time, he takes guitar lessons, studies Korean, and learns how to fly an airplane. He tries <u>things</u> he has never done before, such as breaking into a closed theater or traveling spontaneously.

●●▶ 嘗試的事不只一件,所以用 things

(○) <u>Cult films</u>, also known as <u>underground movies</u>, <u>are</u> <u>films</u> that gain success only within a small, specific group of people.

●●▶ 介紹 film 的類型,最好用複數表示一整「類」

(○) This kind of film has an unclear definition.

●●▶ This kind 強調單一的種類,前後數量最好一致

若要強調影片種類多元,我們可以説 "different kinds of films",複數標記放在 kind 上。對英文使用者來説,名詞的數量標記最好前後呼應一致,若要表達單一種類的東西,最常見的用法可能是 this kind of cat:

This <u>kind</u> of <u>cat</u> makes the best companion. ●●▶ 數量前後一致

若是用複數的 cats,也不能説是錯,只是聽起來怪怪的,同時又會引發另一個問題:動詞該用單數還是複數?

This <u>kind</u> of <u>cat</u>s is easy to find in Taiwan. ●●▶ 以 This kind 為主詞

This kind of <u>cat</u>s <u>are</u> easy to find in Taiwan. ●●▶ 把 This kind of 當數量形容詞

這兩種用法都可能出現，只是側重的主詞不一樣。語言是習慣的產物，習慣有可能依地域、社群而改變，重要的是掌握核心原則：英文名詞有數量的講究，且前後要彼此搭配！

數量的標記通常視使用目的而改變，但也要考慮名詞本身的語意特徵，有些名詞本身即含有多數的概念，如：audience, flock，代表一群人、一群動物，無論用在哪裡，都不能違背「多數」的詞彙語意：

an audience ●●▶ a group of participants

a flock ●●▶ a group of animals

下面這個句子的問題，就是把 audience 和單數主詞混在一起了：

問題句式

(✘) For me, as an audience, watching those dancers on the stage and using their rhythmic movement to express their confidence is really attracting and charming.

　　　　●●▶ me 和 audience 不搭！

正確句式：兩種可能改法

(○) For me, as a spectator, watching those dancers on the stage and using their rhythmic movement to express their confidence is really attracting and charming.

或

(○) For me, as one of the audience, watching those dancers on the stage and using their rhythmic movement to express their confidence is really attracting and charming.

既然 audience 是集合名詞，指「一群觀眾」，卻用來補充描述單數的 me，就顯得矛盾了。可以將 audience 改為 spectator，或是加上 one of the audience 強調其個體化的用法。

另一類名詞，形式上是 the＋形容詞，用來概括所代表的某類型人物，如：the poor, the rich, the sick, the healthy，這些也都是多數的群體概念：

the rich 其實是 the rich people 的簡略說法，用來指具此類屬性的一群人，相當於複數名詞，當然動詞也必須使用複數來搭配。

另外，在某些語境中，雖然使用單數或複數似乎都合乎語法，但在語意上卻有顯著的不同。下面這兩個句子，那一個比較符合真實世界的情況呢？

二選一：

(a)　The Beatles and Bill Gates both got chances to do what they enjoyed doing and to spend their time on their <u>specialty</u>.　●●▶ 兩方的專長都一樣嗎？

(b)　The Beatles and Bill Gates both got chances to do what they enjoyed and to spend their time on their <u>specialties</u>.　●●▶ 兩方各有各的專長？

我們明白，The Beatles 和 Bill Gates 都各自有專精的領域，前者在樂壇登峰造極，後者在資訊業占有一席之地，兩者的專業絕不可混為一談，應用複數 specialties 表示二者各有專精，(b) 句較符合一般的認知。

什麼時候加 s？A Big Trouble with "Trouble/Troubles"

Trouble 這個詞的單複數用法，對許多人而言是個頭大的問題。其實只要掌握一個大原則：trouble 放在片語裡，成為慣用的既定用法，表達其語意「概念」，就不必強調「個

體性」，像是 have trouble、in trouble 或是 get into trouble 等。然而，如果要明確指出一項個別的「煩惱」，也就是強調其「個體性」的用法，就需要有單複數的標記：

1) 片語用法，不強調個體性：

Don't get yourself into trouble.

Every time he is with his older brother, he always gets into trouble.

She has trouble focusing on her work when she drinks too much coffee.

= She has difficulty focusing on her work. ●●▶ 片語用法，不強調個體化

2) 個體化的用法，強調個別的問題：

Please do not take the trouble to travel to Kaohsiung.

The most comforting thing about having close friends is being able to talk about

our troubles. ●●▶ 指各人的種種煩惱，強調個體化的 troubles

類型三 代名詞的問題

「代名詞」顧名思義，就是用來代替前面提過的名詞（所謂的「先行詞」），兩者間有高度的關連性：(1) 兩者的人稱、數目要一致，指代對象是單數，代名詞就用單數；指代對象為女性，代名詞也要有女性標記。(2) 兩者間的指代關係要明確，代名詞和先行詞不能離得太遠，前後關連要一目了然。因此，每次使用代名詞時，都要自問：指代的對象對讀者來說是否清楚？前後是否搭配一致？

1. 「代名詞」的指代對象是誰？前後要一致！

寫作時常出現代名詞和先行詞在人稱、數量上不一致的情形。有了代名詞，卻找不著所搭配的名詞。以下的問題例句一再反映這個疏失，請試著找出下列各句「代名詞」的「指代對象」，確認兩者是否在數量、人稱、性別上彼此搭配？

(✘) In "A Generation in Too Safe a Place," Roger Cohen pointed out the reason why the young generation in London has a difficult time finding a job and cannot make a living on <u>its</u> own. ●●▶ its 是指誰？

(✘) And then, a waiter took our picture and gave it to us. We were surprised and thanked <u>them</u>. ●●▶ them 指誰？有提過嗎？

(✘) A lot of academic materials as well as nice facilities are available at large universities. <u>It</u> can help you learn effectively. ●●▶ it 指什麼？前面提過嗎？

(✘) Sometimes, white lies sound like flattery. However, I regard <u>it</u> as unavoidable in many situations. ●●▶ it 指什麼？搭配一致嗎？

(✘) Love is important, but if <u>we</u> can't trust the one <u>you</u> love, it might be a tragedy. If one day you find your lover tells lies to you, you might start doubting his love.
     ●●▶ 前後兩個代名詞的人稱與指代關係一致嗎？

(✘) Buck understood that if <u>it</u> had not competed for the leadership position, <u>it</u> would have been eliminated by the ruthless conditions.
     ●●▶ Buck 雖然是一隻狗，但用 it 合適嗎？

正確句式

(○) In "A Generation in Too Safe a Place," Roger Cohen pointed out the reason why **the young generation** in London has a difficult time finding a job and cannot make a living on ~~its own~~ <u>their own</u>.
     ●●▶ 代名詞的「數量」須與先行詞一致

(○) And then, **a waiter** took our picture and gave it to us. We were surprised and thanked ~~them~~ <u>him</u>.
     ●●▶ 代名詞的「數量」須與先行詞一致

(○) **A lot of academic materials as well as nice facilities** are available at large universities. ~~It~~ They (or These things) can help you learn effectively.

　●●▶ 除了「數量」要一致，也要考量指代關係是否明確，用 These things 可避免誤認先行詞為 universities。

(○) Sometimes, **white lies** sound like flattery. However, I regard ~~it~~ them as unavoidable in many situations.

　●●▶ 代名詞的「數量」需與先行詞一致

(○) Love is important, but if ~~we~~ you can't trust the one **you** love, it might be a tragedy. If one day you find your lover tells lies to you, you might start doubting his love.

　●●▶ 保持代名詞人稱一致

(○) **Buck** understood that if ~~it~~ he had not competed for the leadership position, ~~it~~ he would have been eliminated by the ruthless conditions.

　●●▶ Buck 為一隻狗的名字，但在此擬人情境中，宜用 he 呼應先行詞 Buck。

　　關於指涉動物的代名詞，理論上似可用無生命的 it，但在愛護動物重視生命的前提下，最常見的還是用人稱代名詞 he/she/they！

　　看完上面這些例子，有什麼發現呢？在寫作文時，常常是「寫了後面，忘了前面」，我們往往急於構思接下來的內容，以致於忽略代名詞究竟要代替誰？請謹記：寫作時必須遵循代名詞單複數的考量，與前面的指代對象要同心同行！

2. 代名詞不可多也不可少

　　代名詞既是代替名詞，本身也可能是句子中的主詞或受詞，用法上仍然遵循英文寫作的大原則，即「主動賓不可少，也不可多」。看看下面這個句子，主詞有沒有「多」了呢？

(✘) David McCullough, though not as famous as Thomas Edison or Neil Armstrong, **he** also succeeded. ●●▶ 主詞是 David McCullough 還是 he？

正確句式

(○) **David McCullough** 主要主詞, though not as famous as Thomas Edison or Neil Armstrong, he also succeeded 主要動詞.

●●▶ 主要子句只能有一個主要主詞和一個主要動詞，he 和 David McCullough 不可同時出現。

　　英文寫作中少不了代名詞的運用，但要如何使讀者知道代名詞指的是誰？就必須仰賴其與指涉對象間的一致性，因此在使用代名詞時，務必檢視：究竟代名詞「指的是誰？」，指代關係清楚嗎？人稱、數目、性別相符嗎？。

3. 「指示代名詞」到底指誰？

　　「指示代名詞」（this, that, these, those），顧名思義就是具有指示作用的代名詞。既然也是「代名詞」，意味著也要展現代名詞和先行詞間所有的搭配講究，無論在**單複數**或是**距離遠近**上，都必須和指代對象協調一致。換句話說，文章中「指示」的是誰？我們必須讓讀者一目了然！

　　看看下面這個段落，最後一句出現的 those 指的是前文中的什麼呢？

　　Sharks have been misunderstood to be threatening and aggressive. Plenty of videos tell us that they appear tamer than we have seen in Steven Spielberg's "*Jaws*." However, those also showed how brutal humans are when catching them.

●●▶ Those 指代什麼？

最後一句中的 those 是用來指涉第二句的 plenty of videos，但在文章中這兩者的距離較遠，其間還出現了許多其他名詞（Sharks, they, "Jaws"），都有可能作為先行詞。這種種原因降低了指示代名詞和其所指涉對象的關連性，讀者在第一時間也就不容易聯想到 those 指的是什麼了。當指示代名詞和先行詞之間相距太遠時，最好再重提一次名詞，使語意更清楚：

正確句式

(○) Sharks have been misunderstood to be threatening and aggressive. Plenty of videos tell us that they appear tamer than we have seen in Steven Spielberg's "*Jaws.*" However, **those videos** also showed how brutal humans are when catching them.

當指示代名詞作為形容詞用時，同樣要注意數量、人稱上的一致：

問題句式

(✘) Every afternoon for **this** four days, when my mother was taking a nap, I just went upstairs and read a novel. ●●▶ 數量一致嗎？

正確句式

(○) Every afternoon for **these** four days, when my mother was taking a nap, I just went upstairs and read a novel.

很明顯地，作者使用的指示代名詞 this 為單數，與後面 four days 的複數形式不一致，應該要改為 these four days。

在使用任何代名詞時，請務必牢記在心：代名詞必須和指涉對象「相親相近」，配搭連結，語意一致，才能夠讓讀者一目了然，容易解讀。

所謂的「不定代名詞」（indefinite pronoun），就是用來指稱不定數量事物的代名詞：

<u>Some</u> of the books are interesting. ●●▶ 不定代名詞用法

多數的不定代名詞都可以當作形容詞使用，後面直接加上名詞，此時便稱為「不定形容詞」（indefinite adjective）。

<u>Some</u> books are interesting. ●●▶ 不定形容詞用法

名詞有可數與不可數之分，修飾名詞的不定形容詞也有可數與不可數之分，用以搭配名詞的數量。例如：

Many +可數名詞： I have **many friends/books/problems/shoes.**

Much +不可數名詞： There isn't **much money/paper/time/coffee.**

Some + 二者皆可： There is **some fruit** on the table.

There are **some books** in my bag.

A lot of +二者皆可: There are **a lot of American tourists** in Paris.

She has **a lot of time** on her hands.

在前後搭配的原則下，代名詞、形容詞與量詞都必須與其修飾的名詞相互呼應，數量一致，運用這個原則來看看下面這三個有問題的句子：

問題句式

(✘) "Living happily ever after" may not be the end of **every** successful **stories.**
　　●●▶ every 是指單數還是複數？

(✘) I think Jeremy Lin could be **one of an example.**
　　●●▶ 單數名詞要標記幾次？

(✘) Although I missed it this time, I still could catch **other opportunity** to have **adventure**!
　　●●▶ 其他的機會有幾個？探險之旅有幾次？

正確句式

(○) "Living happily ever after" may not be the end of <u>every successful story</u>.

•• ▶ every 強調「每一個」，後接單數名詞

(○) 根據語意，有三種改法：

I think Jeremy Lin could be <u>one example</u>.

I think Jeremy Lin could be <u>an example</u>.

I think Jeremy Lin could be <u>one of several examples</u>.

•• ▶ Jeremy Lin 只是「一個」榜樣，有了 one 就不需要 an，保留其中一個即可。

若要強調「其中之一」，就要用 one of the examples!

(○) 根據語意，有兩種改法：

Although I missed it this time, I still could catch <u>another opportunity</u> to have <u>an adventure</u>!

Although I missed this good chance, I still could catch <u>other opportunities</u> to have <u>an adventure</u>!

•• ▶ 用 another 表「另一個」，後接單數名詞；用 other 表其他的多數，後接複數名詞

another vs. the other 怎麼用？

中文說「另外的」、「其他的」，語意好像都一樣，但英文因為有數量搭配的考量，所以要選擇不同的數量形容詞或代名詞：

1) 二擇一：one ... the other

You have two choices: <u>one</u> is to stay in the current job and work harder; the <u>other</u> is to quit and find another job!

2) 之外的「另一個」: one... another, some... another.

We have solved several problems, but there is <u>another</u> issue we need to face.

3) 其他一些：some... others 或 other + 複數名詞

The students in the front rows raised their hands, but <u>the other students</u> remained silent.

Some students raised their hands, but <u>(the) others</u> didn't. ●●▶ 加 the 是強調「可知的」；不加 the 則是單純與 some 的語意對應。

從上述幾個常見的問題可以發現，名詞與前面的修飾語必須緊密配合，數量一致，正如同代名詞與指涉對象的關係一樣，兩者密不可分。一旦數量概念不合，就會造成語法不當、語意不清的問題。因此在使用名詞時，對其修飾語也不容馬虎。

類型五 **其他常見誤用情形**

1. Champion 還是 Championship？

Champion 為贏得比賽的那位冠軍，用來指在比賽中脫穎而出的人物；championship 指的是優勝的地位，代表獎項或頭銜：

He was the champion. ●●▶ 他是冠軍

He won the championship. ●●▶ 他贏得冠軍盃

Championship 亦有「冠軍大賽」的意思，一般的運動比賽，都是 championship。但是台灣學生常誤把 championship 和 games 合用，造成語意上的重複：

問題句式

(✘)　In his senior year, he captained his school-Palo Alto High School and led them to win the <u>championship of the state games</u>.

　　●●▶ championship 就是 games ！

正確句式

(○) In his senior year, he captained his school team – Palo Alto High School and led them to win the <u>state championship</u>.

Championship 本身就有「冠軍賽」的意思，像是世界盃（World Cup）、超級盃（Super Cup）都算是冠軍賽。因此，原句中的 games 和 championship 兩者是重複的概念，擇一而用即可：

He led the team to win the state championship.

He led the team to win the state games.

He led the team to become the champion in the state games.

2. Result 還是 Consequence？

中文翻譯上，result 和 consequence 都是「結果」，但是兩者的語意其實有差別：consequence 強調常理下必然導致不樂見的「後果」，語意側重「前因…後果」間無可避免的因果關聯；而 result 單純指事情最終的情況，什麼結果都有可能，例如：酒駕的法律「後果」是罰款起訴，但酒駕可能造成的「結果」是意外死亡：

The consequence of driving under influence (DUI) is getting fined and arrested.

The result of his driving under influence was killing an innocent woman.

問題句式

(✘)　Because of this reason, she couldn't get <u>good consequence</u> from her exams.

正確句式

(○) Because of this condition, she couldn't get a <u>good result</u> on her exams.

Result 指的是所得到的最後結果，常常是開放而具體的「成果」。consequence 指某事必然產生的後果，常用來描述事出必有因的「負面後果」。例如：

If you continue to smoke, you will suffer the bad consequences.
My mother always reminds me that there are consequences to my actions.

3. 所有格後面的名詞形式

大家都知道所有格後面要接名詞（如：my friend, my car），但是當後面牽涉到動詞或形容詞時，常常就有問題了。一些簡單的英文謝詞就要注意這一點：

謝謝你的細心周到！	••▶	Thank you for your <u>thoughtfulness</u>!
	••▶	Thank you for <u>being so thoughtful</u>!
感謝你的大力幫助！	••▶	Thank you for your <u>kind help</u>!
		Thank you for <u>being so helpful</u>!
感謝你提供的寶貴建議！	••▶	I appreciate <u>your offering</u> me the valuable advice!
		I appreciate <u>the valuable advice</u> you offered!

請記得：thank 的對象是人（thank＋人＋for＋事），但是 appreciate 的對象不是人，而是事情，後面只能接感念的事項（appreciate＋事）。

所有格與後面名詞間的語意關係也要彼此搭配，釐清究竟「所有」的對象是什麼？例如：「我們不喜歡他所做的決定」是指「他的」決定，而不是他的「做」決定：

(○) We don't like his decisions.	••▶ the decisions he made
(✘) We don't like his making decisions.	••▶ 所有格弄錯了！

下面的問題例句進一步反映出這些誤用：

問題句式

(✘)　You've done a lot for me. I truly appreciate <u>you</u>!
　　••▶ appreciate 的對象是人嗎？

(✘)　As for <u>my making</u> choices, I realized it's not just about overcoming my own fears, but also about having the courage to face my flaws.
　　••▶ 做選擇是「我的」嗎？

最後，所有格後面若是使用動名詞，依然要注意動詞本身的用法，別忘了及物動詞後要直接加受詞：

His leaving the country made her cry for a long time.

Your advice led to <u>my accepting the new job</u>. (= my acceptance of the new job)

結語

　名詞在英文中扮演重要的角色，負責介紹各個人物出場，而名詞的標記就要清楚提示這些人物的真實身分，到底是指哪一個、哪一類，或是哪一些。名詞有數量的區別講求，代名詞另有人稱、性別的講究，都是為求嚴謹的結果。寫作時，一定要把握「名詞出場必有標記」的原則，前後呼應，數量一致，語意搭配！

題 目

一、名詞出場必有標記，請牢記這個原則，以下的句子或文章段落中，有些標記是錯誤的，請圈出來並加以改正。（請注意：不是所有的名詞標記都是錯的）

1. A few days later, when I went to night market near my house with my friends, the air was filled with a familiar smell.

2. I am sorry to tell you that I lost the bicycle you lent me last week. Yesterday, I was riding the bicycle on my way home. Suddenly, it rained dogs and cats, and I was all wet, just like drowned rat. I have no choice but to stop and buy raincoat. Therefore, I parked the bike in front of the convenience store.

3. Walking is a very simple way to exercise. All I need is my feet and shoes. I can walk almost everywhere -- park, street, department store, mountain, college, -- wherever I am.

二、以下這篇填空題，請選出正確答案。[8]

Onions can be divided into two categories: fresh onions and storage onions. Fresh onions are available in yellow, red and white throughout their season, March through August. They can be identified by their thin, light-colored skin. Because they have a higher water content, they are typically sweeter and milder tasting than storage onions. This higher water content also makes much easier for them to bruise. With its delicate taste, the fresh onion is an ideal choice for salads and other lightly-cooked dishes. Storage onions, on the other hand, are available August through April. Unlike fresh onions, ___1___ have multiple layers of thick, dark, papery skin. They also have ___2___ intense flavor and a higher percentage of solids. For these reasons, storage onions are the best choice for spicy dishes that require longer cooking times or more flavor.

1. (A) they

   (B) other

   (C) ones

   (D) it

2. (A) a

   (B) the

   (C) an

   (D) every

寫作修理廠

解 答

一、

1. A few days later, when I went to <u>the</u> night market near my house with my friends, the air was filled with a familiar smell.

2. I am sorry to tell you that I lost the bicycle you lent me last week. Yesterday, I was riding the bicycle on my way home. Suddenly, it rained dogs and cats, and I was all wet just like <u>a</u> drowned rat. I had no choice but to stop and buy <u>a</u> raincoat. Therefore, I parked the bike in front of <u>a</u> convenience store.

   （store 並非已知的）

3. Walking is a very simple way to exercise, and all I need is my feet and shoes. I can walk almost everywhere -- in park<u>s</u>, street<u>s</u>, department store<u>s</u>, mountain<u>s</u>, college campus<u>es</u>, -- wherever I am.（用複數表類型）

二、

1. (A)

這裡要選一個代名詞，回指前一句的主詞，也就是 "storage onions"。所以需要一個複數代名詞 "They"。

2. (C)

名詞 "intense flavor" 前需要一個不定冠詞，因為這是一個新出現的名詞，沒有理由認定是對方已知的，所以選 "an"，搭配母音開頭的字 " an intense flavor"。

Chapter

動詞出場時態相隨

08

中文和英文中的動詞有何不同？

如何表達進行，以及完成的觀點？

如何用動詞表達假設？

She is walking her puppy elegantly.

Be strict with verbs

8.1 動詞的時間標記

　　動詞在句子裡扮演著極為重要的角色，它負責表達事件的核心：發生什麼事？發生事情必然牽涉到發生的時間，英文選擇在動詞上標註時間，這一點和中文有著相當大的差異，例如：

我**昨天**吃了一顆蘋果。　●●▶ 中文仰賴時間副詞表達時間，動詞本身沒有任何相關標記
I **ate** an apple yesterday.　●●▶ 英文在動詞上標記時間，因而動詞有了時態變化

　　中文的動詞不需要標記時間，可藉由「情境」來提示，但是嚴謹的英文卻要在動詞形式上交代時間，因此，動詞出場，時態必然相隨。究竟英文標記時間的方法有哪些呢？在《英文文法有道理》一書中，介紹了四種不同的時段區分及標記方式：

發生時間早於說話時間　●●▶ 過去式　I **ate** an apple.
發生晚於說話時間　●●▶ 未來式　I **will eat** an apple.
發生時間等於說話時間　●●▶ 現在式　I **am eating** an apple.
發生時間不固定、無定點　●●▶ 習慣式　I **eat** an apple every day.（過去、現在、未來都適用）

　　從上面的例子中，我們發現英文使用動詞時，脫離不了時態的選擇，每一次用動詞，都有時間的考量，都要標記時間，這就是「動詞出場，時態相隨」的意義。然而由於中英文的差異，許多學生未能養成動詞與時態搭配的習慣，造成事件的時間不明，或前後時態不一致。看看以下這兩個句子，反映了最常見的兩個時態問題：

> ➤ 時間不明：

(✘)　We go to the market yesterday.
　　●●▶ 動詞沒有時間標記

(○)　We went to the market yesterday.

> ➤ 前後時間不一致

(✘)　I was so upset that I left school and take the bus to downtown with my friend Betty.
　　●●▶ 過去式＋習慣式？

(○)　I was so upset that I left school and took the bus to downtown with my friend Betty.

這兩個問題在台灣學生的作文裡層出不窮，稍不注意就把中文的書寫習慣帶入英文寫作中，忽略英文的動詞必須有時間標記，因為「動詞出場，時態相隨」！

動詞的時態標記，其實有兩方面：單純的「時間」（tense）之外，還有事件進行的樣貌，稱為「時貌」（aspect）。時貌指的是說話者選擇看待事件的方式，將事件進行的情況（temporal properties）與另一「參考時間」關連起來。英文中的時貌可分為簡單式、進行式以及完成式三種觀點：

簡單式：把事件視為一個完整、獨立的事件

The cat chased the dog.

進行式：把事件視為與時間並行、正在發生進行中

The cat was chasing the dog (at that time).

完成式：把事件視為在「相關事件」之前已完成

The cat has chased the dog (by now).

時貌對於台灣學生也是個頭痛的問題。追根究柢，問題出在我們對時貌的溝通目的一知半解，部分學生甚至仰賴某些特定的關鍵字來決定時貌，而不是從整體的語意來考量，所以無法完全掌握時貌的用法。特別是「完成式」的使用，究竟什麼叫「完成」？現在完成和過去完成又有何差別？根據《英文文法有道理》，「完成式」所表達的是「相對的」時間概念，強調在參考時間「之前」已完成：

現在完成 ●●▶ 現在（說話當下）「之前」已完成

I have done my homework by now.

過去完成 ●●▶ 過去某一時間「之前」已完成

I had done my homework by the time I came to class.

未來完成 ●●▶ 未來某一時間「之前」將會完成

I will have done my homework by the time I go to bed.

既然「完成式」是強調相對於參考時間「之前」的概念，就不能用來標記事件本身的時間，不能用來表達事情「在什麼時候」發生！

完成式 + by 參考時間：I have watched it (by now).

簡單式 + 事件時間：I watched the movie *KANO* last Friday.

釐清了「完成式」的溝通意涵，你可否看出下面這個句子有什麼問題？

完成式的誤用：

(✘) She <u>has sent</u> the email to her boss at 7 pm <u>last night</u>.
　　●●▶ 完成式不能用來標記事件本身的時間！

正確用法：

(○) She <u>sent</u> the email to her boss at 7 pm <u>last night</u>.　●●▶ 昨晚發生
(○) She <u>has sent</u> the email to her boss (by now).　　●●▶ 現在之前已完成

　　完成式的誤用往往來自直接翻譯中文的說法：「她昨晚已經寄電子郵件給老闆了」。中文可以說「昨晚已經」，因為中文的時間詞可以自由加在句子裡，但英文的完成式有嚴謹的語意講究，對時間的設定是以「參考點」為主，只能表達「之前完成」的語意。

　　要避免時貌的誤用，就要對英文時貌的意義有完全且精準的理解，「已經」不直接等於完成式，就如進行式也不完全等於「正在」（I'm loving it. ≠ 我正在愛）。進行式是對動態事件近距離的描述，強調與時並進、同時發生、持續進行中（simultaneously on-going）：

　　　Q：What are you doing?
　　　A：I am reading a book.　　　　　　　　●●▶ 當下進行中

　　　Q：What were you doing when I called?
　　　A：I was taking a bath when you called.　●●▶ 當時進行中

　　　Q：What did you do while he was cooking?
　　　A：I was watching TV while he was cooking.　●●▶ 同時進行中

　　因此，進行式中通常會出現一個「共進」的時間點，以下我們就時間與時貌兩大方面來檢視幾個常見的問題類型。

8.2 常見問題分析

類型一 時態不一致

　　由於中文的動詞沒有時間的標記，讓不少人在寫英文句子時，很容易忘記在動詞上標示時間訊息，特別是在書寫長句時，前面的幾個動詞還帶有時態，但寫到後面就忘記加上時態了，造成句子前後時態不一致的情形，句子愈長，類似的情況就愈加顯著。所以，請留意句子中常見「時態不一」的問題：

問題句式

(✘)　I <u>sat</u> there nervously with my hands sweating, because I <u>had finished</u> my food and I <u>don't</u> have any money to pay.　●●▶ 前後句的時態是否一致？

(✘)　He even felt afraid when I <u>asked</u> him questions and <u>glance</u> at him.
　　　●●▶ and 連接的兩個動詞時態是否一致？

(✘)　<u>Every time</u> I <u>had</u> hot noodle soup, it <u>always reminds</u> me of the comfort Tina gave me that night.　●●▶ 前後句的時態是否一致？

(✘)　Thank you very much for <u>organizing</u> the event and <u>gave</u> us the opportunity to visit Hsinchu.　●●▶ and 連接的兩個動詞是否有對等的形式？

(✘)　When I <u>was</u> in senior high school, my friends and I <u>develop</u> a project for children who mostly <u>came</u> from poor backgrounds.
　　　●●▶ 主要子句與關係子句間的時態是否一致？

(✘)　It just <u>happened</u> so naturally that I <u>don't</u> even have a chance to make a decision.
　　　●●▶ 主要子句與 that 子句間的時態是否一致？

正確句式

(○) I sat there nervously with my hands sweating, because I had finished my food and I <u>didn't</u> have any money to pay. ●●▶ 描述過去事實用過去式

(○) He even felt afraid when I <u>asked</u> him questions and <u>glanced</u> at him.
　　●●▶ 連接詞 and 前後動詞的時態要一致

(○) 一般習慣：Every time I <u>have</u> hot noodle soup, it <u>always reminds</u> me of the comfort Tina gave me that night.

(○) 過去習慣：Every time I <u>had</u> hot noodle soup, it <u>always reminded</u> me of the comfort Tina gave me that night. ●●▶ 過去的習慣用過去式

(○) Thank you very much for <u>organizing</u> the event and <u>giving</u> us the opportunity to visit Hsinchu. ●●▶ and 連接的兩個動詞形式要對等

(○) When I was in senior high school, my friends and I <u>developed</u> a project for children who mostly came from poor backgrounds.
　　●●▶ 過去發生的事件需用過去式

(○) It just happened so naturally that I didn't even have a chance to make a decision.
　　●●▶ 描述過去發生的事件需用過去式

　　以上的問題是過去事件忘了加過去標記。然而，並不是把句中的所有時態調整一致就是正確的，時態必須配合語意而轉變。看看下列劃線的動詞，時態和語意間的搭配正確嗎？

問題句式

(✘)　The questions asked are easy ones. Yet when they're in English, my brain <u>tended</u> to be blank.

(✘)　How could I just get up and pretend like nothing <u>happen</u>?

(✘)　During this time, I really felt weary from fighting with my mom, but I gradually <u>realize</u> that actually, she really <u>love</u> me.

正確句式

(○)　The questions asked are easy ones. Yet when they're in English, my brain <u>tends</u> to be blank. ●●▶ 本句描述的是一種習慣，因此用習慣式較為合理

(○)　How could I just get up and pretend like nothing <u>happened</u>?
　　　●●▶ 發生過的事應該用過去式

(○)　During this time, I really felt weary from fighting with my mom, but I gradually <u>realized</u> that actually, she really <u>loves</u> me.
　　　●●▶ 已了解到用 realized，但母愛是永遠的事實，因此用習慣事實式

　　時態選擇主要以「說話當下」（speech time）為依歸，在說話時間之前發生的用過去式，在說話時間之後的用未來式，而事實習慣則是橫貫時間座標，涵蓋過去、現在、未來「一直如此」的時間概念。如下圖所示：

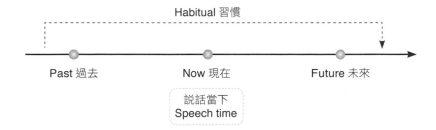

　　習慣式和現在式的時間概念不同，以下兩句話的區別就是最佳寫照：

習慣事實：I eat apples.　　●●▶ 我是吃蘋果的 （一向如此）

現在發生：I'm eating apples. ●●▶ 我在吃蘋果（當下此刻）

時間的標記通常以「說話當下」為基準，但在文學作品中，有時會出現一種特殊的時態用法，刻意將說話者的時間抽離，句子形式上看起來如同現在式或習慣式，但其實是在敘述故事中發生的事，這種標記方式有人稱為「historical present」，也有人稱為「immediate aspect」。在下面這個段落中從第 5 行開始敘事，作者為了隱藏「敘事者」的時間故意將 speech time 抽離，以凸顯故事本身的的臨場感，而選擇用這種特殊的時態：

> "If the funeral had been yesterday, I could not recollect it better. The very air of the best parlour, when I went in at the door, the bright condition of the fire, the shining of the wine in the decanters, the patterns of the glasses and plates, the faint sweet smell of cake, the odour of Miss Murdstone's dress, and your black clothes."
> Mr. Chillip is in the room, and comes to speak to me.
> "And how is Master David?" he says, kindly.
> I cannot tell him very well. I give him my hand, which he holds in his.
>
> — *David Copperfield* by Charles Dickens

　　上文中，除了直接引用的對話外，用來敘事的句子看起來都像習慣式：Mr. Chillip is in the room, and comes to speak to me. 這是作者選擇的一種敘事方式，刻意將說故事的人（作者）和說故事的時間（寫作時間）隱藏，也就沒有「說話當下」的時間考量，只有故事本身發生的時間，如同在時間的真空狀態下，使敘述更為直接、生動，讓讀者有歷歷在目、身歷其境的「立即感」。這是超越一般時間座標的特殊用法，通常用於小說或短篇散文中，故意把敘事時間抽離，製造生動的文學效果。

類型二 時態的相對關係

　　一般情況下，要使用正確的時態，首先需要掌握說話者的「說話當下」（speech time），確立說話時間與事件發生時間的相對關係後，才能決定適當的時態。此外，事件之間的先後關係也要納入考量，特別是在使用完成式時，參考點是設在過去、現在、未來還是習慣性的某一點直接影響到時態的選擇。以下幾個句子，所描述的事件在時間上的相對關係都出了問題：

問題句式

(✘) Before I <u>learn</u> English, I <u>didn't pay</u> much attention to languages. After I <u>learn</u> English, I <u>started</u> to notice the differences between Chinese and English.

••▶ learn English 與 didn't pay attention 的相對關係？

(✘) I sat motionlessly in the classroom as I <u>heard</u> the bad news that I <u>have already expected</u>. ••▶ expect 在 heard the bad news 之前或之後？

(✘) <u>Nowadays,</u> <u>there were</u> several problems that are difficult to solve by curriculum alone. ••▶ why "were"? problems 也存在於說話當下！

正確句式

(○) Before I <u>studied</u> English, I <u>didn't pay</u> much attention to languages. After I studied English, I <u>started</u> to notice the differences between Chinese and English.

••▶ 全句定調在過去，所以都要用過去式，但 learn 用在過去式有「學會」的涵意：I learned English. 而本句指的是單純的學習，故 learn 宜改為 study

(○) I sat motionlessly in the classroom as I <u>heard</u> the bad news that I <u>had already expected</u>.

••▶ expect 是在 heard the bad news 之前，故用過去完成式

(○) <u>Nowadays,</u> <u>there are</u> several problems that are difficult to solve by curriculum alone. ••▶ 現今存在的問題，故用現在式

　　進行貌（即進行式）強調動作事件「正在發生中」（on-going），持續地「與時俱進」。進行貌在動詞的使用上也有所限制。事實上，並非所有動詞都能轉換成進行貌，簡單來說，僅有動態動詞（如：eat, run, read 等）才有進行貌的型態。動態動詞因牽涉到活動的產生，可隨時間不斷變動、不斷前進，所以可以搭配 on-going 的進行貌；相對於動態動詞表活動，另一類靜態動詞（如：know, have, like 等）主要用來表狀態，用來描述較持久、較抽象的心理狀態，不涉及體力、心力的運作，也不會隨時間改變，因此不能用於進行式。

　　大體上說，非動作性的動詞有三類，語意上沒有「與時俱進」的動感，語法上就不能搭配進行貌：

1. 抽象或無形的價值（abstract values）	to be, to cost, to seem, to need, to value, to owe, to appreciate
2. 擁有或存在的關係 （possessive/ existence verbs）	to have, to possess, to own, to belong to, to exist
3. 心理或感知的狀態 （mental/ perceptual states）	to like, to love, to hate, to dislike, to fear, to envy, to mind, to want, to see, to hear

　　要特別注意的是，這些非動態動詞若是真的加上了進行標記，就一定有語意上的變化，產生出具有動態意涵的詞意，才能搭配進行貌，例如：

TO APPEAR

She appears confused.

　　→ *She seems confused.*

My favorite band is **appearing** at the club tonight.

　　→ *My favorite band is giving a performance at the club tonight.*

TO HAVE

I have a car.

　　→ *I possess a car.*

I am **having** fun now.

　　→ *I am experiencing fun now.*

TO HEAR

She hears the music.

> → *She hears the music with her ears.*

She is **hearing** voices.

> → *She is attending to the voices others cannot hear.*

TO LOOK

Nancy looks tired.

> → *She seems tired.*

Farah is **looking** at the pictures.

> → *She is looking with her eyes.*

TO MISS

Mike misses his mother.

> → *Mike is sad because his mother is not there.*

He is **missing** his favorite TV show.

> → *He is not there to see his favorite show.*

TO SEE

I see her over there.

> → *I see her with my eyes.*

I am **seeing** the doctor.

> → *I am visiting or consulting with a doctor.*

I am **seeing** a handsome guy.

> → *I am dating with the guy.*

TO BE

He is tall.

> → *He is high in stature.*

He is being unreasonable.

> → *He is acting in an unreasonable way.*

TO SMELL

I think coffee smells good.

> → *I think coffee has a good smell.*

I am **smelling** the flowers.

> → *I am sniffing the flowers to see what their smell is like.*

TO TASTE

The food tastes good.

> → *The food has a good taste.*

I am **tasting** the tea.

> → *I am trying the tea to see what it tastes like.*

TO THINK

He thinks the science test was too easy.

> → *He considers the test to be too easy.*

She is **thinking** about the question.

> → *She is pondering the question, going over it in her mind.*

TO WEIGH

I used to weigh a lot.

> → *I used to be heavier.*

The doctor is **weighing** the child.

> → *The doctor is determining the child's weight.*

從上面的對照可以明白，並非所有動詞都可以加上進行貌，要看動詞是否具有動態語意，僅有動態動詞才能搭配進行的語意。在選擇時貌標記時，必須考量到動詞本身的語意，畢竟語法與語意兩者是緊密相連的。以下兩個句子，動詞語意和進行貌用法就「不搭」：

問題句式

(✖)　I'm <u>having</u> a cold. ●●▶ have 是否為動態語意？

(✖)　Only when people <u>being</u> honest can they trust each other.
　　　　●●▶ 此句中 be 的語意為何？是動態動詞嗎？

正確句式

(○) I <u>have</u> a cold. ●●▶ have 在本句意指「患有」的狀態，無進行式

(○) Only when people <u>are</u> honest can they trust each other.
　　　　●●▶ Be 動詞在此句中用於連接狀態，無須進行式

　　值得一提的是，進行式和動名詞、現在分詞的形式是一樣的。動詞加上 -ing 也是動名詞的形式。一個動作在進行中，就等於存在於時間座標上，具有名詞般的時間持久性。V-ing 也是分詞構句的形式，為了省略主詞，將句子簡化為不帶時間標記的主動分詞。由於分詞也是一種附屬子句，因此另一種常見的誤用出現在附屬子句中。下列幾個句子，其中的附屬子句都少了帶有時態標記的動詞：

問題句式

(✖)　In the past, big families were common in Taiwanese society, [which <u>fostering</u> the concept of sharing in Chinese culture]. ●●▶ 關係子句中是否有動詞？

(✖)　Besides, the reasons [why teens <u>getting</u> depressed] differ from person to person.
　　　　●●▶ why 所引導的子句中是否有動詞？

(✖)　In the famous novel, *The Call of the Wild*, Jack London illustrated [how a domesticated dog <u>going</u> through the severe environment of Alaska and eventually <u>returning</u> to his primitive instincts]. ●●▶ how 所引導的名詞子句是否有動詞？

附屬子句仍然是一個子句，除了附屬標記外，仍須保持語法語意上的完整，並遵循英文的基本原則：主動賓不可少，必須有一個帶時態標記的主要動詞！

> **正確句式**
>
> (○) In the past, big families were common in Taiwanese society, [which <u>fostered</u> the concept of sharing in Chinese culture].
> ●●▶ fostered 作為關係子句的主要動詞，有清楚的過去式標記
>
> (○) Besides, the reasons [why teens <u>get</u> depressed] differ from person to person.
> ●●▶ get 作為 why 子句的主要動詞，表示一般事實
>
> (○) In the famous novel, *The Call of the Wild*, Jack London illustrated [how a domesticated dog <u>went</u> through the severe environment of Alaska and eventually <u>returned</u> to his primitive instincts].
> ●●▶ how 子句要有動詞，過去式 went/returned，呼應主要子句的過去式

在使用進行貌時，要特別留意動詞的語意，僅有動態動詞在語意上才能與強調 on-going 的進行貌搭配。此外，不要把附屬子句和分詞構句搞混了，帶有附屬標記的子句仍要保有語法和語意的完整性，遵守主動賓不可少的大原則。

類型四　時貌（aspect）的問題：完成式

有別於簡單式與進行式的另一種時貌是完成式，這是讓台灣學生最頭疼的一種時貌。完成式之所以造成這麼大的困擾，主要是因為多數人在概念上，並沒有真正理解什麼是「完成」，以致於在使用上便宜行事，將所有加上「已經」的中文句子全都用完成式表示。

「完成」是一個相對的概念，決定完成與否的基本先決要素在於「參照點」，也就是以什麼時間為基準來看？在什麼時間之前算完成？要先決定參照時間，才能決定事件有沒有完成。

參考點 Reference time

當時態與完成式配搭，可以得到以下三種參考時間，表達三種完成關係：

現在完成式：以**說話當下**作為參考點，在「**現在此刻之前**」已完成

過去完成式：以**過去的時間點**為參考點，在「**過去當時之前**」已完成

未來完成式：以**未來的時間點**為參考點，在「**未來某時之前**」已完成

因此，完成式不是用來表達事件本身發生的時間，而是用來表達事件在參考點「之前」完成的這種相對關係，所以前面提過，下面這種句子是有問題的！

錯誤示範：

(**✘**)　I have already told her yesterday.
　　　我昨天已經告訴她了。

看到「已經」這個詞，想必有不少人直覺會選用完成式來翻譯這個句子，然而，完成式不是用來標記事件的時間，而是標記「在參考時間之前已完成」的相對關係，若是加上 yesterday，就出現時間上的「雙頭馬車」，有兩個時間概念，彼此矛盾：一方面現在完成式意味著以說話當下（現在）為參考點，但句子裡又出現了過去的時間 yesterday，一個句子有兩個時間座標，讓人摸不著頭緒。因此請注意：完成式不能和事件發生的時間點混搭！

正確說法：

(◯) I have already told her (by now).　●●▶ 以完成式表達

(◯) I told her yesterday.　●●▶ 以過去式表達

依照上面所提的概念，請檢查下列句子的完成式是否正確：

問題句式

（✗）She <u>has sent</u> the email to her boss <u>last night</u>. ••▶ 時間衝突！

（✗）Psychologist Robert Sternberg <u>had proposed</u> a triangular theory of love: the components of love are intimacy, passion, commitment. ••▶ 使用過去完成式一定要有過去的參考點，但是句中沒有過去參考點呀！

（✗）Guilt <u>had been eating</u> my conscience at the beginning; I told every single lie with regret. ••▶ 過去完成式的參考點在哪？

正確說法：

（○）She <u>sent</u> the email to her boss last night.

　　••▶ 完成式不能與時間點（last night）混用，以過去式表示即可！

（○）Psychologist Robert Sternberg <u>has proposed</u> a triangular theory of love: the components of love are intimacy, passion, commitment.

　　••▶ 原句中缺少明確的過去時間作為參考點，只能改以「說話當下」為參考點（by now），因此現在完成式更恰當。

（○）Guilt had been eating (at) my conscience <u>since</u> the beginning; I told every single lie with regret. ••▶ 要表示「事件的起點」，介系詞要用 since

類型五　明辨真假：條件句與假設句的時態選擇

　　在英文中，「事實」與「非事實」（真與假）在時態標記上有清楚的區別，這一點是中文所沒有的特性，因此許多學生在面臨假設句與條件句的時候，也容易遭遇問題。其實，若能了解條件句與假設句必須藉由形式來提示「不真」的語意，掌握形意搭配的原則，就能解決大多數的困擾。

➤ **條件句（有可能的假設）**：在未來有可能出現的情況，雖不確定但有可能！

標記方式：以沒有特定時間點的「習慣式」表達「可能條件」，以「未來式」
表達「未來結果」

例如：If you **work** hard, you **will** get a good grade.
習慣式表可能　　　　未來式表結果

➤ **假設句（不可能的假設）**：對既定事實的追悔，既然不是事實，就不能用一般表達
事實的時態，進而使用「時間回返」的方式，表達「與事實相反」：

標記方式：

(1) 現在事實 ●●▶ 以現在式標記

　　　She is short.

　　違反現在事實 ●●▶ 以過去式標記

　　　I wish she **were** tall.

　或　　I wish she was tall.

　　　（were 是形式固定的「反事實」標記，不因人稱而改變）

(2) 過去事實 ●●▶ 以過去式標記

　　　She didn't come home yesterday.

　　違反過去事實 ●●▶ 以過去完成式標記

　　　I wish she **had come** home yesterday.

　　由上述原則可以看出，英文以時態來區分真與假。有可能出現的條件句，用習慣式表示時間不定；但「非事實」的假設不可逆轉，只能選擇用時間上的錯亂（時間倒退）來表示。使用假設句時，一定要先分辨是事實，還是非事實！

問題句式

(✖)　I can't imagine what my life would be like if I never <u>learn</u> English.
　　　●●▶ if 子句是非事實的假設，該用什麼時態？

(✖)　He <u>thought</u> death <u>is</u> another way of living, where he <u>could</u> continue examining
　　　people and <u>won't</u> be killed for doing it.　●●▶ 時態一致嗎？該用什麼時態呢？

正確句式

(○) I can't imagine what my life would be like if I never learned English.

　　●●▶ if 子句為違反事實的假設,故用過去式!

(○) He thought death was another way of living, where he could continue examining people and wouldn't be killed for doing it.

　　●●▶ 整句話為過去的想法,時間必須搭配過去式!

　　時態在英文中扮演了相當重要的角色,既是文法形式的一環,也負有表達語意的作用。藉由動詞時態的掌握,可明確表達事件發生的時間(過去、現在、未來或習慣),事件與參照點相對的進行或完成關係,甚或明斷真假!因此在表達事件時,要特別留意時態的選擇,用心寫出時態與語意彼此搭配的「道地英文」!

寫作練功坊

題 目

一、中英文大不同，也表現在動詞的時態標記上，英文的動詞務必要標記時間，以下的文章段落中有些標記是錯誤的，請圈出來並加以改正。

1. I heard that your parents have been worrying about you for a long while. Do you spend too much time playing video games recently?

2. Penny told me that you are crazy about video games lately.

3. Yesterday, I was riding the bicycle on my way home. Suddenly, it rained dogs and cats, and I was all wet just like a drowned rat. I have no choice but to stop and buy a raincoat. Therefore, I parked the bike in front of a convenience store and went in. At the moment I step out the store, a man was getting on the bike and started riding it.

二、以下這篇填空題，請選出正確答案。

The sun is an extraordinarily powerful source of energy. In fact, the Earth receives 20,000 times more energy from the sun than we currently use. If we used more of this source of heat and light, it ___1___ all the power needed throughout the world. We can harness energy from the sun, or solar energy, in many ways. For instance, many satellites in space are equipped with large panels whose solar cells transform sunlight directly into electric power. These panels are covered with glass and are painted black inside to absorb as much heat as possible. Solar energy has a lot to offer. To begin with, it is a clean fuel. In contrast, fossil fuels, such as oil or coal, release harmful substances into the air when they are burned. What's more, fossil fuels will run out, but solar energy ___2___ to reach the Earth long after the last coal has been mined and the last oil well has run dry.

1. (A) supplies

   (B) has supplied

   (C) was supplying

   (D) could supply

2. (A) continued

   (B) has been continuing

   (C) will continue

   (D) continues

寫作修理廠

解 答

一、

1. I heard that your parents have been worrying about you for a long while. <u>Have</u> you <u>spent</u> too much time playing video games recently?

2. Penny told me that you <u>have been</u> crazy about video games lately.

3. Yesterday, I was riding the bicycle on my way home. Suddenly, it rained dogs and cats, and I was all wet just like a drowned rat. I <u>had</u> no choice but to stop and buy a raincoat. Therefore, I parked the bike in front of a convenience store and went in. At the moment I <u>stepped</u> out the store, a man was getting on the bike and started riding it.

二、

1. (D)

這是一個與現在事實相反的假設，所以用了過去式：If we used....，後面也要搭配過去式的助動詞 it could supply...。

2. (C)

最重要的線索是前面一句的時態是未來式 "fossil fuels will run out"，因此對等連結詞 but 後的子句也要用未來式，故選 (C) will continue。

Chapter

09

主動被動釐清責任

誰主動對誰做了什麼？

誰受誰影響而改變？

主動行事還是被動受影響？

主動分詞與被動分詞的區別？

I'm melted.

The snowman melts.

Be stict about the Active/Passive distiction!

　　英文在「嚴句子」的語性要求下，每一個句子都有主動、被動之分。句子的主詞和動詞之間是「主控」還是「受控」的關係，都必須標記清楚！根據《英文文法有道理》的說明，人是有意志的動物，能主動操控自身的行為，因此，在描述事件時，我們很習慣以主動者的角度切入。被動句與主動句相反，被動句的焦點不是「執行者」，而是放在「受影響」的一方，其主語缺乏主控性。既然所強調的重點不同，在呈現的方式上，也就帶有不一樣的標記。主動句的主詞是有意志、能操控事件發生的「主控者」；被動句的主詞是受影響、被控制的「受制者」。主動與被動兩者所表達的主詞角色完全不同，在標記方式上，就利用動詞形式的轉變來區別。

　　被動句的動詞形式是：Be + Vpp（過去分詞），主要動詞落在表達狀態的 Be 動詞上。這是很有意思的標記方式，因為被動句其實不是描述動作本身的發生，而是描述動作產生的結果狀態。一般表達事件最自然的方式是由「主導者」的角度切入，在 John hit Tom 這個動作發生後，結果就是 Tom was hit.。被動句是用來描述受影響者所處的「改變狀態」，因此形式上以 Be 動詞（狀態連接）加過去分詞 Vpp（類似形容詞）來標記！

　　很多人會直覺的以為英文的被動句就是中文的「被」字句，然而，並非如此！不是所有的被動句在中文都有「被」。換句話說，英文的被動句不一定要翻成中文的「被」。中文在「重情境」的前提下，句子以「主題」為本，其後的小句都繞著主題轉，形成一個「主題 + 闡述」（topic-comment）的基本句式。在這種語境下，對於標記的要求就不似英文如此嚴格，因此中文的被動句未必都包含「被」：

報紙送來沒？	●●▶ Was the newspaper delivered?
房子賣了 1000 萬。	●●▶ The house was sold for $10,000.
作業寫完了。	●●▶ The homework was done.

　　雖然上面的中文句子都沒有「被」，但是從主詞和動詞的關係來看，都是被動關係，因為「報紙、房子、作業」都缺乏主控性，不會自己動，不可能做出「送、賣、寫」等活動。也就是說，這些主語都是「被影響」的產物，所以是被動關係，換成英文，就要用被動句來表達。中文的「被」字句比英文的被動句多了一層語意，除了表達被動關係，還多了不樂意、不預期的負面含意（undesirable）：

他**被打**的很慘，　　　　　●●▶ He was beaten up!

我的車子**被偷**了。　　　　●●▶ My car was stolen.

他的房子**被拍賣**了！　　　●●▶ His house was sold by auction.

當然，在英文強勢的影響下，中文的「被」字句也越來越常見，特別是在表達一些民主運作的概念，負面的語意也在削弱中：

他被選為班長。　　　　　●●▶ He was elected the class leader.

他被提名為總統候選人。　●●▶ He was nominated as the Presidential candidate.

回到英文的原則，只要是被動關係，就要有被動標記！關鍵在於主詞對動詞是否具有主控性。寫作時，一定要考慮每一個主詞所扮演的角色，若非動作的「執行者」，而是「受影響者」，就要加上被動標記！以下，將針對被動句容易出現的幾個問題進行說明提醒。

9.2 常見問題分析

類型一 ▶ 該被動未被動（Under-passivation）

相較於中文環繞主題、不論主動被動的表達方式，英文的要求顯得嚴謹多了。在陳述客觀事實時，英文常把焦點放在「被處置、受影響」的一方，因此被動的表達也很常見。在被動句中，主事者的地位降低，必須以 by 來標記（by whom?），這也成為被動句的一大指標。但究竟如何決定要用主動還是被動？關鍵在於先認清主詞是誰，搭配什麼動詞，並判斷主詞是否具有執行動詞的能力：

The audience 主動主詞 in the front rows raised several questions. ●●▶ 聽眾提出問題

Several questions 被動主詞 were raised by the audience in the front rows. ●●▶ 問題被提出來

以下列舉一些問題句式，都是在該被動的地方沒有用被動。問題可能是不了解動詞的詞意，或是忽略了被動關係：

問題句式

(✘)　But now at least I know the pattern of questions and <u>what should heed</u> while studying.　●●▶ heed 是的主詞是人！

(✘)　As for Jolin Tsai, she is the most famous singer in Taiwan. But even <u>she passed over</u> when she was at an audition.　●●▶ 是誰被 pass over（忽略）？

(✘)　Global warming is known as a natural phenomenon <u>that cause by</u> the green house effect.　●●▶ 既然有 by，表示是「被造成」的，必須用被動！

(✘)　Music is said <u>to perform</u> by special instruments but nowadays people perform it with anything they can get hold of, even everyday objects.　●●▶ music 有主動性嗎？

正確句式

(○)　But now at least I know the pattern of questions and what should <u>be heeded</u> while studying.

　　　●●▶ 由於事情本身不會動，所以用 what should be heeded「什麼事該被注意」或是 what I should heed「我該注意什麼事」

(○)　As for Jolin Tsai, she is the most famous singer in Taiwan. But even she <u>was passed over</u> when she was at an audition.

　　　●●▶ pass over 忽視。Jolin 在選拔會中被忽略，並非自願，故用被動

(○)　Global warming is known as a natural phenomenon that <u>is caused</u> by the green house effect.

　　　●●▶ 暖化是被造成的，是溫室效應導致的，故用被動

(○) Music is said <u>to be performed</u> by special instruments, but nowadays people perform it with anything they can get hold of, even everyday objects.

●●▶ 音樂不會自行表演，是「被演奏」！

被動句的使用是因為動詞與主詞「不搭」，動作的執行者被下放到後面（by whom），反而把「被影響」的一方放在主詞的位置上。這個觀念本身並不難懂，但難的是學生常常對動詞的語意了解不夠，因而不知道該怎麼用。下面的問題句式就和動詞的用法有關：

問題句式

(✘) He wanted to know <u>where was my previous education</u>. ●●▶ 在哪「受教育」？
該用什麼動詞？

(✘) They know what they want and are willing to <u>devote</u> to it. ●●▶ devote 的用法？

(✘) <u>We</u> are appreciated that you can give us a reply at your earliest convenience.
●●▶ appreciate 的用法？

正確句式

(○) He wanted to know where I <u>was educated</u> previously.

●●▶「受教育」是被動的概念 ●●▶ 我被教育 being educated

(○) They know what they want and are willing to <u>be devoted</u> to it. 或
They know what they want and are willing to <u>devote themselves</u> to it.

●●▶ devote 為及物動詞，表示投入「自己」在某件事上，用法是「devote oneself to...」；「自己」是被投入的，當然也可用被動 be devoted to...

(○) **We** will appreciate **it** if you can give us a reply at your earliest convenience. 或
It will be appreciated if you can give us a reply at your earliest convenience.

●●▶ 請記住 appreciate 的用法是「人 appreciate 事」，因此要說 I will appreciate it!

英文中常用的 devote 與 appreciate 常是台灣學生的罩門。這兩個動詞都是及物動詞：devote 表示投入「自己」在某件事上，因此受詞一定是人自己（oneself）；appreciate 表示「人」對「事」的感謝，因此主動主詞是「人」，但被動主詞是「事」：

devote「自己」to「某事」：

He devoted himself to adult education. ●●▶ He is devoted to adult education.

「人」appreciate「事」：

I appreciate your kind help. ●●▶ Your kind help is highly appreciated!

不管問題出在哪裡，根本之道仍是要養成「標記」主、被動的習慣！先找出每個動詞所帶的主詞，再確認兩者間的主控關係，隨時自問：是誰在主導？

類型二 過度被動（Over-passivation）

前面我們看到許多該被動卻沒有被動標記的例子，接下來要看到的是正好相反的情況：太多被動！

要判斷一個句子是主動亦或是被動，關鍵在於主詞是否有「主控性」，是否能執行動詞所表達的動作。一句話的主詞可能是有意志的生物或是無生命的物體，前者比較可能操縱事件發生；然而，後者因為沒有生命，沒有意志，所扮演的角色往往是「被處置」的一方，從而讓人誤以為，只要主詞是物體，就都要用被動句表示。這樣的結論太過倉促，很容易產生問題。看看下面的例子，要描述「冰塊融化」，可以有兩種說法：

The ice is melted. 或是
The ice melts.

雖然冰塊沒有意志，但是冰塊融化是一種物理的自然現象，可以用主動的觀點來描述冰塊自己融化。這是為什麼呢？重點在於「認定」改變的發生由誰主導？

描述物體的狀態改變，有兩種觀點：

1. 外力的改變：The surface of the land was changed by the earthquake. ●●▶ 地表被改變

　　　　　　地貌不會自己改變，是被改變的

2. 自身的現象：The land was sliding and flowing downward. ●●▶ 土地崩塌滑動

　　　　　　土壤自身崩解鬆塌而移動動

　　要強調物體是經歷外力改變時，就會選擇被動式；若要強調自然現象本身的改變，即可用主動。這兩種觀點直接影響到動詞的選擇，有些動詞就是用來表達事件自身的現象，是主動的觀點，無須被動。因此，主被動的標記和動詞語意息息相關，運用這個概念，請檢視下列的句子，動詞語意和主被動標記有無衝突？

問題句式

(✘)　The colorful rainbow <u>was disappeared</u>. ●●▶ 彩虹「消失」是自然變化！

(✘)　In just two months, they made more than one hundred attempts, but <u>all is failed</u>.
　　●●▶ 所有嘗試都「失敗」，是事件自身的結果

(✘)　It was difficult for me to accept that this accident would <u>be happened</u>.
　　●●▶ 事件「發生」是自身的出現

(✘)　Art therapy combines traditional psychotherapy with art expression. It <u>is arisen</u>
　　around the mid-20th century in English-speaking and European areas.
　　●●▶ 藝術治療「興起」也是自身現象！

正確句式

(○) The colorful rainbow disappeared. ••▶ 彩虹自然消失，與外力無關

(○) In just two months, they made more than one hundred attempts, but all failed.

••▶ 試驗失敗是自身現象的結果，不是外力改變

(○) It was difficult for me to accept that this accident would happen.

••▶ 事情自然發生，為事件自身的出現

(○) Art Therapy combines traditional psychotherapy with art expression. It arose around the mid-20th Century in English-speaking European areas.

••▶ 藝術治療本身興起於 20 世紀中葉，為自身的崛起

對於事情的發生、事物的出現，都是描述事件本身的現象，都是由事件為出發點的主動觀點（What happened?），但是請注意動詞 happen、appear、occur 三者的語意搭配：發生在什麼「時候」（When did it happen?），出現則是在「哪裡」（Where did it appear?），出現多少次（How often does it occur?）：

A serious accident happened last week.   ••▶ 意外發生於上星期

It appeared in all the newspapers.   ••▶ 消息出現在報紙上

Accidents may occur again and again.   ••▶ 出事頻繁

特別值得一提的是，有些動詞可以允許兩種觀點，就會有兩種用法：

I flunked the test.   ••▶ 我沒好好用功，考了不及格 (自己要負責)

I was flunked.   ••▶ 我有點無辜，「被」當了（老師主宰）

→The instructor flunked me.

「被當」是指沒有通過考試，在英文裡也可以說：I failed the test. 動詞 fail 也有兩種語意面向：

All his efforts failed.   ••▶ 他的努力都失敗了（事情的結果）

All his friends failed him.   ••▶ 他的朋友都不挺他（對人的辜負）

總之，主動與被動的使用還要搭配動詞語意的考量，詞彙和句式之間有著密不可分的關係！

類型三 被動語句標記的問題

　　前面所提到的問題主要是因為無法掌握使用被動的時機所造成，但其實在被動句的標記上，對英語學習者也是另一門挑戰。

　　在英文中，只要是被動關係就一定要用被動形式來標記，動詞必須改為 Be + Past Participle（過去分詞 Vpp）。其中 BE 動詞為主要動詞，配合各種時態，就衍生出下列形式：

過去被動　He was chased.

現在被動　He is chased.

未來被動　He will be chased.

習慣被動　He is always chased.

　　然而，過去分詞的形式並不規則，有許多變化，造成初學者在被動的標記上常常發生問題，以下即列出幾種常見的被動標記問題：

1. 過去分詞 Vpp（Past Participle）的形式

　　有些動詞的「同伴」較多，在過去分詞的形式上就要特別注意：

問題句式

（✘）　Somebody mocked me and said I snored so loudly that everyone <u>was woked up</u>.
　　●●▶ 過去分詞的形式有誤

（✘）　The American pilgrim leaders <u>have been lightened</u> by Christian teachings.
　　●●▶ 動詞該是 lighten（發光），還是 enlighten（啟發）？

正確句式

（○）Somebody mocked me and said I snored so loudly that everyone <u>was waked up</u>（也可用 <u>woken</u> up or <u>wakened</u> up）.

（○）The American pilgrim leaders <u>have been enlightened</u> by Christian teachings.

由於字源不同，英文有 wake 和 woke 兩個同義詞，兩者的過去分詞形式不同：wake-waked vs. woke-woken 另外還有第三個類似的詞 waken-wakened。在現代英語中，這三個詞幾乎可彼此替代，而且都可用於主動和被動：

Please <u>wake</u> / <u>woke</u> / <u>waken</u> me up when you come back.
I was <u>waked</u> / <u>woken</u> / <u>wakened</u> up by the alarm.

2. Be動詞的不當省略

被動句的完整標記是 BE + Vpp，BE 動詞以及過去分詞都是不可或缺的元素，兩者缺一不可。但是有時學生會忘了被動標記中的 BE 動詞：

問題句式

(✘)　It was clear that the meeting would <u>delayed</u>. ●●▶ 被動式標記不完整

(✘)　It is an honor to <u>admitted</u> to this prestigious university. ●●▶ 少了動詞 Be 動詞

正確句式

(○) It was clear that the meeting would <u>be delayed</u>. ●●▶ BE 在此不可省略

(○) It is an honor to <u>be admitted</u> to study at a prestigious university.
　　●●▶ 完整的被標記，BE 不可少

什麼時候 BE 可以省略呢？大多在省略的關係子句中。當關係子句被簡化時（省略了關係代名詞和 BE），就只剩下過去分詞作為修飾語：

He was selected as a school representative to participate in the Student Forum.
●●▶ He is a representative (who was) <u>selected</u> to participate in the Student Forum.

3. 時態標記个拾

被動句和主動句一樣，都有時態的區別，藉由 BE 動詞來表達時間。因此 BE 動詞的時態選擇也要注意：

> 問題句式
>
> (✘)　In 1949, they <u>are</u> all born in Hsinchu. ••▶ 是「過去」出生！
>
> (✘)　I <u>am</u> scared to death when seeing him. ••▶「受驚嚇」是發生在過去還是現在？

> 正確句式
>
> (○)　In 1949, they <u>were</u> all born in Hsinchu. ••▶ 要用過去式
>
> (○)　I <u>was</u> scared to death when seeing him. ••▶ 要用過去式

4. 分詞形容詞：主動或被動？

最後，被動標記使用「過去分詞」，相對的是「現在分詞」。所謂的「分詞」，不外乎「現在分詞」以及「過去分詞」。但其實這兩者，都與「現在、過去」無關，而是表達「主動」與「被動」之分。因此若改稱為「主動分詞」和「被動分詞」，在語意上將能更容易掌握。分詞單獨出現時可作為形容詞用以修飾名詞，與名詞的語意關係是主動還是被動，就決定分詞的選擇：

現在分詞（主動分詞）	過去分詞（被動分詞）
a selling agent 主動銷售員	a sold item 被賣出的貨
a heart-breaking experience 令人傷心的經歷	a heart-broken person 傷心的人

A heart-breaking experience　••▶ an experience that breaks someone's heart

A heart-broken person　••▶ a person whose heart is broken

由上例中可以看出現在分詞表達「主動」的修飾關係，過去分詞是「被動」的語意。多數人對分詞形容詞的選擇常有疑難，其實是因為不了解現在分詞及過去分詞真正的涵意，用主動分詞和被動分詞來區分，可能就清楚多了！

請檢視下列句子中的分詞形容詞有何不妥之處：

問題句式

(✘) He is really sick and has a <u>life-threatened</u> disease.
　　●●▶ disease 威脅到生命，疾病是主控者，要用主動分詞修飾

(✘) The <u>touched</u> song talked about my personality and our story happened in college life. ●●▶ 歌曲感動人，歌曲是主控者，要用主動分詞修飾

(✘) There were 6 people <u>hurting</u> in the car accident.
　　●●▶ 受傷是是被迫導致的結果，要用被動分詞

(✘) The house is being <u>renovating</u>. ●●▶ 房屋會自己主動翻修嗎？

(✘) He got truly <u>boring</u> to listen to the long, monotone lecture.
　　●●▶ 人的情緒是受外界刺激而被挑起的，要用被動！

正確句式

(○) He is really sick and has a <u>life-threating</u> disease.
　　●●▶「威脅到生命」的疾病：a disease that threatens life

(○) The <u>touching</u> song talked about my personality and our story happened in college life. ●●▶ 歌曲使人感動：The song touches me

(○) There were 6 people (who got) <u>hurt</u> in the car accident.
　　●●▶ 人受傷是「被傷害」的結果，因此該用被動分詞 hurt

(○) The house is being <u>renovated</u>. 房屋本身不具主動性，因此用被動分詞

(○) He got truly <u>bored</u> to listen to the long, monotone lecture.

••▶ 情緒的變化不是自己「主動選擇」的，而是受外界刺激被挑起。情緒的主導者是外界刺激，人反而是受控、被影響的一方，故用被動分詞

同理，I am interested in English writing. ••▶ 被吸引

I was frightened by the news. ••▶ 被嚇到

類型四 ▶ **主語錯置，語意不清**

在英文中，「形式」和「語意」呈彼此配搭的關係，被動句透過 BE + Vpp 的標記表示主詞是「被影響」的對象。此時，描述的主題焦點（即主詞）落在「被動」的一方，而主動句的主題焦點則落在「主控」的角色上，兩者的切入點不同：

主動角色：<u>John</u> broke the window. ••▶ 以「主控的一方」為主題焦點
被動角色：<u>The window</u> was broken. ••▶ 以「受影響的一方」為主題焦點

下面這些句子都有語意不清的問題，請檢視這些被動句的主題焦點何在？

問題句式

(✖) Nature has its rules that humans cannot completely understand. <u>Offending the rules of nature</u> will be punished as people break the laws of society.

••▶ 究竟誰會被 punished ？ Offending the rules of nature 僅代表條件，不是「被處置、被影響」的對象

(✖) <u>This result</u> was got their attention quickly.

••▶ this result 究竟是主動還是被動角色？

正確句式

(○) Nature has its own rules beyond human understanding. <u>People</u> will be punished if they offend these rules of nature. 或

(○) Nature has its rules beyond human understanding. <u>Offending the rules of nature</u> will get people to be punished in the long run.

　　●●▶ people 才是被懲罰的對象，offending these rules of nature 可以是主控的條件，但人才會被懲罰！

(○) <u>This result</u> got their attention quickly.
　　●●▶ This result 在句中擔任主動角色，直接引起注意，因此用 got

類型五　分詞構句的問題

　　前面提過分詞有兩種：現在分詞（表主動）和過去分詞（表被動）。所謂的分詞構句，就是將一個原本完整的子句簡化為附屬子句，用來描述「共時出現」的次要事件。分詞構句通常出現在句首，是用來修飾主要子句的主詞。此時，要特別留意分詞的主詞必須與主要子句的主詞一致，這是我們在第六章一直強調的重點。當出現在句尾時，也要先釐清修飾的對象，才能明確判斷分詞該採用主動或被動。

　　請檢查一下，下面這些句子中的分詞構句是否可用來修飾主要子句的主詞，在語意上是否和主要主詞有清楚的「掛鉤」：

問題句式

(✘)　<u>Surprising</u> by the interesting software, I spent about two hours trying various options already programmed in the system. ●●▶ 分詞主詞是誰？能否主動 surprise？

(✘)　<u>Comparing</u> with daisies, roses are more romantic.
　　●●▶ 分詞主詞是誰？能否主動去 compare？

(✘)　I am writing in response to your point <u>talked</u> about the high cost of freedom.
　　　●●▶ 分詞在修飾誰？主動或被動？

(✘)　Chocolate is a popular kind of snack mainly <u>making of cocoa</u>.
　　　●●▶ 分詞在修飾誰？主動或被動？

正確句式

(○)　<u>Surprised</u> by the interesting software, I spent about two hours trying the various options already programmed in the system.
　　　●●▶ 分詞的主詞為 I，是受外界刺激而感到警訝：I was surprised.

(○)　<u>Compared</u> with daisies, roses are more romantic.
　　　●●▶ 分詞的主詞為 roses，無法主動進行比較，而是被拿來比較，故用被動分詞

(○)　I am writing in response to your point <u>talking</u> about the high cost of freedom.
　　　●●▶ 以主動分詞 talking 來修飾 your point，是由關係子句省略而來：your point [which] talks about the high cost of freedom.

(○)　Chocolate is a popular kind of snack mainly <u>made of cocoa</u>.
　　　●●▶ chocolate 是被製造的，故以被動分詞 made of cocoa 來修飾；原為關係子句 Chocolate is a kind of snack [which is] mainly made of cocoa.

　　選擇主動分詞（現在分詞）還是被動分詞，就要看分詞與主詞間究竟是主動還是被動關係。

結語

　　被動句其實並不難，重要的是養成習慣，清楚表達主詞和動詞間的主、被動關係！這是英文嚴謹的標記講究之一，要釐清主詞和動詞的語意關係。如果不深究被動的溝通目的，只是一味認定有「被」的才是被動句，就會造成該被動卻沒有被動，或是矯枉過正，使用了太多的被動，過與不及的結果，讓人形成「被動句很困難」的錯誤印象。其實，只要了解英文形意搭配的原則，釐清主動被動的語意關係，掌握動詞的標記方式，寫作時充分表達主語究竟是「主導」還是「受控」的角色，這是英文「嚴句子」特性的一種發揮！

題目

一、主動、被動要先釐清，才能清楚傳達主詞與動詞的語意關係。以下的文章段落中有些標記是錯誤的，請圈出來並加以改正。

1. I know you made great efforts on studying, and I was looked up to you then.

2. To play games, you often stayed late, neglected your homework, and blamed by your parents.

3. Badminton lovers are often played indoors, because the shuttlecock is light-weighted and would be easily affected by wind.

4. According to the author, the theory composed of three basic principles.

二、以下這篇填空題，請選出正確合案。

Handling customer claims is a common task for most business firms. These claims include requests to exchange merchandise, requests for refunds, requests that work ___1___, and other requests for adjustments. Most of these claims are approved because they are legitimate. However, some requests for adjustment must be denied, and an adjustment refusal message must be sent. Adjustment refusals are negative messages for the customer. They are necessary when the customer is at fault or when the vendor has done all that can reasonably or legally be expected. An adjustment refusal message requires your best communication skills because it is bad news to the receiver. You have to refuse the claim and retain the customer at the same time . You may refuse the request for adjustment and even try to sell the customer more merchandise or service. All this is happening when the customer is probably angry or ___2___.

1. (A) is correct
   (B) to be correct
   (C) is corrected
   (D) be corrected

2. (A) disappoint
   (B) disappointing
   (C) disappointed
   (D) disappointedly

寫作修理廠

解 答

一、

1. I know you made great efforts on studying, and I <u>was looking</u> up to you then.

   look up to 表示「向某人看齊」，應為主動。

2. To play games, you often stayed late, neglected your homework, and <u>got scolded</u> by your parents.

   blame 是「責怪」之意，但此處用 scold「責罵」才是，且應為被動。

3. Badminton <u>is</u> often <u>played</u> indoors, because the shuttlecock is light-weighted and would be easily affected by wind.

   打羽球的人不會「被打」，應該是「羽球被打」。

4. According to the author, the theory <u>is composed of</u> three basic principles.

   或是 According to the author, the theory <u>consists of</u> three basic principles.

二、

1. (D)

   在 request 後若接子句，可用未來式（之後要做的事）或動詞原形（立即執行），同時工作是被修正，必須選擇被動式 be corrected。

2. (C)

   情緒的變化是人受到外界刺激後的反應，所以人是被影響的，要選擇表示被動的過去分詞。

Chapter 10

說文解字，善於用詞

let/make/cause/allow 有什麼不同？

動詞片語中的介系詞也要注意用法？

形容詞不能只看中文翻譯？

英文的連接用法？

The curse { let / made / caused / allowed } Aurora fall into deep, deep sleep...

哪一個是對的？

Be strict with word usage

詞彙表達語意概念，語意的區分造成詞彙有不同的用法。中式英文的最後一個問題就是詞彙的誤用，關鍵往往在於對詞意的理解不夠完整透徹，對形式的搭配不夠熟悉自在。本章將就常見的字詞誤用，分別說明釐清。

10.1 動詞

　　以下幾組動詞近義詞組，常常造成混淆，必須先認清各個動詞有不同的語意側重。

1. let/make/cause/allow

　　這四個動詞都有「使、讓」的意思，想要區分其用法，必須從詞彙原本的語意來看。這四個動詞中，let 與 make 皆為使役動詞，表達「完全立即」的操控，後面都要原形動詞。但兩者語意有分別：make 本是製作的意思，強調操控產生的結果；let 則是指放開限制後通行無阻，兩個動詞都有立即生效的語意，後面接的原形動詞都是用來標記「必然受控」。但是 make 的強制性高於 let，因受制者如同被製作的物品，是被迫參與，有「迫使某人做……」的意味，執行動作者缺乏主動意願；但 let 則是強調放開操控後立即得到的「自由」，如同閘門一開放，水就奔洩而下，執行動作者仍有主動的意願：

My mother <u>made</u> me go to bed without dinner. ●●▶ 強制產生，我「被迫」去睡覺
My mother <u>let</u> me go to bed without dinner. ●●▶ 允許發生，我「自願」去睡覺

　　和 let 語意相近的是 allow。let 與 allow 都蘊含「允許某人做……」的意思，執行動作者本身有很高的意願執行該動作，但allow僅表達授權和允許之下的可能性，並非完全操控或必然立即產生的結果，因此後面要搭配不定詞表目的，表示接下來可能執行的目標動作，例如：

My parents <u>let</u> me <u>stay</u> out till midnight on weekends. ●●▶ 操控的必然
My parents <u>allowed</u> me <u>to stay</u> out till midnight on weekends. ●●▶ 允許的可能

　　由於語意不同，let 與 allow 在主詞的選擇上也有不同的講究：let 的主詞本身要具有操控的能力，通常是人刻意所為，但 allow 的促成條件不一定是人，有可能是客觀情勢造成的機會：

（○）Living on campus allows me to walk to class. ●●▶ 住校促成的可能

（✘）Living on campus let me walk to class. ●●▶「住校」不具操控性，不適合用 let

至於 cause 這個詞，單純表達因果關係，指出「肇因」和「結果」之間的連結，但沒有完全操控的強制性，也沒有立即發生的必然性。 前面的主詞可能是任何人事物，造成的結果在時間上也一定是後來發生的，所以要用不定詞：

His addiction to drugs <u>caused</u> him <u>to lose</u> his job. ●●▶ 因果有先後，但在時間上不連接

清楚了這四個詞的語意及用法，請看看下面的句子，使用動詞 let 正確嗎？

問題句式

(✘)　However, my life in school never <u>lets</u> me feel bored. ●●▶ School life 有主控意志嗎？ feel bored 是自願的嗎？

(✘)　The thought of quitting my job comes to mind a thousand times every day, but my friends <u>let</u> me stay. ●●▶ friends 有權決定嗎？ stay 符合意願嗎？

(✘)　Studying abroad <u>let</u> him observe closely the humanistic nature of western culture. ●●▶ observe 與 studying abroad 的關係是什麼？

(✘)　In the story "The Boy Who Cried Wolf," the shepherd boy was a liar who repeatedly tricks his neighbors by yelling that a wolf was attacking his flock, and finally <u>let</u> all of his flock eaten by a real wolf, because his neighbors no longer believed him.
　　●●▶ 羊群被吃是牧羊人造成的嗎？

正確句式

(○) However, my life in school never <u>made</u> me feel bored.
　　●●▶ 情緒感受是被引發的，不須特別批准，故用 make 較恰當！

(○) Though the thought of quitting my job comes to mind a thousand times every day, my friends <u>make</u> me stay.
　　●●▶ 說話者想離職，但朋友們使他留下，表示一種「受制」的結果，故用 make

(○) Studying abroad <u>allows</u> him to observe closely the humanistic nature of western culture.
　　●●▶ Studying abroad 提供一個機會，使他能夠觀察西方文化

(○) In the story "The Boy Who Cried Wolf," the shepherd boy was a liar who repeatedly tricks his neighbors by yelling that a wolf was attacking his flock, and finally <u>caused</u> all of his flock eaten by a real wolf, because his neighbors no longer believed him.

●●▶ 小男孩撒謊「造成」羊群被狼吃掉，並非出於主動意願，因此不適合用 let / allow，也不是立即結果，不適用 make，而是選用表自然因果的 cause

2. see/watch/look/read

在英文中，幾個與視覺感官相關的動詞 see, watch, look 常常遭到誤用。想正確的使用這幾個動詞，首先必須掌握它們的語意特徵，雖然在中文裡，這些字都翻譯成「看」的意思，但是怎麼看？是不是刻意地看？看的時間長或短？這些特性在英文中都會造成不同語意，因此要格外注意。

see：主動性低，眼睛睜開直覺進行視覺接收。例如：I <u>see</u> a car near the store.

look：主動性高（intentional），表示使用眼睛的動作，但持續的時間較短。例如：<u>Look</u> at this dress.

watch：主動性高（intentional），表示用心、用腦專注的看，動作持續時間較長。例如：Let's <u>watch</u> a movie.

問題句式

(✘) I was <u>seeing</u> a drama on my computer. ●●▶ 視覺接收還是主動的觀賞？

(✘) I'm not interested in <u>seeing</u> an essay that is written with the same repeated sentence structure. ●●▶ 視覺接收還是主動的「閱讀」？

(✘) I <u>looked</u> many people coming towards me when I was standing in front of the train station not knowing which direction to go. ●●▶ 視覺接收還是刻意的「看」？

正確句式

(○) I was <u>watching</u> a drama on my computer. ●●▶ 專注看的時間長，故用 watch

（ ○ ）I'm not interested in <u>reading</u> an essay that is written with the same repeated sentence structure. ●●▶ 主動性的閱讀用 read

（ ○ ）I <u>saw</u> many people coming towards me when I was standing in front of the train station not knowing which direction to go. ●●▶ 碰巧看見，主動性低，故用 see

　　視覺感知有「自主」與「非自主」之分，就像中文裡的「看」與「看見」是不同的，看了半天可能沒看見。有人問「看電影」到底是 see a movie 還是 watch a movie? 其實兩者皆有可能！若是表達一般去電影院的視覺經驗就可用 see，若是要強調長時間專注盯著看就可用 watch：

Let's go to see a movie tonight!
I'd like to watch a movie/a TV program tonight.

3. talk/chat/discuss/tell

　　這些都是溝通動詞，都有「談」的意思，但細究其語意仍有很大差別：talk 表示交談，chat 則是閒聊，一個較認真嚴肅，一個較輕鬆閒散，語意的重點都在人與人談話這個行為，帶有雙向溝通的意涵，因此用法也很相近：

talk/chat **about**＋事	●●▶ 談話／聊天關於……
talk/chat **to/with**＋人	●●▶ 和……談話／閒聊
We talked/chatted for an hour.	●●▶ 兩方對談／閒聊
I talked/chatted **to** her **about** her career.	●●▶ 我和她談／聊生涯規畫

　　以上 talk 和 chat 的語意都側重兩人交談的行為本身，是不及物動詞（We talked.），若要表達談話的內容，後面一定要加上介系詞 about：talk about something；若是要表達談話對象，一定要加 to 或 with：talk to someone 偏重對話的方向性；talk with someone 則強調談話對象是平行的參與者。另一個動詞 discuss（討論）也表示雙向溝通，但卻是及物動詞，討論必然涉及議題，因此 discuss 的語意側重在討論的事項，可直接以話題作為受詞：

discuss ＋事＋with＋人　　　　●●▶ 和……討論某事

We discussed her career for an hour. ●●▶ 我們討論 [她的職業生涯] 名詞受詞

I discussed her career <u>with</u> her.　●●▶ 我和她討論 [她的職業生涯] 名詞受詞

　　不同於以上三者，tell（告訴）表示單向的告知，我們通常説：告訴誰什麼事，因此 tell 一定有對象，也有內容，後面常有兩個補語：

tell 人＋事　　　　　　●●▶ 告訴某人某事

I told him a story.　　　　●●▶ 告訴他一個故事

I told him that he is a nice guy. ●●▶ 告訴他 [他是個好人] 子句

I told him to stay for the night. ●●▶ 告訴他 [晚上留下來] 不定詞（有「指使」的語意）

問題句式

(✖)　Every day I <u>talked to</u> the myself that I must do my best to finish homework.
　　　●●▶ talk 不可帶子句補語！

(✖)　Everyone started to <u>talk</u> funny things happened in the past year.
　　　●●▶ talk 須搭配介系詞！

(✖)　The five of us <u>chatted</u> our new lives, and the laughter never stopped.
　　　●●▶ chat 須搭配介系詞！

(✖)　I was afraid of my grandpa since he always had a stern face and <u>talked</u> little me
　　　due to his poor health. ●●▶ talk 後要搭配介系詞！

正確句式

(○) Every day I <u>told</u> myself that I must do my best to finish my homework.
　　　●●▶「告訴」自己 + 內容（that 子句）

(○) Everyone started to <u>talk about</u> the funny things <u>that</u> happened in the past year.

(○) Everyone started to <u>discuss</u> the funny things <u>that</u> happened in the past year.
　　　●●▶ talk about 主題（NP）或 discuss 主題（NP）

(○) The five of us <u>chatted about</u> our new lives, and the laughter never stopped.

••▶ chat about ＋主題

(○) I was afraid of my grandpa since he always had a stern face and <u>rarely talked</u> <u>to</u> me due to his poor health. ••▶ talk to ＋對象（需要標記對象的介系詞 to）

4. bring to/take to

　　Bring 與 take 兩者都是「帶」，但在語意上的作用方向不同：bring to 指的是將某人或某物從別處「帶來」，是「趨近」的帶；而 take to 則是將某人或某物「帶走」往別處去，是「帶離」的帶，兩者表達不同的方向性：

Please bring a book to me. ••▶ Please bring me a book. ••▶ 趨近說話者
Please take the book to her. ••▶ 不能說 (✗) take her the book ••▶ 遠離說話者

問題句式

(✗)　Although my father's work sometimes <u>brings</u> him abroad, he still shows his love to my brother and me. ••▶ 將他「帶來」或「帶走」？

(✗)　Despite being told several times, the waiter still didn't <u>take</u> us any water.
　　••▶ waiter 應該將水「拿過來」，不是 take away ！

正確句式

(○) Although my father's work sometimes <u>takes</u> him abroad, he still shows his love to my brother and me. ••▶ 工作常把父親「帶離」國內，故用 take

(○) Despite being told several times, the waiter still didn't <u>bring</u> us any water.
　　••▶ waiter 應將水「帶來」給我們，所以要用 bring 才合適

5. 其他動詞相關問題

動詞補語的類型常是令人頭痛的問題，例如 remain 後要接什麼？

問題句式

(✘) Trot music has <u>remained its popularity</u> in Korea till today.

　　●●▶ remain 的用法？後該接什麼詞類？

正確句式

(○) Trot music has <u>remained popular</u> in Korea even today.

　　●●▶ remain 要接形容詞

此處 remain 的用法類似 stay（Stay healthy!），要接形容詞補語（Remain silent!）不能和 retain 搞混了！

remain + 形容詞：Not many people who win the lottery <u>remain wealthy</u> for long.

retain + 名詞：Trot music has <u>retained its popularity</u> in Korea till today.

最後動詞的使用仍要遵循主動賓不可少、也不可多的原則：

問題句式

(✘) While I was practicing how to ride a bike, I knew that even if I fell on my face, I still had to stand up, wipe the dust off my hands, and keep trying until I <u>success</u>.

　　●●▶ I 後面要接動詞還是名詞？

(✘) There <u>were</u> more than seven thousand people <u>died</u> when the 3/11 earthquake in Japan happened.

　　●●▶ 句中的主要動詞是誰？

正確句式

(○) While I was practicing how to ride a bicycle, I knew that even if I fell on my

face, I still had to stand up, wipe the dust off my hands, and keep trying until I

<u>succeeded</u>.

●●▶ 主動賓不可少，動詞不可少！

(○) There <u>were</u> more than seven thousand people <u>who died</u> when the 3/11

earthquake in Japan happened. ●●▶ 前面已有帶時態標記的 were，後面的動詞

就要用 who 來區隔！

10.2 搭配動詞的介系詞

動詞常需要介系詞的輔助來幫助表達相關的參與角色，而介系詞各有不同的語意側
重。例如：to 用來標記「對象」，是動作的接受者（goal）；for 則是用來標記「受益者」
（beneficiary），不一定和動作直接相關。例如：

The agent sold my house to a rich buyer for me. ●●▶ 為我把房子賣給買家

介系詞 to 所標記的「對象」可延伸為奉獻、期待、或歸因朝向的目標：

He devoted his time to helping others. ●●▶ 奉獻委身的對象

I look forward to seeing you soon. ●●▶ 引頸期盼的對象

He attributed his success to his wife's full support. ●●▶ 歸結原因的方向

還有一些及物動詞轉為形容詞用時，就要加上介系詞：

A suits B：That dress <u>suits</u> you well. ●●▶ It is suitable for you!

A is suitable：That dress is not <u>suitable to</u> wear at school.

That dress is not <u>suitable for</u> wearing at school!

That dress is suitable for you!

以下列舉一些常見的介系詞搭配問題：

問題句式

(✘)　She went to museums and <u>listened</u> some lectures when she had a leisure time.
　　••▶ listen 的對象要搭配介系詞！

(✘)　Art therapy suits <u>for</u> the people who can't fully express themselves, such as children, mentally handicapped patients, or people with trauma.
　　••▶ suits（適合）是及物動詞，後面不需要介系詞！

(✘)　As for this big event, we've already devoted a whole winter vacation <u>on</u> it.
　　••▶ devote 的對象要用介系詞 to！

(✘)　Music can be defined as noise to some people. For example, rap is the kind of music which is popular among teenagers, but it's also criticized by older generations. So, music is <u>decided to</u> the listener.
　　••▶ 由誰決定是 by！

(✘)　Your encouragement <u>for</u> me is really meaningful and powerful.
　　••▶ encouragement 的對象是 to someone！

(✘)　You've always given me guidance, no matter if it's a reminder <u>for</u> trivial things or a warning <u>for</u> not staying up too late.
　　••▶ 介系詞與名詞搭配有問題！

(✘)　The benefit of art therapy is that it lets patients <u>stay in relax</u>, using a natural way to express themselves. ••▶ 介系詞 in 後要接名詞！

正確句式

(○) She went to museums and <u>listened to</u> some lectures when she had a leisure time.
　　••▶ listen to + 受詞

(○) 或 She went to museums and <u>heard</u> some lectures when she had a leisure time.
　　••▶ hear + 受詞

(○) Art therapy <u>suits</u> the people who can't fully express themselves, such as children, mentally handicapped patients, or people with trauma.
　　••▶ suit 為及物動詞，直接加受詞

(○) As for this big event, we've already devoted a whole winter vacation to it.

●●▶ devote 搭配的介系詞為 to，表目標，即奉獻的對象

(○) Music can be defined as noise to different people. For example, rap is a kind of music, which is popular among teenagers, but it's also criticized by older generations. So, music is decided by the listener.

●●▶ 由聽的人決定要用 by，被動句中的主事者放在句尾：by whom

(○) Your encouragement is really meaningful and powerful to me.

●●▶ 對象用 to 標記，我是鼓勵的接收者對象！

(○) She always gave me guidance, no matter if it's a reminder of/about trivial things or a warning not to stay up too late.

●●▶ 關於什麼的 reminder 後接介系詞 of 或 about，但 warning 不要做什麼，可直接加不定詞。

(○) The benefit of art therapy is that it lets patients stay relaxed, using a natural way to express themselves.

●●▶ 用形容詞 stay relaxed 或是 stay in + 名詞（如：stay in relaxation）

動詞和介系詞間相互搭配，形式和語意都要兼顧：

stay in + 名詞：Open communication allows us to stay in harmony.
stay + 形容詞：Stay calm, and everything will be okay.

　有些名詞來自於動詞，例如名詞 encouragement 與動詞相關，可與不同的介系詞搭配，側重不同的面向：
鼓勵的對象：Her kind words were a source of encouragement to me.

●●▶ 對人的鼓勵，用 encouragement to someone

鼓勵的內容：The act passed at the last session for the <u>encouragement of immigration</u> has been put into operation. ●●▶ 對移民一事的鼓勵

鼓勵去做的事：There was little <u>encouragement to believe</u> that the act will be put into operation. ●●▶ 用不定詞表示要去做的事

　　名詞 warning 的用法也來自動詞 warn，因側重不同面向而有幾種不同用法：

單純的對象：This is a warning <u>to all nations</u>!

警告某人要注意某事：The heart attack was a warning <u>for him to get in better shape</u>.

警告某人關於某事：Did you warn her <u>about</u> the wild dogs?

警告勿做的事：The police issued a warning <u>against</u> domestic violence.
　　　　　　　My mother warned me <u>against</u> dating him. Now I see why.

10.3 形容詞

　　形容詞用來修飾名詞，兩者間的搭配也有形式和語意的講究。有些形容詞只能修飾「人」，有些只能修飾「物」，例如：a tiring trip vs. a tired tourist。使用形容詞時，要搞清楚修飾的是什麼，再選擇適當的形式。通常形容詞的詞尾透露不同的語意，以 -able 為字尾，就帶有「能夠」的意思，如：taxable 是「可被課稅的」；以 *-ful* 為字尾，就帶有「full of」的意思，如：truthful, restful。請比較：

They are respectful to the President. ●●▶ full of respect ●●▶ 表現出尊敬的態度

The President is a respectable person. ●●▶ worthy of respect ●●▶ 值得尊敬的人

問題句式

(✘)　Furthermore, Shikaku usually appears when something <u>unexpectable</u> and cheerful happens. ●●▶ unexpectable 的語意不適用此句！

(✘)　The first week of school was definitely <u>tired</u>. ●●▶ 只有人才會感到 tired！

(✘)　Since National Chiao Tung University is not located in the downtown, you might feel <u>inconvenient</u> when you want to go off campus.

　　　●●▶ 造成不方便的不是人！ 不能說 I am inconvenient. (✘)

正確句式

(○) Furthermore, Shikaku usually appears when something <u>unexpected</u> and cheerful happens.

　　●●▶ 句中所想要表達的是 unexpected「意想不到的」，並不是「不能」被期待

(○) The first week of school was definitely <u>tiring</u>.

　　●●▶ 外物讓人產生情緒，外物是主動（The week is tiring.），人是被動（We are tired.）

(○) Since National Chiao Tung University is not located in the downtown, you might feel <u>inconvenienced</u> when you want to go off campus.

(○) Since National Chiao Tung University is not located in the downtown, it might be <u>inconvenient</u> for you to go off campus.

　　●●▶ 外在事物造成不便，人是被影響的，例如：It is inconvenient for me to go out.

英文的詞類有清楚的形式區別，作為形容詞用，就要有形容詞的形式：

(✘)　The sun is so <u>brightly</u> and <u>warm</u> that it seems to breathe new life into the earth.
　　●●▶ 前後修飾語的詞性不一致！

(✘)　Everything became so <u>chaos</u>.　　●●▶ 詞性不對！形式不對！

(✘)　I hope I will not be too <u>sorrow</u>.　　●●▶ 詞性不對！形式不對！

(✘)　I am writing in response to your point about the high cost of <u>free</u>.
　　●●▶ 詞性不對！形式不對！

正確句式

(○) The sun is so <u>bright</u> and <u>warm</u> that it seems to breathe new life into the earth.

    ●●▶ bright and warm 前後修飾語的詞性要一致

(○) Everything became so <u>chaotic</u>. ●●▶ chaos 為名詞，chaotic 才是形容詞

(○) I hope I will not be too <u>sorrowful</u>. ●●▶ 名詞 sorrow + ful，sorrowful 為形容詞

(○) I am writing in response to your point about the high cost of <u>freedom</u>.

    ●●▶ the cost of freedom 介系詞要與名詞共用，兩者缺一不可

10.4 比較級

比較級的語意與形式也同樣存在著對應的搭配關係。比較句的重要標記就是 than，用來連接兩個被比較的物件，兩者之間必須具同質性，才能夠進行比較。我們可以比較 Bob 和 Patrick 的身高，卻不能把 Bob 的身高和 Patrick 的體重進行比較。比較級的另一個標記落在形容詞上，就是眾所熟知的形容詞單音節加 -er 與多音節加 more 的規則。要寫出一個正確的比較句，要注意形容詞的標記與 than 所連接的同質關係都必須兼顧。比較級最常見的問題出自最簡單的表達，「他比我大三歲」怎麼說？可以有兩種說法：

He is three years older than <u>I am</u>. ●●▶ 將 than 視為連接詞

He is three years older than <u>me</u>. ●●▶ 將 than 視為介系詞

Than 本為連接詞，但近年在口語中，愈來愈多的人將 than 視為介系詞，隨之普遍的用法就出現兩種形式：

較正式的說法： I walk faster than he does.●●▶ than 做為連接詞

較口語的說法： I walk faster than <u>him</u>.●●▶ than 做為介系詞，後接受格

問題句式

(✘) Tired of studying, I began focusing on the music club. By joining the band, I learned something <u>important than</u> homework. ●●▶ 形容詞比較級沒出現？

(✘) The <u>air conditioner in this room</u> is colder than <u>that room</u>. ●●▶ 比較的對象不一致！

(✘) My <u>Geography professor</u> is more energetic than <u>Biology</u>. ●●▶ 比較的對象不一致！

(✘) I speak more loudly than <u>they</u>. ●●▶ 比較的範圍不一致！

(✘) We are one year older than <u>last year</u>. ●●▶ 比較的範圍不一致！

正確句式

(○) Tired of studying, I began focusing on the music club. By joining the band, I learned something <u>more important than</u> homework. ●●▶ 要有比較級標記 more

(○) [The <u>air conditioner in this room</u>] is colder than [<u>the one in that room</u>].
●●▶ 比較的應是「這間房裡的冷氣」和「那間房裡的冷氣」，比較雙方須具同質性。

(○) [The <u>Geography professor</u>] is more energetic than [<u>my Biology professor</u>].
●●▶ 比較的對象應該一致，都是「教授」，不能將「教授」與「學科」相比。

(○) [I speak] more loudly than [they do]. (i.e., I speak more loudly than they speak.)
●●▶ 比較「我說話」和「他們說話」兩件事。

(○) We are one year older than <u>we were</u> last year. ●●▶ we are 和 we were 的比較。

10.5 轉承連接詞

　　許多寫作的書都提到文章要有條理，要善用連接副詞，但是連接副詞到底怎麼用？語意有何講究？卻是問題連連。以下來看看幾組連接副詞的用法：

1. Besides vs. In addition (to)

雖然兩者都可翻譯為「此外還有」，但必須注意：besides 承接先前的語意，提供用意相同卻更重要的資訊。因此，使用 besides 時，前後兩句的主旨必須一致，且將重點微妙地轉到後一句，例如：

Besides being a great piano player, Aunt Sally is a great cook.

Tommy was happy to help me move. Besides, he had nothing better to do.

In addition (to) 原意是數學上的加總，用來表達尚未提到的其他可能，語意上沒有 besides 那麼講究，只是附加額外訊息：

In addition to house chores, she has to take care of the kids.

Tommy is coming for dinner. In addition, he will help us move.

問題句式

(✘)　Joining SAA is a good opportunity to practice speaking English. Besides, many foreign students' native languages are French and Spanish.

●●▶ besides 在此不適用，因為語意重點並非後加的這一句！

正確句式

(○) Joining SAA is a good opportunity to practice speaking English. Besides English, many foreign students' native languages are French and Spanish.

●●▶ 把 besides 當介系詞用，為轉換重點預做準備。

---

2. Exception vs. In addition (to)

中文說「除了……以外」在語意上其實有兩種含意、兩個不同的面向：

1) 一種是「除了……以外還有　」，有增加補充、涵蓋在內的意思，如：in addition (to), besides：

Libraries offer various other services <u>besides</u> lending books.

<u>In addition to</u> a thick fog, there was heavy swell.

2) 另一種是「除了……之外，其他都不一樣」，有排除、對比的功能，如 except, except for：

We go to school every day <u>except</u> Sunday.

This book is good <u>except for</u> a few mistakes.

問題句式

(✘) <u>Except from</u> convenient shopping, Taipei also has great scenery to offer to tourists.

　●●▶ 「附加說明」還是「除此之外」？

正確句式

(○) <u>In addition to</u> convenient shopping, Taipei also has great scenery to offer to tourists.

　●●▶ Taipei 提供的不僅是 shopping，還有美景，要用涵蓋加總的 in addition to

---

3. Despite vs. Besides/In addition to

　　常發生混淆的還有 despite 的用法。despite 是介系詞，表達對比式的轉折（in spite of, even though），意即「儘管如此」，仍然如何。

<u>Despite</u> a low GPA, she still got admitted to a medical school.

　●●▶ 儘管平均成績不高，她還是進了醫學院。

<u>Despite</u> the bad weather, we still went on hiking.

　●●▶ 儘管天候不佳，我們仍然去爬山。

問題句式

(✘) <u>Besides to</u> insufficient English learning, her linguistic creativity is amazing.
　　●●▶ 兩句的關係「增加補充」還是「對比轉折」？

(✘) <u>Despite</u> being engineering-orientated, [the Department of Foreign Languages and Literatures] of NCTU provides lessons in different fields, holding diverse activities, and cultivating students' interpersonal skills.
　　●●▶ despite 所指出的情況和主詞外文系有關嗎？

正確句式

(○) <u>Despite</u> insufficient English learning, her linguistic creativity is amazing.
　　●●▶ 對比式的轉折，要用 despite （= even though, in spite of）

(○) [<u>Despite being</u> engineering-orientated], [NCTU] has the Department of Foreign Languages and Literature, which provides lessons in different fields, holding diverse activities, and cultivating students' interpersonal skills.
　　●●▶ 原句的說法把「外文系」和 engineering-orientated 連在一起，但 engineering-orientated 應該是指學校──「交通大學」才對！因此應該將主詞還原為 NCTU。

10.6 對等連接詞 vs. 從屬連接詞

　　兩個子句之間的連接，可以用對等連接詞做平行的連接，也可用附屬連接詞表明主從關係：

對等連接：He likes music <u>and</u> he plays the piano. ●●▶ 平行獨立
附屬連接：He likes music <u>though</u> he doesn't play any instrument. ●●▶ 主從分明

台灣學生很愛用 not only...but also...，這也是一種對等連接，語意上用於強調超出預期，不單只發生一種情況：

He has not only quit smoking but also started to exercise.

以下列舉常出現的一些問題：

問題句式

(✖) Although there is no actual dialogue in the film, but it creates more imagination and the audience can have more time to pay attention to the facial expressions and other details of the movie. ●●▶ 兩個附屬連接詞，沒有主要子句！

(✖) By providing a long-term, cross-cultural working experience, we hope students will not only understand the culture and actually understand the meaning of "Global Mobility." ●●▶ 正確的對等連接詞是 not only...but also...！

(✖) Volunteering abroad can not only meet your expectations and it has a positive influence on your future career. ●●▶ 應是 not only...but also！

正確句式

(○) Although there is no actual dialogue in the film, it creates more imagination and the audience can have more time to pay attention on the facial expressions and other details of the movie.
●●▶ although 標記從屬子句，有別於獨立的主要子句；主要子句無須任何標記。

(○) By providing a long-term cross-cultural working experience, we hope students will not only experience the culture but also understand the meaning of "Global Mobility." ●●▶ not only...but also... 也是一種對等連接。

(○) Volunteering abroad can not only meet your expectations but also become a positive influence on your future career. ●●▶ not only...but also... 連接兩個對等子句。

Coordination 指的是對等平行的連接結構。當我們要提到數個性質相同、語意相關、結構相當的概念時，就需要對等連接詞 and/or/but/yet/nor 等，將這些概念以平行、平等的方式串連在一起。對等連接可用於各種詞類，但在使用對等連接詞時，要特別注意前後連接的內容是否詞性相同、語意相關、形式相當。簡單的說，就是要「物以類聚、同質相親」：

對等連接：X, Y, and Z （x, y, z 的形式和語意都一致）

1. 形容詞的連接問題

當好幾個形容詞排在一起時，要確定形式和語意都具有同質性，意即詞性一致、語意相關、形式類同：

問題句式

(✘) I felt heart-broken, grief-stricken, and lost my mind.
●●▶ and 前面兩個是形容詞，後面是動詞，不對等！

(✘) Although I only had eighteen years with her, I am grateful that she educated me well, teaching me to be independent, strong and never give up.
●●▶ and 連接的詞性前後不對等！

正確句式

(○) I felt heart-broken, grief-stricken, and lost.
●●▶ and 連接的詞性必須一致，lost my mind 可替換為語意相近的形容詞 lost 或 crazy

(○) Although I only had eighteen years with her, I am grateful that she educated me well, teaching me to be independent, strong and persevering.
●●▶ 為保持詞性一致，以 persevering 替換，或是改為連接兩個不定詞片語。

(○) Although I only had eighteen years with her, I am grateful that she educated me well, teaching me [to be independent and strong] and [to never give up].

••▶ and 連接兩個不定詞片語

2. 動詞的連接問題

連接動詞也是一樣的，要確定所連接的動詞，在語意和形式上都有明顯的一致性：

問題句式

(✘)　Therefore, I am very comfortable speaking English in public, including giving a speech, presentation or hosting. ••▶ or 連接的都是動名詞嗎？

正確句式

(○) Therefore, I am very comfortable speaking English in public, including [giving speeches and presentations] or [hosting an event].

••▶ 原句中所連接的三者詞性語意並不一致；host 後面也缺少相對應的受詞，因此改為 [giving speeches and presentations] or hosting an event]。要建立一致性，必須兼顧語意與形式！

3. 名詞的問題

「物以類聚」應用在名詞的連接上，就是同一類的名詞才能在一起，同一類的東西才能用 and/or 連接。每次連接一串東西時，都要搞清楚到底在連接什麼跟什麼！

問題句式

(✘)　The career of one of the most famous rock bands, the Beatles, and the story of one of the richest men in the world, Bill Gates are both familiar figures.

••▶ career 和 story 不是同一類的東西！

正確句式

(○) [The Beatles], one of the most famous rock bands, and [Bill Gates], who is one of the richest men in the world, are familiar figures.

　●●▶ 改為用人物當主詞，人名和人名連接，保留原句的 figures

或是：

(○) [The success of one of the most famous rock bands, the Beatles], and [the rise of one of the richest men in the world, Bill Gates] were both familiar stories.

　●●▶ 改變句中的用字，連接披頭四的「成功」與比爾蓋茲的「崛起」

4. 詞組、子句的連接問題

　　當我們想把好幾件事連在一起時，常常會忘記其間的關係，而寫得愈長愈容易出錯。詞組和子句的連接除了詞類、語意的搭配，還有長短的問題，每個子句的訊息量要平衡。所以連接兩個句子時，不要太長，一個句子一個事件，構思要清楚，結構要平衡，語意才會通順。

問題句式

(✘) I love basketball, playing basketball with classmates every Wednesdays, watching basketball games, **and** am a big fan of Jeremy Lin.

　●●▶ love 子句和 am 子句的形式、類型、長短都不搭！

(✘) I couldn't hear her anymore, telling me not to stay up late **and** eat more vegetables.

　●●▶ 到底 and 連接的是什麼？ not 又涵蓋了什麼？容易造成誤解！

(✘) There were people making many sacrifices **and** protesters yelled for their rights.

　●●▶ 一邊是 making，一邊是 yelled，兩個形式完全不搭！

(✘) I **not only** spent time with my teammates and got to know each of them better, **but** I also learned a lesson: Never underestimate your opponent and got prepared at any time. ●●▶ 一邊是原形動詞 underestimate，一邊是 got prepared，兩個句式完全不同！

正確句式

(○) I love basketball. I enjoy [playing basketball with classmates every Wednesday] and [watching basketball games]. I am also a big fan of Jeremy Lin.

●●▶ 原本的句子太長，訊息不清；改寫成短句後語意關係就較能釐清。

(○) I couldn't hear her anymore, telling me [to eat more vegetables] and [not to stay up late].

●●▶ 為了避免 not 造成語意模糊，可以換一下位置，肯定的 to eat 先講，not to 放到後面，如此才不會造成混淆。

(○) 或：There were [people making many sacrifices] and [protesters yelling for their rights]. ●●▶ 名詞片語包含分詞修飾，形意也必須相等，兩個名詞詞組的架構要平行對等。

(○) 或：There were people [making many sacrifices] and [yelling for their rights].

●●▶ 也可改為兩個平行的分詞片語，共同修飾 people，同樣地，分詞的結構要一致。

(○) I not only spent time with my teammates and got to know each of them better, but I also learned a lesson: Never underestimate your opponent and get prepared at all times. ●●▶ 兩個祈使句型，形式必須一致。

　　最後，來做一個小小的測驗，請把下面這個冗長的句子重新組合，使結構更嚴謹，語意更順暢：

問題句式

(✘) Life is simple. A student staying up late will feel warm while eating breakfast his or her mom made for him or her, or a worker after hard working in a factory, and going home so late feels happy while he or she watching his or her lovely children soundly sleep.

●●▶ 主要子句在哪裡？重點在哪裡？

修正建議：長句改短句，將兩件事分開來講，先講 student，再講 worker：

正確句式：

(○) Life is simple. A student will feel warm after staying up late and eating breakfast made by his mom. Or a worker will feel happy coming home after working hard at the factory to see his children sleeping soundly.

●●▶ 原本複雜糾結的語意可藉由結構上的區隔，來釐清重點，一一交代。

結語

　　使用連接結構可以把事情串連起來，但也容易使句式結構變得較冗長，語意變得較複雜，句子的重點反而模糊不清。別忘了，英文是個重點在前、主從分明的語言，要將重點說清楚、結構簡潔，讓人能一目了然，才是最有效率的表達方式。

寫作練功坊

題 目

一、中文和英文有些類似的詞彙，詞性可能不同、用法也可能不同，因此正確的詞意和詞類搭配是非常重要的。以下的句子中有些標記是錯誤的，請圈出來並加以改正。

1. When I first saw this ad, I felt ironic and contradiction between the girl and the people around her.

2. I will work part-time job after graduate to give you a new bike.

3. Because of curious about what does it taste like, I ordered one for a try.

4. The owner of the street food stand and James saw the luggage, which is belong to the businessman after ten minutes.

5. To avoid these assumed effects happening, my suggestion is that you should talk to them on this event.

6. Power or Strength does not absolutely decide the affect.

7. Almost everywhere I can walk, for example, park, street, department store, mountain, college, wherever I thought.

8. The temperature is lower than day, the wind is comfort, the smell of grass is full of atmosphere.

一、以下這篇填空題，請選出正確答案

　　Many people like to drink bottled water because they feel that tap water may not be safe, but is bottled water really any better? Bottled water is mostly sold in plastic bottles and that's why it is potentially health threatening. Processing the plastic can lead to the release of ___1___ chemical substances into the water contained in the bottles. The chemicals can be absorbed into the body and cause physical discomfort, such as stomach cramps and diarrhea. Health risks can also result from inappropriate storage of bottled water. Bacteria can multiply if the water is kept on the shelves for too long or if it is exposed to heat or direct sunlight. ___2___ the information on storage and shipment is not always readily available to consumers, bottled water may not be a ___3___ alternative to tap water. Besides these safety issues, bottled water has other disadvantages. It contributes to global warming. An estimated 2.5 million tons of carbon dioxide were generated in 2006 by the production of plastic for bottled water. In addition, bottled water produces an incredible amount of solid waste. According to one research, 90% of the bottles used are not recycled and lie for ages in landfills.

1. (A) harmful

　 (B) harmfully

　 (C) harms

　 (D) harmed

2. (A) Although

　 (B) Despite

　 (C) Since

　 (D) So

3. (A) worse

　 (B) bad

　 (C) well

　 (D) better

 解 答

一、

1. When I first saw this ad, I just felt ironic and contradictory about the girl and the people around her.

2. I will find a part-time job after graduation to make money and buy you a new bike.

3. Because I was curious about what it tasted like, I ordered one for a try.

4. James and the owner of the street food stand saw the bag of the businessman ten minutes later.

5. To avoid these undesirable consequences, my suggestion is that you should talk to them in this regard.

6. Physical power or strength alone does not absolutely determine the result of the game.

7. I can walk almost everywhere-- in parks, streets, department stores, mountains, college campuses, -- wherever I go.

8. The temperature is lower at night time than that of the day time, the breeze is comfort, and the smell of grass is refreshing.

二、

1. (A)

這裡空格後是一個名詞組 "chemical substances"，所以要選一個可以修飾名詞的形容詞。

2. (C)

這裡傳達的是因果關係，子句要用於解釋原因，因此要選可以表達原因的附屬連接詞 "since"。

3. (D)

本文一直在比較（美國）自來水和瓶裝水的好壞，並且明確說出瓶裝水的問題，在比較的前提下，這裡當然要選擇比較級 a better alternative。

NOTES

Actions Speak Louder than Words

實戰演練

坐而讀不如起而行，本書的第三部分，提供實戰演練的機會與寫作範例，期許讀者都能百戰百勝！在實戰練習寫作以前，要先懂得分析文章條理。寫作與閱讀是息息相關的，懂得怎麼分析文章，就懂得什麼是寫作的條理。以下是一封通知社區住戶有關遮雨棚工程的 e-mail，請依照前面所談的寫作原則來分析一下！請找出最重要的一句話（Topic sentence with a controlling idea），具體的細節（Supporting details），以及有力的總結（Thesis/Conclusion）：

From: Adrianna, the Property Management Assistant

This notice is being sent out to advise all Palo Alto Central residents about the upcoming awning replacement work. Starting tomorrow, Friday May 15, 2014, Canvas Awning will be on-site painting the frames that are being recovered. Note that only the parts of the frames that are exposed will be painted. The awning installation is expected to take another week to a week and a half to complete. During this work crews will be on ladders and directly outside your windows.

All residents' cooperation is greatly appreciated in this process.

三進式的分析如下：

➤ **最重要的主題句 (Topic Sentence)**：This notice is being sent out to advise all Palo Alto Central residents about the upcoming awning replacement work.

➢ **具體的細節 (Supporting details)**：

Starting date: Starting tomorrow, Friday May 15, 2014, Canvas Awning will be on-site painting the frames that are being recovered.

Type of work: Note that only the parts of the frames that are exposed will be painted.

Duration of work: The awning installation is expected to take another week to a week and a half to complete.

Impact of the work: During this work crews will be on ladders and directly outside your windows.

➢ **有力的總結 (Concluding thesis)**：All residents' cooperation is greatly appreciated in this process.

　　依照這樣三進式的分析方法來進行閱讀與寫作，就可慢慢建立清晰的構思條理。平常寫 email 時也可按照這樣的思維來建立三個簡單的步驟，如下文所示：

　　E-mail 三部曲：先說目的（重點）●●▶ 再談細節（細節）●●▶ 最後總結（結語）：

Dear ABC Online Customer:

We're writing to let you know the statement for your checking account ending in 7788 is now available online.

To see your statement, log on to www.ABC.com.

If you aren't enrolled in Paperless Statements and think you've received this message in error, please call our Customer Support Team immediately, using the phone number on the "Contact Us" page on ABC Online. Please do NOT reply directly to this automatically-generated e-mail message.

Sincerely,

Online Banking Team

　　本書所提出的寫作訣竅絕不是「紙上談兵」，而是可以實際運用在各式各樣的寫作需要上。為了進一步示範 Think English, Write English 的重要性，本書的第三部分將針對台灣學子必須面對的寫作挑戰，提出實際的建議。

Chapter

大學入學考試 作文訣竅應用

11

大學入學考試──英文作文試題介紹

大學入學考試目前共有「學科能力測驗」及「指定科目考試」兩種。

學科能力測驗（簡稱「學測」）包括國文、英文、數學、社會、自然五考科，旨在測驗考生是否具有接受大學教育的基本學科能力，是大學校系初步篩選學生的門檻。英文科測驗範圍包括高一、高二必修科目英文。英文作文占 20 分。

指定科目考試（簡稱「指考」）包括國文、英文、數學甲、數學乙、歷史、地理、公民與社會、物理、化學、生物十考科，旨在檢測考生是否具備校系要求的能力，是大學考試入學招生管道的主要依據。英文科測驗範圍包括高一、高二、高三必修科目英文，英文作文占 20 分。

不論學測或指考，英文作文的分數比重都相當高。因此，掌握英文作文高分絕對是勝出的關鍵。

本章將教你如何將之前所學的 G-S-G 三句話原則應用在大考英文作文中。

大學入學考試閱讀測驗中，經常會問到有關主題（general topic）、焦點（narrow focus），及主旨（main thesis）的問題。其次，跟隨焦點的特定細節（details）也常常是考題之一。因此在閱讀時要養成分析的習慣，對每一句話的功能及 G-S 或 S-G 的關連都要清楚的掌握：

The majority of Indian women wear <u>a red dot</u> between their eyebrows [Topic]. While it is generally taken as an indicator of their marital status, the practice is primarily related to the Hindu religion [Focus]. The dot goes by different names in different Hindi dialects [G on name], and "bindi" is the one that is most commonly known [S on name]. Traditionally, the dot carries no gender restriction[G on gender]: Men as well as women wear it [S on gender]. However, the tradition of men wearing it has faded in recent times, so nowadays we see a lot more women than men wearing one [Thesis].

1. **Why** did people in India start wearing a red dot on their forehead? (**Asking about the "purpose" → the focus**)

   (A) To indicate their social rank.　　(B) To show their religious belief.
   (C) To display their financial status.　(D) To highlight their family background.

   <u>The position of the bindi</u> [Topic] is standard: center of the forehead, close to the eyebrows [Focus]. It represents a third, or inner eye [S on position]. Hindu tradition holds that all people have three eyes [G on eyes]: The two outer ones are used for seeing the outside world, and the third one is there to focus inward toward God [S on eyes]. As such, <u>the dot signifies piety and serves as a constant reminder to keep God in the front of a believer's thoughts</u> [Thesis].

2. What is the significance of the third eye in Hindu tradition? (**Asking about "meaning of the third eye" → the thesis**)

   (A) To stay in harmony with nature.

   (B) To observe the outside world more clearly.

   (C) To pay respect to God.

   (D) To see things with a subjective view.

11.2 作文題目示範

學測考題：看圖說故事

我們可以用 G-S-G 三進法來描述每一張圖片，進而組成一篇有條理的文章。

說明：1. 依提示在「答案卷」上寫一篇英文作文。

2. 文長至少 120 個單詞（words）。

提示：請仔細觀察以下三幅連環圖片的內容，並想像第四幅圖片可能的發展，寫出一個涵蓋連環圖片內容並有完整結局的故事。

(102 年大學學測)

訣竅：每一幅圖都說三句話 → 活用 G-S-G 三進法

第一句：先鎖定主控點，交代圖中人事時地物的重點

第二句：選擇與情節相關的細節，具體描述

第三句：歸納所描述的細節，提出小結，以承接下圖

G ➡ John had a busy day.

S ➡ He was so tired that he threw himself on the MRT priority seat without paying attention to the old man standing in front of him.

G ➡ John felt uneasy but he chose to ignore the man in need.

G ➡ The next day John took a day off and played basketball with his friends.

S ➡ He accidentally fell onto the ground and broke his ankle bones.

G ➡ It really hurt and he had a terrible day!

G ➡ On the third day he had to take the MRT to school, even though he was on crutches.

S ➡ He got on the train slowly and looked for a priority seat. But the seat was taken by a young girl with a book in hands. John looked at her hoping that she would yield the seat. But the girl kept reading her book, ignoring him on crutches. Gs ➡ John was angry and frustrated [because it was really difficult to stand still with a broken foot]S.

G [Paragraph] ➡ He kept staring at the girl, but could not say anything.

G ➡ John thought about himself and his behavior in the past.

S ➡ He realized how self-centered he was when he chose to take the priority seat and ignored the old man in front of him. Gs ➡ He experienced the pain and frustration the old man might have had.

G [Paragraph] He said to himself: "I will yield the priority seat to anyone who is in need and pay more attention to people around me! I need to change!"

G Conclusion ➡ Wow, what a bright day he might have.

　　看圖説故事最適合用 G-S-G 三進原則來鋪陳，每一幅圖都可以發揮三句話原則，先點出圖中人事時地物的重點，然後描述與情節相關的細節，最後再提出歸納細節的小結，總結前圖，承接後圖。

寫作練功坊

題目一

廣告在我們生活中隨處可見。請寫一篇大約 120-150 字的短文，介紹一則令你印象深刻的電視或平面廣告。第一段描述該廣告的內容（如：主題、故事情節、音樂、畫面等），第二段說明該廣告令你印象深刻的原因。

　　請檢視以下這篇加了提示的範例，想一想是否已達到本書所教你的寫作要領，再仔細閱讀後面的寫作修改與建議。

> 　　Nowadays, there are lots of advertisements around us. Some of which are promoting the latest products of their companies. Some are advocating the recent campaigns. Among these ads, the most impressive one to me is a picture posted on the Internet a few months ago. In the middle of the picture sit a pale girl from a civil war country. People around her thumbs up, and the girl look at them with anxiety (any other details?).
>
> 　　When I first saw this ad, I just felt ironic and contradictory between the girl and those people. But after I read the interpretation, I fully understood what it meant (then, describe what it meant!). We (why 'we'?) are fortunate to live in democratic countries, while there are still lots of people living chaos (relation with the picture?). We often feel sympathy of their situation, so we give a "Like" on Facebook and send it to other people. Some people (other people? some people?) might think this action will help them (who are 'them'?) depart from the plight, but actually, it won't change anything. And what they (who are they?) really need is our concrete helps. (does this conclusion explains your feelings?)

下圖呈現的是美國某高中的全體學生每天進行各種活動的時間分配，請寫一篇至少 120 個單詞的英文作文。文分兩段，第一段描述該圖所呈現之特別現象；第二段請說明整體而言，你一天的時間分配與該高中全體學生的異同，並說明其理由。

（**103 年大學指考**）

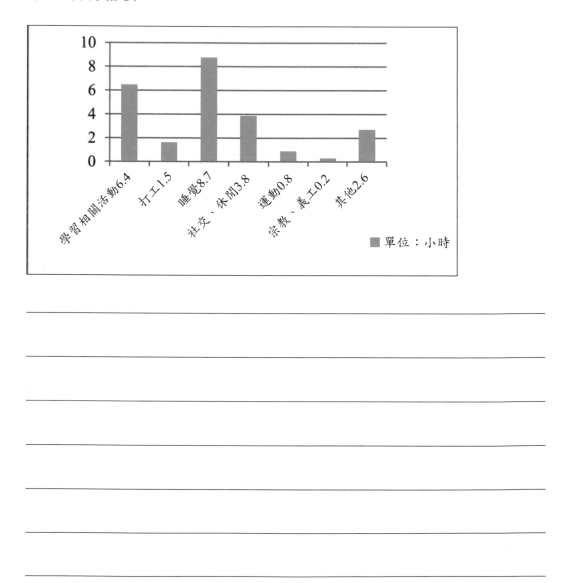

_____

_____

_____

_____

_____

_____

 寫作修理廠

本書「寫作修理廠」中所有的修正改寫都是依照三個原則進行：

1) 應用本書所強調的 G-S-G 三段式思考及寫作原則來做修正。

2) 盡量保留原文想要表達的意思，不另外添加，但是必要時會加上一些語句，使語意更為連結，更有條理。

3) 在語意可通，語法可行的前提下，盡量做最少量的修正。

題目一 修正與建議

問題分析

1. 中式寫法，重點和細節都沒有交代清楚：根據題目指示，第一段應該要描述畫面的內容（如：主題、故事情節、音樂、畫面等），但上文的第一段只有最後兩句和畫面有關，至於主題、情節、畫面的細節都沒有交代。

2. 第二段應該要交代印象深刻的原因，具體描述實際的感受，但上文只了說 "I fully understood what it meant"，卻沒有交代 "what it meant" 的實際內容。

3. 本文的重點是「令你」印象深刻的廣告，所以要以個人的感受為主，盡量以第一人稱 I 的角度來書寫。

修改建議

1. 依照 G-S-G 三進原則，第一段先破題並聚焦（topic sentence with a narrow focus），指出印象最深刻的畫面是什麼，然後描述具體細節（supporting details），再以綜合性的小結（thesis statement）承上起下，連接下一段。

2. 第二段也一樣，以三個 topic block 搭配 G-S-G 原則來寫三件事：a) 説明第一印象是什麼（the ironic contrast），b) 細談 contrast 的細節，解釋感受的具體內涵，c) 然後帶出另外一種 contrast 來作結論。

3. 慎用人稱代名詞：英文的嚴謹在於人稱觀點要保持一致，不要變來變去，一會兒 I，一會兒 we，一會兒 they。改變人稱代名詞時，都要先確定是否已充分指明對象。

Among all the visual stimuli I have seen, the most impressive one is a picture of a pale, helpless girl, sitting on a dirt-filled road [General topic with a narrow focus]. The picture was posted on the Internet a few months ago to promote peace talks [Specific details about where, when and why]. The little girl was surrounded by a group of war-ridden grown-ups who all had their thumbs up and smiled, but the little girl looked up to them with her puzzled eyes [Specific details about the picture]. I saw a face full of anxiety and uncertainty, in contrast to the jubilant adults [General sum-up of the impression].

The picture strikes me as an ironic contradiction between the girl and the surrounding adults [General impression with a narrow focus]. After I read the interpretation, I fully understood what it meant [Support of the focus]. The picture depicts civil war through the puzzled and fearful eyes of the little girl [General about what it meant]. She sees emptiness and cruelty in the military conflicts that are beyond her comprehension [Specific about what it meant]. As the adults were cheerful about winning a battle, the little girl seemed to question why there were wars in the first place [Sum-up of what it meant]. Besides what the little girl sees, I see another contrast in the picture [General introduction of another contrast]. I see how fortunate I am to live in a democratic country, while there are still lots of people living in chaos [Specifics about the contrast]. I felt sympathetic of their situation, so I gave a "Like" on Facebook and sent it to my friends [Specific consequent]. But "Likes" won't change anything; only concrete actions may change the plight of war [General conclusion]!

修正與建議

以下是一篇學生的寫作及修正。

G: According to the table, we know that the students in one American high school student how to assign their daily time in senior high school spend less time in learning than in other activities.

S: In their daily schedule, they only spend an average of 6.4 hours in learning-related activities but more than 8 hours in other activities, including part-time work, social and recreational events, sports and exercises, and community or religious services.

G: It This conforms to our image of American students in general.

S: We think that American students they tend to engage themselves more in extracurricular activities than studying time in studies.

G: All of our Such an idea about American students is from watching American movies and TV drama, and it comes close to what the chart shows. which influence us strongly.

G: My daily life is very different to from those of the American students in senior of high school because I am a Christian.

S1: My family and I spend a lot of time praying and reading the Bible every day.

S2: In addition, I usually pull an all-nighter stay late to prepare for exams, so that I have less time to sleep and do part-time jobs.

G: To sum up, it can be I am sure that American students have more flexible time to us than Taiwanese students. Hoping I hope we could I can have more extracurricular activities as the American students have one day.

According to the table, we know that the students in one American high school spend less time in learning than in other activities. In their daily schedule, they only spend an average of 6.4 hours in learning-related activities but more than 8 hours in other activities, including part-time work, social and recreational events, sports and exercises, and community or religious services. This conforms to our image of American students in general. We think that they tend to engage themselves more in extracurricular activities than in studies. Such an idea about American students is from watching American movies and TV drama, and it comes close to what the chart shows.

My daily life is very different from those of the American students because I am a Christian. My family and I spend a lot of time praying and reading the Bible every day. In addition, I usually stay late to prepare for exams, so I have less time to sleep and do part-time jobs. To sum up, I am sure that American students have more flexible time than Taiwanese students. I hope I can have more extracurricular activities as the American students have one day.

Chapter

TOEIC 寫作測驗訣竅應用

12

TOEIC 口說與寫作測驗介紹

TOEIC 口說與寫作測驗（TOEIC Speaking and Writing Tests）是一項職場中用來評估受試者是否具備有效英語溝通能力的檢定測驗。

寫作測驗共有三種題型，題數 8 題，測驗時間 60 分鐘，題目結構如下：

內　　容	題　數	作答時間	題目概要
Write a sentence based on a picture 描述照片	5	5 題共 8 分鐘	使用兩個指定單字（片語），造出與照片內容一致的句子。
Respond to a written request 回覆書面要求	2	每題 10 分鐘	閱讀 25～50 字左右的電子郵件後撰寫回信。
Write an opinion essay 陳述意見	1	30 分鐘	針對題目設定的議題，陳述意見並說明理由及例子作為佐證。

TOEIC 寫作測驗主要是評量考生職場寫作的能力，評分重點在文章的整體組織，使用文法是否允當正確，以及字彙的運用能力，由 ETS 認證的評分人員進行評分，評分級距及更多關於此項測驗的說明，請參考台灣區官方網站 www.toeic.com.tw。

本章將針對「回覆書面要求」及「陳述意見」兩大項考題，配合之前教授的 G-S-G 三句話原則，進行寫作技巧的指導與演練。

　　寫作構思的三句話法則，即 G-S-G 三進法，不只幫助寫作，同時也能夠增進閱讀能力。為什麼呢？因為 G-S-G 三進法是一個通則，放諸四海皆準。當你能夠使用 G-S-G 原則洞悉別人寫作的路程，就是幫助自己找到寫的途徑。那麼該從何開始呢？一般常見的閱讀測驗即是別人寫的作文，那麼別人是如何寫出閱讀測驗的文章呢？也是藉由 G-S-G 原則來完成。因此，以下我們將介紹各個考試當中所出現的閱讀測驗，來教你一一破解文章密碼！

　　首先，由於多益是用來測試商業英文的能力，因此可以發現，多益的閱讀包含 2 到 3 個問題，而考題本質通常也都與 G-S-G 三進法對應。舉例來說，商業書信溝通首重目的（purpose），因此非常多的題目會出現 "Why" or "What is the purpose of..."，通常這種題目的答案，都與主題句 （topic sentence）當中的焦點（narrow focus or controlling idea）相關，而明確的目的通常在主旨句中會進一步說明（thesis statement）。關於細節的許多題目像是 "What will...do?" 或是 "Who is...?" 等，探討人、事、時、地、物的問題，通常會在段落中間的特定細節找到答案（supporting details）。而關於事情的結果（outcome）、重要性（importance）、或意義（significance），以及事情後續的回應（expected response）等相關訊息，往往可以在最後的總結找到（final conclusion）。

例1

OFFICE MESSAGE

TO: Takashi Matsumoto
FROM: Karen Lang
TIME: 9:30, Thursday

(Telephone)　　Fax　　Office Visit

MESSAGE:
Karen Lang from C&P Accounting called [Topic sentence]. She wants to arrange a new meeting time with you [Thesis statement]. Instead of on Monday at 11, can you see her on Tuesday at 1:30 [Detail about time]? She'll be able to go over the contract with you then [Detail about what to do]. She'll try to contact you again this afternoon. [Conclusion: what to be expected]

Taken By: Mike Nguyen

---

1. **Why** did Ms. Lang call Mr. Matsumoto? （Asking "why" ➡ 目的 / 重點）

    (A) To reschedule an appointment with him

    (B) To ask if he will be able to meet a deadline

    (C) To inquire where a meeting will take place

    (D) To request that he send a new contract

2. **What** will Ms. Lang probably do? （Asking "what to expect " ➡ 結果 / 結語）

    (A) See Mr. Matsumoto on Monday

    (B) Call Mr. Matsumoto again this afternoon

    (C) Contact a representative at C&P Accounting

    (D) Make a reservation for a lunch meeting

例2

Northwood Community Center

March Employee of the Month

Emplyee: Linda Ahn
Classes: Watercolor Painting
            Pen and Ink Drawing
Interests: Photography

Art Instructor Linda Ahn is one of the most popular figures at our community center `Topic with a narrow focus` . She teaches on Tuesday and Saturday mornings and Thursday nights `Detail about time` , and her classes are usually filled to capacity `Detail about popularity` . In May, she is going to start teaching an afternoon beginner's drawing class on Mondays and Wednesdays `Thesis: a new class` . She has added a great dimension to our center `Conclusion` .

---

1. What is **the purpose** of the information? (Asking about the "purpose" ➡ Topic / title)

    (A) To publicize the opening of a community center

    (B) To explain some painting techniques

    (C) To advertise a gallery exhibit

    (D) To describe an employee

2. **On what day** of the week does Linda Ahn teach an evening class? (Asking about time detail)

(A) On Monday

(B) On Tuesday

(C) On Wednesday

(D) On Thursday

3. According to the information, **what will happen** in May? (Asking about the main event / thesis)

(A) A new employee will start working.

(B) An afternoon class will begin.

(C) The building will close for renovations.

(D) Enrollment for classes will resume.

(TOEIC Official Test-Preparation Guide)

12.2 作文題目示範

Directions: Read the question below. You have 30 minutes to plan, write, and revise your essay. Typically, an effective response will contain a minimum of 300 words.

There are many ways to find a job: newspaper advertisements, Internet job search websites, and personal recommendations. What do you think is the best way to find a job? Give reasons or examples to support your opinion.

(TOEIC Online Writing Sample Test)

Sample answer:

提示：構思的方法可運用前面所學的 **G-S-G** 鋪陳法來發揮：

G-Topic S with focus:

Internet job websites are the most useful way for finding a job.

3 Further elaboration:

They provide easy and convenient accesses to job opportunities in numerous fields and offer detailed information about the job requirement.

G-Thesis statement:

Making the best use of modern technology, job websites are innovative and effective in helping job seekers to locate a job of their interests.

An example:

G-Topic S: One of the most famous job websites in Taiwan is XYZ Human Resource Bank, which has helped many of my friends find their ideal jobs.

S- The website has a huge database about job openings for over 30 different professions. It allows a user to specify the type of job, the location, and the position sought with a simple search function. A list of jobs with detailed descriptions will pop out for further selection.

G- XYZ helps to connect the job seekers and the job providers directly. The application process may begin by just pressing a button "Apply".

Reasons:

G- Internet job websites have several advantages over the traditional ways of finding jobs.

S_1- They are faster and more efficient than newspapers as they offer search functions for pre-sorted categories of information. **S_2-**They are more open and reliable than personal connections since they do not rely on relational factors. **S_3-** With a user-friendly design, they may also alleviate some of the anxieties a job seeker may have.

G- Given all the advantages, I will certainly go to an Internet website such as XYZ if I need a job in the future.

Conclusion

G- Internet websites are the fastest way to access the widest selections of job opportunities.

S- The are quick, easy, inexpensive, efficient and fair to all users.

G- In this digital age, I am sure Internet job sites will become the most popular aid for finding jobs.

以下將針對 TOEIC 考題中讀寫的部分做深入的分析，將台灣學生常出現的問題找出來，並提出修正建議。希望透過明確的修改建議，讓讀者體會到寫作時該有的考量，並建立有條不紊的寫作習慣。

1. 回覆書面要求

　　這種類型的題目通常會提供一封來信，然後要求針對來信中所提出的問題或請求，寫出一封書面回覆。寫作的訣竅是先掌握來信的目的與主旨，然後針對題目的指示，按照 G-S-G 三進原則來構思回答：

題目一

In this part of the test, you will show how well you can write a response to an e-mail. Your response will be scored on

• the quality and variety of our sentences

• vocabulary

• organization

Directions: Read the e-mail below.

From: J. Rice
To: H. Garner
Subject: Computer problems
Sent: March 17, 8:30 A.M.
Hello Mr. Garner,
I am still unable to use my computer. I have not been able to get any help from the technical help group. As a manager, would you be able to get me help more quickly?
Thank you,
James Rice

Directions: Respond to the e-mail as if you are Mr. Rice's manager. In your e-mail, describe ONE thing you are doing to help and ask TWO questions.

以下提供一篇寫作範例。請檢視這篇範例回覆，看一看有什麼問題，想一想是否已達到本書所教的寫作要領，然後再參考後面的寫作修改與建議。

From: H. Garner
To: J. Rice
Subject: Respond about computer problems
Sent: March 18, 10:30 A.M.
Dear James Rice, Thank you for the incoming letter. I am writing on behalf of our technical help group to express our deeply apology for causing the inconvenience. Our technical group spends three days finding compatible system with your computer but unfortunately failed. We guess that you may be able to install inappropriate software or download illegally so that you can't turn on your monitor, isn't it? Now, we've deleted all the software and re-install it and make sure there's no problem with it. And, if there's a warning happened on web page, please let us know. Thank you, Garner.

In this part of the test, you will show how well you can write a response to an e-mail. Your response will be scored on

• the quality and variety of our sentences

• vocabulary

• organization

Directions: Read the e-mail below.

From: J. Mason
To: F. Carvajal
Subject: Problem during your stay
Sent: February 16, 3:17 P.M.
Dear F. Carvajal, We understand that you experienced some problems during your recent stay at Summit Hotel. We regret any inconvenience to you and would like to make sure that these problems don't happen again. Could you please describe the problems that you experienced? John Mason Manager, Summit Hotel

Directions: Respond to the e-mail. In your e-mail, describe TWO problems you had during your hotel stay and make ONE suggestion.

以下提供一篇寫作範例。請檢視這篇範例回覆，想一想是否已達到本書所教的寫作要領，然後再參考後面的寫作修改與建議。

From: F. Carvajal
To: J. Mason
Subject: Re: Problem during your stay
Sent: February 17, 5:17 P.M.
Dear Mason, 　　I would like to identify two problems during the accommodation in the Summit Hotel. Firstly, when I got into the room, I found it was totally different from my reservation. My request was the magnificent sea view, but the scenery, in reality, was full of skyscrapers and advertisements. Moreover, some disposable toothbrushes and combs were used. The housekeep didn't check thoroughly on the condition of these consumables. Although it was an unpleasant experience in staying in the hotel, I would like to give one suggestion. It would be much better if the employee help customer check on the details of the reservation and some requests of client before they checked in. Keep up and good work. Carvajal

寫作修理廠

題目一 修正與建議

| From: H. Garner |
| To: J. Rice |
| Subject: Respond about computer problems |
| Sent: March 18, 10:30 A.M. |

Dear James ~~Rice~~,

    Thank you for your ~~incoming~~ letter regarding your computer problems. I am writing on behalf of our technical help group to express our deep~~ly~~ apology for causing ~~the~~any inconvenience and to let you know what we have been doing. Our technical group ~~spends~~has spent three days trying to find~~ing~~ a compatible system with your computer but unfortunately all the efforts failed. ~~We guess that you may be able to install inappropriate software or download illegally so that you can't turn on your monitor, isn't it? Now, we've deleted all the software and re-install it and make sure there's no problem with it. And, if there's a warning happened on web page, please let us know.~~

    In order for us to offer help more quickly and effectively, I would appreciate your answers to the following TWO questions:

1) Have you installed anything inappropriately or download any illegal software?
2) Was there any noise when you tried to turn on the computer?

    Once I get more information from you, I will decide what to do next and contact you within the next 24 hours.

Thank you for your patience and cooperation!
H. Garner
Manager

修改說明

1. 信件開頭如何稱呼收信者？較親近自在的，可用 Dear + First name (Dear James)；較客氣正式的，可用 Dear + Title + Last name (Dear Mr. Rice)。

2. 第一句話要把 topic 定義清楚，信件回覆是有關電腦的問題。

3. 第二句要把目的說清楚，不僅要道歉，也要說明已經做了什麼。

4. 按照題目要求，必須提出兩個問題，因此可針對顧客的希望（to get help more quickly），明確地把問題提出來。

5. 回覆顧客的信要客氣婉轉（多用些詞：I would appreciate it if you can...），答覆要盡量明確肯定（I will ... within the next 24 hours），最後的致謝也是禮多人不怪（Thank you for your patience and cooperation）。

6. 依照 G-S-G 法則，TOEIC 書面回覆的內容結構大致如下：

前言：感謝或問候：Thank you for your....

主體：G- 言明主旨目的：I am writing to.... 或 I would like to....

S- 交代相關細節：Who has done what? When, where and why?

What happened was.... 或 It is found that....

G- 給予承諾或要求：I will.... 或 Could you please....

結語：道歉、致謝，或等待回音

修改後版本

Dear James,

Thank you for your letter regarding your computer problems. I am writing on behalf of our technical help group to express our deep apology for causing any inconvenience and to let you know what we have been doing. Our technical group has spent three days trying to find a compatible system with your computer but unfortunately all the efforts failed.

In order for us to offer help more quickly and effectively, I would appreciate your answers to the following TWO questions:

1) Have you installed anything inappropriately or download any illegal software?

2) Was there any noise when you tried to turn on the computer?

Once I get more information from you, I will decide what to do next and contact you within the next 24 hours.

Thank you for your patience and cooperation!

H. Garner

Manager

題目二 修正與建議

Dear Mr. Mason,

Thank you for your inquiry about the problems I experienced during my stay at Summit Hotel. I would like to identify two major problems. ~~during the accommodation in the Summit Hotel.~~ Firstly, ~~when I got into the room,~~ the room I had was totally different from ~~my reservation~~ what I had made reservation for. My request was a room with the magnificent sea view, but my room was not facing the sea and the only scenery, in reality, was full of skyscrapers and advertisements. ~~Moreover~~ Secondly, I found that some disposable toothbrushes and combs you provided were actually used and left unchanged. The housekeeper didn't check ~~thoroughly on~~ the conditions of these consumables thoroughly. It was truly disappointing to see used stuff in the room.

修改說明

1. 一開始還是要禮貌的感謝來信詢問，然後陳述問題。
2. 重點先講，言明問題有兩個，作為有力的 general statement。
3. 客觀描述問題時，可直接用 the room I had 作主詞；要把問題說清楚，因此加了一句：The room was not facing the sea.
4. 有兩個問題，既然用了 firstly，就要用 secondly。
5. 描述第二個問題時，也要儘量說清楚，因此加了幾個字：The disposables you provided were actually used and left unchanged.
6. 注意 G-S-G 法則，最後還是有一個 general 的結語。

~~Although~~ It was indeed an unpleasant experience to stay in the hotel, and I would like to give one suggestion: It would be much better if ~~the~~ your employees can ~~help customer~~ check on the details of the reservation and clean the room carefully before clients check in.

~~Keep up and good work.~~ Thank you for taking note of the two problems!
Carvajal

1. 因為要明確指出（assert）這是不愉快的經驗，所以用主要子句，不能放在附屬子句當作背景資訊。

2. 提出的建議也要明確完整，既然有兩件事，最好建議中都要提到。

3. 最後的結語，再次禮貌的謝謝對方關注這兩件事。

修改後版本

Dear Mr. Mason,

Thank you for your inquiry about the problems I experienced during my stay at Summit Hotel. I would like to identify two major problems. Firstly, the room I had was totally different from what I had made reservation for. My request was a room with the magnificent sea view, but my room was not facing the sea and the only scenery, in reality, was full of skyscrapers and advertisements. Secondly, I found that some disposable toothbrushes and combs you provided were actually used and left unchanged. The housekeeper didn't check the conditions of these consumables thoroughly. It was truly disappointing to see used stuff in the room.

It was indeed an unpleasant experience to stay in the hotel, and I would like to give one suggestion: It would be much better if your employees can check on the details of the reservation and clean the room carefully before clients check in.

Thank you for taking note of the two problems!

Carvajal

2. 陳述意見

　　這個部分要寫的是較為正式、說理性質的短文。需要切實運用 G-S-G 三進原則來陳述意見，有清楚的主控觀點（controlling idea）、明確簡潔的主旨（thesis）、有力的支持例證（supporting details），以及呼應主旨的結論（conclusion）。

題目一

In this part of the test, you will write an essay in response to a question that asks you to state, explain, and support your opinion on an issue. Typically an effective essay will contain a minimum of 300 words. Your response will be scored on

· whether your opinion is supported with reasons and/or examples

· grammar

· vocabulary

· organization

Question: Think about a job you have had or would like to have. In your opinion, what are the most important characteristics that you and the people you work with should possess to be successful in that job? Use reasons and specific examples to illustrate why these characteristics are important.

請檢視以下這篇範例，想一想是否已達到本書所教你的寫作要領，再閱讀後面的寫作修改與建議。

Traits of a Successful Engineer

"What makes an engineer successful?" In the modern edge, people would like to know the answer of the question because the professional knowledge is just the prerequisite to be successful. Unlike the engineer in the past, collaborating with colleague in different background and thinking independently would be the two critical characteristics to be successful.

In the brand-new world, cooperating with others become a crucial trait to be successful. A new product, such as a machine tool or tablet PC, require a lot of people with different background to cooperate with each other. Take me for example, I have experience in cooperating with a company to design a new machine tool. During the period of cooperation, I, as a graduate student, have to communicate with both the engineers in different departments. I have to assure the design of machine tool match the request of R&D department and it can be manufactured by the workpeople. It's significant to realize both the need and limitation of product by communicating with people in different departments.

Another feature to be successful may be thinking independently. According to Kuo, Ciou-Tsung, the personnel directive of UMC, a company requires the people who could think independently as the practical skills, such as operating a machine or typing minutes, could all be trained, but it difficult to train a person "think" independently. A man thinking independently means he could identify the problem and get a solution. Moreover, it also means the start of innovation since when he starts thinking the defects of product, it makes the product progressive.

In the changeable world, abundant knowledge would not be the only element leading an engineer to the success. The newest technology may be outdated soon due to the fact pace of innovation. However, collaborating with others and thinking independently are, undoubtedly, the two characteristics making an engineer successful.

寫作修理廠

修改建議

Traits of a Successful Engineer

"What makes an engineer successful?" ~~In the modern edge~~age, People like me would like to know the answer to the question because ~~the professional knowledge is just the prerequisite to be successful~~ it requires more than professional knowledge to succeed in the industrial world. Unlike the engineers in the past who could work on their own, in the modern age, collaborating with colleagues ~~in~~ from different backgrounds and thinking independently would be the two critical characteristics to be a successful engineer.

修改說明

1. 一開始的問題並不是每個人都要問的，而是工程業界的人才想問的，因此要避免用籠統的 people。

2. 過去的工程師和現在有什麼不同？要稍加說明，因此加上關係子句說明。

3. 最後一句將過去和現在做對照，藉此表達主旨（thesis statement）。

In the ~~brand-new~~fast-changing and highly specialized world, cooperating with others becomes a crucial trait ~~to be successful~~ for engineers. A new product, such as a machine tool or tablet PC, requires ~~a lot of~~ a group of people with different backgrounds to cooperate with each other. Take ~~me~~ my work for example, I have ~~experiences in cooperating~~ cooperated with a company to design a new machine tool. During the period of cooperation, I, as a graduate student, ~~have~~had to communicate with both the engineers in different departments. I ~~have~~had to ~~assure~~make sure the design of the machine tool match the request of the R&D department and it can be manufactured by the ~~workpeople~~production line. It~~'s~~ is ~~significant~~ important to ~~realize~~ understand both the needs and the limitations of the product by communicating with people in different ~~departments~~fields. Thus, teamwork is crucial in the job of an engineer.

1. 這一段有一些用詞的問題：形容詞的選擇要貼切主語，a brand-new world 是指一個全新的世界，文意不通，所以改為 fast changing and highly specialized；a lot of people 太過廣泛，改為 a group of people；動詞的使用要形意相符，realize 是指頓時的瞭悟發現，並非持久的理解 understand。
2. 既然是談工作，舉例時最好用工作經歷做例子，而非自己這個人。
3. 時態也要注意，談過去的工作經驗就要用過去式。
4. 同樣的詞組要避免重複使用，in different departments 可改為 in different fields、in various departments 或 with different expertise。
5. 回到 G-S-G 法則，最後一句最好有個段落的總結。

Another feature ~~to be successful~~ of a successful engineer ~~may be~~ is thinking independently. According to Kuo, Ciou-Tsung, the personnel directive of UMC, a company ~~requires~~needs ~~the people~~ employees who ~~could~~ can think independently. ~~as the~~ Practical skills, such as operating a machine or typing minutes, could all be trained, but it is difficult to train a person to "think" independently. ~~A man~~ An engineer who thinks~~ing~~ independently means he or she ~~could~~can identify the problem and get a solution. Moreover, it also means the start of a possible innovation since ~~when he starts thinking~~ a solution to the defects of a product ~~to makes the product progressive~~ may lead to a new improvement.

1. 要注意語意的關連：要談的另一個特性是成功工程師所具備的，是所有關係：a feature of a successful engineer，而非不定修飾：a feature to be successful（✘）。
2. 用詞的精準要加強：有關主旨的論述要肯定明確，既然認定有兩項特質，就要確定的說出來，用 is，而不是 may be；動詞 require 是要求某人做某事，後面接要求去做的事。
3. 公司需要什麼樣的員工，用 employee 比泛指 people 來得精準。
4. 獨立思考可促成產品的改進，整句話的鋪陳可以更客觀有力！

~~In the changeable world~~ In the field of engineering, **abundant knowledge** ~~would~~ may **not be the only element leading** ~~an engineer to the~~ **to success.** The professional expertise of an engineer should also include teamwork and problem-solving skills. No matter how fast t**he newest technology** may develop, ~~be outdated soon due to the fact~~fast pace of innovation. ~~However,~~ collaborating with others and thinking independently are, undoubtedly, the two important **characteristics** ~~making an engineer successful.~~ required of a successful engineer.

修改說明

1. 整篇文章中用了好幾次 In the ＿＿＿ world，為了避免重複，並且強化語意關連，可改為更精準更相關的範圍設定，如：In the field of engineering。

2. 中間加了一句話 The professional expertise should include...，使前後的語意更為連接，既然 knowledge 不是唯一的要素，那什麼是必要的呢？

3. 最後的轉折要有清楚的關連：在迅速改變的科技發展中，重要的人才特質顯然不外所談的兩項，結語再次呼應首段的主旨！

修改後版本

Traits of a Successful Engineer

"What makes an engineer successful?" People like me would like to know the answer to the question because it requires more than professional knowledge to succeed in the industrial world. Unlike engineers in the past who could work on their own, in the modern age, collaborating with colleagues with different backgrounds and thinking independently would be the two critical characteristics to be a successful engineer.

In the fast-changing and highly specialized world, cooperating with others becomes a crucial trait for engineers. A new product, such as a machine tool or tablet PC, requires a group of people with different backgrounds to cooperate with each other. Take my work for example, I have cooperated with a company to design a new machine tool. During the period of cooperation, I, as a graduate student, had to communicate with the engineers in different departments. I had to make sure the design of the machine tool match the request of the R&D department and it can be manufactured by the production line. It is important to understand both the needs and the limitations of the product by communicating with people in different fields. Thus, teamwork is crucial in the job of an engineer.

Another feature of a successful engineer is thinking independently. According to Kuo, Ciou-Tsung, the personnel directive of UMC, a company needs employees who can think independently. Practical skills, such as operating a machine or typing minutes, could be trained, but it is difficult to train a person to "think" independently. An engineer who thinks independently means he or she can identify the problem and get a solution. Moreover, it also means the start of a possible innovation since a solution to the defects of a product may lead to a new improvement.

In the field of engineering, abundant knowledge may not be the only element leading to success. The professional expertise of an engineer should also include teamwork and problem-solving skills. No matter how fast the newest technology may develop, collaborating with others and thinking independently are, undoubtedly, the two important characteristics required of a successful engineer.

Chapter 13

TOEFL / SAT 作文訣竅應用

TOEFL / SAT 測驗介紹

「托福」測驗（Test of English as a Foreign Language, TOEFL）旨在測試母語非英語者之英語能力，如果想申請美加地區大學或研究所，「托福」成績單是必備文件之一。

「托福」網路測驗（TOEFL iBT）是經由網際網路方式進行，測驗項目包含：閱讀（Reading）、聽力（Listening）、口說（Speaking）及寫作（Writing）。每項分數 30 分，總分 120 分。每個項目至少需作答一題才計分，寫作只能以打字方式完成。

SAT（Scholastic Assessment Tests）測驗是由美國大學委員會（The College Board，大約 4,300 所美國大學共同組成的文教組織）委託教育測驗服務（Educational Testing Service，簡稱 ETS）定期舉辦的世界性測驗，做為美國各大學申請入學的重要參考條件之一。

SAT 測驗分為 SAT Reasoning Test 和 SAT Subject Test 兩種。SAT Reasoning Test 共有三個單元，包含寫作（Writing）、數理（Mathematics）與批判性閱讀（Critical Reading）。

寫作（Writing）

測驗型態	測驗範圍	應試時間
作文（25 分鐘）、選擇題（35 分鐘）	文法、應用、字彙	60 分鐘

即使 TOEFL 或 SAT 的寫作篇幅都較長，還是可以運用 G-S-G 的原則來鋪陳一篇架構完整的文章，本章將以這兩項測驗的範例來詳加說明。

在托福閱讀考題中，我們觀察到，G-S-G 法則也適用於分析托福的閱讀段落。下列的敘述中，有一個清楚的條理：每一個概括（general）的論點出現時，後面必然緊接出現一個細節（specific detail）來支持，運用 G-S 互補的原則來鋪陳：

Meteorite Impact and Dinosaur Extinction

There is increasing evidence that the impacts of meteorites [Topic] have had important effects on Earth [Focus] [G], particularly in the field of biological evolution [S]. Such impacts continue to pose a natural hazard to life on Earth [Thesis] [G]. Twice in the twentieth century, large meteorite objects are known to have collided with Earth [Support] [S] .

If an impact is large enough, it can disturb the environment of the entire Earth and cause an ecological catastrophe [G]. The best-documented such impact took place 65 million years ago at the end of the Cretaceous period of geological history [Example] [S]. This break in Earth's history is marked by a mass extinction [G], when as many as half the species on the planet became extinct [S]....

(TOEFL iBT online Sample Questions)

在 SAT 考試中，閱讀測驗被稱為 Critical Reading，因為閱讀就是牽涉到條理的思辨。以下是一份 SAT 的短文，文章的內容清楚呈現 G-S-G 的條理，由 Topic 加上 narrow focus，到 Supporting details，再到 Thesis，顯示出緊湊的關連：

While many rivers have long been utilized and harnessed by the people near them, **the Mekong River** （湄公河） [Topic], though it snakes through five countries in Southeast Asia, has eluded human control until recent times [Narrow focus]. [Why?] The narrow water level in dry seasons impedes travel down the river [Reason 1], as does the Mekong's habit of splitting into wide networks of smaller channels [Specifics for reason 1]. Annual flooding during the monsoon season thwarts attempts at long-term agriculture [Reason 2]. But in recent years, modern technology and a burgeoning human population have begun to encroach upon the Mekong's independence `Recent change`. <u>Soon the Mekong may be as readily manipulated as many of its peers around the world</u> `Thesis`.

1. The author's use of personification in lines 2-4 portrays the Mekong River as

   (A) Willfully independent

   (B) Monumentally important

   (C) Inherently destructive

   (D) Sublimely sacred

   (E) Uniquely situated

2. The reference to "annual flooding" in lines 8-9 serves to

   (A) Provide supporting evidence for a prior assertion

   (B) Resolve the conflict between two points of view

   (C) Confirm the impracticality of technological innovation

   (D) Analyze the veracity of the author's argument

   (E) Support the argument against the river's development

這兩個題目,剛好針對「主題焦點」的內容與「具體細節」的內容來出題。第一句的主要子句就為全篇定調,點出主題(湄公河)與主控點(逃脫控制直到近年),指出湄公河一直逍遙自由,直到近年才開始被開發利用。接著就解釋湄公河因水域狹窄,又連年犯濫,因此過去很少開發,但由於近年科技發達,人口增加,它也難逃像其他河川一樣被利用開發的命運。

問題 1 是問作者對湄公河的擬人化寫法,把他描述成什麼?
答案是 (A) Willfully independent,因它過去一直不受控制。

問題 2 是直接問第 8~9 行提到湄公河每年氾濫成災,其用意是什麼?
答案是 (A) Provide supporting evidence for a prior assertion,支持前一句的論點:eluded human control until recent times.

Some students like to take distance-learning courses by computer. Other students prefer to study in traditional classroom settings with a teacher. Consider the advantages of both options, and make an argument for the way that students should organize their schedules.

（摘自 Barron's TOEFL iBT）

G-Topic S with a controlling idea:

Learning may be done in different ways. Distance-learning and traditional classroom instruction may have different advantages and both serve to facilitate learning.

S- Further elaboration:

Distance-learning allows a more flexible and convenient schedule while classroom instruction allows more face-to-face interaction.

G-Thesis statement:

Both options require the students to organize their schedules appropriately and make sure they are actively involved in either settings.

Advantages of distance learning:

G- Distance learning is innovative in utilizing modern technology.

S_1- It provides a convenient less-costly access to instruction with the use of computers.

S_2- Learning can be done in any place, at any time, with any participants.

G- It facilitates learning in a learner-centered setting that overcomes the limitations of traditional classrooms.

Advantages about classroom instruction:

G- Classroom instruction is done in a more humanistic way.

S- It allows students to directly interact with the teacher and enhances the personal connection to both sides.

G- Though students are confined in a classroom, they may focus more on the subject, engage more in discussion without being distracted easily.

Conclusion

G- Given the advantages of both options, the most important lesson for a student is to organize the schedules in a manageable and fulfilling way.

S₁- Some classes may be effective with distance learning such as general lectures while other courses may require more classroom instruction such as art or manual creations.

S₂- Availability is also a factor that needs to be taken into consideration.

G- The best way of learning is to tailor one's needs with a wise selection of courses and a easy-to-manage schedule.

題目一

Think carefully about the issue presented in the following excerpt and the assignment below.

> Some people like to live by the old expression, "If you can't say anything nice, don't say anything at all." This expression reflects the widely shared belief that one should always try to be polite and to have consideration for another person's feelings. While such an approach may make it easier to get along with people, no real relationship can truly thrive unless it is built on a solid foundation of truth.

Assignment: Is it more important to avoid hurting people's feelings or to tell the truth? Plan and write an essay in which you develop your point of view on this issue. Support your position with reasoning and examples taken from your reading, studies, experience, or observations. (200 words)

請檢視以下這篇範例,想一想是否已達到本書所教你的寫作要領,再閱讀後面的寫作修改與建議。

　　"Should I tell him/her the truth?" Similar questions pop up in our mind all the time. While some hold the opinion that people should always be considerate, others may believe being able to tell someone the ugly truth is the very essence of a real relationship. For such dilemma, I argue that we should consider the possible effects of telling the truth, and do what could benefit the person you are thinking if you should tell the truth to.

　　The possible effects of telling the truth can be extremely complex, but it will be easier if we put others' benefit into consideration. For most people, they prefer not to tell the truth simply because they are afraid people who are told the truth will start to hate them. While this, indeed, happens a lot, but if we believe telling people the truth will benefit them in the long run, we should do it.

Take myself as an example. When in high school, I participated in a student research project about Taiwanese pop music, and my research instructor didn't give me any opinion throughout, but kept telling me I had done a great job. I believed him, assuming I would certainly get tons of positive feedback after I published the research essay. Later, I showed my essay to another teacher who told me she was interested in the topic and would also like to take a look at the research essay I was working on. She went over my essay and told she would like to have an appointment with me discussing the essay. During our meeting, she pointed out I should have organized my essay in a more direct and simple way to make it clearer, and that a couple of sentences and words could be ambiguous to the reader. She even also marked the logical fallacies she was aware of.

While I had a hard time accepting it as she was painstakingly showing me the defects of my essay. Now, looking in retrospect, I have to admit that not until that very moment did I realize the research essay I was so proud of actually contained many mistakes and there were large room for improvement. Her constructive criticism had benefitted me significantly, and the "ugly truth" she revealed made me convinced that sometimes, telling truth to someone can be of true importance, especially when that someone being told the truth can benefit from learning the truth. If there hadn't been a teacher that tried to tell me the truth, I would not have been able to learn that much from the research for sure.

In his famous inspirational commencement address at Stanford, Steve Jobs confessed as he recounted the painful memory of being fired from Apple, "It was awful tasting medicine, but I guess the patient needed it." Similarly, the ugly truths people don't welcome can be, in fact, important, or even necessary, medicine for them because they might have a disease—things they can improve—that needs to be treated. Therefore, if, after careful consideration, we still believe that telling the truth can be beneficial, we are supposed to do it, despite the bad feeling that people might have.

Think carefully about the issue presented in the following excerpt and the assignment below.

> Identifying with a group makes people feel secure with and trust one another because of what they have in common. They might share the same interests, language, beliefs, ethnicity, or cultural background. However, by limiting their identities to a specific group, people may miss important opportunities to connect with and understand others.

Assignment: Should people focus on enjoying the present moment instead of following a plan for future achievement? Plan and write an essay in which you develop your point of view on this issue. Support your position with reasoning and examples taken from your reading, studies, experience, or observations. (200 words)

請檢視以下這篇範例，想一想是否已達到本書所教你的寫作要領，再閱讀後面的寫作修改與建議。

In Renaissance England, "yourself" carried more meaning than it does today. As we can see in many Shakespearean plays, in addition to serving as a reflexive pronoun, it also referred to the best possible potential one was expected to realize. Although such characteristic has disappeared in modern English, I argue that to live out "ourselves", or to reach our self-actualization, as most people might have put it since Goldstein, people should follow a plan for a better future that is closer to our own dreams.

I was admitted to an English Instruction department three years ago, but I have decided to make some changes after learning that staying in this department cannot really satisfy me. When I was a freshman, I took a Western literature class, in which I got a chance to engage myself in the literary pieces from the ancient world to early modernity, from the Bible and Homer to Dante and to Cervante's Don Quixote. While the education program as well as the core subjects related to English instruction didn't interest me, I enjoyed myself analyzing literary texts, contemplating on the social and cultural issues reflected in the texts and thinking over the significance that lies between the lines. It is certainly that I can stay in the English Instruction department, keeping taking the classes that aren't really interesting to me. The classmates are nice; the professors are helpful and friendly. However, owing to my indelible passion toward literature, I manage to transfer to other literature-based English departments, such as those in NTU and NCCU.

After the decision is made, I left the group of people I know very well. I wrote email to completely unfamiliar professors, hoping they could grant me the permission to audit the classes. Later, even though I got to sit in literature classes in NTU and NCCU, I was surrounded by a group of complete strangers that seemed to know one another very well. It was scary. It was intimidating. Nonetheless, as the class proceeded, the anxiety of trying to blend into a new environment was replaced by the euphoria brought by literature. I am not sure if I can successfully be admitted to another school, but I am sure I have benefitted a lot during the process of trying to stick to the plan for future achievement—I got to meet new groups of people and make friends them, and to explore deeper in the study field of literature, discussing with the teachers and fellow classmates about the pieces we had read, all of which were unlikely if I had not been trying to take action pursuing my own goal.

Staying away from our comfort zones is hard. Being willing to sacrifice in order to stick to our plans for our own dreams can be even harder. Whenever I feel exhausted and depressed while pursuing my personal goal, I thought of Dante. "Midway along the journey of our life / I woke to find myself in a dark wood, / for I had wandered off from the straight path." Thus he opens the Comedy, a fictional spiritual journey that made his name supreme among the authors of world literature. Giving up enjoying the present moment, from some people's perspective, means going astray. However, all the wanderings, according to Dante, with firm belief and clear mind, lead to eternity. Only by undergoing all the hardships can we truly be "ourselves"—those that have reached the fullest potential we have.

修正與建議

"Should I tell ~~him/her~~ the truth?" Similar questions pop up in our minds all the time (Topic S). While some hold the opinion that people should always be considerate and say something nice, others may believe being able to tell someone the ~~ugly~~ truth is the very essence of a real relationship. For such a dilemma, I argue that we should consider the possible ~~effects~~ consequence of telling the truth, and ~~what could benefit the person you are thinking if you should tell the truth to~~ what is to the best interest of the person who may need the truth even though it may not be welcome.

第一句以問句破題，頗有巧思；最後一句點出主旨句（thesis statement），但語意要完整、清楚、明確。同時前後要保持一致的人稱：our minds... we，不可再變成原句中的 you。

The possible effects of telling the truth can be extremely complex, but it will be easier if we ~~put~~ take others' benefit into consideration. For most people, they prefer not to tell the truth simply because they are afraid ~~people (who?)~~ ~~who are told the truth will start to hate~~ ~~them(who?)~~ of being hated or treated with hostility. While this, indeed, happens a lot, ~~but~~ we should still do it if we believe telling ~~people~~ someone the truth will benefit them in the long run~~, we should do it~~.

第二、三段應就主旨句加以申論。本段一開始就明確定調，以 topic sentence 點出重點：The effect may be complex, but it will be easier if...，接著應解釋為何 complex，又為何會 easier？

Take myself as an example. ~~When~~ In high school, I participated in a student research project about Taiwanese pop music, and my research instructor didn't give me any negative opinion throughout the whole time. He kept telling me I had done a great job. I believed him, assuming I would certainly get tons of positive feedback after I published the research essay. Later, I showed my essay to another teacher who told me she was interested in the topic and would also like to take a look at the research essay I was working on. She went over my essay and told me that she would like to have an appointment with me ~~discussing~~ to discuss the essay. During our meeting, she pointed out several problems of my writing (G). She said that I should have organized my essay in a more direct and simple way to make it more clearer, and that a couple of sentences and words ~~could~~ may be ambiguous to the reader (S1). She even ~~also marked~~ commented on the logical fallacies she was aware of (S2). The harsh truth was indeed undesirable, but definitely beneficial to me! (G)

本段以自己為例，詳細描述個人的相關經歷。有細節、有例證，但仍要注意 **G-S-G** 的鋪陳方式，結尾最好加上一句總結。

I had a hard time accepting the truth that there are so many defects of my essay, as ~~she~~ the teacher （代名詞離所代替的名詞太遠了，而且是新的一段，有必要再提老師）~~was~~ had painstakingly showed ~~showing me the defects of my essay~~. But now, looking back in retrospect, I have to admit that not until that very moment did I realize that the research essay I was previously so proud of actually contained many mistakes and ~~there was~~ it had ~~large~~ a lot of room for improvement. The constructive criticism from the teacher had benefitted me significantly, and the "ugly truth" she revealed made me convinced that sometimes, telling the truth to someone can be of true importance, especially when ~~that someone being told~~ the truth can benefit the hearer from ~~learning the truth~~ facing the real problems. If there hadn't been a teacher that tried to tell me the truth, I would not have been able to ~~learn that much from the research for sure~~ make any improvement on my research project.

這段描述對個人經驗的反思，從而相信說真話是對人有益的，這是一段重要的論證，不僅引出全篇主旨，並帶入後面的總結。

In his famous and inspirational commencement address at Stanford, Steve Jobs confessed that as he recounted the painful memory of being fired from Apple, "It was an awful-tasting medicine, but I guess the patient needed it." Similarly, the ~~ugly~~ undesirable truth people don't welcome can be, in fact, the most important, or even necessary medicine for them because they might have a disease—things they can improve—that needs to be treated. Therefore, if, after careful consideration of the consequence, we still believe that telling the truth can be beneficial to the person involved, we ~~are supposed to~~ should take the courage to say what is true, despite the bad feeling ~~that people might have~~ it may initially arouse.

最後一段引用 Steve Jobs 的名言來強化自身的經驗,並以「良藥苦口」作為譬喻,是很生動有力的連結,最後的總結句再次呼應第一段的主旨句,前後一致。

題目一

修改後版本

"Should I tell the truth?" Similar questions pop up in our minds all the time (Topic S). While some hold the opinion that people should always be considerate and say something nice, others may believe being able to tell someone the truth is the very essence of a real relationship. For such a dilemma, I argue that we should consider the possible consequence of telling the truth, and what is to the best interest of the person who may need the truth even though it may not be welcome.

The possible effects of telling the truth can be extremely complex, but it will be easier if we take others' benefits into consideration. For most people, they prefer not to tell the truth simply because they are afraid of being hated or treated with hostility. While this, indeed, happens a lot, we should still do it if we believe telling someone the truth will benefit them in the long run.

Take myself as an example. In high school, I participated in a student research project about Taiwanese pop music, and my research instructor didn't give me any negative opinion throughout the whole time. He kept telling me I had done a great job. I believed him, assuming I would certainly get tons of positive feedback after I published the research essay. Later, I showed my essay to another teacher who told me she was interested in the topic and would also like to take a look at the research essay I was working on. She went over my essay and told me that she would like to have an appointment with me to discuss the essay. During our meeting, she pointed out several problems of my writing (G). She said that I should have organized my essay in a more direct and simple way to make it more clear, and that a couple of sentences and words may be ambiguous to the reader (S_1). She even commented on the logical fallacies she was aware of (S_2). The harsh truth was indeed undesirable, but definitely beneficial to me! (G)

I had a hard time accepting the truth that there are so many defects of my essay, as the teacher had painstakingly showed. But now, looking back in retrospect, I have to admit that not until that very moment did I realize that the research essay I was previously so proud of actually contained many mistakes and it had a lot of room for improvement. The constructive criticism from the teacher had benefitted me significantly, and the "ugly truth" she revealed made me convinced that sometimes, telling the truth to someone can be of true importance, especially when the truth can benefit the hearer from facing the real problems. If there hadn't been a teacher that tried to tell me the truth, I would not have been able to make any improvement on my research project.

In his famous and inspirational commencement address at Stanford, Steve Jobs confessed that as he recounted the painful memory of being fired from Apple, "It was an awful-tasting medicine, but I guess the patient needed it." Similarly, the undesirable truth people don't welcome can be, in fact, the most important, or even necessary medicine for them because they might have a disease—things they can improve— that needs to be treated. Therefore, if, after careful consideration of the consequence, we still believe that telling the truth can be beneficial to the person involved, we should take the courage to say what is true, despite the bad feeling it may initially arouse.

In Renaissance England, the word "yourself" carried more meaning than it does today. As we can see in many Shakespearean plays, it ~~also~~ referred to the best ~~possible~~ personal potential one was expected to realize, in addition to serving as a reflexive pronoun. ~~it also referred to the best possible potential one was expected to realize~~. Although such a characteristic has disappeared in modern English, ~~I argue that to live out "ourselves", or to reach our self-actualization, as most people might have put it since Goldstein, people should follow a plan for a better future that is closer to our own dreams~~ the significance of 'self' has never been neglected. In order to live out "oneself", or reach self-actualization, as Goldstein put it, I argue that one should follow a plan for future achievement, instead of just enjoying the present moment.

1. 第一句為 Topic sentence，以 "yourself" 的意義來定調，很有巧思。
2. 第二句將主要子句移到前面，重點先講，同時避免連續用兩個不甚相關的附屬子句。
3. 第三句前後的語意要相關，前面提到消失的 characteristic 是與 self 的意義有關，下一句突然接 I argue，有點突兀不搭，因此改為針對 "self" 來發揮，並轉接下一句。
4. 最後一句先以目的子句指出 argue 的緣由，用以銜接上一句，然後言明 argue 的主張，帶出主旨句（Thesis statement）。

My own experience is a good illustration. I was admitted to ~~an English Instruction department~~ a program on Applied English that focuses on teaching English as a foreign language, but I ~~have~~ decided to make some changes after ~~learning~~ realizing that ~~staying in this department~~ studying TEFL cannot really satisfy me. ~~When I was a freshman~~ In the first year, I took a ~~Western literature~~ class of western literature, in which I got a chance to engage myself in the literary ~~pieces~~ works from the ancient ~~world~~ time to early ~~modernity~~ modern days, from the Bible to Homer, and then from Dante and to Cervante's Don Quixote. While the ~~education~~ curriculum of Applied English ~~as well as the core subjects related to English instruction~~ didn't interest me, I enjoyed myself analyzing literary texts, contemplating on the social and cultural issues reflected in the texts and thinking ~~over~~ about the significance that lies between the lines. It is ~~certainly~~ that I ~~can~~ could stay in the TEFL program, ~~keeping~~ taking other classes that aren't really interesting to me. My classmates are nice; the professors are helpful and friendly. I could just enjoy "the present" and forget about the future. However, owing to my indelible passion toward literature, I ~~managed~~decided to transfer to ~~a literature-based~~ literature-oriented English departments such as those in ~~NTU~~National Taiwan University (NTU) ~~and~~or National Chengchi University (NCCU).

1. 第二段要給例證，仍須依照 G-S-G 鋪陳原理，第一句要指出重點 (G)，作為本段的 topic sentence。
2. 第二句交代主修科目及決心轉變的原因，請注意系所領域的講法；同時要想清楚究竟是什麼使人不滿足？應該是所學的的科目，而不是系所本身。
3. 第三句用單純的時間片語，指出客觀的時間（不需要用 I）；系所的整體課程可用 curriculum。From... to... 如同連接詞，前後要對等。
4. 第四句要加上 other classes，別忘了還有一門是喜歡的課。
5. 加上一句 I could just enjoy "the present" and forget about the future，來強調呼應第一段的主題，同時凸顯接下來的轉折。

The process was not easy. After the decision to transfer ~~is~~was made, I left the group of people I ~~know~~knew very well. I wrote email to completely unfamiliar professors, hoping they could grant me the permission to audit ~~the~~their classes. Later, even though I got to sit in literature classes in NTU and NCCU, I was surrounded by a group of complete strangers that seemed to know one another very well. It was scary. It was intimidating. Nonetheless, as the class proceeded, the anxiety of trying to blend into a new environment was replaced by the euphoria brought by literature. I am not sure if I can successfully ~~be~~get admitted to another school, but I am sure I have benefitted a lot ~~during~~in the process of trying to stick to

~~the~~my plan for future achievement—I got to meet new groups of people and make friends with them, and to explore deeper in the study field of literature, discussing the texts we read with the teachers and fellow classmates ~~about the pieces we had read~~, all of which were ~~unlikely~~unattainable if I had not been trying to take action pursuing my own goal.

1. 依照 G-S-G 法則，第一句要給一個 general statement，做為整段的開場。
2. 注意時態，描述過去事件要保持過去式。

Staying away from ~~our~~one's comfort zones is hard. Being willing to sacrifice in order to stick to ~~our~~one's plans and dreams ~~for my own dreams~~ can be even harder. Whenever I feel exhausted and depressed while pursuing my ~~personal~~ goal, I ~~thought~~ would think of Dante. "Midway along the journey of our life / I woke to find myself in a dark wood, / for I had wandered off from the straight path." Thus he opened the *Divine Comedy*, and embarked on a fictional, spiritual journey that made his name supreme among the authors of world literature. Giving up enjoying the present moment, from some people's perspective, may mean going astray. However, all the wanderings, according to Dante, with a firm belief and clear mind, may lead to eternity. Only by undergoing all the hardships can ~~we~~you truly be ~~"ourselves"~~ "yourself"—~~those that have reached the fullest potential we have~~fully exercising the great potentials in YOU!

1. 第一句依照 G-S-G 法則，給了一個 general statement，做為整段的開場。
2. 把 we 改為 one's 作為客觀的人稱代名詞，中文裡常隨口用「我們」，但英文裡要避免隨便轉換人稱。
3. 表達不確定的可能，可用 may，如：It may mean...。
4. 最後將 "ourselves" 改為 "yourself"，呼應文章一開始的 topic sentence，前後一致，有始有終！

題目二

修改後版本

In Renaissance England, the word "yourself" carried more meaning than it does today. As we can see in many Shakespearean plays, it referred to the best personal potential one was expected to realize, in addition to serving as a reflexive pronoun. Although such a characteristic has disappeared in modern English, the significance of 'self' has never been neglected. In order to live out 'oneself', or reach self-actualization, as Goldstein put it, I argue that one should follow a plan for future achievement, instead of just enjoying the present moment.

My own experience is a good illustration. I was admitted to a program on Applied English that focuses on teaching English as a foreign language, but I decided to make some changes after realizing that studying TEFL cannot really satisfy me. In the first year, I took a class of western literature, in which I got a chance to engage myself in the literary works from the ancient time to early modern days, from the Bible to Homer, and then from Dante and Cervante's Don Quixote. While the curriculum of Applied English didn't interest me, I enjoyed analyzing literary texts, contemplating on the social and cultural issues reflected in the texts and thinking about the significance that lies between the lines. It is certain that I could stay in the TEFL program, taking other classes that aren't really interesting to me. My classmates are nice; the professors are helpful and friendly. I could just enjoy "the present" and forget about the future. However, owing to my indelible passion toward literature, I decided to transfer to a literature-oriented English department such as those in National Taiwan University (NTU) or National Chengchi University (NCCU).

The process was not easy. After the decision to transfer was made, I left the group of people I knew very well. I wrote email to completely unfamiliar professors, hoping they could grant me the permission to audit their classes. Later, even though I got to sit in literature classes in NTU and NCCU, I was surrounded by complete strangers that seemed to know one another very well. It was scary. It was intimidating. Nonetheless, as the class proceeded, the anxiety of trying to blend into a new environment was replaced by the euphoria brought by literature. I am not sure if I can successfully get admitted to another school, but I am sure I have benefitted a lot in the process of trying to stick to my plan for future achievement—I got to meet new groups of people and make friends with them, and to explore deeper in the field of literature, discussing the texts we read with the teachers and fellow classmates, all of which were unattainable if I had not been trying to take action pursuing my own goal.

Staying away from one's comfort zones is hard. Being willing to sacrifice in order to stick to one's plans and dreams can be even harder. Whenever I feel exhausted and depressed while pursuing my goal, I would think of Dante. "Midway along the journey of our life / I woke to find myself in a dark wood, / for I had wandered off from the straight path." Thus he opened the Divine Comedy, and embarked on a fictional, spiritual journey that made his name supreme among the authors of world literature. Giving up enjoying the present moment, from some perspective, may mean going astray. However, all the wanderings, according to Dante, with a firm belief and clear mind, may lead to eternity. Only by undergoing all the hardships can you truly be "yourself"— fully exercising the great potentials in YOU!

 題目一

Read the following passage and the lecture which follows. In an actual test, you will have 3 minutes to read the passage. Then, answer the question. In the test, you will have 20 minutes to plan and write your response. Typically, an effective response will be 150 to 225 words. Candidates with disabilities may request additional time to read the passage and write the response.

READING PASSAGE

Critics say that current voting systems used in the United States are inefficient and often lead to the inaccurate counting of votes. Miscounts can be especially damaging if an election is closely contested. Those critics would like the traditional systems to be replaced with far more efficient and trustworthy computerized voting systems.

In traditional voting, one major source of inaccuracy is that people accidentally vote for the wrong candidate. Voters usually have to find the name of their candidate on a large sheet of paper containing many names—the ballot—and make a small mark next to that name. People with poor eyesight can easily mark the wrong name. The computerized voting machines have an easy-to-use touch-screen technology: to cast a vote, a voter needs only to touch the candidate's name on the screen to record a vote for that candidate; voters can even have the computer magnify the name for easier viewing.

Another major problem with old voting systems is that they rely heavily on people to count the votes. Officials must often count up the votes one by one, going through every ballot and recording the vote. Since they have to deal with thousands of ballots, it is almost inevitable that they will make mistakes. If an error is detected, a long and expensive recount has to take place. In contrast, computerized systems remove the possibility of human error, since all the vote counting is done quickly and automatically by the computers.

Finally some people say it is too risky to implement complicated voting technology nationwide. But without giving it a thought, governments and individuals alike trust other complex computer technology every day to be perfectly accurate in banking transactions as well as in the communication of highly sensitive information.

LECTURE TRANSCRIPT

(Narrator) Now listen to part of a lecture on the topic you just read about.

(Female professor) While traditional voting systems have some problems, it's doubtful that computerized voting will make the situation any better. Computerized voting may seem easy for people who are used to computers. But what about people who aren't? People who can't afford computers, people who don't use them on a regular basis— these people will have trouble using computerized voting machines. These voters can easily cast the wrong vote or be discouraged from voting altogether because of fear of technology. Furthermore, it's true that humans make mistakes when they count up ballots by hand. But are we sure that computers will do a better job? After all, computers are programmed by humans, so "human error" can show up in mistakes in their programs. And the errors caused by these defective programs may be far more serious. The worst a human official can do is miss a few ballots. But an error in a computer program can result in thousands of votes being miscounted or even permanently removed from the record. And in many voting systems, there is no physical record of the votes, so a computer recount in the case of a suspected error is impossible! As for our trust of computer technology for banking and communications, remember one thing: these systems are used daily and they are used heavily. They didn't work flawlessly when they were first introduced. They had to be improved on and improved on until they got as reliable as they are today. But voting happens only once every two years nationally in the United States and not much more than twice a year in many local areas. This is hardly sufficient for us to develop confidence that computerized voting can be fully trusted.

Question: Summarize the points made in the lecture, being sure to explain how they oppose specific points made in the reading passage.

請檢視以下這篇範例,想一想是否已達到本書所教你的寫作要領,再閱讀後面的寫作修改與建議。

The reading passage discusses three major drawbacks in the traditional voting system currently adopted in the United States. In the lecture, the professor addresses the claims made in the article and provides counter arguments against the critics' proposition to switch into a computerized voting system. First of all, critics argue that people with poor eyesight can easily mark the wrong candidate given the numerous names listed in the ballot. They believe that such a mistake can be avoided once voters have access to easy-to-use touch-screen with candidates' names enlarged. However, the professor casts a doubt on the accessibility of the computerized system. She argues that not everyone feels comfortable with using computers. The fear and/or confusion of using the computerized voting system might even prevent some voters from voting.

Secondly, although it is true that human beings might make mistakes in counting the votes, the professor argues that the possibility of such an error occurring in the computerized system cannot be entirely eliminated either. She contends that counting errors made by the computerized voting system are even more difficult to repair than the traditional manual counting system. Finally, critics cite the extensive and reliable use of computerized systems in daily life such as banking transactions to refute the risk of implementing the voting system. The professor points out that the reliability of computer technology for banking and communications have been improved based on constant feedback from the users. However, since voting is not a daily or weekly event, feedback on voting system is unlikely to obtain constantly, thus the reliability of the computerized voting system will be more difficult to establish.

Read the question below. In a real test, you will have 30 minutes to plan, write, and revise your essay. Candidates with disabilities may request a time extension.

Typically, an effective response will contain a minimum of 300 words.

Question: Do you agree or disagree with the following statement?

A teacher's ability to relate well with students is more important than excellent knowledge of the subject being taught.

Use specific reasons and examples to support your answer.

請檢視以下作文範例,再閱讀後面的修改建議

　　Teachers play many roles in the classroom; they can be knowledge deliverers, group activity facilitators, or even simply observers. Among all the roles that a teacher plays, transmitting knowledge seems to be the most important task that a teacher is expected to perform in the classroom. Thus, teachers' knowledge of the subject being taught is a strong indicator of their teaching efficacy. However, I believe that a teacher's ability to relate well with students is much more important than the depth of his or her subject knowledge. To illustrate this point, I would like to share the results of an interesting group discussion that I had in one of my undergraduate courses.

　　The topics that my classmates and I discussed were "Who are your favorite and the least favorite teachers? And why?" We reflected back on the teachers we had from kindergarten up till college and shared characteristics that made them the favorite and the least favorite teachers. While people have different perceptions of good and bad teachers, one of the common traits that emerged from the favorite teachers was the care they invested on students. As for the least favorite teachers, we unanimously agreed that bad teachers were the ones that behaved the opposite way. They did not care about their students. After the discussion, we came to the conclusion that teachers normally equip more or less the same depth of knowledge on the subject being taught, but what makes them drastically different from one and another are the different ways they delivered the same knowledge and how they care about the learning of their students.

My favorite teacher is one of my undergraduate English professors. He always delivered his lectures with enthusiasm. What made him likable was not only his wide knowledge of the English language but also the ways he interacted with the students. He was very approachable and showed great patience in answering questions in and outside of the classroom. On the contrary, one of my math teachers in senior high school was on the other end of the spectrum. She taught her lessons as a robot, failed to make eye contact with us, and left the classroom immediately once the class was over. I believe that she knew the formulas and equations well enough to be a math teacher, but I think she failed to relate with her students and thus was not qualified as an educator.

In sum, an adequate understanding of the subject knowledge is the prerequisite to being a teacher. However, being a "good" teacher goes beyond mastering the subject matter. The ways a teacher deliver the knowledge content and how his or she interacts with students are more crucial to the success of education.

題目一　修正與建議

(Topic sentence) The lecture is doubtful about the criticisms of the current voting system as stated in the reading passage. The reading passage discusses three major drawbacks in the traditional voting system currently adopted in the United States. In the lecture, the professor addresses the claims made by critics in the article and provides counter arguments against the proposition to switch ~~in~~ to a computerized voting system (Thesis statement).

First of all, critics argue that people with poor eyesight can easily mark the wrong candidate given the numerous names listed in the ballot. They believe that such a mistake can be avoided once voters have access to easy-to-use touch-screen with candidates' names enlarged. However, the professor casts a doubt on the accessibility of the computerized system. She argues that not everyone can use or feel comfortable with using computers. The fear and/or confusion of using the computerized voting system might even prevent some voters from voting.

Secondly, although it is true that human beings might make mistakes in counting the votes, the professor argues that the ~~possibility of such~~ same kind of "human error" ~~occurring in the computerized system~~ cannot be entirely eliminated from a computerized system. ~~She contends that counting~~ The errors made by ~~the computerized voting system~~ a computer program may be worse and ~~are~~ even more difficult to repair (or remedy) than the traditional manual counting system.

Finally, critics cite the extensive and reliable use of computerized systems in daily ~~life~~ use ~~such as~~ and banking transactions to refute the risk of implementing the voting system. However, the professor points out that the reliability of computer technology for banking and communications have been improved based on constant and frequent feedback from the users. However, since voting is not a daily or weekly event, feedback on voting systems is ~~unlikely~~ less likely to obtain, thus the reliability of the computerized voting system will be more difficult to establish or improve.

(Conclusion) In sum, the lecture opposes all three seemingly "advantages" of computerized voting systems, pointing out that computer is not accessible and familiar to everyone, computer programs may be equally fallible, and the lack of frequent use will make it hard to improve and stabilize a computerized voting system.

修改說明

1. 即使是寫 summary，仍要注意 essay writing 的結構原則與鋪陳方式：

   開頭要破題聚焦（topic sentence）

   第一段要言明主旨（thesis statement）

   中間各段有條理地鋪陳細節（supporting details）

   最後要有提綱挈領的總結（summarizing conclusion）

2. 既然是寫 summary，文字要力求精簡直接，避免過長的贅字或句子。

題目二

修改建議

Teachers play many roles in the classroom; they can be knowledge deliverers, group activity facilitators, discussion leaders or even simply observers. Among all the roles that a teacher plays, transmitting knowledge seems to be considered the most important task that a teacher is expected to perform in the classroom. Thus, it is commonly recognized that the teachers' knowledge of the subject being taught is a strong indicator of their teaching efficacy. However, I believe that a teacher's ability to relate well with students is much more important than the depth of his or her ~~subject~~ knowledge. To illustrate this point, I would like to share the results of an interesting group discussion that I had in one of my undergraduate ~~courses~~ classes.

The topics that my classmates and I discussed were "Who are your most favorite and ~~the~~ least favorite teachers? And why?" We reflected back on the teachers we had from kindergarten up ~~till~~ to college and shared characteristics that made them the most favorite and or the least favorite teachers. While ~~people~~ we have different perceptions of good and bad teachers, one of the common traits that emerged from the discussion of favorite teachers was the care and time they invested on students. As for the least favorite teachers, we unanimously agreed that bad teachers were the ones that behaved the opposite way－they did not care about their students.

After the discussion, we came to the conclusion that teachers normally equip more or less the same depth of knowledge on the subject being taught, but what makes them drastically different from one ~~and~~ another are the different ways they delivered the same knowledge and how they care about the learning of their students.

My favorite teacher is one of my undergraduate English professors. He always delivered his lectures with enthusiasm. What made him ~~likable~~ popular was not only his wide range of knowledge of the English language but also the ways he interacted with the students. He was very approachable and showed great patience in answering questions in and outside of the classroom. On the contrary, one of my math teachers in senior high school was on the other end of the spectrum. She taught her lessons as a robot, ~~failed to~~ made no eye contact with us, and left the classroom immediately once the class was over. I believe that she knew the formulas and equations well enough to be a math teacher, but I think she failed to relate with her students and thus was not qualified as an educator.

In sum, an adequate understanding of the subject ~~knowledge~~ is the prerequisite to being a teacher. However, being a "good" teacher goes beyond mastering the subject matter. The ways a teacher delivers the knowledge content and how he or she interacts with students are more crucial to the success of education.

修改說明

這是一篇很好的文章，內容完整、結構整齊、文法正確，但是仍有幾個問題要注意：

1. 作者在第一段前面三句所陳述的看法和接下來要主張的立場很不一樣，為了避免似是而非的疑慮，建議在前面陳述他人看法時，加上清楚的標記，表示所說的是一般人的看法而已：Transmitting knowledge seems to be considered.... It is commonly recognized (by others) that...。

2. Favorite 是特別喜歡的，通常不加 most，但在此用 most favorite 是為了和 least favorite 做對比。例如：What is your most favorite and least favorite celebrity?

3. 維持一致的人稱是文章有條理的第一步，my classmates and I 合併為 we，而不是 people！

Chapter

14

如何撰寫履歷：
申請工作與學校

　　不論是申請學校或是求職，一份脈絡清晰完整的履歷表絕對是一項利器，因為在還未見到面之前，這份履歷就代表了個人的形象，展現個人的思維邏輯、表達能力。這是唯一讓他人能夠初步認識你的機會，因此一定要寫得精簡扼要且傳達出重點，並記得要妥善管理、定期維護自己的履歷表。一份完美的履歷才能夠讓人留下深刻的第一印象，進而獲得下一步的審核或面談。

　　有的學校或公司行號，甚至會要求寫自傳或回答申論題，這時就更需要靠寫作來支持你的論點、行銷個人特色。言不及義的文章只會讓人對你的思維邏輯能力大打折扣，文章寫得動人，自然而然就會吸引主考官的目光。

　　培養好的寫作能力，在求學、職場生涯中都是相當重要的，是會跟隨著你一輩子的基本能力。本章就將教你如何善用 G-S-G 法則，在需要表現自己的任何時刻都能展現優雅寫作的自信。

14.1 申請學校

14.1.1 College Essay

　　國內大學或研究所的申請，常須要撰寫一篇自傳式的短文或讀書計畫；國外的大學則要求至少要寫一篇 college essay。目的都是要藉由簡短而精緻的文字，了解申請人在成績分數之外個人的特質與熱情。因此，自傳不是流水帳，讀書計畫更不是制式的短、中、長程計畫而已。書寫的目的應該是要介紹「個人化」的經歷：凸顯個人成長過程中特別的經歷與感受，又如何藉此找到學習的興趣與方向。這個終極目標在各大學提出的自傳問題中清楚可見：

➢ Describe the world you come from – for example, your family, community or school – and tell us how your world has shaped your dreams and aspirations.（美國加州大學）
➢ Tell us about a personal quality, talent, accomplishment, contribution or experience.（美國加州大學）
➢ Write about someone who has influenced your life or a time that you have experienced great change.（美國康乃爾大學）

　　既然強調「個人化」的經歷與特質，就要避免千篇一律、一成不變、制式化的內容，不須鉅細靡遺地細數家珍，大家都一樣的就不用贅述，無關個人的也不用多提，只要鎖定一個「最特別、最深刻、最個人、最不一樣」的人、事、物，作為核心主題，藉由描述事物本身，來凸顯經歷背後的意義，然後闡明這個經歷對個人學習態度與興趣的影響：正如加州大學網站上一再強調，自傳（personal statement）必須具備「個人化」的意義：

Your personal statement should be exactly that – personal. This is your opportunity to tell us about yourself – your hopes, ambitions, life experiences, inspirations. .... Be open. Be reflective. Find your individual voice and express it honestly.
(http://admission.universityofcalifornia.edu/how-to-apply/personal-statement/)

　　在申請過程中，college essay 可能是最具挑戰的一步。為了引起審閱人的興趣，學生總是絞盡腦汁，力求生動脫俗，雋永深遠。究竟有什麼寫作訣竅呢？讓我們再次回到本書

一再強調的三句話原則！

第一步：確定最重要的人／事／物——以不落俗套的方式破題，點出主軸焦點

第二步：選擇相關有意涵的細節——生動地描述經歷過程的實際細節

第三步：歸納出印象深刻的意義——畫龍點睛式的總結，慧點地呼應主題

　　以下是一篇可供參考的文章，作者選擇描述自己在高一時，由台灣飛往美國的心路歷程，這是他人生中的一個很大的變動。藉由登機前的傍徨來回顧自己過去的成長經歷，以及面對未來的省思，在反思的過程中，終於認識自己並找到方向，最後再以登機的行動來表明面對挑戰的勇氣與信心。

全篇的鋪陳可按照前五章所介紹的寫作策略來分析：

 範例 1

Describe the world you come from – for example, your family, community or school – and tell us how your world has shaped your dreams and aspirations.

A Plane Ride

　　"Flight BR0018 flying to San Francisco is now boarding." I sat motionlessly in the Taoyuan International Airport. How could I just get up and walk out like it was another ordinary day in life? With this flight I was moving to Palo Alto, California, and for the first time since kindergarten, I was leaving Taiwan, not for summer programs, not for community services, not even for family vocational trips, but for permanent residence. With this flight, I was walking out of my comfort zone surrounded by loving and caring families and friends, and cushioned by the familiar faces at school that I've known since grade one. Into the unknown of California, I could not help but feeling pressured and immobilized.

　　"Well, what're you waiting for?" my mother, hands on her hips, stared at me, speaking in the familiar Mandarin that I heard every day. I wondered exactly what I was waiting for. I had been ecstatic and eager to leave Taiwan, a place I considered humid, buggy, and boring at times. But now, minutes away from taking off, I was hesitant. I wasn't sure when I would be able to eat my grandma's delicious *jiaozi* (dumplings), to sit down with my grandpa for a game of Chinese chess, or to play another basketball game with my teammates again.

Growing up in a highly traditional Chinese family with a Christian faith, huge expectations were heaped upon me. I was the only grandson that carries the forefather's last name, LEE. My entire extended family wished for a son, and was so grateful when I was born. They named me "Matthew," a biblical name that stands for "gift from God." From the very moment I was born I was expected to achieve above and beyond. I was supposed to be well-mannered, intelligent, and outstanding. My aspirations and dreams had been driven by a clear force: expectations and obligations. I was expected to get good grades, so I aspired myself to study hard and become the top student. I was expected to play an instrument, so I practiced hard with my violin. Straight A's, talent shows, extra-curricular activities, social skills — in every aspect of my life, I felt motivated by other people's expectations. As I grew up, the expectations became motivations. Even now, as I was about to step onto an unfamiliar continent, I was expected to adjust perfectly and continue obtaining high marks in a foreign campus.

But as the long line of boarding passengers grew, a new-found strength came over me. I began to realize that I, Matthew Lee, expected myself to succeed and do well in the journey ahead. It was not about what had been asked of me anymore, but what I wanted to do for myself. After having lived my life to meet the expectations defined by parental, familial and cultural roles and duties, I found a fresh stream of inspiration: I was finally ready to motivate myself. My dreams and aspirations were going to be my own.

"I'm coming." I got up, picked up my bags, and boarded the plane. I didn't know what sort of courage came over me in those precious seconds as my mother stood and waited for me before the boarding gate, but I knew I was resolved and invigorated. Confidently, I put my fears behind me, tucked my own expectations under my jacket, and walked onto the plane that would take me to an exciting adventure.

分析說明

第一段 破題聚焦

以機場的原音重現 "Flight BR0018 flying to...."，點出事件的場景，一開頭就採用敘事的生動手法，直接引述播音細節，再破題，聚焦於離開台灣的這個重大轉變（I sat motionlessly in the airport.）。這是將 General-to-Specific 倒過來，變成 Specific to General（S-G），因此顯得不落俗套。接著以心中明確的問題來延伸離開的衝擊，最後用小節（thesis statement）"With this flight, I was walking out of my comfort zone surrounded by loving and caring families and friends..." 來承上啟後，帶出要開始談的成長背景。

接下來，中間兩段是具體的細節與真實的感受，最後兩段是轉折與總結。

第二段 成長環境

開頭仍舊是 S-G 的運用，直接引述母親的問話，藉由媽媽的角色，帶出個人之外的環境，並由熟悉的「語言」來喚起熟悉的記憶、熟悉的環境、想念的事物，提供成長的細節：Humid weather, grandma's delicious jiaozi (dumplings), grandpa's chess.

第三段 家庭背景

由大環境轉到家庭，藉由描述名字的意義來顯明家庭所加諸的期望，與過去一直被要求的努力。陳述的方式依循 G-S-G 的原則：首先概括描述重點 (G): My aspirations and dreams had been driven by a clear force: expectations and obligations. 接著舉例加強說明 (S): I was expected to get good grades, so I aspired myself to study hard and become the top student (example1). I was expected to play an instrument, so I practiced hard with my violin (example 2). Straight A's, talent shows, extra-curricular activities, social skills (more examples)，然後再下一個小結：in every aspect of my life, I felt motivated by other people's expectations (G). 最後一句再將過去和現在連結，過去到現在都存在一樣的 expectation。

仍是由外而內的襯托寫法，當排隊人群如泉湧增加的同時，內心的反思也如潮水發生了轉折性的改變，從被動的期望到主動的改變：I began to realize that I, Matthew Lee, expected myself to succeed and do well in the journey ahead. 過去他人加諸的期望已經內化為自身的動力，成為自己對自己的期望：I found a fresh stream of inspiration: I was finally ready to motivate myself. My dreams and aspirations were going to be my own.

第五段

以短短的引述 "I'm coming." 來反映個人主動的回應，將登機的場景融入個人內在的轉變。

登機前收拾的動作細節，正好反映收拾內心的步驟。即將展開的飛行旅程代表即將要展開的人生旅程，堅定自信的走上飛機，就代表自己主動迎向人生的挑戰。

範例 2

What matters to you, and why? (400 words)

My family matters the most to me. Throughout the changes in my life, it is my father, my mother and my sister that have remained constant and assuring. The relationships between us have been seeded in unbreakable bonds, nourished by accepting understanding, and grown over one and a half decades of laughter and tears.

My dad has always been "that guy." As the CEO of his company, he worked hard and often returned home after nine p.m. In our scarce time together we managed to know each other. He is a visionary entrepreneur, always standing on the bright side when things turned dim. He was the peacemaker when arguments arose and the laid-back guy in the midst of turmoil. He could even make impromptu songs to tease and cheer. From him, I inherited a positive attitude and sense of humor. I see in him the kind of friend I hope to be.

Discipline was my mother's cup of tea. Being a professor in university, she knew how to eloquently instruct me. She is my coach, my caregiver, and my nightmare all at the same time. When she was authoritative with me, I learned to be self-assured. When she frustrated me, I exercised self-control and self-esteem. When she set expectations for me, I turned to be self-motivated and self-paced. Finally, when she complimented me, I knew I had earned it. My mom represents the kind of parent I hope to be.

I have a sister who is four years older. She always knew about the cool new things earlier than I, grasped the trendy fads better than I, and gave the correct answers to my math homework faster than I. She is calm and determined, and I've lived my life to catch up with her. As she graduated from Cornell, she became a role model I wanted to follow. My sister is the adult person I hope to be.

Each of my family members has affected me in unique ways. They are an integral part of me and a defining factor of my life. Every memory we shared adds joy, and every crisis we faced together adds understanding. My family is my strength and support. It matters!

分析說明

這篇文章言簡意賅地把家人對自己的重要性，分段描述。第一段整體介紹後，每段描述一個人，突顯其人的特點以及對自己的意義。最後再回到家庭的共同經歷，並有力的總結：It matters!

熱情的展現：服務學習及社區工作

近年學校很鼓勵學生從事自願服務工作，在服務學習中，可以展現個人的熱情與志趣。因此除了履歷、自傳之外還可提供第三種文件：有關服務學習或其他重要活動的心得感想，說明個人在參與服務中的收穫與成長。

以下提供一篇學生申請美國大學的補充資料，陳述個人在動物園服務的寶貴經驗、文圖並貿，生動有趣。

My Valuable Experiences - ZOO

When I set foot on the winding, dirty street before the Hsinchu Zoo, I did not expect this street to take me anywhere significant. Little did I know, it led me to a path that would impact me deeply.

My volunteer work at the zoo is one of my major experiences with exotic animals. The zoo itself is relatively small. Precisely for this reason, the other volunteers and I interacted directly with the director of the zoo. Through him, we had first hand experience with the animals. The first day I arrived, we followed a zoo keeper on his round to feed the animals. We entered the cages

➢ **African Spurred Tortoises**

➢ **Cages for transportation**

and were able to observe the animals from a close range. The zoo keeper briefly pointed out characteristics of the animals as we helped distribute the food. Then, he took us to newly arrived African Spurred Tortoises and told us to "walk" them. So, we spent time watching these giant tortoises sunbathe while the tourists asked us about them.

The times following the first day were also filled with just as much learning and new experiences. Because the zoo often receives exotic animals confiscated from local people, we are usually involved in moving animals into new habitats. This is an especially difficult job because animals are quite territorial and they hate to be disturbed. The first time we moved

> **The python that bit my friend**

> **Baby magpies and bread worms as food**

two macaws in with other macaws, we witnessed brutal fights over territory and social status. In addition, some of the animals that we move can be quite dangerous. When we tried moving a python, my friend was bitten by her. Luckily, pythons are not poisonous and my friend was fine. But because he was bitten, imagine how nervous we were when we carried the python by hand to her new habitat. Another time, we transferred snapping turtles and we only dared to prod them with sticks when they wouldn't come out of the transfer containers. One of the turtles turned right around and snapped the end of my stick off. The force that was transferred through the stick from his bite ran all the way up my arm.

Sometimes when we receive confiscated animals or animals donated by other people, the animal is not ready to be moved in with the rest of its kind. These animals stay in a special area and we take care of them. We feed them, play with them, and do what we can to make

> **Guinea pigs**

> **BowBow sleeping after eating**

them comfortable. The best example is the baby Formosan Rock-Monkey named BowBow. She's too young to be entered into the monkey pack so we are the ones that entertain her and act as her group. We even take her on walks through the zoo so she can get used to the sights and smells of the outside.

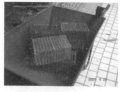

> **Rat traps**

Because the animals in the wild spend almost all their waking hours searching for food, animals in the zoo easily get bored from a lack of things to do. The zoo keepers have taught us to entertain them by giving them incentive to move around. The first way we can do this is by giving the animals

> **Bear enjoying his fish**

snacks that they may not necessarily eat but will definitely spike their interests. For example, we throw dry dog food at the monkeys and the pack will run to catch them. We catch live rats from the zoo and give it to the reptiles or eagles for them to chase. We fish from our ponds and throw the fish to the bears and the tigers. The second way is to give the animals food that they

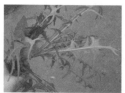   

don't normally eat. The director went as far as teaching us how to identify plants and berries in the zoo that certain animals love to eat. We fed ostriches, deer and peacocks all sorts of hand picked greens.

> **Sticks for the new**

In addition to interacting with the animals themselves, we often have to modify their existing habitats. As the zoo gets new additions, we are responsible for making the habitat livable. For example, we transferred rocks, branches, and dead leaves to the new snake cage and tried to design the placement of these materials so that the snake enjoys them. Another

> **Covering with tarp**

> **Python's new cage**

time, we renovated the snapping turtle pen by planting new water plants and transferring more fishes into the pen.

> **Picking up branches**

Furthermore, because Taiwan is prone to typhoons, we often have to do preparations for the typhoon or repair the zoo after a typhoon. Once, we spent three hours trying to cover a large bird containment with tarp. Another time, we helped clear away fallen branches in that containment and transfer them out. All of this required a lot of team work, willingness to do hard work, and on the spot ideas so that our work could be done efficiently and well.

Another major part of working at the zoo is the educational opportunities for us to participate in. We watched veterinarian school students from National Taiwan University do check ups on the monkeys. The veterinarian students used blow guns to shoot down the monkey and then they laid her down on a table and did blood tests. Later on, the veterinarian taught us how to make the blow

> **Treating a lame goat**

darts and we shot at inanimate targets. We participated in the veterinarian's work as he administered drugs and did blood tests. He taught us how to get blood samples from

> **Taiwan Unv. students with monkey**

rabbits and how to give shots to goats. When an animal died, the veterinarian would dissect it and we saw how different the animal's composition is from ours. Such valuable experiences are hard to find.

Lastly, we participated in helping the zoo educate

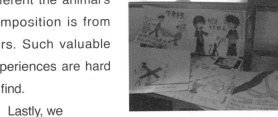

> **Campaign to stop the tourists from feeding the animals**

> **Packing fruit and vegetable ice for activity**

others. The largest contribution on our part is probably supplying the zoo our English abilities. Since we are bilingual, we often translate the information into English for English speaking tourists. In addition, the zoo often holds educational activities for the tourists and we help prepare for those. All of these activities test our creativity and team work. From these experiences I've improved my communication with peers and with others.

My Valuable Experiences – Animal Hospital

From my voluntary work at the Hsinchu zoo, I realized that merely loving animals was not enough to make me a good animal caretaker. I became eager to gain experience with saving animals. Through the help of the veterinarian at the zoo, I started a part-time job as a trainee at Fleur Animal Hospital in January, 2007, as I offered to work there for free. At the animal

➢ **Co-worker and Me**

hospital, my duties included front desk, customer service, surgery preparation, medicine distribution, documentation, cleaning, etc. My experience at the hospital has not only fortified my knowledge in animal clinical works but also helped me grow in my attitude toward executing tasks and facing new challenges.

Quality and Professionalism

The lesson that struck me first is the importance of doing things right. While the director of Fleur, Dr. Wang, is a very nice person, he is always very strict about the quality of works. He expects precision in everything my colleagues and I do. If there's anything we don't quite understand, we have to ask no matter what. We are constantly reminded to paying attention

➢ **Director**

to details and double-checking crucial procedures especially when handling medicines and helping surgery. His serious attitude makes me realize how different it is working at a professional business as opposed to being a volunteer at a zoo. There is little room for accidents and no room for negligence. Under Dr. Wang's guidance, I have polished my diligence as well as my knowledge and techniques in animal clinical work.

Taking Challenges

At the animal hospital, I was pushed to do things I was not comfortable with. In the beginning, I secretly avoided picking up phone calls because I often did not know the information to tell the customer or the correct procedure to transfer calls.

When Dr. Wang found that out, he made me pick up all the calls for a month. With some initial struggles, I gradually became competent as a front desk receptionist and excelled in taking care of registration, documentation, and providing customer service information. Through this special learning process, I feel that both my self-confidence and capability are greatly enhanced.

➤ **Preparing**

Surprise

One day in May, Dr. Wang approached me and said that he was going to start paying me for my work. He recognized my hard work and was pleased with the progress I made. He thought that I deserved to be treated as his regular employee. This gave me a great sense of accomplishment that I was able to live up to the standards in real professional fields.

Ultimate Test

The hospital held a special activity in honor of the hospital's "birthday" in September. We gave out free rabies shots and discounts on all sorts of things. As a result, my colleagues and I faced a major flux of customers for the entire day. The work was a blur of taking the papers from the desk to the doctors, constantly doing blood tests, washing the equipment,

➤ **The shots**

preparing shots, and other various tasks. As the end of the day approached, I felt a wave of success washing over me.

Overall, the animal hospital job brought me to a new level in my pursuit to becoming a professional in veterinary. I am ready to take the next step by entering my college education in this field.

Write about someone who has influenced your life or a time that you have experienced great change.

_____

_____

_____

_____

_____

_____

_____

_____

_____

_____

_____

範　文

The Game of *Xiang-qi*

"Time for the game!" my grandfather called out to me. He was a great *Xiang-qi*, or Chinese chess, player. Every day after dinner, we sat down, face to face, and played a game of chess. Every time we played, I wracked my brain to find ways to beat him, but ended up defeated. I tried various approaches, maneuvered my steps, but he always managed to get ahead of me. When I captured one of his Pawns, he would have my Cannon under siege in the next move. Everywhere I turned, he had a counterattack up on his sleeve to crush me. Frustration came to capture me, but I sat down with grandpa and played a game of *Xiang-qi* every night.

I stare intently at his face, looking for signs of wavering emotion that I can tactically draw upon, but I see nothing. His poker face gazes back at me as he calmly tramples my armies with his.

"Life is much like Xiang-qi," grandpa says after an extended silence. "Every move you make must be deliberated, calculated, and carried out with confidence."

"But I'm always losing, Grandpa."

"That's OK, Matt. Playing chess is not just about winning or losing; it is about the choices you make. You choose to immerse yourself in a competitive game and take every move gracefully and enjoyably. You learn to pursue your heart and win a victory of trying, no matter what the outcome is," Grandpa wrapped up the conversation with a swift move and ended the game with a checkmate, "Jiang Jun!"

I came to California in my junior year and stepped into a completely new game. There were new rules to learn and new moves to make in the unfamiliar environment. I loved basketball, but I couldn't continue to play on the varsity team; I enjoyed math and was placed in the most advanced class, but I got a C+ on the final; I used to play first violin in a youth orchestra, but the heavy schoolwork filled my schedule. I once chaired the drama club, but now had to re-start with a minor role. The moves I needed to make were all as critical and challenging as those in the *Xiang-qi* game.

A few months after I settled in Palo Alto, my grandpa passed away. I'll never have the chance to know if I would be able to beat him some day. But it doesn't matter anymore. I kept playing my favorite sport of basketball every Saturday; I continued to challenge my math ability in the hardest math lane; I auditioned for a violin seat and got to play Bach again; I joined the choir and sang a 16th century cantata; and I stood on stage to rehearse my lines for drama night. As I sat down and looked over the chess board, the seat opposite to me, across the battlefield, was vacant. But the solid *Xiang-qi* pieces have engraved the words in me: "pursue your heart and win the victory of trying."

分析說明

這篇文章藉由 "和爺爺下象棋" 來帶出人生中最重要的人物與時刻。一開頭的細節描述在第一段最後一句做了一個小節：Frustration came to capture me, but I sat down with Grandpa...every night. 很有技巧的表明全篇的主旨：雖有挫折，卻不放棄。

接著進一步藉由真實的對話回應主旨句，並帶出下一段中人生要面對的轉變與挑戰。最後以爺爺過世來凸顯他的影響力。人雖遠去，但一起下象棋的珍貴經驗卻永存不朽。

14.1.2 個人簡歷與自傳式說明

　　為了使學校有較完整的個人資料，有時學生會提供一份精緻完整的簡歷與自傳式的問答說明。學生簡歷最重要的是個人背景與學業成績，因此將這這幾項放在最前面：

Personal information

Education

Honors and awards

　　接下來可說明與興趣相關的學習活動、社群服務、社團職責等，然後總結個人的特質與能力。接著建議對家庭的教育背景加以說明，有些美國大學很重視家庭教育傳統，通常父母親讀的學校會偏好自己校友的孩子，因為如此可形成一種對學校的忠誠支持：

Skills-building activities and clubs

Work experiences and community services

Summary of qualifications

Family legacy

　　最後提供一份較詳細的自傳式說明，以問答方式來引發好奇，再精簡陳述重點。問答式的自傳說明提供清楚易懂的小標題，可幫助釐清個人的特點與經歷，閱讀起來有條理、有重點，不致乏味冗長。在說明的最後（或是最前面），可以進階圖表清晰呈現一路努力的軌跡，來凸顯自己有明確的方向與行動。問答式的標題可包括：

➢ **The environment I grew up in**

➢ **The most influential person**

➢ **What are my aspirations and what have I done to achieve them?**

➢ **My monumental experiences**

➢ **The roadmap – steps to reach my goal**

　　書寫申請資料的祕訣是理性中帶有感性，條理中重點分明。由審閱者的角度來設想可能會提出的問題，可能會想知道的訊息，按照三句話原則來思考，運用 G-S-G 的鋪陳方式，使文章一目了然，趣味盎然！

履歷表加上自傳就是一份完整申請學校的文件，以下提供一份完整的範例：

Mark H. Lin

marklin@gmail.com

H: 650-123-4567　　C: 650-987-6543

25 Madison Avenue, CA 94306, USA

Personal Information

- **Date/Place of Birth:** April 21, 1994/Boulder, Colorado, U.S.A.
- **Nationality/Ethnicity:** U.S. Citizen/Asian Chinese
- **Intended Major:** Economics
- **Academic Strengths:** Business Law, Economics, Accounting, Math, English, Chinese
- **Interests:** vocal and instrumental music, financing, marketing, basketball, drama, creative writing and reading

Education

- **Academic Performance**
  - ✓ GPA: 3.818 (un-weighted, out of 4.0)
  - ✓ SAT I: Total Score 2280 (Critical reading 710, Math 800, Writing 770)
  - ✓ SAT II: Biology-E 760, Chinese 800, Math-2C 740, Literature 720
  - ✓ PSAT: Total Score 213, Percentile 98 (Critical reading 66, Math 72, Writing 75)
  - ✓ AP Classes: Biology (5), Chinese Language (5), Environmental Science (5), Psychology, Macroeconomics, English, Calculus BC,
- **Palo Alto Senior High School, Palo Alto, CA**
  - ✓ 2010-present, related courses taken:

Economics: Grade A　　　　　　　　　AP Economics (Spring 2012)

Business Law 1 and 2: Grade A+

- **Summer College for high school students at Stanford, Palo Alto, CA**
  - ✓ 2011 Summer: Accounting for Managers and Entrepreneurs MS&E 140/240

- **Educational Program for Gifted Youth (EPGY), Stanford, Palo Alto, CA**

  2009 Summer: Topics in Economics: Grade A

- **Bilingual Department at National Experimental High School (NEHS), Taiwan 2000-2010 Grs.1 – 10:**

  ✓ Full-scale English curriculum: same as American public school system

  ✓ Additional Chinese curriculum: Chinese language and Chinese Social Studies

Honors and Awards

- **National Merit Scholarship Recipient (PSAT/NMSQT), 05/2011**
- **Palo Alto High School's Annual Science Awards for AP Environmental Science, 05/2011**
- **Certificate of Appreciation and Acknowledgement 01/2009 - 06/2010**

  ✓ English tutoring to local disadvantaged students, Nightlight Angel Program

  ✓ After School English Tutoring Program

  ✓ Key Club participation - 63 hours from 07/2008 to 06/2009

- **Student of the Month, NEHS Bilingual Department**

  ✓ for Responsibility 09/2008

  ✓ for Honesty 03/2009

- **Notable Athletic Accomplishment in 2008-2009 and 2009-2010**

  ✓ Junior Varsity Basketball team

- **Top 3 GPA Honors**

  ✓ 1st highest GPA in fall semester, Grade 09, 02/2009

  ✓ 3rd highest GPA in spring semester, Grade 9, 08/2009

- **Award for Well-balanced Excellence (Junior High Graduation Honors), 06/2008**
- **Outstanding Academic Performance (Junior High Graduation), 06/2008**

Skills-Building Activities and Clubs

- **Key Club (Kiwanis International, ongoing), Member, grades 7-11, 2006- present**

  ✓ Representative at 04/2011 California-Nevada-Hawaii District Convention

  ✓ Head of Food at IBSH Charity Night 2009 (performance and dinner event),

- ✓ Head of Unplugged 2010 (charity performances)
- ✓ Tech Head of Charity Night 2010
- **Drama Club/Thespian Society (ongoing)**
  - ✓ Member of National Experimental High School Drama Club, grades 7-9, 2006-09
  - ✓ President of International Bilingual School in Hsinchu Drama Club, grade 10
  - ✓ Member of the Thespian Society at Palo Alto Senior High School 2010-present
  - ✓ Participant in One Acts Productions at Palo Alto Senior High School 05/2011
- **Organized Sports: Junior Varsity Basketball**
  - ✓ Member of JV Basketball at National Experimental High School 2008-09
  - ✓ Captain of JV Basketball at International Bilingual School in Hsinchu 2009-2010
- **Model United Nations, Delegate (ongoing)**
  - ✓ Taichung Model United Nations (TAIMUN): Delegate of Afghanistan 2010
  - ✓ Hsinchu Model United Nations (HSINMUN): Delegate of Denmark 10/2008
- **Bilingual Department Student Council (BDSC)**
  - ✓ Activity Council, grades 7-10, 2007-08
- **NEHS StudentTutoring Program**
  - ✓ Reading and English tutor, grades 8-10, 2007-10
- **Music: Instrument Violinist (ongoing)**
  - ✓ Peninsula Youth Orchestra, Violin I, 2011- present
  - ✓ Hsinchu Youth Philharmonic Orchestra, Violin II and I, 2007-2010
- **Future Business Leaders of America**
  - ✓ Member 2010-present
- **Paly Entrepreneurship Club**
  - ✓ Member 2011-present
- **Music: Vocal Tenor (ongoing)**
  - ✓ Musical Performance, lead vocalist, 2008-2009
  - ✓ Productions of Les Miserables, Hairspray
  - ✓ Concert Choir Tenor, 2011-present

✓ Palo Alto High School Madrigal Singers Tenor (advanced vocals) 2011-present

✓ Crystal Children's Choir, Tenor and dancer, 2004-2008

Work Experiences and Community Services

- **Loveast Culture Exchange LLC, 2011**
  - ✓ Assistant to Chief Executive Officer
  - ✓ Junior financial analyst
- **American Disaster Relief (ADR) at Palo Alto Senior High School**
  - ✓ Member, 2010-present
- **Relay for Life, Campbell and Palo Alto 2011**
  - ✓ Fundraising and 48 hours walk for cancer patients
- **Week Without Walls, Cebu, Philippines 07/2010 (Cement house building and painting)**
- **Paid English Tutor, Hsinchu Grace Church 2009**
  - ✓ Taught beginning English to Chinese 1st-3rd graders
- **Tutoring/Administration Assistant, International Bilingual School at Hsinchu 06/2009**
- **UrbanPlan, 2010**
  - ✓ Served as financial analyst
- **Recycling Community Service 07/2010**
  - ✓ 30 hours of volunteer at school recycling site

Summary of Qualifications

- Highly motivated for a career in economics/business administration
- Focused training in major areas of business development
- Responsible, efficient, goal-minded and teamwork-oriented
- Talented in music, drama and social networking; skillful with Java, Office, Videomaker
- Fluent (reading, writing, listening, speaking) in English and Mandarin

Autobiographic Statement – My passion and Pursuits

The Environment I Grew Up In

I grew up in two different environments and cultures that are contradictory on the surface but complementary down in the roots. I was born in Boulder, Colorado on April 21st, 1994. From my early age on, I traveled frequently between Taiwan and the United States. As a child, I didn't understand what the impact was to be placed in two drastically different cultures. All I noticed was that I had two homes, two groups of friends, two kinds of food, and two languages. When my family finally settled in Hsinchu, the "Silicon Valley" of Taiwan, I attended a bilingual school that was established exclusively for families like mine. Immersed in both Taiwanese and American curricula, I began to see and experience first-hand how the two cultures set different values, goals and means of education. When my English teacher taught me to be creative and self-assuring, my Chinese teacher would emphasize conformity and submission. While the two sets of rules don't overlap, they actually complement each other and make a balanced whole. I learned to be confident to myself but humble to others, brave in attempts but reserved in the outcome. As the only grandson to my grandparents, I had great expectations placed upon me to carry on the family legacy. While my American upbringing urged me to be independent and self-sufficient, I was willing to play my role in the family and commit myself to the bigger mission. Over the years, new challenges kept piling up, piano and violin lessons, sports and orchestra, summer programs and community volunteer works, I managed to balance my life between the Western enjoyment and the Eastern perseverance. When I moved back to California in 2010, I had to make lots of tough decisions to adjust myself socially and academically. Fortunately, I have learned to make use of the strengths of both realms to strive for the best.

The Most Influential Person

The most influential person in my life is my grandfather. He was a professor in botany, a great player of Chinese chess and an amateur singer of Peking opera.

Although I have an encouraging father and a loving, disciplinarian mother, my grandpa is the one who truly shaped me to become what I am today. As the only direct grandson of his, I was the one who carries the family name, and my grandpa would boldly and directly let everyone know that I was what he cared most about. He was a calm, strong and wise man, mentally and physically; he always beat me in chess and wrist-wrestling. As he had gone through all the life-threatening trials in the Chinese civil war and established himself miraculously in Taiwan, he got lots of interesting stories to tell me. He would always advise me to make balanced and intelligent choices. He had high expectations of me, but he didn't expect me to invent cure to cancer or solve world hunger; rather, he expected me to just live my life to the fullest in a meaningful way. To this day, I believe I haven't disappointed him. From a very young age, I was exposed to various activities and lessons to grow to be a well-rounded person. At times, these things filled up my spare time and strained me to a point that I felt like giving up, but the words and stories told by my grandpa would pop up and gave me new strength to hang on. Today, as a senior applying to college, I'm proud to say that I continue to practice violin as a hobby and passion, I continue to sing in Paly choir for love and joy, and I continue to strive for the best in my grades as well as my characters. My grandfather instilled a sense of excellence within me and inspired me to exercise all my potentials. He passed away in February and I remembered my promise: I won't let him down.

What Am I Passionate about?

Career-wise, I am curious and passionate about the business world. My father is a CEO leading a start-up company, and I have always wanted to know more about the various dimensions in business development, financial planning and entrepreneur "adventures". Starting from my freshman year, I have been accumulating knowledge and experiences in related fields. I love dealing with numbers and multi-factor decision making.

Outside the classroom, I was drawn to a number of activities that I persisted in and devoted myself to. As a young boy, I found myself enjoy straightening things up and helping people out. I decided to engage myself in community services as a life style. I have been a member of the Key Club (high school branch of Kiwanis International) since eighth grade. I am concerned with both environmental and social issues, and the best way to made a difference was by mobilizing the whole community. When I serve others, at a retirement home entertaining the elderly or at a beach cleaning up trash, I feel that I have spent my time doing something meaningful. I have always been dedicated to and enjoyed community services.

Music has been a natural part of me ever since I could remember. My parents both agreed that I have some musical talents and encouraged me to further develop them. I started piano lessons since age five, violin lessons since six, and concert choir when I was eight. Later, I've even picked up rock drums and string guitar on my own. People often asked me how I could bear to have so many musical commitments at once, and I simply told them: I love making music. When I play my instruments or sing my heart out, I enjoy it and feel happy. The music that I create through years of practice and dedication is like a symphony of melodies, a satisfying treat for me. I wish to continue making music with an inextinguishable fire for music.

Both of my parents played college varsity basketball in Taiwan. I was introduced to the basket on my father's shoulders even as a toddler and I started playing serious basketball when I was in ninth grade, a relatively late age for basketball players. Soon I found that I loved basketball more than any other sports I had played such as soccer, tennis and badminton. Basketball suits my temperament: it requires tactics, teamwork, dedication, and competitiveness. I worked hard on the court and was appointed as the captain of the junior varsity team in my sophomore year, an accomplishment I still feel good about. The next year, I moved to Palo Alto and basketball seemed to be slipping away given the fact that I was not good enough to enter the varsity team here. However, I hung on to my passion and continued to sharpen my skills by playing with friends twice a week, in hope of participating in intramural games in college. I won't give up basketball no matter what.

There are many more things I enjoy doing, but the above four things have been the most consistent passions in my life.

What Are My Aspirations and What Have I Done to Achieve Them?

I am fascinated with money and the way it works. My fascination with money began on the day of Chinese New Year, back in 1999. As a tradition, elders would hand out "red envelopes" to younger children and grandchildren, and it was the first year I was old enough to receive some of my own. I remember laying out my "spoils" on my desk, gazing at the multitude of bills that are thousands worth in New Taiwan Dollars. A clear sensation ran over me: How lovable money is!

That simplistic childhood obsession has matured with more time and further interest in the business world and economic operations, a field that I decided to pursue when I was only twelve years old, in seventh grade. I asked my parents to subscribe to TIME magazine, and with each monthly issue I kept track of the world economic changes: I worried for the global economy during the 2006 housing bubble, I sweated for the brink of bankruptcy in Greece, and I still fret over the current credit crisis that is has been hitting the American economy. I kept myself immersed with the current topics on the "business" section, and anticipated that one day I will be writing the stories.

My family has a positive impact on my pursuit. Both my parents obtained doctoral degrees and put a heavy emphasis on academic achievement, but they are open to all career possibilities as long as I put my heart and efforts on the pursuit. They were supportive of the activities I was interested in and encouraged me with their cheering hands and financial support.

Persistently from my freshman year, I've tried to enroll in classes and programs that would better prepare me and enrich my experiences. In the summer of 2009, I attended the Educational Program for Gifted Youth (EPGY) at Stanford, enrolled in the class of "Topics in Economics." In my junior year 2010-2011, I took the elective courses of "Economics" and "Business Law" at Palo Alto High. In the summer of 2011, I was accepted into Stanford Summer College in the class "Accounting in Managers and Entrepreneurs." All of these classes and experiences have helped consolidate my decision to pursue a business career.

From a childish obsession to a career decision, I am aspired to take up an enterprise in business development. Although the topics on business are so wide ranging, from bank investments, stock broking, to futures trading, I've found myself interested in almost all of them. The next step I need to take is to pursue this goal in higher education, majoring in Business or Economics. I believe my decade-long dream will eventually come true with a solid training in college and graduate school.

My Monumental Experience

During the summer of 2011, I was hired as "Assistant to Chief Executive Officer" at a relatively new company based in Mountain View, CA. It's called Loveast Culture Exchange LLC. The company ventures to bridge the East and the West, bringing Chinese students and scholars overseas to America for education or work. Taking it seriously as my first paid job and internship, I did not know it would turn out to be an invaluable learning experience.

On the very first day, July 18th, 2011, I was tasked with formatting letters and designing official logos to represent the company's visions. Starting from scratch, I learned through grasping the key guidelines and browsing the internet to let my creativity fly. I formatted letter headings and official papers to make them ready to be sent as signature documents. The second day, Wednesday July 21st, I was tasked with making a financial spreadsheet of local high schools and colleges, adding in information from college tuition, financial aid to housing options, I created a spreadsheet that clearly displayed the data and allowed easy comparisons of the items. I learned how to create user-friendly spreadsheets of financial information in the process.

I was kept busy all summer till August 24th. Over the weeks, I helped my boss review the Loveast Culture Exchange LLC Income Sheet and Budget Sheets, check for discrepancies and make future projections. I became the junior financial analyst for the company, overlooking and finding programs that would be the most cost efficient for foreign students to stay in America on a temporary visa. I was also the treasurer in charge of fund-raising for the Loveast-sponsored student union. The two-month working experience strengthened my commitment to studying business and I learned how to get things done right in the real business world.

At the same time, I studied at Stanford Summer College, taking a course on Accounting for Managers and Entrepreneurs. My last summer in high school was filled with studies, work, and real life adventures. Was it difficult? No. Was it boring? No. Did I love it? Yes. I loved every single minute I was at my work, doing things that were new and fascinating to me. My intensive summer job at Loveast as an intern assistant to the CEO served as a cornerstone that grounded my desires to become a Business major.

The Roadmap – Steps Taken to Reach My Dream

In the chart below, I diagramed the important activities I have taken to build up my strengths and to accumulate relevant experiences for the pursuit of my dreams.

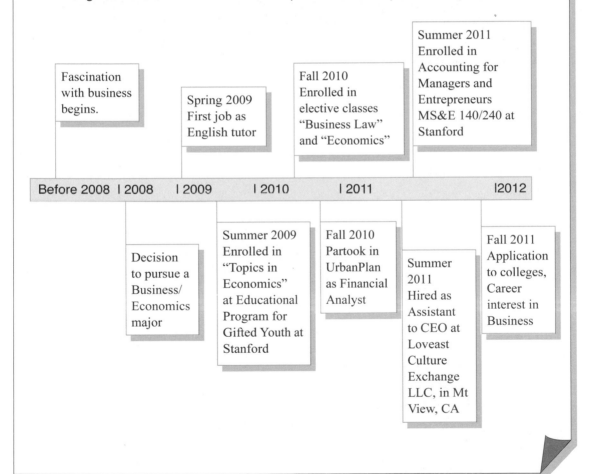

Fascination with business begins.

Spring 2009
First job as English tutor

Fall 2010
Enrolled in elective classes "Business Law" and "Economics"

Summer 2011
Enrolled in Accounting for Managers and Entrepreneurs MS&E 140/240 at Stanford

Before 2008 | 2008 | 2009 | 2010 | 2011 | 2012

Decision to pursue a Business/ Economics major

Summer 2009
Enrolled in "Topics in Economics" at Educational Program for Gifted Youth at Stanford

Fall 2010
Partook in UrbanPlan as Financial Analyst

Summer 2011
Hired as Assistant to CEO at Loveast Culture Exchange LLC, in Mt View, CA

Fall 2011
Application to colleges, Career interest in Business

寫作練功坊

Name _____

Personal Information

_____

Education

_____

_____

Honors and Awards

_____

_____

Skills-building Activities and Clubs

_____

_____

Work Experiences and Community Services

_____

_____

Summary of Qualifications

_____

_____

14.2 求職履歷表

原則不變：三句話原則

英文寫作的原則，如同人生其他的定理：原則不變，一以貫之！在求職或申請學校時，需要寫履歷自傳，但怎麼寫呢？還是要回到英文的溝通習慣：重點先講，細節隨後！運用「三句話」原則，可歸納出寫履歷的三項基本要素：

最重要的話：求職的目標
最具說服力的細節：有利的學經歷
最令人印象深刻的總結：個人化的特點

最重要的話：求職的目標（**Objectives**）

從雇主的角度來看一封履歷，最重要的話當然是你求職的目的是什麼？要找的工作性質與內容是什麼？是不是切合雇主的需要？因此在一開始交代姓名與基本聯絡資料之後，就可以直接說明申請工作的目標。因為是最重要的話，所以要簡潔有力，重點清楚，最好不要超過三項，每項 1-2 行。以下是一位出版社編輯的求職目標：

Objectives

- Position sought: a Chief Editor's role in a publisher where I can maximize my editorial and marketing experiences to develop integrated product portfolios for various language learning publications
- Job responsibilities: buying book rights from abroad, seeking potential writers, managing editorial process, writing copies for products, and creating marketing strategies
- Career goal: "to Bring World Languages to Taiwan and Bring the Chinese Language to the World."

最具說服力的細節：有利的學經歷（Education and Experiences）

　　既然有了清楚的求職目標，接下來就要提出有力的證明，詳細交代過去相關的學經歷，佐證自己是有能力完成工作的最佳人選。因此求職目標之下，可進一步說明相關的各項專業經歷（Professional Experiences）。請注意，條列專業項目的原則仍然是重點在前：最重要、最相關的先說！

　　各項工作經驗的說明，必須簡潔扼要，條理一致。先交代公司雇主、職位職稱、雇用時間之後，可以分項條列的方式凸顯重點。以下提供同一編輯的部分專業經歷及學歷說明，作為範例。請注意，學歷和經歷相輔相成，兩者的先後順序可就申請的目標來決定。如果是申請學校，最好要把學歷放在前面（請參考 14.1 節申請學校的說明）。

Professional Experiences

ABC Publishing Co., Taipei, Taiwan

Editor   June 2009 –

- Propose and develop language materials for English, Mandarin, Japanese, Korean, and French learning.
- Review and buy rights of foreign publications and create Traditional Chinese or bilingual editions.
- Work with book writers, editors and illustrators and create language learning materials for different levels.
- Manage book publication process, from editing, proofreading, publishing to marketing.

DEF Publishing Co., Taipei, Taiwan

English Editor   September 2007 – May 2009

- Translated articles and edited GEPT/TOEIC test preparation series.
- Planned and designed Freshman English and Freshman English Listening and Speaking textbook series for vocational colleges in Taiwan.
- Delivered presentations to school teachers and received adoptions from school.
……

Education

Graduate School of Business, XYZ University, NY, USA　　　July 2006 – June 2007

Master of Science in Marketing

- XYZ University Journal: VP of Communications, Editor, Reporter
- XYZ Marketing Association (XMA): Active member
- Ambassador of the university

UVW University, Taipei, Taiwan　　　September 1997 – June 2001

Bachelor of Arts in English

- Recipient of the Honor Student Award
- Western Painting Club: President
- English Association Committee: Director of Publicity & Public Relations
- English Graduate Performance Committee: Publicity & Public Relations Officer
- English Playlet Contests: Stage Design Leader, Actress
- Arts & Culture Center, Exhibit Team: Volunteer

最令人印象深刻的總結：個人化的特點

　　交代了專業背景，說明了學經歷之後，已提供完整的佐證細節，最後還要說什麼呢？一般履歷的最後會提供比較個人的特點說明。若是雇主對你的專業資歷很有興趣，也許會想多了解你這個人，因此可簡要說明你的特長、技能、興趣。此外，有些公司會希望進一步了解你過去的表現與其他人對你的評價，因此可提供 2-3 位過去工作的主管或同事作為推薦人（References）。

　　履歷的最後加入一點增強專業性向的個人化介紹，可使人印象更為深刻，但原則是點到為止，不可過多過長，且要與專業結合，以求相得益彰的效果。以下提供個人化特長及外部參考人說明的範例：

Personalities, Skills & Interests

- **Personalities:** Out-going, friendly, cheerful, responsible and punctual; an excellent team player with good people skills
- **Computer Skills:** Proficient in MS Office and SPSS; Familiar with Photoshop, Illustrator, Flash, InDesign, SoundForge
- **Language Skills:** Fluency in Mandarin Chinese, Taiwanese, English and basic Japanese and Spanish
- **Interests:** Arts, design, literature, drama, music, movies, dancing, travel, and sports

References

- Dr. A. Lin, CEO, ABC Publishing Co., PHONE and EMAIL
- Dr. B. Lee, Director, DEF Publishing Co., PHONE and EMAIL
- Dr. C. Liu, Chair, UVW University, PHONE and EMAIL

一份完整的履歷範本

　　一份完整的履歷到底該有多長？一般求職的 resume，要看工作職位的高低而定，一般職務以一頁為原則，因為雇主沒有時間看太長的履歷，因此要怎麼扼要地提示就是各有巧妙了！若是較高階職務，因為經歷豐富，也許需要更多的頁數，但也不可過長。然而學術 CV 則另當別論，因為須包含研究論文出版的介紹，可能越長越好。

　　以下針對求職需要，提供一份完整的履歷範本：

Linda Lin

0931-123-456

linda.lin@gmail.com

Objectives

- Position sought: a Chief Editor's role in a publisher where I can maximize my editorial and marketing experiences to develop integrated product portfolios for various language learning publications
- Job responsibilities: buying book rights from abroad, seeking potential writers, managing editorial process, writing copies for products, and creating marketing strategies
- Career goal: "to Bring World Languages to Taiwan and Bring the Chinese Language to the World"

Professional Experiences

ABC Publishing Co., Taipei, Taiwan

Editor   June 2009 –
- Propose and develop language materials for English, Mandarin, Japanese, Korean, and French learning.
- Review and buy rights of foreign publications and create Traditional Chinese or bilingual editions.
- Manage book publication process, from editing, proofreading, publishing to marketing.

DEF Publishing Co., Taipei, Taiwan

English Editor   September 2007 – May 2009
- Translated articles and edited GEPT/TOEIC test preparation series.
- Planned and designed Freshman English and Freshman English Listening and Speaking textbook series for vocational colleges in Taiwan.
- Delivered presentations to school teachers and received adoptions from school.

GHI Company, Boston, MA, USA

Bilingual Marketing Specialist   October 2007 – May 2009

- Coordinated and represented the company to exhibit at conferences, workshops, and events.
- Executed company events, such as Karaoke Contest, Company Anniversary celebration events, Holiday Book Fair, etc.
- Wrote copy of press release, advertisement, catalogues, and graphic (e)mail.
- Presented and introduced materials of Chinese learning series for school textbook adoption.

JKL Company, NY, USA

Research Associate Intern   September 2007 – October 2007

- Developed qualitative and quantitative analysis to explore consumer insights and satisfaction, driving consumer loyalty.
- Generated statistics information, wrote market analysis report and prepared presentation materials.

MNO Publishing Group, Taipei, Taiwan

English Editor   July 2001 – June 2006

- Designed the entire textbook product package. The textbooks earned "Best Quality Textbook Award" from Ministry of Education, Taiwan.
- Handled the development and publication of the monthly interactive English learning magazine.
- Delivered presentations and demonstrations on textbook promotions at high schools nationwide.
- Conducted market analysis and executed sales force education training.
- Earned "Outstanding Contribution Award" from the company in 2004.

Education

Graduate School of Business, XYZ University, NY, USA   July 2006 – June 2007

Master of Science in Marketing

- XYZ University Journal: VP of Communications, Editor, Reporter
- XYZ Marketing Association (XMA): Active member
- Ambassador of the university

UVW University, Taipei, Taiwan   September 1997 – June 2001

Bachelor of Arts in English

- Recipient of the Honor Student Award
- Western Painting Club: President
- English Association Committee: Director of Publicity & Public Relations
- English Graduate Performance Committee: Publicity & Public Relations Officer
- English Playlet Contests: Stage Design Leader, Actress
- Arts & Culture Center, Exhibit Team: Volunteer

Personalities, Skills & Interests

- **Personalities:** Out-going, friendly, cheerful, responsible and punctual; an excellent team player with good people skills
- **Computer Skills:** Proficient in MS Office and SPSS; Familiar with Photoshop, Illustrator, Flash, InDesign, SoundForge
- **Language Skills:** Fluency in Mandarin Chinese, Taiwanese, English and basic Japanese and Spanish
- **Interests:** Arts, design, literature, drama, music, movies, dancing, travel, and sports

References

- Dr. A. Lin, CEO, ABC Publishing Co., PHONE and EMAIL
- Dr. B. Lee, Director, DEF Publishing Co., PHONE and EMAIL
- Dr. C. Liu, Chair, UVW University, PHONE and EMAIL

寫作練功坊

請就本書學到的英文寫作要領,掌握 G-S-G 原則,寫出自己的一份完整的履歷表,未來無論是要升學或是就業,一份漂亮的履歷表絕對能凸顯自己的優點,為未來加分。

Name _____

Contact Information

_____

_____

Objectives

_____

_____

Professional Experiences

_____

_____

Education

_____

_____

Personalities, Skills & Interests

_____

_____

References

_____

_____

結語：

　　這本書所教的寫作訣竅，首重構思的條理，其次是句子的組成，然後到實際的演練，再再提醒讀書英文寫作是有理可循，有方法可行，且有訣竅可掌握的。希望讀完本書後，英文寫作不再是苦惱的煎熬，而是人人享受的過程。

英文達人必讀系列

英文寫作有訣竅！三句話翻轉英文寫作困境

2014年10月初版　　　　　　　　　　　　　　　　定價：新臺幣390元
2023年10月初版第八刷
有著作權・翻印必究
Printed in Taiwan.

著　　　者	劉　美　君
叢書編輯	李　　　芃
文字編輯	陳　俞　汶
	林　岱　瑩
	Hannah O'Brien
校　　　對	謝　佳　倩
	林　昀　彤
	陳　香　伶
插　　　畫	桂沐設計
封面設計	江　宜　蔚
內文排版	楊　佩　菱

出　版　者	聯經出版事業股份有限公司	副總編輯	陳　逸　華
地　　　址	新北市汐止區大同路一段369號1樓	總編輯	涂　豐　恩
叢書主編電話	(02)86925588轉5317	總經理	陳　芝　宇
台北聯經書房	台北市新生南路三段94號	社　　　長	羅　國　俊
電　　　話	(02)23620308	發行人	林　載　爵
郵政劃撥帳戶第0100559-3號			
郵撥電話	(02)23620308		
印　刷　者	文聯彩色製版印刷有限公司		
總　經　銷	聯合發行股份有限公司		
發　行　所	新北市新店區寶橋路235巷6弄6號2F		
電　　　話	(02)29178022		

行政院新聞局出版事業登記證局版臺業字第0130號

國家圖書館出版品預行編目資料

英文寫作有訣竅！三句話翻轉英文寫作困境
/劉美君著 . 初版 . 新北市 . 聯經 . 2014年10月(民103年) .
336面 . 18×26公分（英文達人必讀系列）
ISBN　978-957-08-4456-6（平裝）
[2023年10月初版第八刷]

1.英語　2.寫作法

805.17　　　　　　　　　　　　　　　　103017242